PLAYING THE

GAME

$ $ $

SARA RICKOVER

ISBN for paperback edition: 978-0-9853244-1-4

ISBN-10 for paperback edition: 0985324414

Rickover Publishing
Playing the Game

Second printing July 2020

Play the game for more than you can afford to lose . . . only then will you learn the game.

Winston Churchill

DEDICATION & ACKNOWLEDGMENTS

My thanks to my first readers Ellen, Tresia, Tom, and Mary for their encouragement and plot suggestions; to my book club and writing critique groups for their input and technical corrections; and to my beta readers Peg, Tim, Betty, and Marsha for their sharp eyes and attention to detail. All of you have helped to make this a better story.

This novel is dedicated to administrative professionals everywhere. They are the ones who keep businesses running

PlayLand Organizational Chart

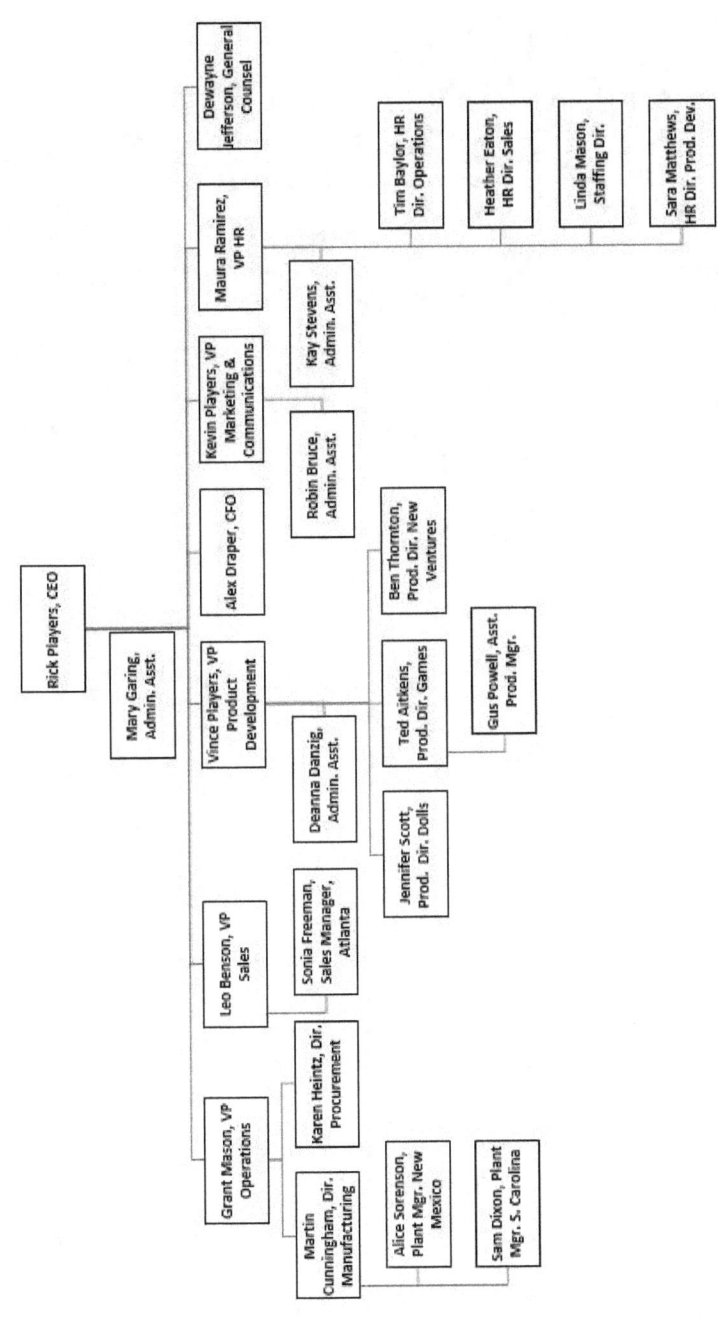

CHAPTER 1: SUNDAY, JANUARY 7

Rick Players looked up from his snowmobile at the jagged peaks of the Rockies. A cold wind stung his cheeks, and he smiled at its bite.

It was the last afternoon of his twin teenage sons' winter break. For this day only, Rick had ignored his job as CEO of PlayLand, the toy company his family owned. Just one afternoon with his boys. That's all he wanted.

Well, if he were honest, he wanted out of the job altogether. He hadn't realized when he took over from his father that leading PlayLand would cost him his freedom. There was more to life than work, he was coming to realize. But two thousand employees and all the children who bought the company's toys depended on him. Even today, he had his damn cell phone clipped to his belt.

Rick shifted his snowmobile into gear, and gunned the engine to launch himself across the deep powder.

"Race you!" he yelled, as he rocketed past the two fifteen-year-olds sharing another machine. He could still beat them, he knew he could. And that wasn't the beer he'd had at lunch talking either.

Rick glanced back. The boys had narrowed the gap. Damn, they're good, he thought, feeling both pride and competitiveness. He went full throttle and felt the surge of power. Speed! He loved it.

One of the twins whooped a challenge as the boys drew closer.

Rick veered down the hill to head them off. Too late to stop, he saw a ditch yawning in front of him. He tried to turn, but the snowmobile pitched forward. His body flew. *Shit! This is going to hurt.*

But he didn't feel a thing.

$$$

Maura Ramirez sat in her office at PlayLand's headquarters on Sunday afternoon. She liked to begin her Mondays with flexibility, so she worked most Sundays.

Her phone rang, and she answered.

"Maura, it's Kevin. Rick's in a coma at St. Luke's."

"Good God! What happened?" Rick was Maura's boss. Her friend, too.

"The old fool was snowmobiling," Kevin said. "Racing with his kids. He's in ICU. Doctors say he has a fractured skull. And broken bones."

"Will he be all right?"

"Doctors won't say." Kevin's voice shook.

"God, I'm sorry. How can I help?"

"Christ, I don't know."

"Is his family there?" Maura asked.

"Yeah. Paige and the boys. Vince, too."

"Who else needs to know?" Maura asked. "Employees?"

"I guess. Can you handle it?" Kevin asked. "I've got my hands full."

"What about the media?" Maura tried to put her concern for Rick aside to think logically. "We'll need to be ready if word gets out. Can you get me an update from the doctors?"

Kevin sighed. "I'll text you what I can. We don't know much."

"I'll shoot you a draft when I get it done." Maura hung up and dropped her head in her hands. *Christ, Rick!*

Rick was the best boss Maura had ever had. He drove his staff hard, but passionately promoted the games and dolls PlayLand made, grinning as much as the kids who bought the company's toys. Over the years Rick had developed the company's most successful product lines, making PlayLand a national force in the toy industry.

And he treated employees fairly, which made Maura's job running Human Resources easier. She wouldn't be able to push the employee changes needed to keep the business afloat without Rick to back her up.

What would PlayLand do if Rick died? He **was** the business.

$$$

Maura left her office much later than she had planned. It had taken hours to work with Kevin on the press release and employee communications. By the end of the afternoon, Kevin reported Rick was still in critical condition. The hospital had done a CT scan on Rick's brain, which showed a skull fracture, with rising intracranial pressure.

"The neurologist says he's a three on the Glasgow Coma Scale, whatever that is," Kevin told her. "He's not responding, even to pin pricks to his arms. No movement at all."

"Jesus. Is he at least breathing on his own?" Maura asked.

"Yeah, that much is good. They'll do an MRI tomorrow. Maybe we'll know more then."

"Let's hope so."

"He also has three broken ribs and a broken leg," Kevin continued. "The doctors say it's a miracle he doesn't have more internal injuries. The snowmobile must weigh six hundred pounds. The twins found it on top of him."

As she walked down PlayLand's empty halls, Maura thought again about how dreadful losing Rick would be—to employees, to the company's financial status, . . . and to her personally.

And where's Vince? she wondered, thinking of the middle Players brother. All afternoon she had only talked to Kevin, the youngest of the three brothers. Vince seemed to stay out of critical corporate issues, even though he managed Product Development, the lifeline of the business.

Maura drove out of the employee parking lot in the dusk and glanced back at the low, bulky profile of PlayLand's headquarters. Red, blue, and yellow stripes matching the company's bright logo lined the exterior walls—a playful expression of the company's creative mission. Maura enjoyed the fun environment. Too bad there were so many financial problems this year.

And no one to fill in behind Rick. As head of HR, she should have focused on leadership development, but Rick had always said there would be plenty of time. She should have pushed him.

On her drive home, Maura worried about all the things she had on her plate. Succession behind Rick would be a major issue, if Rick's health were permanently impaired. Improving employee relations. Management training. Increasing the diversity of the employee base as consumers themselves became more diverse.

The current financial environment wouldn't let her do everything she wanted, not when PlayLand needed to cut payroll and benefits costs. Cost reduction was hard. Could they do it without Rick?

$ $ $

Maura walked into chaos at home. Between her husband Carlos and her two kids, one of them was always on the outs with another.

"Mom," her fourteen-year-old daughter Liz said, "Rafe wants Dad's car, so Dad can't take me to soccer practice. We need to leave now."

"Can't Rafe wait and drop you off?" Maura asked.

Liz rolled her eyes. "Dad said he didn't have to. He said you'd do it."

"I don't need this now, Liz." Maura sighed. "Carlos?" she called, "Can you take Liz? Sorry I'm late. Had a crisis. Rick's in a coma."

"Rick? Good God, what happened?"

"Tell you later. It's bad."

"Yeah, I'll take her." As usual, Carlos would come through.

Maura fed Liz a late dinner after practice. Her daughter prattled on about her upcoming *quinceañera*, while Maura listened with half an ear and watched her cell phone for email so she could field questions about Rick's condition.

It was after ten o'clock before Maura and Carlos were alone, and then only because they went to their room and shut the door.

"What happened to Rick?" Carlos asked, rubbing Maura's feet after she collapsed on their bed.

"Snowmobile accident. Some broken bones, but Kevin says the doctors are more concerned about his head."

"Rick's got a hard head," Carlos said. "He'll pull through."

"I hope so. Kevin's worried. Me, too. For Rick and his family. And it's a terrible time for the business. Rick's the only one who can handle most of our problems."

"You can't handle them?" Carlos asked, nibbling her neck. Carlos, a tall, dark and handsome Latino, had attracted Maura since they met as juniors in college.

"Nope," Maura said. "I'm just the HR person."

"I thought you said HR ran the show."

"I only say that to make you think I'm important."

"Oh, I think you're important," Carlos said, as he bent to kiss her.

$ $ $

Grant Mason sat in front of the fireplace in his den, sipping a single malt Scotch. What would Rick's injury mean for PlayLand? he wondered.

Ten years earlier, Rick had recruited Grant from a small plastics firm to reengineer PlayLand's manufacturing and sourcing functions. Now Grant was Vice President of Operations. At fifty-eight, maturity gave him an air of assurance. But his stern expression made people nervous, and he often had to remind himself not to frown so he wouldn't seem threatening.

Grant frowned now. Operations employees knew Rick was the force behind PlayLand. Rick didn't hide in his office like a lot of CEOs. He visited the plants and talked to people. Employees would fret about Rick's condition.

Production would plummet. Grant would have to get out to the Lakeview plant to keep employees focused on churning out product.

He began to relax as he planned his week. Grant might look like an executive, but he was a tinkerer at heart. He smiled at the prospect of time at the plant.

His wife Linda entered the room and sat beside him on the sofa. "You got Maura's message about Rick?" she asked. Linda, the Staffing Director at PlayLand, reported to Maura. "We'll have to decide on a successor for Rick."

"He's not dead," Grant replied. "Just hurt."

"Make sure Maura knows you want the job."

"Do I?" Grant's scowl returned.

"You know you could do it. Better than Vince or Kevin."

"Oh, so I wouldn't be supplanting Rick. Just his brothers?"

"If Rick comes back, there's no need for a successor," Linda said. "But even if he gets better, we need a contingency plan. Neither Vince nor Kevin would be a good CEO. It's my job to make sure the company deals with this, even if the Players family doesn't want to. I'm going to talk to Maura tomorrow."

"If you're going to talk to her, why do I have to?"

"Well, I can't speak for you. She'd think I'm out for our self-interest."

"Aren't you?" Grant asked. Linda often pushed him to get involved in corporate politics. He stayed out of her plotting when it didn't involve Operations. For months, she'd told Grant he should be the next CEO, even though it didn't seem likely Rick would leave the family's business. At least it hadn't been likely until today.

"Will you talk to Maura?" Linda pressed.

Grant scowled. "You're really scheming, aren't you?"

"Just thinking ahead. Maura's resisting succession planning. But she'll have to deal with it now."

"I already manage a huge budget and the biggest division. Why should I take on more responsibility? PlayLand isn't in great shape. Being CEO is asking for trouble."

"You know you're the best one to do it."

"All right. I'll talk to Maura."

$ $ $

Late Sunday evening, Kevin Players sat on a plastic chair in ICU beside his brother Vince. Machines beeped rhythmically, monitoring Rick's heart rate, blood pressure, respiration, and brain waves. He heard the constant patter of voices from the nurses' station and the squeaks of carts rolling down the hall.

The doctors hadn't given a definite prognosis. "He has some injuries in the cerebral hemispheres," the neurologist had said. "His brain is still swelling, though not as rapidly as earlier. If it continues, we may need to surgically extract some of the dead tissue. Or at least relieve the pressure caused by the swelling. All we can do is wait."

Now Kevin and Vince sat waiting. Kevin leaned back and stretched his arms over his head. They needed to make some plans about the business. Kevin didn't want an argument, but Vince wouldn't do a damn thing unless Kevin brought it up.

Kevin squinted at Vince. "We have to decide what to do about tomorrow's officer meeting."

Vince grunted.

Vince was forty-six, several years younger than Rick, but eleven years older than Kevin. Vince's hair was thin on top, Kevin noticed in surprise. Rick hadn't lost any hair yet. Kevin ran a hand over his own head. Would he go bald like Vince in another ten years? Would he get Vince's paunch, or Rick's six-pack abs?

"If we cancel, it'll seem like no one's running the show," Kevin said.

"But you heard the doctor. How can we go on, business as usual?"

"The doctor said anything could happen," Kevin argued. "We've got to think about how people will react. Employees. Customers. Lenders. What'll they do if they think no one's in charge?"

"How can we keep going without Rick?" Vince asked.

"I don't know," Kevin said. He stretched again. He'd expected some resistance, but Vince wasn't helping at all. "We have to give the impression things are under control. Starting with the meeting tomorrow. Can you lead it?"

"Me?"

"You're head of Product Development. You're next in the family after Rick. People will expect you to do it."

"Christ!" Vince groaned. "What's on the agenda?"

"How the hell should I know? Rick keeps his own agendas."

Vince grimaced. "What should we say? You're the great communicator."

Kevin shrugged. "Give the group an update on Rick. Then ask everyone for status reports. It's mostly for show. So the rest of the company thinks we know what we're doing. Even without Rick."

Vince nodded. "Okay. But you back me up."

"Sure." Kevin closed his eyes and leaned his head back against the wall. With his eyes still closed, he asked, "What's on your plate this week?"

"Nothing much Monday. Staff meetings. A couple of new product meetings on Tuesday and Wednesday. Don't remember after that."

"Paige gave me Rick's cell phone," Kevin said. "I looked at his calendar. There's a big meeting with Toy Mart sometime this week with our Sales group. One of us should go. I think it's mostly about marketing programs. I can get up to speed. I'll go."

Vince grunted again.

Kevin decided that meant Vince didn't care who went to Toy

Mart. "He was also getting ready for the bank meeting next week," Kevin said. "It'd look pretty weird for me to go. No reason for Marketing to be there. You'll have to cover that one. Alex will know the details. Talk to him."

Vince glared at Kevin. "Hell, you know I hate financial crap."

"Alex can handle the numbers. Just act like an owner," Kevin replied. Sometimes he didn't think Vince cared about the family business. Kevin had been the kid brother all his life, but now he spent half his time pushing Vince.

"All right." Vince belched. "I'll call Alex."

Relieved that he had covered the immediate business issues, Kevin turned to the family problems—the bigger challenge, he thought. "We're going to have to watch Paige," he said.

"Why?" Vince asked.

"She was hysterical this evening," Kevin said. "She's worried about Rick, obviously. And pissed at him for racing with the boys. She said he must have been drunk. But his blood alcohol was legal." Kevin shook his head. "I don't know if she can cope."

"Christ," said Vince. "I couldn't deal with a wife when I was married. How can we handle Paige and PlayLand both?"

Kevin squirmed to get comfortable in the small chair. Paige had always been a handful. Spoiled her whole life, first by her father and then by Rick. She'd freaked out when Jason broke his arm last year. "I don't know," he said. "But we've got to."

$ $ $

Throughout the night, the hospital monitors continued to beep, assuring the nurses that Rick Players was alive, at least for the time being.

CHAPTER 2: MONDAY, JANUARY 8

Maura Ramirez went to work early on Monday. Kevin had said the officers' staff meeting would go on as scheduled, but she wasn't sure what to expect. What was there to talk about, other than Rick? She had planned to bring up cutting labor costs. But without Rick, the group couldn't—or wouldn't—decide anything. Should she even raise the issue?

When Maura arrived in her office, the voicemail light on her phone blinked. Her email held a screenful of unread messages. Most were from people wanting information about Rick. She responded to as many high-priority calls and messages as she could.

Before she knew it, it was 8:30. Time for the meeting.

Maura grabbed her headcount reduction file, still not sure whether to talk about it, but wanting to be prepared. She headed down the hall to the executive conference room near Rick's office.

Alex Draper, the Chief Financial Officer, sat in his usual seat at the conference table, files and calculator and laser pointer arranged in front of him. Alex was a good number-cruncher, his analytics as precisely trimmed as his dark curly hair and bristly mustache. But Maura had never seen him smile at any of PlayLand's products.

Dewayne Jefferson, General Counsel, loomed over Alex with a cup of coffee and a coconut doughnut in his hands. "Lining your pencils up, Alex?" Dewayne said. "Too bad you can't get profits to line up as neatly."

Dewayne, a large African American, wore a dark grey suit, blue button-down shirt, and red foulard tie—impeccably attired as always. Maura suspected he used his imposing size and intellect to

15

intimidate his adversaries, in the courtroom and at PlayLand.

As Dewayne twitted Alex about his pencils, Grant Mason, the Vice President of Operations, strode into the room. Despite being one of the older officers at PlayLand, Grant radiated energy. Employees told Maura they were afraid of his furrowed eyebrows and stern mouth. Only those who worked closely with Grant knew that, though he was hardheaded, he considered new ideas thoughtfully.

He was one of Maura's favorites on Rick's staff. She smiled at Grant as he sat.

Grant shot her a quick grin back, then frowned. "Any word on Rick?"

She shook her head.

Leo Benson sauntered in about eight forty. Leo had spent his entire career—over thirty years—in the Sales group. He hustled customers, but reacted negatively to his peers' ideas. For Leo, it was Sales against the rest of the world, and Sales was always right.

Leo settled into his seat. A gold chain flashed around his neck and another shone on his wrist. His right hand sported a heavy diamond ring, an award from early in his career for achieving top sales for five years running.

"Where are Vince and Kevin?" Leo asked. "They called this meeting."

No one answered.

At 8:45, Kevin and Vince walked in together.

"Any word on Rick?" Grant asked as the others murmured the same concern.

Kevin shook his head. "Nothing new."

The Players brothers all had the same nose and ears, but whenever Maura saw them together, she noticed how different they were. The injured Rick was the oldest and also the broadest, built like the football player he had been in college.

Vince, the tallest, had not kept himself in shape. The green plaid sweater and rumpled corduroy slacks he wore today emphasized his generous stomach. Maura stifled a sigh as she glanced at Vince.

Kevin's ready grin made him the most attractive, in Maura's opinion, though he was the least physically imposing. She also found him the most personable, the easiest to get along with.

Kevin motioned Vince toward the head of the table where Rick usually sat.

Vince cleared his throat as he took Rick's chair, then said, "Thanks, everyone, for your concern about Rick. We really appreciate it. He's still in a coma. Doctors don't say when he'll come out. We'll let you know if anything changes." Vince looked toward Kevin, who nodded.

"Let's go around the room," Vince continued. "See what's happening. If you needed anything from Rick this week, we'll figure out what to do. Where we can, we'll wait until Rick's back. Who wants to start?"

Leo stirred his coffee, diamond ring flashing. "Rick and I were supposed to meet with Toy Mart on Thursday," he said. "I'll handle it. Just preliminary. To feel them out about our new action figure line. Rick was only going because Toy Mart's our largest customer."

"I'll go," Kevin said. "They'll expect special marketing terms. But we have to be sure we don't overcommit. We can't afford much this year."

Leo shrugged. "Suit yourself," he said. "No need. But if you want to go, I've leased a jet. We leave at seven thirty Thursday morning."

"I'll be there," Kevin said.

Alex tapped his pencil on the files in front of him. "Haven't you seen the financials, Leo? No money for jets."

"The plan was for Rick and me and a couple of Sales guys to go. Toy Mart's in a podunk town in Wisconsin. If we fly commercial, we end up spending three days out of the office for a three-hour meeting. Our time's worth something."

Alex stood and passed copies of a spreadsheet around the table. "Kevin's right about not overcommitting. We can't promise Toy Mart or anyone else anything this year. These projections show the trouble we're in."

Alex turned on a projector displaying a PowerPoint slide of the spreadsheet he had distributed. He flashed his laser pointer at the bottom line. "We're losing money. Cash flow is eroding every week. At this rate, our whole line of credit will be used up by June."

He showed another slide. "Every division needs to control costs until we negotiate a bigger line. Rick and I have—or had—a meeting scheduled with the banks next week. What do we do about that meeting? How will the banks react if they think Rick is incapacitated?" Alex's diction was as precise as his sculpted mustache.

"Vince will work with you and the banks until Rick is back," Kevin said.

Vince looked up from his hands. "Yeah," he said. "Let's talk later this week, Alex. You can show me specifics. Even if Rick wakes up today, he can't travel next week. Not with broken bones."

"Okay," Alex said, his head bobbing up and down. He peered around the room above his glasses. "Does everyone understand? We can't spend any money this year." He tapped his pencil on the table to emphasize his words.

"Oh, come off it." Leo waved his hand dismissing Alex, his ring flashing. "How can I sell new product without marketing dollars?"

"We have some ideas to keep the marketing costs down," Kevin said. "Isn't that right, Vince?"

"Got my staff brainstorming," Vince replied. "Both the New Ventures folks and Jennifer Scott in Dolls."

Leo snickered. "That sweetie's a doll herself. But what does she know about action figures?"

"Give her a chance," Kevin said. "She's pretty sharp."

"Okay, Alex," Vince said, "Anything else we need to know from Finance?"

"Keep costs down, and let me know ASAP about budget overruns." Alex turned off the computer screen and went back to his seat.

"Grant?" Vince asked, turning to the Vice President of Operations.

"So far, we're on track with production planning. We've only seen specifications for the first few action figure SKUs, but we should get the others soon from Product Development. I assume we're still on schedule?" Grant frowned at Vince.

Vince nodded.

"Everything else is in good shape," Grant continued. "Costs for raw materials are up, but we've switched to some cheaper vendors. I think we'll hold product costs level with last year." He scowled. "But labor costs are up. That's the weak link in our projections."

That was her cue, Maura decided. She wished Rick were there to back her up. She leaned forward. "Both salary and benefits costs are shooting up. We'll probably need to reduce staff this year. But as a first step, I recommend we don't hire anyone unless absolutely necessary."

"But I have open sales territories," Leo said. "Turnover in the field is sky-high. I need to fill those jobs."

"If you have to, you have to," Maura said. "But if we lay people off later, you'll have a bigger mess then. Better to hold the territories open."

Alex tapped his pencil nervously. "Maura's right. Labor is the fastest growing item in our budget. Why would we hire more employees, given our current projections?"

Grant glared, leaning back in his chair with his arms crossed. "Leo and I have the most people. I hear what you're saying, Maura, but sometimes we have to fill open jobs."

Maura shook her head. "I'm not telling you to cripple the business. Just be careful. My staff's working on a headcount reduction plan. We'll have it ready soon." She wouldn't present the plan now. If they wouldn't even agree to stop hiring, no way would these guys lay people off. Only Rick could make them do it.

"Can we agree to be careful?" Vince asked. "If it seems like we need to get tougher, we'll revisit the issue. Maybe when Rick is back."

Maura watched in disgust as the rest of the group nodded. Vince had cut off the debate without reaching resolution. Leo would do as he damn well pleased. Grant wouldn't add employees unnecessarily, but he would run Operations the way he thought best. Only she and Alex seemed concerned about the rising labor costs. Typical.

$ $ $

After the staff meeting, Vince headed back to his office. Alex followed him. Vince's stomach and head hurt after listening to all the damn bickering, and he needed a few minutes alone. But when he got to his office, Alex still trailed him, like a small dog yapping at his heels.

"What is it, Alex?" he asked, not caring that he sounded fretful.

"When can we talk about the bank meeting?"

Vince sighed. "Now, I guess. Deanna, can you clear the next hour?"

His assistant nodded.

Vince's office held the same executive furniture as Rick's, but Vince's office was smaller and the plush guest chairs were too big for the space. Even Alex, a small man, had to squeeze to sit in front of Vince's desk.

"Okay," Vince said. "Talk."

Alex spread his papers out on Vince's desk. "What do you know already?" he asked.

Vince wasn't sure how to respond. Should he pretend to understand what Alex was talking about? He wouldn't be able to fake that for long. Not with Alex.

Vince wished he had paid more attention to his dad and Rick over the years. His father, Richard Players, had given his three sons stock in PlayLand years ago. Vince cashed his dividend checks each quarter, but he didn't focus on the company's performance. He was stressed enough managing Product Development, without worrying about the big picture.

"Start with the basics. I'll let you know if I've already heard it," he said.

Alex showed him the prior year's profit and loss statement. "We made a small profit last year, even after deducting interest and taxes. But the profit was substantially lower than the year before."

Vince knew this much. "Okay. What about this year?"

"It's like Grant said. All our expenses are up. Plastic costs are up because of oil prices. Shipping costs are skyrocketing, both to get raw materials to the plants and completed product to the warehouses. Maura mentioned labor costs. Wages are part of the problem, but employee health care is going through the roof."

As he spoke, Alex pointed to various lines on the current financial statement, and showed Vince the percentage increases. Every line item Alex mentioned had gone up by more than ten percent over the prior year.

Vince rubbed his forehead, which felt like it was in a vise. "I didn't realize things were this bad."

Alex tapped his pencil on the bottom line. "If we stay on this trend, we'll have a loss this year. For the first time in PlayLand's history."

Vince wanted to bolt, but that wasn't an option. "What can we do?"

"There's more." Alex flipped to a cash flow statement. "As you know, we have a twenty-million dollar line of credit, split equally between two major banks." Alex underlined the bottom figure on the cash flow statement. "I've projected the cash we'll need to keep paying our bills until revenue from the new action figure line kicks in. At our current rate, we'll run out of cash by June—only five months away. Maybe sooner. And that's assuming that sales of existing products don't slide, that the product cost estimates on the action figures hold true, and that the new product sells at the pace we forecast."

Alex pointed to another line on the statement. "Our interest costs increase as we borrow more money, which compounds the problem. But we can't avoid borrowing. Not if we're going to pay employees and suppliers."

"So what do we do?" Vince asked again.

"We need more credit from the banks as a cushion."

"But you said that increases our interest costs." Vince rubbed his tender stomach. He wondered if he had an ulcer, but he didn't have time to get to a doctor, not while he was doing half of Rick's job.

"That's right. So we have to get our cost structure down. Product costs. Labor. Overhead. We have to attack expenses across the board."

"Isn't that rather dramatic?" Vince didn't want to make any changes without Rick. Rick would second-guess whatever Vince did.

Alex drew circles around the loss projected for the year. He pushed his pencil so hard the lead broke and skittered across Vince's desk. "We need dramatic action. Unless you want this to be the first time in PlayLand's history we lose money. We're bleeding. Besides, the banks won't increase our credit unless we show them we can turn this ship around."

"What did Rick say about all this?"

"He saw these numbers for the first time last week. We hadn't decided on a plan of action yet. But I told him the same thing I'm telling you. We need to cut costs. Hard and deep."

"What about money to launch the action figures?"

"That's another reason to cut other expenses." Alex rapped his pencil on the spreadsheet again. "The action figures have to save the top line, so we need to invest in them. But we can't go overboard."

This was why Vince hated finances. Alex was known as a doomsayer for good reason—he acted like everything was the end of the world. Vince didn't know enough to tell whether Alex had overstated the problem.

"We have to launch the new line by summer, or we won't have the manufacturing and distribution kinks worked out before the Christmas season," Alex continued. "Christmas is make-or-break. We have to hang on until then."

It all sounded circular to Vince. They couldn't spend money or the business would crater, but they had to spend money to dig out of the hole they were in.

Vince pinched the bridge of his nose. "So what do we tell the banks?"

"What I just told you." Alex gathered up his spreadsheets. "But you need to back me up when we talk about cutting costs. I don't know what specifics we can have ready by next week, but they'll want details. Maybe all we can hope for is time to get our act together. You need to get the rest of the officers on board."

"Okay," Vince said. "Send me a copy of what you want to give the banks. We'll talk again before the meeting. You can tell me what to say." He sighed. "Maybe Rick'll wake up, and we can get his input."

$ $ $

Vince walked down the hall for a cup of coffee after his meeting with Alex. He didn't need the caffeine, nor more acid in his stomach, but he had to escape.

When he returned, his phone's message light blinked. Maura had called, wanting an update on Rick. He groaned. One more damn thing. His head still spun after listening to Alex, and his gut churned from the coffee.

Vince called the hospital ICU and asked about Rick.

"He's still unconscious," the nurse said. "Vital signs normal. The doctor will be here around four o'clock. You could see him then. By the way, Mrs. Players is here, in the waiting area."

Vince dialed Paige's cell phone. "Paige," he said, "I talked to the nurse. She says Rick's the same."

"They let me see him for a little bit," Paige said. "He looks so pale and old. Not like Rick at all." She sniffled into the phone.

"What do the doctors say?"

"He still has a poor rating on ... what do they call it? The Glasgow scale? The neurologist said most people this deep in a coma after twenty-four hours don't recover fully." She hiccupped, as if she'd been crying a long time. "If he doesn't respond to pin pricks soon, his chances of recovery get worse."

"But yesterday the neurologist said anything can happen," Vince reminded her. "He said not to worry for another day or two."

"I can't take this," Paige wailed. "And the boys. I sent them to school, but they're so upset. You see what his drinking is doing to our family."

"Now, Paige," Vince said. "The beers Rick had didn't have anything to do with the accident. That's what the blood tests showed. He fell in a ditch. That could happen to anyone."

"But if he hadn't been drinking . . . ."

"Rick's always taken risks. Mother used to say Rick attracted danger like lint." Vince had hated it when their mother laughed at Rick's recklessness. He'd felt like such a pansy by comparison, never able to match his older brother. "HR wants to put out another statement, but it sounds like there's nothing new to say. I'll try to get to the hospital this afternoon."

Vince hung up and called Maura. "No news is good news," he told her. "I'll get you an update later."

Vince leaned back in his chair, staring at the ceiling of his cramped office and rubbing his gut. He had put Maura off for a few hours.

The calendar on Vince's cell phone beeped. Time for his meeting with two staff members, Ben Thornton and Jennifer Scott. Shit, he thought. This would be worse than Alex.

Ben was the New Ventures Director. His group had created the action figure line, the only new product in the pipeline, so it had damn well better be successful. If the action figures didn't make a ton of money, Vince would have to sack Ben, even if he was Rick's college buddy. But Ben would probably find a way to blame someone else. He always did.

Jennifer was the Doll Director, a title that caused all the guys to smirk that she still played with dolls. She was young and dressed like the fashion dolls she developed. But she was the best Product Director on Vince's staff, despite her youth and curves.

Vince sighed, thinking about the argument that was sure to develop between Ben and Jennifer. He hated choosing sides.

Ben arrived first. "Hey," he said, sitting without any invitation.

Vince had still been in grade school when Ben had visited the Players home with Rick. But it irritated Vince when Ben presumed familiarity.

"What's the news about Rick?" Ben asked. He sounded genuinely concerned, but Ben was good at schmoozing.

Vince gave Ben a brief update, then repeated the news when Jennifer arrived and asked the same question.

"Looking good, Jen," Ben said as she sat. "As pretty as those dolls you make." Vince watched Ben ogle Jennifer from head to foot, taking in her short plaid skirt and tight sweater. Ben was old enough to be her father, and Vince rolled his eyes in disgust.

"You're such a prick, Ben," Jennifer said, not even looking at him.

Vince grimaced at their squabbling. "Let's talk about the product launch. Ben, you've managed the action figures so far. What's your plan?"

"Show it off at Toy Fair next month. We need final prototypes, if not actual production units by then. And we should get it in front of our major customers. It's unlike anything PlayLand has done before. The retailers will eat it up."

Generalities. That's all Ben ever gave him, Vince fumed. "Okay, but how will we hype it?" he asked.

"That's Kevin's department. I asked him last week, but he never got back to me." Ben sounded wronged.

"Do you have any ideas of your own?" Vince asked. It was like pulling teeth to get Ben to say anything concrete.

"A few, but I wanted to run them by Marketing first," Ben said.

Vince sighed and turned to Jennifer. "What would you do?"

"Of course we'll be at Toy Fair, but we need to do more. I've thought about how we can make a bigger splash. If they were dolls—"

"They're not dolls, Jennifer." Ben interrupted. "They're action figures. For boys. You can't package them in pink boxes and hope they'll sell." He grinned at Vince.

Jennifer tossed her honey-colored hair and scowled, but otherwise ignored Ben. "If they were dolls," she repeated, "I'd use books to introduce the characters. Tell their stories to the kids. Boys don't read as much as girls, so maybe chapter books won't work. But what about comic books? I've never produced comics, so I don't know the costs yet. They can't be too expensive, can they? The biggest problem could be finding an author and artist to produce them quickly. I don't know if we can have a prototype done by Toy Fair. But I'd like to explore it."

"It'll never work." Ben winked at Vince. "Toy Fair's only six weeks away. You don't know the line. How can you develop stories?"

Jennifer leaned toward Vince. "Let me try. I've seen the mock-ups. Surely we can put stories with them. Give me a week of a product manager's time. I'll get cost estimates. Give me a chance." She looked directly at Ben for the first time since the meeting started. "Unless you have a better idea," she said.

Vince could see Ben staring at Jennifer's breasts. Ben had one arm thrown over his chair toward Jennifer. He wasn't touching her, but his fingers were damn close to her shoulder. Did Jennifer notice? Vince hoped she wouldn't make an issue of it.

"As I said, I haven't talked to Kevin," Ben said. "I'm sure his group has something planned. Comics would be a huge distraction from the figures themselves. And my hunch is they'll cost too much."

"Okay." Vince rubbed the back of his neck to calm his tension headache. The meeting was derailing, like every other meeting with Ben and Jennifer. He was going to have to choose. Maybe he could put it off.

"Jennifer," Vince said, "You've got a week to put together your comic book proposal. Ben, give her access to the people working on the line. In the meantime, Ben, get Kevin's input. We'll meet again next week to decide. We need to launch with a splash, so think big.

We can scale back if the costs get out of hand."

Ben and Jennifer left, Ben making a show of letting Jennifer exit first.

$$$

Maura ate lunch at her desk, trying not to get mustard on the file in front of her. Dewayne appeared in her door. "Got a minute?" the General Counsel asked.

"If you don't mind my pastrami." Maura took off her reading glasses and looked up at Dewayne. "What's up?"

"New lawsuit, filed by a former employee," he said, unbuttoning his jacket as he sat.

Maura's furniture was delicate for an executive office. Dewayne's bulk filled the light oak guest chair. If he leaned back, the legs might break, she thought.

"A reverse race discrimination case," Dewayne continued, his fingers steepling over his large stomach. "EEOC didn't even investigate, just gave him a right to sue letter. He filed the lawsuit as soon as he could. Plaintiff's a white guy. Says we fired him to hire more minority women. Clearly bogus, but we need to respond."

Maura frowned. The situation didn't sound familiar. "Who was the employee and where did he work?"

"Steve Williams. Former Sales employee in Atlanta. Worked for Sonia Freeman, the Sales Manager down there. She's Black." Dewayne's jaw tightened.

Dewayne was the highest ranking African American employee at PlayLand. He bristled whenever anyone criticized another Black employee. Maura had heard him vent about how minorities needed to be twice as good as anyone else to get half the credit. She suspected that's why he was always so prepared—doing his part to be twice as good.

"I know Sonia," Maura said. "Good manager. She wouldn't have fired Williams without good reason."

"Don't you approve employee terminations?" Dewayne asked. His glare came across as an accusation.

"I can't remember them all. I'd need to see his file." Maura took another bite as she thought. "Atlanta. We fired a guy there who'd been on a medical leave."

"Oh, great. So he has a potential disability claim, too?" Dewayne slumped in the chair, which only made him look larger. "Don't you HR types talk to Legal when you have a messy firing?"

"If it's the guy I'm remembering, he refused to do his job. That's why we fired him. Seemed pretty straight forward. Let me pull his personnel file, and I'll call you."

Dewayne stood and buttoned his jacket. "Have someone bring me the file when you get it. We need to gather our records for the early disclosure meeting in federal court."

$ $ $

As she left the meeting with Ben and Vince, Jennifer tried not to be steamed at how Ben treated her. Lots of guys at PlayLand belittled her work, but Ben was the worst.

She had better marketing skills than Ben. Better ideas than Vince, too. She hated wading through Ben's bullshit just to be heard. All because she was young and female. She had an M.B.A. in Marketing; they should take her seriously. Vince should have stopped Ben, but how could she confront one of the Players boys?

Jennifer had one of the smallest offices at PlayLand. But it had a window. She had insisted on converting the former mini-conference room into her office when she was promoted. All the male Product Directors had windows, and she deserved the same perks. Maura Ramirez had told her not to be so aggressive, but what had worked in Maura's day didn't work now. If there'd been a larger office with a window, Jennifer would have insisted on that.

Back in her office, Jennifer dialed Karen Heintz, head of Procurement. "Hey, Karen, Vince gave me the go-ahead to explore comic books. I need your help. We need to figure out what they'll cost, and whether we have vendors who can do the books on spec or if I'm going to have to hire someone. I've only got a week. Ben'll try to stop me any way he can. While staring at my boobs the whole time."

"Whoa," Karen said. "Slow down. What's this about?"

"I'm trying to get the action figures assigned to Dolls. Ben wants to keep them. It's not like he did anything on the line himself. Rumor has it Gus Powell in Games developed the idea, and Ben took it for New Ventures. I want to sell comic books to promote the action figures."

"What do you need?" Karen asked. "Sourcing for comic book production, and who could do the actual creation?"

"Yeah. And whether we can get mock-ups in time for Toy Fair in late February."

"Yikes. That's tight."

"Well, can you help? If you start on the sourcing, I'll set up a meeting tomorrow. You, me, Gus, and whoever else Ben lets me use. But we can't count on anything from Ben."

$$$

Vince left PlayLand in midafternoon and drove to the hospital. His stomach and head throbbed. First Alex and the financial problems, then refereeing Ben and Jennifer.

If Ben hadn't been Rick's college roommate, Vince would have canned him years ago. Ben was a pompous prick who'd never accomplished anything. All he did was treat other employees like crap. Like he did Jennifer.

But Vince couldn't do a damn thing about Ben. Not as long as Rick stood by his old pal.

He steeled himself for the scene he would face at the hospital. Paige would be in tears.

Vince was as put out as Paige at Rick's stupidity on the snow-mobile. The old fart had left them with a shitload of trouble. Now everyone wanted Vince to take charge. Hell, he didn't even want his own job, let alone Rick's.

Vince had gone on the professional golf circuit after college, but hadn't managed to cover expenses. Now he wished he'd stuck it out a few more years. But it had been easier to fall into the job his father gave him than to cut a few more strokes off his game.

Besides, everyone knew Rick would take over from their dad, so Vince hadn't had to work very hard. All he had to do was avoid screwing up.

When Rick became CEO, Vince was named Vice President of Product Development. Vince wanted his father to think he was a success, so he took the job. Rick had promised he'd help Vince, and he had.

Until now, Vince thought. Now Rick left him holding the bag. How was Vince supposed to launch the action figures and handle the banks without Rick? Damn Rick for getting himself hurt.

Vince entered ICU and found Paige sobbing, as anticipated.

"Nothing's changed," she said. "His eyes haven't opened, but he does pull away when he's poked with a needle. No response to anything anyone says."

"When's the last time a doctor saw him?" Vince asked.

"The chief neurologist will be here at four."

"Let's wait to see what he says." Vince sat next to Paige.

"Thanks for your support." Paige squeezed his fingers and smiled through her tears. Her hand looked very small in his beefy one. "I don't know what I would have done without you and Kevin."

"We don't have a choice, do we? We need to get Rick back. So he can take care of all of us."

"Don't sell yourself short." Paige's voice was sharper than Vince expected. "Rick always said you could do more if you tried."

That was his problem, Vince thought. He didn't try, and he didn't want to. He wanted Rick to handle everything.

The neurologist droned on about Rick's vital signs. "We still see significant brain activity, so that's good," he said. "But typically there's been a decrease in brain swelling by this point after a trauma. At least his intracranial pressure is no longer increasing. And I'm worried about the shallowness of his breathing. We may have to put him on a respirator."

"When will he get better?" Paige asked.

"I can't tell you."

"When will you know?"

The doctor shrugged. "Most people who get to a hospital right after an accident eventually come out of their comas. He could make a fast and full recovery, or it could take a long time, or he could end up in a vegetative state. If that happens, you'll have some very difficult decisions to make."

"But when will we know?" Paige repeated.

"We just need to wait. It could be weeks."

"Weeks," Paige said, her eyes welling again.

CHAPTER 3: TUESDAY, JANUARY 9

Maura arrived at PlayLand early again on Tuesday. She needed to review her headcount reduction file before meeting with her staff of eight Human Resources Directors. Maura's staff met every Tuesday morning. It was her opportunity to tell them what she could from the officers' meeting on Monday.

The HR conference room was drab—laminated tables on rollers to accommodate various training programs, chairs lightly padded in utilitarian plaid tweed, flipcharts and easels in the corners. A few of PlayLand's products languished on shelves along one wall, but they were discontinued SKUs which no one had updated in the last year.

HR should pay more attention to the company's products, Maura thought, as she did every time she entered the room. But no one took the time to make the changes.

When her HR staff had gathered around the table, Maura announced, "We have a new employee lawsuit. From a former Sales employee. Steve Williams. Worked in Atlanta for Sonia Freeman. Anyone remember him?"

"He was a deadbeat," Petra Terrell said. She managed the Employee Performance and Development function and reviewed terminations before Maura approved them. "Guy wouldn't do his job. Claimed to have agoraphobia. Said he couldn't leave his house, which was a problem for a Sales rep."

"Steve called me after he was fired," Clarice Washington, Director of Diversity, said. "He claimed Sonia wanted to replace him with a woman of color. Sonia said Steve insisted on doing his job over the phone. Sonia told him he had to make in-person sales calls."

"Petra, why'd you say he was a deadbeat?" Maura asked.

Petra shook her pen back and forth impatiently. "He'd been making sales calls for years. Then he just stopped."

"We reorganized Sales last year," Heather Eaton said. Heather was the HR liaison with the Sales Division. "Right around June 1. We wanted the reps to call on the largest stores in each territory. To build stronger relationships with the retailers and see how consumers like our product."

"And it's worked well," Petra said.

"I don't know when Steve's problem started," Heather continued. "But it was obvious by June he couldn't handle the job. With the face-to face calls he had to make, he couldn't hide in his home office any longer."

"Did we try to accommodate his agoraphobia?" Maura asked.

"I talked to Legal," Petra said. "They said if all the sales reps had to make in-person calls, we should be okay to fire him." Petra shrugged. "What more do we have to do?"

"Heather," Maura asked, "could the job have been done out of his house?"

"Not the way we restructured it. Steve was reasonably successful before then. But everyone else made the transition. Some reps don't keep up with the call schedule, but they all know it's part of the job."

Maura turned to the Diversity Director. "Clarice, what do you think?"

Clarice lifted a delicate shoulder shrouded in an African caftan. "White guy saying he was fired for race and gender reasons? He'll have a hard time with that. But it could get dicey if all the facts come out. We reorganized the job so he couldn't do it."

"So his best claim is disability discrimination?" Maura asked.

"Yeah," Clarice said. "But we're making his case for him here. He never mentioned disability to the EEOC."

Maura sighed. "Does he have a lawyer?" There were plenty of white guys who felt the world was out to get them. Sonia Freeman wouldn't have fired Steve Williams because he was white or male. But had she taken the time to try accommodating his agoraphobia? Maura didn't know.

"There was someone listed in the EEOC paperwork," Petra said.

"The EEOC charge only dealt with race and sex, not disability. But as soon as we say Steve wouldn't make sales calls, you can bet the lawyer will amend to raise a disability claim." She slumped in her chair. "We can't do anything without someone suing."

As the discussion about Steve Williams wound down, Maura pulled her headcount file in front of her. "Okay," she announced. "New topic. But it needs to stay in this room. Don't talk to the managers in the divisions you support yet, and don't talk to anyone else in HR."

She had their attention. "We need to think about a major reduction in force at PlayLand. What would happen if each division cut its personnel by ten percent?"

She watched her staff recoil. Tim Baylor grimaced. He supported Operations, which had the largest employee population and would lose the most people in a layoff.

"But Sales just reorganized last year," Heather said. "Leo will throw a fit if we do it again."

"I know," Maura said. "Cutting heads would be hard. I'm hoping we don't have to. But I want HR out in front, not playing catch up if Finance says we have to slash costs. Every division will say they can't cut jobs. Let's think it through before we propose anything."

Petra scowled. "Do you really think we'll need a ten percent cut?"

"I don't know," Maura said. "But I want to be ready. Give me your recommendations by the end of the week. And be prepared to talk about the problems you think we'll face if we move forward."

$ $ $

Grant spent most of Tuesday morning at PlayLand's main production plant on the outskirts of Lakeview, about five miles from headquarters. He traveled regularly to all six manufacturing sites, but the Lakeview plant got most of his attention. Monday's production numbers were substantially lower than quota, which prompted the Tuesday visit.

Grant would have found reasons to get to the plants even if it wasn't part of his job. He loved the hum of activity, the thrill of watching completed products stack up for shipment to the warehouse. When office work stifled him, Grant went to the plants to feel his job was worthwhile.

Heat and noise energized him as he walked into the plant. The shine of primary colors on the product packaging gave the plant a festive look, and the smell of fresh plastic filled the air.

Grant yearned to get to the production area to inspect toys coming off the lines, but instead he went directly to Martin Cunningham's office. Martin was Director of Manufacturing for PlayLand and oversaw all six plants, while also serving as general manager of the Lakeview plant.

"What was up with yesterday's numbers?" Grant asked as he walked into Martin's spartan office, furnished with a metal desk, shelving and file cabinets. "Or should I say 'down'?" This plant handled half the plastics production for PlayLand. If the plant didn't make quota, the schedule for the action figure line was in jeopardy.

"Employees are scared," Martin said bluntly, leaning back in his chair to look up at Grant. A short pudgy man, Martin was a genius with equipment. "Worried about Rick and about what his accident means for PlayLand. Not many toys made yesterday. And I doubt we get back on pace until we know about Rick. Any updates?"

"Not good," Grant said, being equally direct. "Best I can tell, there's been no change since the accident."

Martin rubbed his crew cut. "Wow. I thought Rick would bounce right back."

"Yeah, well, a blow to the head can stop anyone. But we can't let Rick's condition slow us down. Doesn't matter if folks are worried, we need to keep them focused. We need to make quota. Let's get out there."

The two men walked the plant floor, stopping at several machines to talk to operators. The injection molding equipment spitting out plastic parts ran smoothly, but there was a hush on the floor instead of the usual buzz of voices above the throbbing machines.

"How's Rick?" was the most frequent question they heard.

"Still unconscious," Grant told them. "We're all praying for him and his family. But we have to get our toys made on schedule. No matter what, stay focused. Our customers depend on us. Get those components off your machine and on to the next workstation."

Grant bought lunch in the plant break room, eating the same warmed-over catered food as the employees. About midafternoon, he drove back to headquarters and the quiet clicks of fingers on keyboards. The noise and heat levels were lower than at the plant, but so was the energy.

As Grant sat down at his desk, Alex Draper called.

"Have you seen my email?" Alex asked.

"No. I just got back from the plant."

"Did you talk to Martin about yesterday's numbers? That's what my email was about."

Grant frowned. Why was Alex nagging him? But he told Alex about his visit to the Lakeview plant. "Give them a couple of days to catch up," he concluded. "We'll meet quota."

Alex sighed. "I know I'm obsessing," the CFO said. "But with business so bad, I need to look at everything. I'm not singling out Operations."

"I push my people as hard as I can without bringing a union down on us. We'll be back on track by the end of the week."

"We'd better be. I'm watching every nickel going into product cost. We have to deliver on budget and on schedule. Vince and I need to show the banks good cost trends next week."

"We'll do what we can, Alex. Operations never lets you down."

"There's always a first time, Grant."

$$\$ \, \$ \, \$$

Jennifer Scott, Karen Heintz, and Gus Powell gathered in the Doll Room—the room Jennifer's department used for most of their meetings. Dolls of all sizes, shapes and states of dress sat on shelves and were heaped on a corner of the long conference table. It looked sloppy to anyone outside the department, but Jennifer got jazzed sitting in the middle of the products she loved.

"Who else is coming?" Karen asked.

"Ben said he'd send a product manager from New Ventures," Jennifer responded. "But I'm not holding my breath. He hasn't exactly supported my involvement in the action figure launch. Let's go ahead. What did you learn about the comic book costs?" She crossed her legs beneath the table, pulling one leg up to sit on. After Ben's reaction to her short skirt yesterday, she was in grey slacks today. And she'd made sure her maroon sweater covered the low cut of her pants.

"Printing comic books is comparable in cost to newsprint flyers.

Like those we usually make," Karen said. "Paper costs are about the same. Finishing costs for comics are a little higher because the books are stapled. But the hitch is that hiring freelancers for design work is a lot more expensive than having our ad agency do a photo shoot for the flyers."

"So what can we do?" Jennifer said, frowning.

"If we use a start-up firm, the comic books are within our budget. That's a win-win. The start-up gets PlayLand as a customer and our connections with toy stores, and we get low prices. But we'll have to cut back on Saturday TV ads to make it work."

"What do you think, Gus?" Jennifer turned to him. "I'm told you thought up these characters. Can we come up with stories that would play well in comic books?"

"Yeah." Gus looked down at the table, his face hidden by hair almost as long as Jennifer's. Gus had a reputation for being spacey and quirky. But creative. Jennifer hoped working with him would be worth the effort.

"So, do you like the comic book idea?" she asked.

"I should. It's my idea." Gus still mumbled into his hair.

How could he say that? Jennifer had come up with the idea over Christmas—something fresh to persuade Vince to let Dolls manage the action figure line. "What do you mean?" she asked.

Gus peered at her through his black eyeglass frames. He stood and paced as he talked. "I told Ben. Didn't he talk to you? I developed these characters. In college. I wanted to do a comic strip then. But I didn't know how to get it published. When I joined PlayLand, I talked to Ted about making a video game out of them. But he wasn't interested." Ted Aikens was the Product Director for Games, Gus's boss, and Ben's and Jennifer's peer.

Gus kept pacing, turning with each new sentence. "I kept after Ted, but he didn't want them. Finally, he sent me to Ben. To see if New Ventures could use my characters. Didn't hear back. Then last fall Ben came to me. With the sketches I'd given him. Said he needed a new product line. Said he wanted to make them into action figures. That's how the new line got started. But I can take these guys back to comic books. That's what they were to begin with."

Gus paced faster as he talked. Jennifer could almost smell his palms sweating. But now she had the answer to her question. Gus had started with comic books, and Ben hadn't told anyone. That sleaze! Now she had had the same idea. Surely it would work. "Do you have the drafts you showed Ben?" she asked.

"You bet." Gus said, spinning on his heels back toward the conference table to face Jennifer. "I'd never throw my drawings out."

"Can you get them now?"

"Back in a moment," Gus called over his shoulder as he hurried out.

"He's like a little kid, isn't he?" Jennifer said when he was gone.

Karen smiled. "Yeah, but he's talented. Have you seen his cubicle? Full of stuff he's drawn. If we can get him assigned to us full time, we might not need an outside artist. That would take our costs down. Then we could do more TV advertising."

"What about promotional T-shirts and other products? This could be really big." Jennifer pushed her hair out of her face as she leaned forward. "I'll see how much space Vince thinks we can get in the stores. Can you talk to the Licensing Department? See what they think we can do?"

"Licensing reports to Ben," Karen said.

Jennifer frowned. "So? Let's see what they say anyway."

Gus returned, his arms full of rolled up art paper. He spread the pages out on the table and weighted down the corners with dolls he pulled off the pile on the table. "Here's the main character," he said, pointing. "Adolpho. The leader. The strongest. Then there's Beowulf, the dragon slayer, with swords for arms. And Camero. With photographic vision. Delphi's the smart one. Got a computer for a brain. There are several more. PlayLand is starting with six action figures, but I have more. Each one has bionic properties. Different bionics. But as a team they are invincible."

He sounds like a ten year old boy, Jennifer thought. But then, that was the target consumer. She wrinkled her nose. "Are you stuck on those names?" They sounded weird to her.

Gus squinted. "I like them."

"Have you done any product testing? What do preteen boys think of the characters?"

"I don't know." Gus's jaw jutted out stubbornly. "They're my guys. I named them."

"Can I take these to Vince and ask him if we can test your stories as comic books? And test the names? You can be there and see what the reaction is." Jennifer leaned across the table toward Gus.

He blushed and stammered, "Do what you want. But I want my drawings back when you're done."

$$$

Midafternoon on Tuesday Kevin left the Marketing group offices on the third floor of headquarters and strode downstairs two flights to see Leo in Sales.

He detoured through the Communications group, also on the first floor, which reported to him. He hated having them so far away from his office, but he did his best to touch base with them several times a week. He usually found some problem to resolve on his walk-throughs, or learned something useful he couldn't pick up from the third floor.

Today someone asked about sending out an updated press release on Rick. "There's no new information," Kevin said. "Tell anyone who calls that we're guardedly optimistic."

Leo was on the phone when Kevin arrived, schmoozing a retail buyer. Leo motioned him to sit.

Kevin amused himself looking at Leo's bookshelves. Trinkets from sales conferences dating back thirty-five years. Framed pictures of Leo with the company founder, Richard Players, and Sales executives throughout PlayLand's history, all shaking Leo's hand as he received awards. The smiling faces and clasped hands looked like politicians' mementos. But then, Kevin thought, Leo was as smooth as any politician.

When Leo hung up, Kevin said, "Sorry to drop by without calling, but I thought you should brief me before the Toy Mart trip on Thursday."

Leo's gold bracelet flashed as he crossed his hands over his stomach, which had only the hint of a paunch despite his sixty years. "Okay. Here's the *Reader's Digest* version. Toy Mart wants exclusive rights to our new products for a minimum of six months, and they want a guaranteed decrease in our prices on existing products for the next year."

"Can we do that?"

Leo grinned. "Hell, no. But that's what they'll ask for."

Kevin frowned. He had hated the constant battles with customers when he was a Sales manager, but Leo treated it like a football game, each side battling for yardage. "So what do we do?" he asked.

Leo put his tasseled loafers up on his desk. "All we need to do is promise exclusivity for Toy Mart among the big chains."

"And prices?"

"Shit, we'll just whine to Toy Mart about how high energy and material costs are. We can't give price concessions until Grant cuts product costs. I'd like to give Toy Mart what they want, but we can't reduce our margin. Alex would kill us."

"Will that make Toy Mart happy?"

Leo shrugged. "It'll put 'em off until Toy Fair. I have a tee time with their CEO then. I'll butter him up. By then we'll know what we can sell to other chains. Thursday's meeting is just a skirmish." Leo smoothed his hair back and narrowed his eyes. "How's Rick really doing?"

"What do you mean?" Kevin asked, surprised at Leo's shift in the conversation.

"Maura's updates are pretty bland," Leo said. "Is Rick going to be okay? Toy Mart will ask. They don't like Vince. Rick's the only one they trust on product development. I can sell, but I can't sell sawdust. We need new products. Pronto."

"He's still in a coma," Kevin said. "The doctors think he'll probably come out of it, but the next few days are critical. We're hopeful, but only time will tell."

Leo twisted his diamond ring nervously. "Then there really isn't anything to say."

Kevin shook his head.

$ $ $

Maura heard Linda Mason's heels clicking down the hall as she approached Maura's office. The Staffing Director wore a grey pantsuit that showed off her slim figure. Maura felt frumpy by comparison. She took off her reading glasses.

"How's Rick?" Linda asked as she sat across from Maura.

"Nothing new," replied Maura.

"His accident shows we need a better succession plan," Linda said. "We don't have much of a plan for any of the officers, and we have no one slated behind Rick. What'll happen if he doesn't return?"

Maura sighed. "We can't do anything now. Even if we put together a plan, who would approve it? Nobody's asking. The person who should be asking is in a coma."

"But we still need a plan." Linda leaned forward. "Don't you think we owe the company our best recommendation?"

Maura shrugged. "In theory, yes. But if the Players family doesn't want to talk about succession, what can we do? And who do we talk to? Rick's out of the picture. At least for now."

"But that's precisely why we need a plan," Linda said.

"Okay. So we put together a plan. Then what do we do?" Maura twirled her glasses as she thought out loud. "Let's say you and I put together a list of CEO candidates. Both internal and external candidates. In a public company, we'd take our list to the CEO and/or the Board of Directors. They'd decide how to proceed. But our CEO is unconscious. And as a family-owned business, we don't have an outside Board of Directors. I don't even know the legalities of who's in charge without Rick here."

"We can evaluate the internal candidates. Have it ready. When Rick is back, we talk to him, and get him to endorse one or two successors. Or else he authorizes us to do an external candidate search. At least then we'll have some direction." Linda shook her head. "I told you months ago we should be working on this."

"You're right," Maura said. "And I told you I wasn't getting any support from Rick." She frowned at Linda. "For now, go ahead and evaluate our best candidates. In case Rick doesn't return. Whom do you have in mind?"

"The officers of the major divisions," Linda said. "Vince. Leo. Grant. And I'd probably put Kevin on the list, because he's the founder's son, though he's still pretty young. Anyone else you'd add?"

Maura hesitated before responding. This was going to get touchy. "You know, Linda, if Grant is on that list, you can't manage this project."

"But I'm the Staffing Director. It's part of my job."

Maura shook her head. "You're smart enough to know both your credibility and Grant's will suffer if you're managing the succession plan and he's a leading candidate," she stated. "Do you know if Grant even wants the job?"

"Why don't you ask him?" Linda said. "He and I don't talk much about his career at home. I know he's thought about it, but I don't know how much he wants it." Linda paused, then continued. "Let me evaluate the other candidates. I'll include Grant's career history in my write-up. But I won't give an opinion on his qualifications. You can add your personal evaluation of him. Not show me. Then we'll have something, in case we are asked. You can take it forward."

Maura nodded. "All right."

Linda stood to leave. "If Rick comes back, you should review the plan with him. You have a good excuse to raise the issue again, given his accident. And if he doesn't come back, at some point someone will have to replace him. We'll have a recommendation ready."

Maura sighed. "I hope Rick returns for lots of reasons. One is— I'd rather not deal with CEO succession in crisis mode."

$ $ $

After Linda left, Maura called Grant. She didn't want Linda to get to him first.

"How's the morale in Operations?" she asked when he was on the line.

"Mostly shock," Grant replied. "Employees wonder if we're telling them the truth about Rick. Production is down. The quicker we have a firm prognosis, the better they'll respond. Even if the news is bad. They just need to know."

"I've been pushing Vince and Kevin for more information, but they don't know anything," Maura said. She took a breath. "Different topic." She paused again. "I just talked to Linda. She's working on succession planning. HR needs to have something in place."

Maura was silent a moment, but Grant did not speak. She continued, "This is a confidential conversation, obviously. But I need your help, so I hope you'll keep this quiet."

"All right," Grant said.

"Linda can't manage succession planning if you're a candidate to replace Rick. As your wife, she has an obvious conflict of interest. Now, speaking confidentially, as your friend and as head of HR, I think you're a strong candidate. But before I propose you as a successor, I need to know if you're interested. Because of Linda. It'd be Linda's project if you're not on the list. But if you are, then I have to handle it. So what about it?"

Grant was quiet for an uncomfortably long minute. "You know I love Operations," Grant began slowly. "But I'd be foolish to turn down an opportunity to be CEO. Will it hurt Linda if I'm a candidate?"

"I can manage it," Maura said. "But I wouldn't want her to miss the opportunity for visibility with Rick and other family members."

"Let's put it this way. I'm interested. But if it doesn't happen, I would end my career happy running Operations for PlayLand. I love what I do."

"Okay. I'll take it from here," Maura said. "I don't have a clue how far this will go. But it's work HR needs to do even if . . . when Rick returns. Thanks."

$ $ $

When he got home Tuesday evening, Grant tossed his sport coat on the back of the hearth room couch and poured himself a Scotch. He glanced over at Linda in the kitchen. She was stirring a pot that smelled like homemade soup.

"Maura called me this afternoon," he said. "Thanks for letting me bring things up by myself."

"She asked me whether you wanted to be CEO," Linda said. "I had to tell her we'd talked. But I didn't speak for you. What'd you tell her?"

Grant took his drink into the kitchen and leaned against the granite-topped island across from the stove. "I told her I was happy in Operations, but wouldn't turn down the CEO role."

"Well, that makes it sound like you really want the job." Linda turned to him with her hands on her hips. "Couldn't you show more excitement?"

"I'm not sure I am excited. This is a terrible time for PlayLand. Anyone who takes over now would inherit a mess. Plus, my candidacy will hurt you."

"What do you mean?"

"Maura says you can't handle the succession plan if I'm a candidate."

"Oh, I'm not worried about that." Linda smiled at Grant, and put her arms around his neck. "You're the best candidate we have, and you know it."

"I'm not sure the Players family would agree."

"Neither Vince nor Kevin is ready." She kissed his cheek, then turned back to her cooking. "And that's my professional opinion."

"What about your future with PlayLand?" Grant asked. "If I did become CEO, you couldn't continue in HR, could you?"

Linda shrugged. "That'd be a great problem to have, don't you think?"

$ $ $

After work, Kevin drove to the hospital. Vince hadn't been able to answer all Kevin's questions, despite his conversation with the neurologist Monday. "Talk to the doctors yourself," he had told Kevin. So today, it was Kevin's turn to go to the hospital.

Vince wasn't taking any responsibility, Kevin fumed. Vince didn't like working with Alex on finances. He groused about Ben and Jennifer, but let them do whatever they wanted. He wouldn't make the call on how to market the action figures. Kevin felt like the only competent Players brother at the moment.

Kevin met Rick's wife at the hospital. "How's it going?" he asked.

"I'm so scared." Paige wiped her eyes with a tissue. "The doctors still don't say when he'll wake up. I can't talk to the boys without crying."

"Hang in there. Let me find the nurse and get caught up. We'll talk to Jason and Jacob together."

"No change," the ICU nurse told him.

Kevin looked in on Rick lying pale and shrunken in the bed. Rick had always seemed larger than life to Kevin—eighteen years older, and off to college before Kevin was born. When Rick had come home on breaks, he had loomed like a conquering hero over his baby brother.

Kevin hadn't really known Rick until they started working together at PlayLand. And Kevin hadn't realized the breadth of Rick's responsibility as CEO until this week, when he and Vince divided Rick's schedule between them.

Rick had the weight of the world, or at least of PlayLand, on his shoulders. He had to know everything—cash flow, product costs, labor and equipment productivity, marketing plans, customer negotiations, employee relations. Kevin wondered whether he would ever be able to step into his oldest brother's shoes, much as he had wondered the same thing as a four-year-old stepping into Rick's football cleats.

"Hey, Uncle Kevin," one of the teenaged twins said as they entered their father's room. "How's Dad?" Kevin could never tell them apart by voice alone. He had to watch them awhile before he could distinguish Jacob, the quieter one, from Jason, the marginally taller one.

"About the same," Kevin said.

"He looks so old." The boy seemed close to tears. Maybe the twins had inherited their mother's weepiness, but Kevin hadn't seen it in them before. He thought they were pretty level-headed kids, for teenagers.

Kevin replied, "Hey, dude, you thought he looked old before he got hurt."

Whichever twin had spoken made a sound that was a cross between a laugh and a sob. The other twin punched Kevin's bicep. Kevin caught them both in a hug, stretching an arm around each boy's shoulders.

"How are you two doing?" he asked. These two kids were the only nephews he had. Vince had a daughter, but she lived with her mother. The twins were the only third-generation Players around.

Jason spoke first. "All I can think about is Dad."

"I keep seeing the accident over and over in my head," Jacob added. "I was driving our snowmobile. Maybe I distracted him."

Kevin looked the boy in the eye. Damn, he thought, they're as tall as I am. "Jacob, it wasn't your fault. You didn't know he was headed for a ditch."

"Maybe I'd have seen it if I'd been watching." Jacob rubbed the back of his hand across his eyes.

"Hey," Jason said. "I wasn't driving anything. I should've been looking."

"Nothing stops your dad when he's after something," Kevin said. "And he was after beating you down the hill."

"He's such a dumb ass," Jason said.

Jacob grinned weakly.

Kevin ruffled Jacob's hair. They were all right, he decided. At least for the moment. "Okay," he said, "You guys go take care of your mother. She's a basket case."

"Crying again," muttered Jason.

As the three of them turned to leave, an alarm sounded from one of the monitors hooked up to Rick. Immediately, three nurses and a doctor swarmed into the room, thrusting Kevin and his nephews out of the way. Paige ran in as the doctor shouted orders and the nurses called out Rick's vital signs.

"He's crashing."

"No heartbeat. Start CPR stat."

Kevin, Paige, and the boys watched as the medical team swung into action. One of the nurses pushed them out to the waiting area. "We'll come tell you as soon as we know what's going on," she said.

The four of them sat in silence.

After the longest fifteen minutes of Kevin's life, the doctor came out. "He's stabilized. Heart rate and breathing steady. But I don't have to tell you, this isn't a good sign."

$$\$ \$ \$$$

The white light around Rick Players was so bright, so beautiful. He had watched it forever, it seemed. It bloomed and beckoned, calling him with brilliance so sweet he could taste it. Hands appeared in the light, reaching out, their touch soft, yet powerful. He yearned for the comfort of the deep womb at the center of the light.

Then the light receded. The hands pushed away. The taste turned bitter. And he wanted to cry, if only he could.

CHAPTER 4: THURSDAY, JANUARY 11

Dressed in a grey suit and red tie, Kevin met Leo at seven thirty Thursday morning at the executive airport in Lakeview. He hated to leave town after Rick's heart stoppage the day before, but the trip couldn't be postponed.

Several hours later, when they got off the small private jet Leo had leased to take them to Toy Mart, a bitter wind blew across the tarmac from Lake Michigan. "Christ," Leo said, buttoning his camel overcoat and pulling on gloves over his diamond ring. "Give me the dry mountain air over this lake cold any day."

At Toy Mart's headquarters, Leo introduced Kevin. After the usual chitchat, Leo launched into the purpose of the meeting. "PlayLand has a fantastic new action figure line," he said. "It expands our reach into the preteen male market. We're here to give Toy Mart, as our most valued customer, a look before Toy Fair next month."

Leo spread out photographs and described the characters and their bionic properties. "Kevin's Marketing group is developing the launch plan now. We'll unveil our campaign at Toy Fair."

The Toy Mart executives listened politely. Kevin had been at enough customer meetings to know politeness didn't mean they'd agree to anything.

At the end of Leo's pitch, the senior Toy Mart executive announced, "We're looking for both product exclusivity and price concessions. What can PlayLand do for us?"

Kevin watched Leo's eyes gleam as he shifted from product spiel into negotiating. "Given the draw we think this line will have with consumers, PlayLand won't do both," Leo said. "Is exclusivity or price more important to Toy Mart? We'll do our best to sell your needs back in Lakeview."

As Kevin expected, Toy Mart's answer was, "They're both important."

"Of course they are," Leo countered. "But we can't do both. How can I help you the most?"

Kevin was impressed. Leo held his ground, while seeming to want the best for his customer. On the morning flight, Leo had bemoaned the change in customer relationships over the last twenty years. "It's no longer a chase," he'd said. "Retailers are like accountants now. They only look at the quarter's bottom line."

As Leo had predicted, Toy Mart pressed hard. "I need something on price as well as product exclusivity," their lead spokesman said. "We have some room to negotiate, but I can't give up either entirely. Make me your best offer."

"You're making my life difficult, as always," Leo said with an easy grin on his face, no hint in his voice that PlayLand was desperate for Toy Mart's business.

"That's my job. Otherwise, I'd be working for PlayLand. Get back to me when you have something to offer."

On the jet back to Lakeview, Kevin said, "We didn't get very far with them, did we?"

"Oh, they're just throwing their weight around," Leo said. "That guy at the end, he's the new buyer for their boys' department. Like all newbies, he has to make his mark. I told you they'd want a price cut."

"Yeah, but you said they'd back off."

"I'll call them tomorrow. We'll work it out. We'd be in a much better position, though, if we could give them the action figures as an exclusive, at least for some period of time. What's Vince say about the timing of the launch?"

"I haven't talked to him. He was at the hospital all day yesterday. I'll call when we get back. Ben's hounding me, too. He wants some marketing ideas."

Leo snorted. "What ideas has he given you?"

"What ideas has Ben ever given anyone?" Kevin shrugged. "I don't know what Rick sees in Ben. He's never impressed me as having any substance. But I'll work with him. We need to make the launch a success."

"How bad is business anyway?" Leo twisted his diamond ring, as if his finger itched. He sounded casual, but his nonchalance seemed feigned. "You must get the straight scoop, being part of the family."

Kevin didn't want to tell Leo more than what Rick told the officers as a group. Not that Kevin had much more information than the rest of them. "Oh, you know. We need more cash, and our revenue stream is flat. You've heard Alex."

"But how bad is it really?" Leo leaned across the narrow aisle in the plane toward Kevin.

"I think we'll be all right by the end of the year. But like Alex said, we have some hard months ahead." It was Kevin's turn to hide his anxiety, something his communications and marketing role required him to do every day. "If we can weather this year, we should be able to get back on a growth track."

$ $ $

Word of Rick's downturn on Tuesday buzzed through PlayLand's halls all day Wednesday, and Maura responded to frantic questions from managers and media. So when she arrived at work Thursday, with no sign Rick's condition had worsened again, she was relieved.

Maura opened an email from Linda Mason, titled "Succession Analysis Attached." The succession plan might be more important than she had suspected, Maura mused. She read Linda's summary of each of the PlayLand executives who were candidates to replace Rick Players.

"Vince Players: Age 46; currently Vice President of Product Development. Worked for PlayLand since age 24 (22 years). Started as supervisor in Manufacturing. Average reviews. After two years moved to a Product Manager role in Games. Average reviews. After two years promoted to purchasing role in Asia. Mediocre reviews. Moved back to headquarters in another Product Manager role after two years. Average reviews. After two more years moved to Sales Manager role in Detroit. Mediocre reviews. Promoted to Product Development Director in 1997. Average reviews. After four years, in 2001, promoted to Vice President of Product Development when Rick Players promoted to CEO.

"Strengths: Respected as a family member. Knows our existing products. Also knows Operations and Sales.

"Weaknesses: Does not have broad knowledge of the business; particularly weak in financial acumen. Does not have strong reputation as a manager; not a good motivator of people. Not creative — no new product launches since he took over product development."

Maura could tell Linda had tried to give a balanced assessment of Vince. But there wasn't much to say. Vince managed to get the job done, but he was negative and indecisive.

Maura moved on to Linda's assessment of the next candidate:

"Leo Benson: Age 60; currently Vice President of Sales. Started at PlayLand in 1970, a year after graduating from college, as entry level sales representative. Strong performance, at top of his district. Promoted to Sales Manager after five years. Continued strong performance. Promoted to Regional Sales Manager in 1981. Performance compared to sales objectives strong some years, not others. Promoted to Vice President of Sales in 1994; still holds that position.

"Strengths: Knows our customers well. Strong customer relations skills. Strong advocate for Sales division.

"Weaknesses: No experience outside of Sales. Has not increased sales during the last few years, though he blames the lack of new product. Not viewed as a team player by employees outside of Sales."

Maura smiled at Linda's accurate picture of Leo. He'd been a loyal employee, but he didn't have the personality to be CEO. He was more loyal to the Sales division than to the overall success of PlayLand.

Maura was surprised Linda had even included the next candidate on her list, not because he didn't have the knowledge, but because Alex also didn't have a CEO's demeanor.

> "Alex Draper: Age 46; currently Chief Financial Officer. Began career at a major public accounting firm, where he was PlayLand's outside auditor. Hired by PlayLand in 1994 as Accounting Manager. Strong performance ratings. Moved to Tax Manager in 1998. Continued strong performance. Promoted to CFO in 2003. Good performance since that time.

> "Strengths: Thorough understanding of PlayLand business. Works well with bankers and auditors. Respected for his financial expertise within the company.

> "Weaknesses: Knows product costing, but not product development. Not creative — no understanding of marketing. Not tested as a manager outside Finance. Not a strong communicator."

After reflecting on his track record, Maura conceded that Alex was a possible contender for the CEO role. But he wasn't a strong leader, as his nervousness and stridency since Rick's accident had shown.

Besides, the Players family had always focused on product development and manufacturing over finances. What would the family want for the future? Maybe because of PlayLand's cash flow problems, it was time for a strong financial manager to take the helm. But Alex?

Then Maura turned to Linda's description of Kevin Players.

> "Kevin Players: Age 35; currently Vice President of Marketing & Communications. Started with PlayLand in 1994, as supervisor in Manufacturing. Good reviews. After two years moved to Product Manager position. Good reviews. Promoted to Sales Manager position in Los Angeles. Strong performance. Sent in ideas for how sales force could market products locally. After three years in Sales, returned to headquarters as Product Development Director for Games; worked closely with the Marketing group. Instrumental in launching video game line. Strong performance

ratings. Promoted in 2005 to Vice President of Marketing; added Communications responsibilities in 2006.

"Strengths: Quick learner. Excellent communicator — a natural at the communications function. Respected both internally and externally.

"Weaknesses: Little depth in any function, though has done well in Manufacturing, Product Development, Sales, and Marketing. Needs more financial acumen. Still inexperienced relative to other candidates."

Maura could tell Linda liked Kevin. Most people did, including Maura. If it were ten years in the future, Kevin would be a strong CEO candidate. Unfortunately, he didn't have enough experience yet.

And finally, Linda had started a recap on Grant:

"Grant Mason: Age 58; currently Vice President of Operations. ROTC in college; Army veteran, honorable discharge. After military service, joined plastics manufacturing company making housewares, where he worked from 1974 until 1998. Rose through the ranks from frontline supervisor to Chief Operating Officer. When larger company bought his employer, he took severance package in the reduction in force after acquisition. Joined PlayLand as Vice President of Operations in 1998. Still in that position.

"Strengths: . . .

"Weaknesses: . . .

As Maura and Linda had agreed, Linda left the qualitative assessment of Grant blank.

Maura turned to her keyboard to add her commentary on Grant. More than half the company's employees worked in Operations, so she dealt with Grant frequently. He was fair to employees, and worked well with Human Resources. He was her favorite candidate, and that's what she would tell Rick or anyone else. But she made sure her written assessment was objective.

> "Strengths: Deep knowledge of manufacturing, distribution, and procurement. Experience mostly in plastics. Excellent manager of people; one of our best communicators with employees. Understands costs.

> "Weaknesses: Limited experience outside of Operations. Little knowledge of product development. Financial acumen beyond product costing unknown."

When Maura finished, she leaned back in her chair. It's a good start, she thought. A good overview of the top candidates. Of course, the Players family might decide to replace Rick with someone from outside the company. Or they might insist another Players family member lead the company.

But, of course, the best thing would be if Rick recovered quickly.

Now, what should she do with this analysis? Maura didn't know whom to involve next.

Rick had run the company single-handedly since Maura had been at PlayLand. His title had been Chief Operating Officer then, but his father hadn't been active. Maura had heard Richard Players was now completely incapacitated by Alzheimer's. She couldn't talk to him.

Maura thought Rick held his father's proxy. She had no idea who had Rick's proxy, if anyone.

It would be awkward to talk to Vince or Kevin. PlayLand didn't have an independent board of directors; the family ran the company. Maura decided to talk to Dewayne Jefferson. He would know the legalities of who was in charge.

$ $ $

By the time he got back to his office late Thursday, Kevin was dragging. He hadn't slept much all week because of Rick. And the trip to Wisconsin had ended with Leo sulking when Kevin wouldn't give him the inside scoop.

Now Kevin wanted to go home, but he still needed to talk to Ben

Thornton. He and Ben had only traded phone calls since before Rick's accident.

Kevin's office in the Marketing Department was less formal than Rick's or Vince's, and messier. He threw his coat on a side chair and moved a few stacks of paper from the desk to the floor so he could put his feet on his desk. He loosened his tie as he sat and dialed Ben.

"Ben, it's Kevin. You wanted to talk about the action figures."

"Yeah. Jennifer has this crazy idea about comic books. You're the expert marketer. I need your help. She shouldn't spend our marketing dollars on some harebrained scheme. And she shouldn't stick her pretty little nose into New Ventures anyway. Let her play with dolls."

"What do you think we should do?" Kevin ignored the condescension toward Jennifer in Ben's voice.

"That's your job. You're head of Marketing. Or do you need to put one of your people on it?"

As usual, Ben passed the buck to someone else. Kevin wondered again why Rick kept Ben around.

"Actually, I think comic books are kind of clever," he said. "Why don't you think they'll work?" Ben might be right, but there was something about Ben that made Kevin want to argue.

"You can't be serious," Ben said. "She had no cost figures. She's got no talent lined up for storyboards or artwork. She can't get it done by Toy Fair."

Kevin decided to give Ben something. "Well, typically we'd do a product giveaway and coupons in weekend flyers. We could do that." But he didn't want to. He wanted to let Jennifer try her idea. All Ben was doing was complaining about Jennifer. "But why not try something different this time?"

Ben snorted. "You aren't sure comics will work, are you?"

Kevin rolled his eyes at Ben's negativity. "No. So have a backup plan using the more traditional approach. But let Jennifer do her thing. Vince can make the call once we get more details on both."

Kevin was irritated at Vince as well as Ben. Vince should have resolved the argument between Ben and Jennifer, instead of Kevin getting dragged into the brawl.

"Thanks," Ben said. "I'll tell Vince we've talked. I'll put together a traditional promotion, like you suggested. Let me know what you think, if Jennifer brings you any details on comics."

Kevin hung up and turned away from the phone. Jennifer Scott stood in his doorway.

"Kevin, can I show you something?" She bounced into his office, smiling, her long hair and dangly earrings swinging. She carried a roll of large papers. "Vince isn't in, and I have to show someone."

"Is it comic books?"

Jennifer's face fell. "You talked to Ben."

"Just got off the phone with him. He doesn't think much of the idea." Kevin smiled. "But he never thinks much of anything you do. Why doesn't he like you, anyway?"

Jennifer tossed her head. "He asked me out a couple of years ago. Right after I was promoted to Director, when he had that line of activity kits that flopped. I told him I didn't want to get involved with anyone at work. He's bad-mouthed me ever since. Not that I care. He's old enough to be my dad. Not my type, personally or professionally."

Kevin's jaw clenched, though it was none of his business whom Ben dated. "Show me what you have," he said, gesturing at the chair across from him. "Just put that file on the floor."

Jennifer moved the file, sat, and unrolled a packet of drawings. "You know Gus Powell, don't you? In Games? He mostly works on board games, but he's a real artist. Look." She gestured at the sketches. "So, it seems Gus developed some characters before he came to PlayLand. He couldn't get Ted to use them, so he pitched them to Ben. Ben turned them into the action figures we're about to launch."

Jennifer leaned her arms on Kevin's desk to hold the rolled paper open. Her eyes sparkled. "Gus could draw the comics for us. But I think we need some product tests. I'm not convinced the names are right. And I want to get some reaction to the stories we come up with. It might be difficult working with Gus because these are like his babies. Like some of the doll designers. They practically breast feed their creations."

Kevin smiled at Jennifer's enthusiasm. A nice contrast to Ben's negativity.

"Let me see." Kevin turned the drawings toward him. He was

surprised; Gus's illustrations looked professional. They weren't finished, but the characters depicted were colorful and distinctive. "These are really good. What's the story line?"

"As best as I could get it from Gus, they're superheroes in a future universe, each with special bionic powers. That idea isn't necessarily new, but the world they come from is a mix of technical and nature. Machines and the environment intertwined. There could be some great plots developed. As I said, we need some product tests and focus groups with some preteen boys." She wrinkled her nose. "Do they call preadolescent boys 'preteens'? I'm so used to dealing with girls, I'm not even sure what the market segments are for boys."

"What do you need from me?" Kevin leaned back in his chair.

Jennifer grinned, looking like she was seventeen instead of almost thirty. "Nothing really. I just wanted to show off what I had to someone, and Vince wasn't there." Then her face sobered. "But since I caught you, what do you think? Seriously. Can we sell action figures with the comic books as a hook? What about licensing to third parties?"

Kevin nodded. "It's got potential. What about timing? Can you be ready by Toy Fair?"

"If Gus works with me for the next month, I can have prototypes by Toy Fair. And comic books on the shelves by late spring. That'd be a few weeks before the first action figures launch."

"I'll tell Vince it's worth pursuing. But you should know I told Ben to work on a backup plan. Just in case the costs or timing on this don't work."

Jennifer made a face at the reference to Ben, but didn't object. "Do you have anyone who can work with me on focus groups?"

"I'll get you someone. But you'll have to get tests underway next week if you want results in time to draft the comic prototypes."

"I'm on it." Jennifer rolled up the drawings.

Kevin watched her as she almost danced out of his office. He'd always made it a rule not to date PlayLand employees. But he wondered if he was Jennifer's type.

$$$

It was only Thursday, but Vince had already had a rough week. He hated winter. He couldn't stay focused when he couldn't play a couple of rounds of golf a week. He'd washed out on the PGA circuit, but golf was still the only thing that relaxed him.

He had to deal with the turf war between Ben and Jennifer. And Leo said Toy Mart wanted both price breaks and exclusive product. Alex would never support price reductions, not with PlayLand's balance sheet out of whack, so Vince would have to come up with exclusives for Toy Mart. And Rick wasn't around to bail him out.

Simply thinking about these problems made Vince's stomach hurt. He wasn't cut out for the business world like Rick and his dad. Maybe he should have stayed on the pro circuit after all.

The downturn in Rick's condition Tuesday night had panicked Vince. Until then, he'd been confident Rick would wake up soon. Once Rick was conscious, he'd take care of everything. But if Rick didn't wake up, what would Vince do?

He'd never talked to his father or Rick about who would succeed Rick as CEO, but everyone would expect Vince to be next in line. Vince had always assumed Rick would stay at the helm another fifteen or twenty years.

At least, that had been the plan until Sunday. Would Vince have to step up now? He already had more than he could handle on his plate.

He needed to know where he stood. He picked up his phone and called Maura. "It's Vince," he said when she answered. "I know this is a weird question, but you HR types are probably used to it. Did you and Rick do any work on succession planning behind Rick?"

Maura was silent, which worried Vince. Christ, why didn't she want to talk to him?

Then Maura spoke hesitantly. "HR is always noodling. Why?"

"You know Rick's heart stopped Tuesday night. What if he doesn't get better? Someone needs to think about what's next." Vince tried to sound casual.

"Has anyone asked you?"

"No," Vince said. "I'm just thinking out loud. I thought we should be prepared."

"It's kind of awkward, Vince, because of the family situation. Even though HR typically does work on succession planning, without your dad or Rick in the loop, we don't have any direction."

Maura was usually more forthcoming. Vince wondered what she

was hiding.

"Then we're in the same boat," Vince said. "No one's giving me any direction either. All I want to know is, if Dad has a good day and we talk, or if Kevin and I talk, or if Rick wakes up and I talk to him, can I tell them you have something?"

"You can tell them I could pull some thoughts together quickly and give them my perspective."

Vince decided to press her. "Do you have anything you could give me now?"

She was silent again for a moment. "Vince, I can't do that. I'll have to deal with Rick or your father on this, unless they're both completely out of the picture. Then I don't know what I'd do. I guess Dewayne would have to tell us. But let's be frank. You'd be a candidate to replace Rick. That's why it's awkward. And you can assume most of the other officers would also be candidates. And, of course, the company could look outside of PlayLand as well."

"Okay. I get it." A pain flashed through Vince's stomach. He still didn't know where he stood. What did she mean he'd be a candidate? And which other officers did she think were candidates? "Dad's condition is pretty iffy most days. The whole reason for me asking is because Rick might not wake up. If it seems appropriate, I'll mention it to Dad. And, of course, we all hope Rick wakes up soon, and it's a moot point."

"Yes, we do," Maura said.

$ $ $

After talking to Maura, Vince had had enough for the day. He packed up his briefcase and stopped by Kevin's office on his way out. "I'm going to the hospital," he said. "Any news?"

"Heard from Paige an hour ago," Kevin replied. "Nothing new."

"Leo called me about Toy Mart," Vince said. "He wants exclusive action figures for them. How the hell am I supposed to do that? We're scraping as it is to get prototypes ready for Toy Fair."

Kevin shook his head. "It was a miserable meeting. Toy Mart wants price concessions and product exclusivity. Leo says they'll cave. But if we don't have something to give them, I don't know how hard we can push."

"Another thing," Vince said. "You've got to help me with Jennifer and Ben. They're fighting again. Ben says he tried to get in touch with you. Meanwhile, Jennifer is doing her own thing. I wish the two of them could get along."

"I talked to Ben. He's working on a generic plan." Kevin hesitated, then continued. "You know, Vince, their squabbles are your own fault. You've let that situation fester. She's worth two of him, and you know it." Kevin grinned. "She's better looking, too." Then his face turned serious. "When . . . if . . . Rick comes back, we have to convince him Ben only causes trouble around here. And if Rick doesn't come back, we'll have to deal with Ben ourselves."

Vince didn't respond. There didn't seem to be any point to replying.

"Jennifer tells me she's working on comic books to hype the action figures," Kevin said. "Do you like the idea?"

Vince shrugged. Now Kevin was pushing him, too. "Sounds expensive. I asked her to make a business case and get back to me next week. What'd you think?"

Kevin leaned back in his chair. "I liked what she had. If the numbers hold up, I'd go with her idea. But it's your call."

Vince turned to leave. He debated whether to raise his conversation with Maura with Kevin. After a moment, he turned back to his brother. "Say, did you know HR's working on a succession plan for Rick?"

"I hadn't heard. But I would've assumed they had something." Kevin didn't sound concerned.

"Have you ever seen it?" Vince frowned at his younger brother.

Kevin shook his head. "Nope. I'd think they'd talk directly to Rick. Or to Dad before Rick. I've only been a vice president for a couple of years. I'm still getting a handle on Marketing and Communications." He gave a mock salute to his brother. "It's all yours, pal."

Vince snorted. "I've got enough to do."

"Then we'd better hope Rick gets better and saves both our hides," Kevin replied.

Vince's stomach ached for the whole drive to the hospital. He dug an antacid out of his pocket as he walked into St. Luke's and headed for ICU. His heart sank when he saw Paige. Another problem.

"Vince," she said, "Thank God you're here."

"What happened?" he asked.

"That's just it," Paige said. "Nothing's happening. I'm spending all my time here, with no response from Rick. The boys came after school, but they left for soccer practice. I'm all by myself again." She started to cry.

"Paige, you've been crying for five days now," Vince said. "Maybe you should go home."

"How can I think about anything but Rick?" she said, wiping her eyes. "I know I'm a problem for you and Kevin, and you have the business to run, but I'm so alone."

"How can I help?"

"Just let me vent." Paige smiled through her tears. "You've always been a good brother to Rick and a good friend to me."

Vince sat beside her and patted her hand. She took his hand and held it tightly. The doctors came through on evening rounds, and Vince asked about his brother.

"We can keep him in intensive care for a few more days," the neurologist said. "But your family should start planning where to move him if there isn't any change. We're not doing anything for him here that couldn't be done in another, less expensive environment. A nursing home handling long-term acute care could keep him comfortable and monitor his condition as well as we can."

"What are you saying?" Vince asked. "We need to move him? It's only been five days."

"I can authorize him to stay in the ICU awhile longer, but I suggest you start exploring other options. If he wakes up, it's another story. Then we'd want to put him into rehab."

Paige's tears flowed again. Vince called Kevin on his cell phone and told him the news.

"A nursing home?" Kevin said. "That's pretty drastic. Can't they keep him in the hospital?"

"For now, yes, but for how long? Should we tell Dad Rick is sick?" Vince said. "I didn't mind waiting a couple of days, when we thought Rick would come out of it quickly. But if Rick isn't going to wake up, we're going to have to make other plans. Maybe if Dad has a good day . . . . And how are we going to manage the business without Rick?"

"We can manage PlayLand for a while longer," Kevin said. "I hate to look like we can't cope without Rick. If Dad's coherent, he'll only worry. If he's not coherent, he won't understand. And he'll forget as soon as we tell him."

"But we can't cope without Rick," Vince said.

Vince returned to Rick's room and sat back in the chair next to the bed. The monitors around Rick whirred and beeped.

"Rick, you've left an awful mess," Vince said. He took a deep breath and sighed, the sound of his exhale echoed by the ventilator breathing for Rick. "If you're going to stay in the land of the living, I suggest you come back now."

Vince dozed next to Rick's hospital bed through the evening. Over time, his stomach quieted, lulled by the rhythmic sound of the monitors. Finally, he went back to his empty townhouse to sleep in a real bed. He deserved a little peace to help him get through the rest of the week ahead.

$ $ $

At home that evening, Maura curled up on the bed next to Carlos. "I've always been glad PlayLand was a privately held company so I didn't have to worry about share price," she said. "But I got my fill of private company problems today."

Carlos put down his book and glanced at her over his reading glasses. He had only grown more handsome as he aged, Maura thought. "What happened?" Carlos asked.

"Vince wants to know if we have a succession plan for Rick's role."

"Isn't that what you've been doing?"

"Yes, but I don't like talking to Vince about it. He all but asked me who's leading the list. I had to tell him he was out of line. Most of the officers are potential successors. It's not my call to say who's at the top of the list. But I can't tell Vince to go ask Rick. And I don't know who else to talk to. I'm pretty sure Richard is out of the loop."

"What about talking to Vince and Kevin together?"

"That's your Latino sense of family," Maura said running her hand down Carlos's cheek. "I don't think the Players boys have ever talked about succession. Rick never seemed to talk to them any more than to any of the rest of the officers."

"That's because you are all so brilliant," Carlos said, pushing Maura over on her back and kissing her. "At least the one I know is."

"You're changing the subject," Maura said, smiling.

"That's because I'm brilliant, too."

Chapter 5: Friday, January 12

Kevin's telephone rang early Friday morning. He shook his head groggily, sat up in his lonely king-size bed, and grabbed the phone.

"Hello." He glanced at the clock. Five o'clock.

"Kevin, it's Paige," she said in tears. "It's Rick."

"What happened? Why didn't someone call me?" Kevin assumed the worst.

"He's moving. Groaning a little. The hospital just called. I'm going over. Can you come?"

"Be there as soon as I can. Is he conscious?"

"No. But he's better. I know he'll get better." Paige sounded hopeful, though Kevin could tell she was still crying.

Kevin showered and shaved quickly. Was this really a good sign about Rick? Or had Paige blown a small improvement out of proportion? He'd know soon enough. But he hoped Rick was waking up; they needed him.

Kevin took the elevator from his top-floor loft apartment to the parking garage. He'd bought into an early wave of loft conversions. The neighborhood was still chic, though prices had fallen.

At the hospital, he waited with Paige and Vince for the neurologist to start his rounds.

"There's definitely some improvement," the doctor said. "He's moving on his own and making sounds. His eyelids have fluttered. These are his first responses since the accident. His Glasgow score is up to a six or seven. We'll wait to see what happens next."

"Won't he continue to get better?" Paige asked.

The doctor shook his head. "Sometimes the patient remains in a coma at this stage. I don't want you to get your hopes up."

"Can we talk to him?" Kevin asked.

The doctor smiled. "Talking to him is more for your benefit than his. Some people think coma patients can hear. It can't hurt, but don't expect him to respond. Or to remember any of it if he wakes up."

"I'll sit with him today," Paige said. "You guys go to work. I'll call you if there's a change. And I want Jason and Jacob with their father today."

Vince offered to bring the boys to the hospital. Kevin sat with Paige by Rick's bed until Vince and the twins returned, then he left for the office.

When Kevin arrived at PlayLand, he called Maura. "Good news for a change," he said. "Rick's showing some signs of progress." They drafted an updated bulletin and sent it to the division heads. As word spread, it felt like the entire building took a deep breath and relaxed.

$$$

Maura hoped the worst of Rick's illness was behind them. If Rick got better, she wouldn't have to deal with a succession plan. Not until she could talk to Rick himself.

The discussion Maura had had with Vince the day before troubled her. The Players family might assume the next oldest son was the logical candidate to succeed Rick, but Maura couldn't recommend Vince. Where would that leave her if the family disagreed?

Maura knew she managed Human Resources well. Rick listened to her and backed her up with the rest of his staff. But if the next CEO didn't have confidence in her, she wouldn't be successful, and she wouldn't be able to make a difference to employees or the business. Unfortunately, succession issues were the type of problem that got HR people in trouble with company owners.

But she had more immediate problems. Like the lawsuit Steve Williams had filed. She needed to talk to Dewayne. The best defense in any lawsuit was always the truth. But in this case the truth would highlight the plaintiff's disability claim.

They'd been right to fire Williams, Maura still believed. He had ignored orders to call on his customers. But PlayLand had changed the rules on a guy whose agoraphobia limited his ability to do the job. Who knew what a jury might do?

She also should push harder for headcount reduction, even if the other PlayLand officers didn't want it. She'd have to battle her peers, and also help employees whose lives would be uprooted without their jobs.

Alex would back her. In fact, he'd want to go further than Maura. Grant would argue, but in the end he'd be reasonable. Leo would fight any changes in Sales. Only heaven knew what Vince would do. The support functions—IT, Legal, Marketing and Communications, Human Resources—weren't big enough to matter. But they would all have to participate.

Maura hated pushing headcount reductions, but payroll was a huge part of the cost structure—it had to be cut. The only alternative to cost cutting was increased sales, but she could only work on what she could influence, and that was headcount.

The HR Directors had submitted their proposals to her. Maura started putting salary and benefit costs next to personnel numbers and worked on a company-wide recommendation. She would share it with Alex and Grant first, she decided. They would be constructive, even if they disagreed with the specifics.

$ $ $

Jennifer hated talking with Legal. The attorneys always had some reason she couldn't do what she wanted. But she swallowed hard and called Dewayne Jefferson.

"I need some advice about licensing new characters," Jennifer began when Dewayne answered. "We want to market the new action figure line with comic books. And I'd like to license the characters to third parties on other merchandise. We could make a big splash if we do this right."

"Who holds the copyrights in the characters?" Dewayne's voice boomed into her ear.

"What? Well, we're developing them with Gus Powell's help. He works in Games. So, I guess we do. Don't we?" She hadn't thought about any copyright problems. Ben should have sorted that out.

"Did Gus develop them for PlayLand?" Dewayne asked.

"Well, sort of. He says he started working on them in college. Then he worked with Ben Thornton on our new line."

"Are they his, or are they PlayLand's?"

Jennifer felt like she was being cross-examined. Wasn't

Dewayne supposed to be on her side? "Kind of both, I guess," she said, scowling at her phone.

"The law doesn't have a 'kind of both' status." Jennifer imagined Dewayne steepling his fingers as he talked into his speakerphone. "The characters are either Gus's or they're PlayLand's as a 'work made for hire.' You can't even think about licensing until we know who owns them."

All Jennifer could say was "Oh." She'd expected a damper, but Dewayne might shut down the whole product launch.

"Set up a meeting," Dewayne ordered. "Bring Vince, so we can determine our options. I'll get our intellectual property attorney involved. We can't launch the action figures until we understand the facts."

"Okay," Jennifer said.

She slammed her phone down. This always happened when Legal was involved. They'd killed a new doll line two years ago, just because it looked a lot like a competitor's line. Of course, the PlayLand dolls looked like the other doll line, Jennifer fumed. PlayLand had to compete with the competitor's hot new product. She'd made sure the PlayLand dolls had trendier clothes and sharper hair styles. But the dolls had to look like what girls wanted to get them to buy PlayLand's line.

Jennifer called Karen Heintz in Procurement. "What do you know about 'works made for hire'? Legal says we might not be able to develop the action figures using Gus's characters."

"It has something to do with where they were developed—by Gus here while he worked for PlayLand, or when he was on his own. Is that what Legal's worried about?"

"Yep."

"Why didn't Ben get the ownership resolved a long time ago?" Karen asked. "We're gearing up for production already, for God's sake."

"That's what I thought," Jennifer said. "I need to talk to Vince. I want him to hear this from me. Not Dewayne or Ben."

Jennifer ended the call and lowered her head into her hands, pushing her hair back out of her face. Vince would blow up, she was sure of it. He never wanted to hear about problems. But if PlayLand couldn't sell the action figures, they had a major problem. Beyond major. Monumental.

She'd have to think about how to approach Vince. Was there anyone who could tell her what Ben and Gus had talked about regarding the action figures?

The only people she could think of were Vince or Kevin. Vince would have mentioned any concerns about ownership if he'd known about them. So she guessed he was in the dark.

Jennifer walked down the hall to Kevin's office, her heels clicking briskly. "Kevin, got a minute?"

"What's wrong? You're not as excited as yesterday."

"I just talked to Legal. Dewayne is always so negative."

"Yeah, well, that's his job. He's usually right."

"Dewayne asked if PlayLand has the rights to the action figures Gus developed in college. Do you know if anyone's talked to Gus?"

"Shouldn't Ben have talked to Gus?"

"Ben or Vince." Jennifer sighed. "I'll talk to Vince, but I wondered if Ben mentioned anything to you."

"No, I assumed the rights had been worked out. That should have been done months ago." Kevin rubbed the back of his neck. "If we can't launch the new line, we're cooked. We won't have anything to promise Toy Mart or the bankers."

"Toy Mart?" Jennifer hadn't heard of any problems with Toy Mart.

"Leo and I met with them yesterday. The head Toy Mart buyer wants terms. Both price discounts and product exclusivity. That's what it'll take to get a big order from them."

"I'll let you know what Vince says," Jennifer said.

"Assuming we proceed with the action figures, do the comic books look like they'll pan out?" Kevin asked.

"Procurement says the costs will work. If Gus can create the artwork and story lines quickly enough. We only have a few weeks to get a mock-up done before Toy Fair."

"Keep me posted." Kevin grinned as Jennifer turned to go. "And hang in there. It's a great idea."

Jennifer smiled back. "Thanks."

Jennifer walked down the hall, still smiling. Talking to Kevin always made her feel better. Unlike Vince.

Her mood dropped when she arrived at Vince's office. But she had to tell him about the problem with Gus. "Vince, we need to talk."

Vince looked up, scowling. The last of Jennifer's good humor evaporated as she sat. "Legal's worried about whether we have the rights to the action figures," she said.

Vince's frown deepened. "Of course we do. They were developed in New Product."

Jennifer took a deep breath. "Did you know Gus created them when he was in college? Before he ever worked for PlayLand."

Vince's face went white. Jennifer could see him gulp. "Christ, no," he said. "I knew Gus had worked with Ben, but I didn't know they were from his pre-PlayLand days."

"Well, that's what Gus says. So you and Ben never talked about Gus?"

"Why would I have even thought to ask Ben?" Vince shouted, as he threw his pen down on his desk. "It's Ben's fucking job to make sure we have the rights to new products." He slumped in his chair. "Shit."

"So Dewayne wants me to set up a meeting. You, me, him, and Gus."

Vince shook his head. "I want to talk to Ben first. We need Product Development together before we meet with Legal." Vince paused. "I guess I'd better call Ben."

"Okay," Jennifer responded. Did Vince want her to talk to Ben? Jennifer wondered. But Ben would never tell her the truth. Vince had to step up; he was the boss.

"Dewayne wants to talk soon," she said. "I'll set the meeting up for early next week. Can you get to Ben this afternoon?"

Vince waved his hand vaguely, dismissing her.

Had she been too direct with Vince? Jennifer worried as she left his office. He hated conflict, and she'd dumped a doozy in his lap.

She went back to Kevin's office. "Vince didn't know anything," she said. "He's going to talk to Ben. I hate being the one to tell Vince."

"Why's that?" Kevin asked.

Jennifer hesitated. For a moment she'd forgotten Vince was Kevin's brother. She'd vented with Kevin like he was her friend. "Oh, you know," she said, "You always hate to bring your boss a problem."

"Well, he needs to deal with this," Kevin responded. "Don't feel bad."

$ $ $

Vince leaned back in his chair and grimaced at the ceiling. He didn't need another crisis, but he had one. If Ben had known PlayLand might not own the rights to the action figures and hadn't told Vince, he'd screwed up royally. And if Ben hadn't known about the problem, he was incompetent. Either way, Vince had a catastrophe on his hands, and it was all Ben's fault.

This was the type of question Vince always took to Rick. He never knew how hard he could push Ben. Rick always took Ben's side. No one else even liked Ben.

Hell, his life would be so much easier if Rick just woke up. But Vince couldn't wait for Rick to get better. This was too important. He had to know what rights PlayLand had in the action figures. And he had to know before he met with Legal.

Vince sighed, then went to Ben's office. The conversation with Ben couldn't wait for a secretary to set up a meeting. Jennifer had made it clear Legal was pushing. Vince had to be a step ahead of Dewayne, which wouldn't be easy.

That was another thing. When did Jennifer start meeting with Legal, rather than letting Vince talk directly to Dewayne? PlayLand's procedures were falling apart, and Vince didn't know what to do about it.

"Hey, Vince, what's up?" Ben leaned back and put his feet up on his desk as Vince sat across from him. It irritated Vince when Ben was so informal. Vince's family owned the damn company, not Ben's.

"We have a problem," Vince began.

"Won't the comic books work? Do they cost too much?" Ben chortled, folding his arms behind his head. "I knew Jennifer's idea wouldn't pan out. Boy's market isn't like her frilly little girl world."

"It's not the comic books, Ben. Legal's wondering whether we even have the rights to the action figures."

"Shit," Ben slammed his feet to the floor and leaned over the desk toward Vince. "Did Jennifer call Legal? What the fuck for?"

"She says Gus developed the action figures when he was in

college."

"So?" Ben settled back in his seat, grinning. "Is that the problem? Gus and I have a deal. Why'd she call Legal?"

"A deal?"

"Yeah, Gus gets 'creative credit,'" Ben used his fingers for quotes. "And PlayLand gets the action figures. I told him that's the only way the line would ever get produced. He wants the crap out in the market, and he's willing to give up his rights as long as he gets some recognition within PlayLand. He wants a better job here."

"Did you talk to Legal to see if that would work?" Vince asked.

"Shit, Vince. You know Legal always wants it buttoned down in their underwear. I don't have a written contract with Gus, if that's what you mean. But he understands the situation. I told him if we got the action figures to market, I'd do my best to get him out of Games. Games loaned him to me for this project, but I said I'd get him moved into New Ventures permanently. Games is a wasteland, particularly that board game crap. Gus has a hard-on about his action figures. That's all he wants."

Vince sighed. His head hurt, and he wasn't getting through to Ben how serious this was. "We need to meet with Dewayne, and see what he says. We can't fuck this up, Ben. If we don't have the rights to the action figures locked down tight, Legal won't let us take the product to market. I don't have to tell you what that will mean for New Ventures or the company."

"No problem, Vince. I've got Gus in my pocket."

$ $ $

After Vince left, Ben closed his office door. He usually kept the door open so he could watch who came to see Vince. And who headed down the hall toward Rick's office. Ben liked his office. Good location and he'd hassled Procurement until they found him decent furniture. Not quite as nice as what his old pal Rick had, but not bad.

Now Ben stewed over how to handle the fucked up mess with the action figures. If that fucking Jennifer hadn't wormed her way into the product launch, Ben could have kept it under control. He could let Gus have his fucking action heroes, and Ben would get credit for launching a new product line, which would keep him on Rick's good side.

Ben had worked hard since college to stay on Rick's good side, even when he wanted to puke at sucking up to Rick. He mimicked what Rick did—clothes, classes, friends, the way he cut his hair. Rick was Ben's highway out of hell, his road out of the trailer park. The football scholarship had only got him halfway where he wanted to be. Rick was the first class ticket.

Ben seethed, remembering all the times he had helped Rick, clearing the way for Rick on the football field and off. Ben tackled, so Rick could run. Lineman Ben made the holes for quarterback Rick to throw through. Ben had Rick's back during their barroom brawls. Rick owed him, and Ben made sure Rick never forgot it.

But for years Ben had had crappy jobs at PlayLand in Manufacturing and Sales. Still, he smiled for Rick. Even married Rick's friend. She'd had a fucking fortune, which hadn't hurt. Ben had hoped marriage would get him away from Rick, but his wife had made him sign a prenup. So after the divorce, Ben crawled back to Rick.

Then there was Nicole; Ben had really covered Rick's ass then. Of course, Ben thought smiling, he'd covered Nicole's ass as well, but that wasn't any hardship. Until after they were married. Ben had found out too late she was a drunk. He should have realized that was the only reason she'd hooked up with Rick in the first place.

So now Ben was back at PlayLand. Making toys, and working for that asshole Vince. Hell, Vince was just Rick's kid brother. Vince should be reporting to Ben.

Ben needed the action figures to be a success. If they were, maybe he could get Rick to promote him over Vince. If Rick would wake the hell up.

Why the fuck had Rick been playing with his goddamn sons anyway? Fuck Rick for risking his life; Ben needed Rick. If Vince took over PlayLand, he'd boot Ben out in a frigging minute.

Ben didn't know who he was most pissed at—Gus, Jennifer, Vince, or Rick. They were all getting in his way or letting him down. And he had to clean up the mess.

Ben picked up his phone and dialed Gus. "Say, Gus, what have you been telling Jennifer?"

"Nothing. She met with me. I told her all the stories about

Adolpho and my other characters. Same as I told you last fall."

"Yeah? Well, now she's butting in. We may not get them out to market."

"But she said she wanted to develop comic books. Remember? I told you I wanted to draw comics and I had some story lines? She wants my stuff." Ben could hear Gus's voice rising in pitch.

"Calm down, Gus. If we wait for comic books, who knows when the action figures will see the light of day? It could be another frigging year. Is that what you want? If that happens, I don't know if I can save a spot for you in New Ventures."

"You promised, Ben." Gus's voice rose another notch. "You said if I gave you the drawings and worked on the specs, you'd move me into New Ventures. I did what you said. Got the characters into production. Now Jennifer wants my comic books. Why can't I work with her?"

"The comics aren't a done deal yet. Vince hasn't made the call."

Gus continued as if Ben hadn't said anything. "Jennifer says we can do comics. She says we can draw them while the figures are in Manufacturing. I've always wanted to do a comic book. And you promised you'd get me out of Games. I can't keep working with these assholes anymore."

Gus babbled on. Ben couldn't rely on him to talk to Vince or Dewayne. He'd have to handle it himself. But he had to keep Gus on his side.

"Look, Gus, if you go play with Jennifer and her dolls, don't come crying to me when it doesn't work out. Just make sure Legal knows we had a deal, that you gave the action figures to me. I can't get you into New Ventures unless the product gets to market. Don't screw it up."

Ben slammed down his phone, bile rising to his throat. Gus could send Ben's is career up in flames. Gus would fold if Legal pressed. Why wasn't Rick around to salvage this mess?

CHAPTER 6: TUESDAY, JANUARY 16

Maura dreaded the week ahead, even the short week after the Martin Luther King, Jr., holiday. Due to the Monday holiday, the officer meeting had been rescheduled for Tuesday morning, so at eight thirty Maura arrived at the executive conference room.

Alex again sat fussing with his folders, squaring their sides to the edge of the table. Leo and Vince talked in a corner. Rather, Leo talked, his diamond ring flashing as he gestured. Vince looked cowed, even though he was taller than Leo. Kevin stirred sugar into his coffee, while frowning at Leo and Vince. Grant stood alone, scowling into his coffee mug.

Great, Maura thought. Frayed tempers at the first meeting of the day.

Dewayne walked in behind Maura. "Sorry I'm late," he said. "Early call with Atlanta counsel. You guys get seated while I get my coffee." His voice boomed across the room, and at his direction the rest of the officers moved toward their chairs.

Maura saw Vince hesitate as he passed his regular chair and moved on to the head of the table. Rick's seat.

When the group had settled, Vince said, "No change in Rick's condition. He's still moving some, but not conscious. We'd hoped for more improvement. It's been over a week since the accident. We're considering next steps."

"What does that mean?" Maura asked.

"Long term care," Kevin replied.

Maura felt the room still. Kevin's words implied Rick's condition might be permanent.

Vince continued, "The neurologists say there's nothing ICU can do that can't be done elsewhere. But we're not quite ready to make that call yet."

"Does that mean Rick isn't coming back as CEO?" Dewayne asked the question on everyone's mind.

"We don't know." Vince's voice was clipped.

"What'll we do?" Grant asked.

"For now, same as we have been," Vince said. "We all know our jobs. We can keep managing our divisions."

"But who'll deal with conflicts between divisions?" Maura asked. "That's the real issue."

"Let's try to keep those to a minimum," Vince said.

Maura overheard Leo mutter, "Shit." More loudly, for the group to hear, Leo said, "Sooner or later, we're going to need someone to make decisions around here. What'll we do? Flip a coin? Vote? Will each division get one vote? Or weight our votes by budget or personnel?"

"Give us some time. The family needs time to sort through the implications." Kevin spoke mildly, but Maura heard tension in his voice. Was he irritated at Leo or at Vince?

"Let's get on with the agenda," Vince said. They hadn't resolved the decision making issue, but it was clear Vince wouldn't lead a debate on that topic. Not today. Maybe never. Maura would have to talk to Dewayne about the legalities of an absent CEO.

"Next topic is the action figure line," Vince continued.

"I've told Toy Mart we'll give them price concessions and exclusivity," Leo said. "What specifics can we offer, Vince?"

"That's premature," Vince snapped. "I told you so last week. We're still sorting out the marketing program."

"Hell, Vince, you can't keep stalling like a junior product manager." Leo slammed his fist on the table. "They're our biggest customer. We have to meet their timeline. What will we do to keep our space in their stores?"

"I'm still working on it."

"When will you know what you're doing?" Leo leaned back in his seat, radiating disgust.

"Some of us don't throw tantrums to get what we want," Vince shouted, his face red. "We can't all be great gladiators fighting the competition. I have a brother maybe dying, and you want me to referee two of my product directors in a pissing contest? Well, you're going to have to wait your fucking turn to get a piece of me."

Maura stared at Vince. It took a lot to get him to show any emotion, but when he did, he said more than he meant.

"Calm down, Vince," Grant said quietly, but with a frown. "Leo, quit being an asshole. Surely your relationship with Toy Mart is strong enough to buy us a little time. They'll give us some slack due to Rick's situation."

"I've been trading on my relationship with them for the past month." Leo strode to the side table to refill his coffee cup. "Toy Mart started this conversation before Christmas. I can drag it out a little longer. But it won't be long before their buyers turn into piranha. They know we're drowning. They'll eat us before we're dead. And I'm the one they'll eat first."

"We can't promise too much." Alex sounded nervous. "We're losing ground on our cash position. And we fell off production pace last week."

"You don't have the most recent numbers," Grant said. "We worked overtime through the holiday weekend and caught up."

"How much did the overtime add to expenses?" Alex asked. "You need to keep Manufacturing on pace to keep our costs in line."

"Christ, Alex, I know how product cost is calculated." Grant's voice was testy, and his frown deepened. "Let me run Operations. We'll get back on track. I'll meet my budget."

"Timing is everything this year, with our cash flow in the tank." Alex worried like a terrier. But Maura could tell he didn't want conflict; he fidgeted with his pencils and wouldn't meet Grant's eyes.

"Okay," Vince said, "We can't solve this problem now. Let's do what we can to stay on budget and on schedule. Next topic is the reduction in force."

Maura updated the group on the discussions her staff had had. "We're playing with a ten percent reduction in headcount. But I don't think an across-the-board cut is the way to go," she concluded. "The divisions all have different problems. We'd be better off tailoring our cuts by division. Those groups working on the new product line need to focus on getting it out. We can retrench more heavily in other areas."

"You're saying Operations and Product get to keep their staffs?"

Leo asked.

"No. Every group needs to downsize. But different reductions in each division."

"Sales cut heads last year." Leo's jaw was set.

"You can't be exempt this round." Maura wished Leo would push Toy Mart as hard as he bullied his peers at PlayLand.

"I'm not cutting until Rick says I have to." Leo smirked. Maura couldn't respond to that remark.

"None of us like to cut staff, Leo," Kevin said. "I don't want to cut Marketing. But we have to take our cost problems seriously. What do you suggest?"

"I'm just the Sales guy," Leo replied. "Let the bean counters decide how to cut costs."

"Maura and I are trying to do exactly that," Alex said. "But you keep pushing back."

The meeting continued in a similar tone. As Maura had feared, they couldn't resolve anything without Rick.

$ $ $

Maura went directly from the executive meeting to her HR staff meeting. She was still fuming over the disagreement among the officers about the reduction in force, but she tried to be objective with her staff. "HR's going to have to make the best recommendation we can. We need to analyze which divisions should cut deeper and which groups need to keep most of their people. Let's get to work."

They spent the rest of the morning arguing about options and recalculating payroll savings in each division until they agreed on a proposal.

"All right," Maura said, "Now I need to try to sell this. I doubt it'll fly exactly as we've outlined here. But it's a great place to start. I'll keep you posted."

$ $ $

After the HR meeting, Maura headed to Alex's office, bringing her HR staff's spreadsheets with her. Alex only respected numbers, but her group had done enough financial analysis to impress him.

Alex turned to her with a glum expression. His office was neat, the furniture simple. Maura was sure if she opened any random drawer in the file cabinets behind his desk, each file would be neatly labeled.

"If we can reduce headcount by an average of ten percent," Maura began, "we can get our labor costs back in line with two years ago."

"You can get to ten percent?" Alex perked up. He turned on his desk calculator and advanced the lead in his mechanical pencil. "Let's see."

Maura put on her reading glasses and reviewed her numbers. Alex jotted notes and tapped on his calculator.

As she finished, Maura said, "Now, remember, there are short-term costs associated with getting these long-term savings. In the next few months, this'll have a negative impact on cash flow. We'll have to pay severance to terminated employees, so we won't break even for about seven months. Can we manage that?"

"Why do we have to pay severance?" Alex didn't look up from his calculator as he spoke.

"We'll never hire good people again if they don't think they'll get a reasonable severance package if they're let go. I assumed a standard package, what we've done in the past. But two weeks' pay per year of service times average tenure of fifteen years is thirty weeks' pay. That's how long it'll take to break even."

"What else are you assuming?"

"Within each division, we've assumed equal cuts by department," Maura said. "If we hit some departments harder than others, costs will vary depending on the salaries and tenure of employees in those departments."

"Should we cut each department the same?"

"Probably not," Maura said. "But before we talk to the other officers, you and I need to work together. Rick's not here, so I need you to back me up. Plus, the bankers will want to know what we're considering."

"Okay," Alex responded. "What'll the other officers say?"

"Will you support the reduction in Finance?" Maura asked. "I can do it in HR, though we'll have to cut back on employee services."

Alex's jaw tightened. Maura knew he didn't like cutting Finance any more than she liked cutting HR. But he nodded. "We all have to play to make this work."

"Exactly," Maura said. "But the support areas like HR and Finance aren't big enough to make much difference in our cost structure.

"So we need Operations and Sales?"

"Yes, and Product Development," she said. "We can vary the percentage cuts by division, but it has to add up to ten percent across the board to reach the total I showed you."

"I'll cut Finance," Alex said. "But we'll get pushback from the others. No one wants his own division hurt. They'll all argue they need the people they have."

Maura nodded, then leaned forward. "Does the business really need to cut costs so much? If not, we don't need this distraction. Cutting jobs isn't how I want to spend my time if it isn't critical. I'd rather hire or train people any day than fire them."

"Well, we can't add HR programs in our current environment." Alex frowned and tapped his pencil on the spreadsheets Maura had given him, then underlined the bottom number. "Do we really need the severance costs? We don't have any cash to spare. We already need to increase our credit line. I need to think about how to time our cash needs, and whether the banks will support us. They might, if we show we can cut costs in the longer term."

He tapped the spreadsheets again with his brow furrowed, then entered a few numbers in his calculator. When the calculator had spat out an answer, he nodded at Maura. "Can you talk to Grant and Leo by the end of the week? We need to know who's on board before we talk to the banks."

"Sure. But can I tell them you and I agree on the need to reduce payroll? This can't be just an HR scheme. Because no one's going to like it."

"Okay," Alex said. "And ask them, if they can't cut staff, what non-payroll costs can they cut? I bet they don't have any ideas, or we would have heard them already."

$ $ $

Maura spent her lunch hour preparing to meet with Grant. Grant would grill her harder than Alex. The CFO would cut costs any way he could.

Grant would want to protect the employees in Operations,

though he understood as well as Maura and Alex how important reducing expenses was this year. Grant would be one of her best allies if he agreed with her, but he would fight her tooth and nail if he disagreed.

She reviewed her information on Operations. Their salaries were lower than many of the college-educated groups at PlayLand, but they had more tenure. Plus, their health benefits made up a bigger percentage of their income. If PlayLand had to raise insurance premiums, this group would feel it the most.

The cost reductions were going to have to come from somewhere. PlayLand could reduce its employee population and try to get the same revenue with fewer employees, or the company could increase what employees contributed toward health insurance and retirement savings. Grant would understand this dynamic; which direction would he prefer to take?

At two o'clock Maura was in Grant's office, which was austere, but functional. Photos of Linda and his children and grandchildren sat on the credenza behind his desk. Maura smiled at the picture of one of Grant's grandsons, a little boy of about four who frowned the same way Grant did.

Maura launched into her arguments. "You know payroll makes up over half the total expenses of the company. It's over a third of the expense in the Operations group, with machinery and raw materials being the bulk of the remainder."

"That's been true for decades." Grant toyed with a paperclip on his desk, but Maura knew he was listening.

"What's changing," she continued, "is revenues aren't keeping up with payroll increases. Salaries are going up gradually, but benefits are shooting through the roof. Our medical costs alone went up over ten percent last year. And with the aging employee base, retirement costs are going up also. With flat sales, we can't keep all the employees we have."

"Then we need to increase revenue. We need new product." Grant sounded indifferent, as if the rising costs were not his concern.

Maura knew he was just testing her. "New product isn't enough, and you know it," she said. "We need to address employee costs, too. We have two choices. Option one is to reduce the number of employees we have. Option two is to reduce salaries and/or benefits."

"Neither option will make you or me very popular." Grant continued to play with the paperclip.

"Believe me, I wouldn't be here if I thought we could avoid it. The last thing I want to do is lay off employees or cut their pay. But what other choices do we have?" Maura's voice caught.

Grant shrugged. "I have unused capacity in several plants. I can pump more product through our system without hiring more than a few on-call folks, if we had stuff for them to make. And we have other sources for production in Asia. We could solve all PlayLand's problems if we had a pipeline of new product."

"But you and I can't develop new product by ourselves. My job is to manage the employee resources we have. Right now, we need payroll cost reductions. I've done it before, with Rick's backing. I can't get Rick's opinion now, but it's still my best contribution to the problem. I'm asking for your input."

Grant sat forward in his chair with a bounce, looking ready to engage in the debate. "Maura, I'm not blaming you. But you know reducing employee costs is only a temporary fix. First, we have to pay severance. What does Alex say about that? Second, if we do turn the product situation around, we'll have to hire people back. The employees we rehire will never trust us the same again. Third, if we don't get new product in the pipeline, we'll be right back with the same problem in another year or two. I'd rather spend our energies on new product development."

"I hear you." Maura leaned forward also, until she and Grant were face to face across his desk. Grant frowned, resembling the little boy in the picture behind him. "I hope these action figures get to market quickly. But until they do, we have to work the headcount issue. To be perfectly blunt, I'm not sure we can pull this off. Alex is the only officer behind me now. He is worried about severance costs, but he says we need to ask for an increase in our line of credit from the bankers anyway—whether we're paying salaries or severance—so we might as well have a plan to reduce long-term costs."

Grant snorted. "Well, don't expect me to back you on this."

"Okay." Maura decided to retreat. "Let's talk hypothetically.

What would the problems be if we did cut headcount in Operations? What would happen if we reduced your employee base by ten percent?"

"Ten percent!" Grant jumped to his feet, looming across his desk over Maura. "Christ, we'd never be able to gear up for a new product launch. If we ever got the chance."

Maura kept her face calm, despite Grant's aggressive response. "Could you keep producing our current product with ten percent fewer employees?"

Grant paced around his office, jingling the change in his pockets. At least he hadn't thrown her out. He finally said, "With a little overtime during peak periods, probably. But we'd have no flexibility left in our production system."

Maura pressed, her tone still mild. "Which would you prefer? To cut your employee base by ten percent and give the salary increases we've already planned to the ones who remain? Or to give no pay increases this year to anyone, raise health insurance premiums by another fifteen percent, and eliminate the company match on our 401(k) plan?"

Grant stopped pacing and stared at her. "You'd cut the heart out of this company either way. I've been a part of downsizing at a company, and lost my own job at the end of it. People don't recover."

"But which is worse? Firing some people, or cutting everyone's pay and benefits?"

Grant turned to gaze out his office window. "What would the severance be for those who left?" he asked.

"One week per year of service and continued health benefits for hourly employees. Two weeks per year of service, health benefits and outplacement for salaried employees. The same package PlayLand has used before."

Grant returned to his chair and grimaced as he sat. "I don't like either option."

Maura was silent, letting Grant stew.

"I'd have to go for the ten percent headcount reduction," Grant said at last. "I hate laying folks off, but I can't cut their pay. Not with energy and housing prices going up. I'd rather figure out how to keep our best employees happy." He glowered at her. "But you know I'm going to push Vince and everyone else on new product."

Maura nodded. "And I hope you succeed. For all our sakes." She stuffed her papers back in her folder, then looked Grant in the eye. "You're fighting for your people, and I respect that. I wish we agreed on this. But I need to do what I think best, even without your support. I don't see what other choice we have."

$ $ $

Jennifer Scott and Karen Heintz met again in the Doll Room to finalize their cost figures. Jennifer summarized Karen's input. "So we can develop comic books for about the same amount as a traditional promotion campaign—flyers advertising giveaway of an action figure for every three purchased."

"If Gus does most of the artwork and story lines," Karen said. "I assume the costs of a giveaway are already in the marketing plan. Also, we can sell the comics. That revenue will offset the rest of the cost differential."

"Yeah, we have the budget." Jennifer hesitated, but the gossip she had was too good to keep to herself. "So, have you heard the latest?"

"What's that?" asked Karen.

"About Gus." Jennifer lowered her voice.

"No."

"Turns out Ben never got Gus's written permission to use the action figures. Gus created the characters before he came to PlayLand. Ben never resolved the rights."

"Then why are we worrying about a marketing plan?" Karen asked.

"Vince and Ben are trying to sort it out now." Jennifer couldn't help letting a grin spread across her face. "I'm hoping this is the last straw for Ben. Vince already hates him."

Karen snorted. "Everyone hates Ben. Except Rick Players. So far, that's been all that mattered. I don't see Vince getting rid of Ben if Rick is anywhere in the picture."

"But will Rick be around?" Jennifer frowned. "It's been days since the accident."

"He's moving now. I hear the doctors think he might wake up."

"God, I hope so. For the family's and the company's sake," Jennifer said. "But I hope Vince fires Ben first."

$ $ $

Late Tuesday afternoon, Maura went to Dewayne's office. She started by asking him about the reduction in force. He grilled her about the severance terms and lectured her about the need to involve Legal in analyzing whether too many minority or female or older employees were out of jobs because of the reduction.

Maura nodded her head as Dewayne talked. She'd done several layoffs over the years; she knew when to talk to Legal. But she needed Dewayne's help on the corporate governance issue. So she smiled sweetly as Dewayne droned on. When he finished, she asked, "Dewayne, how do we hold this place together without Rick?"

"What do you mean?" He leaned his ponderous body back in his chair and folded his hands across his stomach.

"You were at the meeting this morning. Leo, Grant, and Alex are sparring like ten-year-olds. Vince won't make decisions. Kevin doesn't have the experience. You and I have limited influence outside our groups. How will we get anything done without Rick? What happens if Rick can't come back?"

"I'd hoped we wouldn't have to face that." Dewayne ran a hand over his head. "I have enough grey hair as it is."

"Well, we might have to face it," Maura said. "I've done some thinking about candidates to replace Rick, but who do I talk to? There's no one in charge. PlayLand doesn't have a board of directors that can act without the CEO."

Dewayne steepled his fingers in front of his mouth and looked at her over his hands. "Well, technically, we do."

"We have a board?" Maura was surprised.

"PlayLand is a corporation. Incorporated in Delaware, like most U.S. companies. Every corporation has a board of directors. It's required by law, even though we're not publicly owned."

"Who's on our board?"

"Our bylaws provide for three directors, elected by the shareholders."

Dewayne wasn't volunteering anything. "Who are they?" Maura asked again.

"Rick, Vince, and myself."

"The three of you were elected?"

"Yes. PlayLand has stock, like every company, though the family owns it all. Richard still owns fifty-five percent, and the three sons each have fifteen percent. Rick has Richard's power of attorney, so he votes seventy percent of the stock between his own and his dad's."

"If Rick controls that much stock, what do you and Vince do?" Maura asked.

Dewayne shrugged. "We just sign whatever we need to legally. We don't even meet as a board. Ditto with the shareholders. PlayLand doesn't have shareholders' meetings like public companies do. Rick controls everything, so there's no need."

"Who votes the stock in Rick's absence?"

"Rick's wife Paige can vote his stock if he's incapacitated. She has Rick's power of attorney. But it isn't clear to me who votes Richard's stock if Rick can't. As far as I know, no one else has a power of attorney for Richard. It might take a court order to give someone else the power to vote it."

"Does Paige having Rick's power of attorney mean she acts as a director of PlayLand as well?"

"No. The position of director is personal to Rick. The power of attorney doesn't matter. The shareholders would have to vote for another director to replace Rick. Which can't happen without someone voting Richard's majority shares."

"Then we're stuck with no one in charge?" Maura was confused.

Dewayne steepled his fingers again. "No. Two of the three directors are still here. Vince and me. Each director has one vote, so Vince and I represent a majority of the board. Technically, the shareholders don't choose the officers, the directors do. Therefore, Vince and I could vote in a new CEO. Or an acting CEO. Or whomever else we want to put into any officer position."

"What happens if the Players family disagrees with what you do?"

"Well, once the family sorts out who's voting which block of stock, the shareholders could countermand us. They could replace us as directors with people who would do what they want. And if we do something really stupid, they could sue us for breach of fiduciary duty. But legally, Vince and I can take reasonable actions in Rick's absence and make them stick." Dewayne paused and stared at her. "I'd want Kevin and Paige on board with whatever we do, if at all possible, to minimize the risk of any later disputes."

"Have you talked to Vince about this?" Maura rubbed her eyes. It looked like all roads led back to Vince, which was disappointing.

"No." Dewayne was curt.

"Why not?"

"Vince can't cope with any more responsibility than he already has. That's why you're here, isn't it?" Once again, Dewayne cut right to the heart of the problem.

"Yes, that's why I'm here. So what should we do?"

Dewayne lifted one massive shoulder. "I didn't want to do anything, which is why I haven't talked to Vince." He sighed. "But if Rick isn't going to regain consciousness soon, I'll have to work with Vince to get someone appointed to act as CEO." He looked at Maura. "Do you think we're at that point?"

She nodded. "This morning's meeting was a disaster. The officers carping at each other. Someone needs to make the decisions."

Dewayne hid behind his steepled fingers again, apparently deep in thought. "I'd prefer to meet with Vince, Kevin, and Paige together. Give them the problem to resolve jointly. If the three of them agree on a course of action, it's less likely one of them will sue."

Maura decided to go out on a limb. No harm in asking. "Can I be at that meeting? As I said, I've been thinking about succession behind Rick?"

Dewayne scrutinized her from behind lidded eyes. "Mind if I ask you what your thoughts are?"

Maura had known Dewayne would inquire at some point. But two could play hide and seek. "There are a variety of directions the family could take to replace Rick," she said. "I don't know whether they want to stay with a family member or go with another internal candidate or if they want to look outside. That's where I would begin the conversation."

"You don't want to tell me, is that it?" Dewayne grinned at her.

Maura gave Dewayne credit for intelligence. "That's right. I want some direction from the family."

"But you do have recommendations, depending on the direction they give you?"

"Yes."

Dewayne was silent, watching her. Was he going to cross-examine her further? But he simply shrugged and said, "Sure. Be there if you want. The more the merrier. Should be interesting." He was still grinning when Maura left his office.

$ $ $

That evening, Vince sat with Kevin in Rick's hospital room. Rick stirred and moaned occasionally, but still was not conscious.

The doctors had again mentioned moving him to a rehabilitation center. "We can do some physical therapy here, but he'd be better off in a facility with rehabilitation specialists."

"What is there to rehabilitate?" Vince asked. "He doesn't respond to anything."

"This hospital is designed for acute care," the neurologist explained. "The rehabilitation center is better equipped to prevent muscle deterioration and try to improve his functioning. We can't provide the sensory stimulation it takes to help patients with traumatic brain injuries. TBI patients need individual treatment protocols developed and monitored as their conditions change. That's what the rehab center would do."

After the doctor left, Kevin asked, "What do you think we should do?"

"Isn't it really Paige's decision?" Vince rubbed his forehead. Either his head or his gut hurt constantly these days.

"Paige will listen to us."

"What do you think?" Vince asked.

Kevin was silent for a long while before saying, "It isn't doing anyone any good to have Rick here. Nor for us to spend all our time here. Paige needs to focus on the twins. You and I need to focus on PlayLand."

"We don't have what it takes to save the business." Vince grimaced at a particularly sharp pain in his stomach. "You and I can't push through the cost reductions Alex says we need. Not while we're also trying to launch a new product line. We simply can't do it."

"Vince, we have great people working for us. They'll help."

Vince groaned. "Ben Thornton and Jennifer Scott are in a cat fight. Gus Powell owns the fucking rights to the only product that can save us. Alex is breathing down my neck about costs. Who's helping me?"

"Jennifer has good ideas. You're not giving her a chance."

"I need to keep Ben happy, or he'll run to Rick as soon as Rick wakes up."

"What if Rick doesn't wake up? What will you do with Ben then?" Kevin asked.

"And what if Rick pulls through and questions everything we've done?"

"So? You tell him Ben screwed up. He let us develop a product line we might not even own."

"We still don't have the money to launch the product, even if Legal lets us go forward."

"Why are you so negative?" Kevin stood up and paced the narrow room. "It's always been this way. Someone has an idea, and you spout off all the reasons why it won't work." Kevin walked over to Vince's chair and leaned over him. "Face it, Vince. Saving PlayLand might be up to you and me. I don't like it. You don't like it. But there's no one else. Dad's out of it, and Rick may be, too."

"If Rick doesn't snap out of this soon, I think we should sell. Alex could find us a buyer."

"Yeah? How? Who'd vote Dad's stock? I don't have a clue. We need a lawyer to sort it all out. That'll take time, and someone has to run the place in the meantime."

"Well, we aren't going to resolve this tonight. I'm going home." Vince stood and slouched toward the door. Kevin was as bad as Rick, always telling Vince what to do.

As Vince left, Kevin called out, "We can put off deciding about the business. But we're going to have to decide about Rick in the next few days."

$ $ $

After Vince was gone, Kevin sat with his elbows on his knees and his head in his hands. A heavy sob escaped his lungs. He hadn't cried in years, but Rick had never been near death before, and PlayLand's health was almost as bad as Rick's.

Vince wouldn't help. Kevin would have to deal with Rick and with as much of PlayLand's business as he could.

Paige walked in. "I just got Jason and Jacob off to soccer practice." She sat in the chair Vince had vacated. "How's Rick?"

Kevin sighed. "Same. He's thrashing around a little, but the doctors have him restrained."

"We can't keep on like this." Paige had tears in her eyes. "It's too much, taking care of the boys, and sitting here with Rick as much as I can. I'm so tired."

"I know." Kevin patted his sister-in-law's hand. "Vince and I were just talking. What do you think about moving him to the rehab center? It's your call, but I'll back you up."

"I don't know." Paige's voice rose. "I guess whatever the doctors think best."

"Vince is still hoping Rick will wake up."

"Don't you hope so, too, Kevin?" Paige's tears spilled over.

"Of course. But I'm also thinking about what's best for you and the boys. And for PlayLand. We're all living in limbo. We have to move on. Or life will move on around us. I told Vince we could give it a couple more days, but then we'll have to decide about Rick. And he and I have to make some decisions about PlayLand."

"I'll do whatever you and Vince decide." Paige sighed. "It's too much for me."

$$\$ \ \$ \ \$$

Grant walked into his home that evening and threw his jacket on the back of the couch. A fire in the hearth room burned brightly. Linda brought him his Scotch. "You look tired," she said.

Grant sunk to the couch with his drink. "I'm beat."

Linda curled up beside him. "That's no way for the future CEO of PlayLand to talk."

Grant shot her a disapproving look. "Don't joke about it, Linda."

"Sorry." She smiled. "Bad day?"

Grant leaned his head back against the cushions. "Maura talked to me about headcount reductions. Did you know what she had up her sleeve?"

"Yes."

"If she gets her way, it'd have a huge impact on Operations. Ten percent of our people. Maybe more, if she can't get all the divisions to play, and Operations has to take more than its fair share."

"Ten percent is big," Linda agreed. "But PlayLand went through a downsizing before and came through all right."

"Everyone is so touchy right now, because of the situation with Rick and the poor sales picture. I don't know how employees would react."

"Don't people expect some cost cutting?"

"Maybe. But they won't like it. And if it hits Operations hard, I worry about a unionizing attempt. We'll have to be careful."

"If you have to, can you cut ten percent in Operations?"

"Sure. But what do we do after it's over? We can eke out our current product lines. But we won't be able to make anything new."

"If we ever get any new products." Linda reached out to stroke Grant's hair. "Isn't that the real issue? Will we need more plant capacity or not? If not, then Maura is doing the right thing in cutting payroll."

"Yeah. But it's ugly."

CHAPTER 7: THURSDAY, JANUARY 18

When Jennifer arrived at Vince's office on Thursday morning, she wore a tight, low-cut sweater, though a long skirt and boots covered her legs. Her wardrobe didn't help her professional image, Vince thought as she sat across from him.

"Good news," Jennifer said. "The comic book costs and timeline will work."

Ben appeared in Vince's doorway. Vince hadn't invited him; he must have been lurking in the hallway, waiting for Jennifer to show up.

"Hey, Jennifer," Ben said. "Can I hear what you've got? Okay with you, Vince?" Ben walked in without stopping to hear Vince's answer and sat next to Jennifer. "Nice sweater, Jennifer. Was it made for one of your dolls?"

Jennifer ignored Ben and handed Vince a spreadsheet. "Here's what Procurement gave me. The costs aren't much different than the ad flyers we typically print. The only additional costs are for artwork and story development. But Gus can do that work, so we'll be fine. And the comic books give us revenue, which the flyers don't."

"Where do we stand with Gus?" Vince had to know, though now he'd have to listen to Jennifer and Ben carp at each other. "We're meeting with Legal later this morning."

"I told you, Vince," Ben said. "We're good. Let Gus work on his action figures, then move him into New Ventures later this year. He'll be fine." Ben sounded confident, but Ben always sounded confident.

Ben leaned across the desk toward Vince, blocking Vince's view of Jennifer. Ben's voice turned snide. "But the comics won't give us anything a 'buy one, get one free' promotion won't. This is a huge waste of time. Time we don't have. I keep saying, these aren't dolls. Boys don't read."

"Maybe you don't read, but I've done a little research." Jennifer handed Vince another spreadsheet. "Preadolescent boys buy most of the comic books sold in the U.S. I think the comic book tie-in will work. Besides, it'll get us good press. Because it's new."

"What about shelf space?" Ben asked. "Have you talked to Leo? Will the stores give us space for both comics and action figures? Flyers don't need shelf space."

Vince watched Ben and Jennifer volley for his attention. Finally, he interrupted the arguing, asking Jennifer, "Have you talked to Leo about shelf space?"

"No, but I can." Her voice was subdued. She probably hadn't thought of the space issue, Vince guessed.

"And what about the publication timeline?" Ben smirked as he threw another verbal punch at Jennifer. "Gus has his job in Games. Where's he going to find the time to help you?"

"I assumed you could get Gus assigned to me for the next month or so," Jennifer said to Vince. "He's been working with Ben."

Vince nodded. "If we decide on comics, I can make that happen. You need Gus if that's the route we take."

"But we don't have to go with comics." Ben leaned further across the desk. "Just hire the ad agency to do the flyers."

Vince sighed. He didn't want to decide anything this morning. "Let's get the situation with Legal resolved. Then I'll make the call." He rubbed the back of his head, which throbbed again. "In the meantime, Jennifer, work up a detailed timeline. And check with Leo about shelf space. Ben, have the agency mock up a flyer. Just a sketch. I don't want a big bill. Neither of you should spend much until we resolve the ownership issue."

The two Product Directors turned to leave, Ben gesturing broadly to wave Jennifer ahead of him. Vince said, "Ben, can you stick around a minute?"

"Sure thing." Ben sprawled back into a chair. If he puts his damn feet on my desk, I'll fire his ass, Vince fumed. But Ben didn't presume quite that far.

"This situation with Gus is a real screwup." Vince felt sick thinking about the complications Dewayne would raise. "PlayLand has to have full ownership of the products we develop. It'll look bad for all of us. I want you at the meeting with Legal."

"I'll be there. But don't worry." Ben waved his hand, flicking away the problem like a buzzing insect. "Gus and I have a deal. If it hadn't been for Jennifer mucking around, you'd never have heard a thing."

"That's part of the problem. I need to know about any issues with new products. You kept this from me."

"Sorry, boss." Despite his apology, Ben didn't sound concerned. "I guess I just wanted to look good." Ben stood, smiling. "You'll see, nothing will come of it."

$ $ $

Later that morning, Vince walked down the hall to the Legal Department. Heavy law books lined the conference room walls. Vince had been in caves that were brighter. He felt trapped by the heavy atmosphere and by Dewayne's looming presence across the table. Ben walked in right behind Vince, and Jennifer arrived a few minutes later. She sat as far down the conference table from Ben as possible.

"Jennifer, tell me again what you heard from Gus," Dewayne commanded.

"He said he developed the characters during college. Gave them names and everything. He told me he wanted them to be comic book characters, but Ben told him PlayLand could use them as action figures."

"Gus clearly created the characters before he started work here?" Dewayne asked.

"Yes," she said.

Dewayne turned to Ben. "You knew Gus developed these characters in college?"

"Sure," Ben said with the same small wave of his hand he'd used in Vince's office. "I told him I'd make him a deal. Get him out of Games if PlayLand used his characters. I said comic books weren't our thing, but we could get action toys into stores."

"Unfortunately, it isn't that simple," Dewayne said. "Copyright law says Gus still owns the rights to the characters, unless he sells them to PlayLand."

90

"Sell?" Vince asked, bile rising in his gut. "He's an employee, for God's sake. Doesn't he have to do what we want? We can't increase our costs. Plus, I don't want to pay one employee, when dozens of people work on product development."

"Gus isn't expecting any money," Ben interrupted. "All he wants is a different job."

Dewayne responded to Vince, without any comment on what Ben said. "PlayLand would best be served legally if we pay Gus a fair price for the characters. Otherwise, there's a risk he'd sue us later. I know it's awkward to pay employees beyond their regular salary, but he didn't create these characters at PlayLand."

"What's a fair price?" Vince asked.

"Hard to say," Dewayne said. "Feel him out. We don't want to overpay. But we need him, and we don't want him to think we're taking advantage of him."

"Who should talk to him?" Vince asked.

"I'll do it," Ben said. "He'll do what I tell him."

"No." Dewayne shook his head emphatically. "You've done enough, Thornton. We need someone new. Someone with authority. Vince."

One more damn thing, Vince thought. Hell. "Why not Jennifer?" he asked. "She's working well with Gus."

"You're a vice president and a Players family member," Dewayne said. "It should be you. How fast can you get to him?"

"I'll see." Vince didn't want to talk to Gus. But PlayLand had to get the rights to the characters. The new product line was all the company had.

$ $ $

Ben went back to his office. Christ, so now Gus gets money out of the Players boys? When Ben had been the one who pushed the shitty product into the pipeline? Nothing would have happened without Ben, and Dewayne hadn't suggested paying Ben extra. Ben decided to play nice with Gus for now, but he'd play hard ball if he had to.

Ben picked up his phone and called Gus, getting Gus's voice mail. "It's Ben," he said into the machine. "Say, looks like the action figures are moving ahead. I have Vince ready to move you out of Games. He might even want to meet with you this afternoon.

91

Stick to what we've talked about. Tell him about our deal. Don't fuck this up, pal."

$$$

The meeting with the Players family was scheduled for Thursday evening. Maura drove to the gated subdivision in Lakeview where Rick and Paige lived. She had attended a couple of parties there over the years, but she didn't know Paige well.

Dewayne, Vince, and Kevin already sat in the formal living room when Maura arrived. A fire burned in the marble fireplace. Paige was serving wine and hors d'oeuvres, fluttering about her guests as if this were a social call. When everyone had a glass in hand, Paige sat beside Dewayne.

"I told you why I thought we should get together," Dewayne said, his bulk filling the largest chair in the room. "We need to be clear on the legal ramifications of Rick's incapacity."

"Legal ramifications?" Paige looked puzzled.

"Our corporate bylaws require PlayLand to have certain roles. Rick is the incumbent in several positions. If he isn't available, the company needs to replace him." Dewayne explained how shareholders elected directors and directors elected officers, just as he had to Maura. "Our bylaws say we need three directors. We also need a CEO. At some point, we need to clarify the lines of authority in the company and fill these positions."

"So Rick is an officer . . . and a director . . . and a shareholder of PlayLand?" Paige said, wrinkling her forehead.

"That's right." Dewayne nodded, his hands folded across his stomach. "You can vote his shares as shareholder because you have his power of attorney. But unless the family has done something I don't know about, you don't have the authority to vote his father's shares. Only Rick has that power of attorney. Rick, Vince, and Kevin together hold forty-five percent of the shares. A minority, if no one can vote Richard's shares. So the three of you can't replace Rick as a director without court intervention."

"But you and Vince can replace Rick as CEO, because you're two-thirds of the directors." Paige's voice was crisper. Her eyes narrowed.

She's not as flighty as she seems, Maura thought.

Dewayne shrugged. "If we need to replace Rick as CEO, Vince

and I have the authority to make the change. Whenever we decide it's in the best interest of the company and shareholders."

"Is it best to replace him as CEO now?" Paige asked, looking around the room.

Vince cleared his throat and rubbed the back of his neck. "Well, now, Paige, I don't think we have to do anything yet."

"But we need to know who's running the company," Maura said. She couldn't insist that Paige, Vince, and Kevin act, but she couldn't let them ignore the problem.

"Who *is* running the company?" Paige asked.

"We're each running our own division," Kevin said. "We're fine, as long as there aren't any conflicts."

"There are bound to be disagreements," Maura told Paige. "There always are. It'd be better to clarify the chain of command now, before anything major happens." She glanced at Dewayne for confirmation, but he had settled into his seat with a little smile on his face.

"Who do you recommend we replace Rick with?" Paige looked directly at Maura.

"That depends. Do you want an interim CEO to hold things together until Rick's medical condition is more certain? Do you want to replace Rick long term? Do you want an internal candidate or do you want to look outside of PlayLand?"

"Hold on," Vince said. "Who's saying anything about replacing Rick long term?" He stood up and paced the room, rubbing his gut.

"I'm simply outlining options," Maura said.

Paige's eyes welled up as she turned to Dewayne. "Do we have to replace Rick?"

"No." Dewayne reached out and patted her arm. "You don't have to do anything you don't want to."

"But Maura's right," Kevin said, looking at Paige. "We should make a decision before problems develop. Rick's always been the referee when divisions butt heads."

"Is that happening?" Paige asked.

"No more than usual," Vince said.

"But as finances get more strained in the months ahead, we're likely to have more conflicts," Maura said.

"Strained?" Paige asked.

"Cash flow is tight," Kevin said. "Didn't Rick tell you?"

"No." Paige shook her head. "He doesn't tell me much." She bit her lip.

"Well, last year wasn't great, and this year is looking worse," Kevin said.

"We have the new product coming," Vince added.

"But until we know whether it's successful, we need to control costs. Cost reduction is always hard unless someone at the top makes it happen." Maura leaned toward Paige. "You don't have to appoint a new CEO to fill Rick's role permanently, but I strongly urge you—well, really, it's Vince and Dewayne who need to decide—to appoint someone as an acting CEO until we know what Rick's condition will be long term."

"Who should it be?" Paige asked.

"It's up to Vince and Dewayne," Maura said. "But here's what I think. It doesn't make sense to hire from the outside in the short term, though we could launch an executive search if you want. For an interim CEO appointment, you should look at the current executives. There are three large divisions. Vince runs Product Development; Leo Benson, Sales; and Grant Mason, Operations."

Paige nodded. "I know them."

"Vince is the most logical choice," Maura said. "He's a family member as well as a division head. Leo and Grant are also well qualified to run the company on an interim basis, but if you appoint either one of them, the other will be ticked off. The smaller divisions are headed by Kevin, Dewayne, Alex Draper, and myself. Of the four of us, Alex as CFO is probably the most reasonable choice, though Dewayne is also a possibility. Kevin has a narrower line position, and HR isn't usually tapped for these jobs. Bottom line, you should choose Vince, Alex or Dewayne."

When Maura finished, there was dead quiet. The silence lasted forever. She should have known no one would speak while they were all together.

Finally, Dewayne filled the void. "Well, we know our options."

No one responded.

Dewayne spoke up again. "It's getting late. Let's sleep on it. We all need to agree before we act. Vince and Kevin, shall I follow up with you tomorrow?"

"Okay," Kevin said.

Vince nodded.

They all rose to go.

As Maura gathered her coat and briefcase, Paige pulled her aside. "Would you stay a minute, Maura? I have a question about Rick's health benefits."

"Certainly." After the others left, Maura followed Paige back into the living room. "What can I do for you?"

Paige waved her hand. "I don't need anything on benefits. I wanted to talk to you privately about this interim CEO appointment."

"Okay."

"What do you think we should do?"

Maura blanked. What did Paige want? "Excuse me?" she asked.

Paige didn't look at all vulnerable now. She looked tough. "Look, Maura, I'm not stupid. I graduated Phi Beta Kappa from Wellesley. I know I haven't handled Rick's accident well. I've been too afraid to make decisions. Maybe Vince or Kevin told you. I may look like all I can do is organize a cotillion for twelve-hundred people or a charity fundraising auction. But I understood what you said tonight. And I think there's a lot you didn't say." She blew out a deep breath, her nostrils flaring. "Do you really think Vince should take over PlayLand, even on an interim basis?"

Maura stalled. "His experience is as good as anyone's."

"Give it to me straight." Paige stood with her hands on her hips. "I've talked to Vince and Kevin daily since the accident. They haven't been much help. Particularly Vince."

Paige stared at the fire. "I'll be honest. I'm used to leaning on men. My father told me what to do until I got married. Then Rick." She turned and looked Maura in the eye. "But I'm not stupid. Vince hasn't been worth shit. He won't make a decision. Is he any different at work?"

Wow! Maura wondered whether Rick had seen this side of Paige before; she certainly hadn't. "No," she said, her answer as direct as Paige's question. "He isn't."

"Then Vince isn't the right guy to take over, is he? Even on an interim basis?" Paige pressed the point as well as Dewayne could have.

95

"No," Maura said.

"So what should we do?"

Maura thought a moment. Paige could handle the truth. "If you want to know who I think should replace Rick on a long-term basis," Maura said, "I'd say Grant. But in the short term, like I said, Grant and Leo will chew each other up. Don't appoint Grant unless it's for real. And it doesn't sound like you're ready to give up on Rick yet." That sounded callous, Maura thought, so she softened her statement, "And you shouldn't be."

"Why not Kevin as the interim?"

"He doesn't have as much experience as the others, and it would look bad for Vince," Maura said. "Someday Kevin might run PlayLand, but appointing him over Vince now would hurt them both. Kevin doesn't need Vince and everyone else breathing down his neck, waiting for him to make a mistake."

Paige nodded. "So that leaves Alex or Dewayne. Or you."

"Not me." Maura shook her head. "The good ol' boys wouldn't accept me."

Paige shrugged. "That's your call, but I'd back you. If not you, who? Alex or Dewayne?"

"I'd like to say Alex. He knows the most about PlayLand's finances, which are the major issue at the moment. But Alex is too fussy. Dewayne has more credibility. Right now, I'd pick Dewayne."

Paige considered for a moment. "If it's Dewayne, is that sending the wrong message in the long term?"

Maura pursed her lips and thought. "Depends on how we position it. Not if we're clear this is only an interim appointment." She sighed and looked at Paige. "But what good does it do for us to be talking like this? It's Vince's and Dewayne's call what we do."

Paige smiled like Mona Lisa. "How do you think I get a million dollars for the auction every year? We're talking about my sons' future. I'll get it done."

$ $ $

The smell of chili greeted Maura when she got home. Carlos stood stirring a large pot, the television blaring in the background. Both teenagers were in the hearth room, Rafe on his laptop and Liz texting on her cell phone. "Glad you could join us," Carlos said, glancing at Maura.

Great. He was pissed at her for being late. Maura made an effort at conversation, asking the kids about school. Neither Rafe nor Liz said much. Nor did Carlos when she asked about his work. She didn't volunteer anything about her day either.

During the mostly silent dinner, Maura mulled over the conversation with Paige. Could Paige get Vince and Kevin to decide on a replacement for Rick? Was Dewayne the right person to put in charge? A part of Maura wanted the family to choose Grant. But a part of her—like the Players family—wasn't ready to admit Rick might not return.

"Mom," Liz interrupted her train of thought. "Mom, have you heard anything I've said?" Carlos glared at her. Rafe kept shoveling in food.

Maura smiled at her daughter. "Sorry, sweetie. I was thinking about work."

"That's a surprise," Rafe mumbled.

Maura ignored her son and asked Liz, "What were you saying?"

"Remember Grandma comes tomorrow? We're still going shopping for my dress on Saturday, right?"

Maura closed her eyes. Damn, she'd forgotten. Carlos's mother was coming to take Liz shopping for her quinceañera dress. Maura had promised to go with them. There went Saturday.

"Yes," she said. "I'll be there. What time on Saturday?" Maybe she could work at home for an hour or two before the shopping expedition. She had to get the headcount reduction presentation ready for the banks.

"I need shoes, too. Flats for church and heels for the party," Liz said.

"That's fine," Maura said. What would Dewayne be like as a boss? she wondered. He liked to show off his intellectual superiority. He knew the law, but how would he make decisions on product?

"Mom," Liz's voice pierced Maura's consciousness again.

"Sorry, Liz. Problems at work."

"No surprise there," Liz said, sulking. "You don't have to go shopping. Grandma and I'll find something."

"I want to go, Liz. I know how important this party is to you."

Liz glared at her mother. "You don't care. If you cared, you'd have booked the hotel this week. You said you would. I'll bet you forgot."

Maura shut her eyes and cursed herself. "You're right," she said. "I forgot. I'll do it tomorrow."

"You forgot last week, too. Mom, we have to get the Hacienda Room. Maria Estanza had her quinceañera there last year. It was perfect." Maura's heart swelled at the sparkle in Liz's eyes. She kicked herself mentally for not paying more attention to her daughter.

"Liz, I'm sorry. I'll take care of it. I promise."

Rafe got up and asked to be excused, as Liz spoke again, "Mom!"

"What?" Maura said.

"The guest list. If we can get the per person cost below forty bucks, can I invite more people? I really want the whole soccer team there."

"How many people is that?"

Thank goodness Carlos spoke up. Let him handle Liz on this. The conversation swirled around Maura, as Carlos talked to Liz about staying within a total budget. Liz argued back. Maura listened with one ear, while thinking again about her conversation with Paige.

"Who's going to pick Grandma up tomorrow?" Liz asked.

Maura tuned back in. "What time does her flight get in? I can't remember."

"About four PM," Liz said.

"I can do it." Maura wasn't sure what was on her agenda Friday afternoon, but this was a chance to make amends with Liz and Carlos.

"Are you sure?" Carlos asked. "I can get Mama."

"No, no," Maura said with more confidence than she felt. "I'll do it. Just leave me a note in the morning."

$$$

The light was back, brighter than ever. Its call was stronger. Rick yearned to follow the light and the ghostly hands that beckoned. He went as far as he could toward the light.

"Flat line. Code Blue," a voice said. Doctors and nurses and technicians rushed to Rick's bed. They shocked his heart, they pumped in drugs.

"Okay," Rick heard someone say, "He's back."

The white light dimmed. Rick wanted it so badly. Why wouldn't it stay with him? Moving away from the light was the hardest thing he'd ever done.

CHAPTER 8: FRIDAY, JANUARY 19

The phone woke Vince early Thursday morning. It was Paige.

"The hospital called," she said, sobbing. "Rick flatlined again last night. They barely got his heart started. He almost died. Vince, I can't keep doing this."

Christ, Vince thought, he couldn't deal with it either. Too much stress. One thing after another. He hadn't slept well after the meeting last night. Now Paige had woken him at some ungodly hour.

Vince squinted at the clock. 6:15. He shook his head and felt the first pain of the day in his gut. Then he tried to focus. "How is he now?" he asked.

"He's back. About like yesterday," Paige said. "Still moaning. But he's not conscious. What are we going to do?"

"Calm down, Paige. What do the doctors say?"

"Same as before. But do they really know? The neurologist wants to move him to the rehab center."

"Have you talked to Kevin?" Vince didn't want to be the only one Paige was leaning on.

"No. I called you first."

Vince sighed. "Let me talk to Kevin. We'll discuss rehab. But I don't want to give up hope on Rick."

"I know, Vince. You're a big help. I know you want what's best for Rick."

"We all do, Paige."

Vince hung up, then called Kevin at home. No answer. Where the hell was he at 6:15 in the morning? Vince showered and dressed, grabbed a cup of coffee from his automatic coffeemaker, and went to work. No breakfast or newspaper this morning. Not today. He had to track down Kevin.

When Vince arrived at PlayLand, he went straight to Kevin's office. Kevin had just arrived, he was still in his overcoat and his hair was wet.

"Been working out?" Vince asked. "I haven't been to the gym since before Christmas."

"I needed a clear head." Kevin hung up his coat. "What's up?"

"Rick flatlined again last night. ICU got him back, but it sounds bad." Vince rubbed his stomach. Already it hurt like he'd been eating Mexican all day.

"Christ," Kevin slumped in his chair. "How's Paige?"

"Crying. So what should we do?" Vince sighed. "Should we give up? Move him to the long-term care place?"

"Hell if I know." Kevin passed his hand over his eyes, sighing. "Is that giving up?"

Vince shrugged. "Let's give it until Monday. See how he does through the weekend." Vince wanted to defer the decision if possible. He turned to leave. "And now I have to go deal with Gus. I don't know what to do with him either."

$ $ $

Vince had asked his secretary to set up a meeting with Gus for late Friday morning. At eleven thirty, Gus hovered outside of Vince's office, waiting. Gus's reticence annoyed Vince as much as Ben's arrogance.

"Come on in, Gus." Vince stood and held out his hand. He recognized Gus, but they hadn't worked together before. According to Jennifer, the guy usually hid in his cubicle. "Have a seat."

Gus's hand was damp when Vince shook it. "You wanted to see me," Gus said as he sat, scooting his chair away from Vince's desk as far as possible in the cramped space.

Vince tried to be affable, to get Gus to calm down. "I thought we should talk about the new action figures. Ben and Jennifer both rave about your contributions. Good stuff. Tell me how you got involved."

"I've worked on these characters for ages. Started doodling when I was bored in classes at college, you know?" Gus voice became more animated. "These guys kept me sane, I'm telling you."

"What did you do with them in college?" Vince asked.

Gus shrugged, a shy smile forming beneath his long hair. Vince wished he could order the young man to at least pull it back in a ponytail. "Just fooled around," Gus said. "For fun. Gave them some names and made them into a team. When I had a rough day, I asked myself how Adolpho—he's the leader of the team—would have handled the situation. After a while, I thought I had some good stories. My friends liked them. I sent the best story lines off to a couple of publishers with some of my drawings. Never got a response."

"Then the characters were seen by someone outside PlayLand? Before you started working here?" Dewayne wouldn't like that, Vince was sure.

"Yeah," Gus bobbed his head up and down vigorously, his hair falling over his eyes. "But no one wanted to work with an unknown like me."

"What have you done with them at PlayLand?"

"Nothing. Just tacked a couple of drawings up on my bulletin board. I know it's weird, but I still liked them, even if no one else did." Gus's voice lowered to almost a whisper. "I don't like telling you this because it makes me sound like I wasn't working. But when I was bored with my job in Games, I'd look at my pictures and dream up new adventures for my guys. Send Adolpho and his crew out on missions." Gus straightened up in his chair. "But you know, I did have a work purpose. I think PlayLand should put my guys in video games. That's what I really want to do. Develop video games."

Vince didn't care what Gus wanted, he just wanted the problem to go away. But the only way Vince could get rid of the predicament was to make Legal happy. "How'd Ben learn about the characters?" he asked.

"He said he'd heard I had some interesting drawings. I don't know how he heard. He asked if I thought PlayLand could do anything with them. I told him I'd tried to peddle them years ago, but didn't get anywhere. I talked about video games. When he asked if he could have my sketches, I said sure."

"Then what happened?" Vince's stomach sunk. Ben had known about Gus's earlier attempts to sell the characters.

"Ben brought the drawings back a few days later. Said he

thought he could get them into the marketplace if we made them into action figures. No go on video games or comic books. He said to trust him. The project wouldn't fly if people thought the idea came from Games. It had to come from New Ventures. So he told me to keep quiet, and he'd help me out"

"What'd he say he was going to do?"

"He knew I thought Games was a dead-end job. Sorry, but it's true. Our Games business sucks. I only took the job because the ad said PlayLand needed a graphic designer. But I've mostly been doing grunt work for product managers. Ben said he could get me a graphic design job in New Ventures. If I kept my mouth shut about where the action figures came from. That's all I knew until Jennifer wanted to meet. I thought Ben had put her up to talking to me, and it was starting."

"What was starting?"

"Ben's promise. He said I could work on action figures, then Jennifer comes wanting me to develop comics. Like I had always wanted."

"You thought the comic book idea came from Ben?"

Gus nodded.

"We're exploring comics as a promotional tool, but I haven't made a decision yet. In fact, we haven't decided for certain to go forward with the action figures." Vince pinched his nose to slow his headache. Damn! It was worse than he'd thought. Ben had duped Gus not only about rights to the characters, but also about why PlayLand was considering comics.

After taking a deep breath, Vince looked at Gus. "If we do proceed, PlayLand will want to do right by you for your creation of the action figure characters. What do you want out of this, Gus?"

Gus stared at Vince with a puzzled expression. "Ben told me I could get a job in New Ventures. Is that what you mean?"

"I can give you a spot on the action figure team." Vince nodded. "Is there anything else? You didn't develop the characters on PlayLand's time. We need to make sure PlayLand owns whatever products we make."

"You mean, like I might have some rights to these?" Gus's eyebrows shot up above his glasses. "Ben made it sound like he was the only one who could push the action figures through. Like I

103

didn't have anything without him."

"Ben might have sold the characters to the rest of Product Development, but you created them. How much time did you spend on them in college?"

"Oh, several hours a week. Less during finals."

Vince decided to be direct with Gus. "If we paid you for your time in college, would you sell all the rights in the characters to PlayLand?"

Gus's eyebrows shot up higher, until Vince couldn't see them behind his hair. "You'd pay me? Gosh, Ben told me they were worthless."

Vince gulped. He hoped Gus didn't notice. "How does ten thousand sound? But you have to agree PlayLand can do whatever we want with your characters."

Gus hesitated. "These guys got me through college. I feel like I'm selling my kids or something. I don't know."

"You don't have to decide right now. I'll have Legal send you a contract while you think about it. But we need a decision soon, or the deal is off. PlayLand has to have the action figure line ready by Toy Fair in February, if we're going to use it at all." Vince stood and shook Gus's hand again. "Thanks for talking to me."

Gus left, and Vince sat, rubbing his forehead. He was pissed. Ben had deliberately underplayed Gus's involvement and overplayed his own influence in getting the action figures sold. Ben had duped Gus, it was that simple. Gus might have been easily duped, but that didn't excuse what Ben had done. And now Vince had to clean up Ben's mess. Without Rick to back him up.

$ $ $

Maura sat across from Vince in his office. The office was stifling and cramped, not conducive to a productive discussion. Vince had dark bags under his eyes, and he hadn't smiled when she walked in. But she couldn't put off talking to him about the headcount reduction. She couldn't wait until he was in a good mood. She had to get back to Alex by the end of the day. And she had to leave early to pick up Estella.

"I need your opinion on the headcount reduction," she said.

"Maura, no one wants a layoff." Vince rubbed his forehead. "I thought that was clear at Tuesday's meeting."

Maura hesitated. It was hard enough to get Vince to make a decision on a good day. If he wouldn't listen to her, she'd never get an answer. "No one wants to avoid this more than I do," she said. "But we have to reduce labor costs. If we can get headcount down across the company by about ten percent, then we can give the raises we planned and we won't have to increase medical premiums any more this year."

"What's the alternative?" At least Vince heard what she said, even if he wouldn't look at her.

"Pay cuts for everyone. Or at the very least, no increases. And premium increases. It boils down to whether we give our better employees decent salaries and benefits and let the bottom ten percent go, or whether we try to keep everyone employed and make them all unhappy."

"No good options then."

"No, but the reduction in force is better for the company. We need our stronger performers to stay motivated until we're back on a growth track."

"Rick never liked layoffs." Vince massaged the back of his head.

"I know. He and I debated every layoff at PlayLand before we made any decisions. Sometimes we decided to proceed, sometimes we held off. But Rick isn't here, so I need to talk to the rest of his staff."

Vince grunted.

"You manage one of the larger divisions at PlayLand," Maura continued. "Your input's critical. Not to mention your ownership role." Maura tried to stay calm, but she was exasperated at Vince's disengagement. She wished she were dealing with Rick.

"Who else have you talked to?" Vince turned toward her, but didn't meet her eye, though she kept her eyes on his.

"Alex, of course. And Grant. Alex is very supportive. Grant doesn't like it any better than you do. But he said he'd rather have a layoff than a pay cut. That's where I land also."

"Who else are you going to talk to?" She should have expected Vince to want to know what everyone else thought before he declared.

"Leo's next on my list."

"What about Kevin?" Vince held his stomach, grimacing.

105

"Kevin only has a small division. I haven't set up time with him, but I can if you want."

"He's an owner, too." Vince frowned. "I want to know what he says."

"Okay." Maura stood to leave.

"Wait." Vince leaned forward. "Have you thought any more about our conversation at Paige's last night?"

"I'm ready to talk whenever you and your family are."

"Rick had another setback last night. We're still hoping he'll pull through, but . . . ." Vince's voice trailed off.

Maura paused, wondering how to phrase her concerns so Vince wouldn't take offense. "You know, you have to plan for the possibility Rick won't come back. His condition doesn't sound good. I hope he comes back as much as you do. But maybe you and Kevin and Paige need to decide on Plan B. I say that as head of Human Resources. The company needs strong leadership."

Vince sighed. "We're looking into long term care. You talk to Kevin about headcount. I'll talk to him about Rick."

$ $ $

Maura headed to Leo's office. Why was Vince so reluctant to state his opinion? He's not stupid, she fumed. But he wouldn't go out on even a very small limb. Not on the headcount plan. Not on Rick's injury. Not even on the new product line.

Heaven help PlayLand if Vince replaced Rick. She'd hate working for Vince. Maybe he wouldn't bother HR, so he wouldn't get involved in the muck. But he wouldn't support her on the tough calls. Not like Rick. Her job would become more difficult, for sure.

"Leo, are you free?" Maura asked when she arrived at the Sales vice president's office. His office always felt like a car dealership to her.

"Hey, Maura, how's it going?" Leo got up to usher her into the seat across from him. She doubted he rose when his male peers entered his office.

"I have something to talk about you won't like." Maura pulled out her papers on the Sales division headcount.

"Isn't that always the case with HR." Leo laughed. "You guys always bring some problem my way. What's this I hear about a former Sales rep in Atlanta suing us?"

106

"Yes. Reverse race and sex discrimination. I don't think it's serious, and one of your better managers was involved."

"Didn't HR approve the termination? How'd we get in this crap?"

"Leo, you know we can't keep people from suing us. Be thankful Sonia's the manager. She'll be a good witness, and I trust her. We did the right thing in firing the guy. But the case could get dicey."

"What do you mean?" Leo scowled.

"Well, the guy suddenly quit visiting accounts. Obviously, we were justified in firing him, but if he claims he had a mental disability, we may look bad because we didn't try to accommodate him."

"Why should we accommodate a guy who doesn't do his job? I tell you, the employment laws are getting worse every day."

"Keep me posted if you hear anything from Legal or your sales folks. I want to stay on top of how we're approaching the case."

"Sure thing. What else?"

"We need to talk about headcount reductions."

Leo's face turned beet red. "Hell, Maura, I told you. Sales reorganized last year. That's what got us into this mess in Atlanta. HR crammed the last reorganization down our throats. Now you want us to change everything again."

"I understand your concerns." Maura said quietly. It didn't help to yell at Leo, she reminded herself, tempted though she was. "Hear me out. Sales are flat, as you well know."

"Yeah, blame it all on Sales. We take shit from everyone. We're on the front line trying to sell the same crappy product we've had for years, but we're the ones who get beat up. When's Product going to come up with something new?"

"I know that's the root problem." Maura's voice remained low. "But we can't count on new revenues. Benefit costs are skyrocketing, and we have to raise salaries every year to stay competitive. Do you want to cut pay and benefits, or do you want to reduce headcount to fund increases?"

"Damn it, Maura, Sales shouldn't have to do either. We reduced costs last year."

"If Sales doesn't participate, then all the other divisions will have to cut by more than ten percent."

"Fine by me. We've done our part. You know damn well Rick wouldn't cut people on a cream cheese approach. Haven't you done any more homework than to tell us all to cut ten percent?"

"Are you telling me Sales can't reduce payroll at all?" Surely, he wouldn't want her to tell their peers Sales wouldn't play ball.

Leo sat back. "Now don't crap in your panties. I'm not saying that. But I'm not going to volunteer any cuts. Go back to the drawing board and decide which divisions are too big. It's not Sales."

"Which division do you think I should be targeting?"

"You're the HR person. You decide. But not Sales."

"Okay. Thanks for your time. I'll see what others have to say." She hadn't made any progress with Leo at all. He wouldn't cooperate without a direct order from Rick.

$ $ $

Maura trudged up two floors from the Sales department toward her office. At the top of the stairs, she glanced at her watch. Still time to stop by Kevin's office and get to the airport on time. She could get all her conversations done before the weekend.

She caught Kevin sitting at his desk staring at the office door. "I need to talk to you, Kevin, but this doesn't look like a good time. Any news about Rick?"

"No, that's not what's wrong. I'm just thinking." Kevin shook his head as if to clear it. "What do you need?"

She sat across from him. "Alex and I are vetting our headcount cuts with the other officers. Vince suggested I talk to you."

"How much of a cut?"

"We need ten percent across the board to keep our payroll costs in control. Otherwise, we'll need to reduce salaries or increase healthcare premiums to get to a viable cost structure. I'd rather cut heads."

"What criteria would you use for letting people go?"

Maura smiled. At least Kevin was thinking, unlike Leo or Vince. "That's the first intelligent question I've heard all day. Everyone else is up in arms about their people getting cut. I don't blame them, but no one other than Alex will get on board."

Kevin leaned forward. "Don't misunderstand me, Maura. I don't want the cuts either, but I want to know how it would work. I haven't been involved in a layoff before."

Maura nodded. "Okay. Here's what happens." She went through the same general spiel she'd given the other officers, then turned to her figures on the Marketing and Communications division. "Here's what it would mean for your group."

Kevin glanced at the spreadsheet, then back at Maura. "Before we get into how it would impact Marketing, help me understand the big picture. How often have we done this?"

"Not often. The last time we did an across-the-board layoff was about five years ago. Since then we've only targeted particular divisions when they reorganize. Like Sales last year. Which is why Leo is fighting any further reductions this year."

"What kind of fallout do we typically get?"

"It isn't pretty. The employees who are let go are usually bitter. And employees who stay feel guilty about keeping their jobs. If we cut too deeply, the people left are overburdened with too much work. Morale definitely suffers. I don't like layoffs, but if costs get out of whack with revenues, the whole company could go bankrupt."

"What do the others say?"

"Leo is opposed. Grant doesn't like it, and hasn't agreed yet. But he would go with a layoff over pay cuts. Alex is in favor; he needs something to take to the bankers next week."

"And Vince?"

"He hasn't declared. He wanted me to talk to you."

"What do you need from me?"

"Just your reaction." Maura pointed back at the figures on Kevin's division. "What would happen if you cut ten percent in your group? Would you want equal reductions in each department, or would you target certain groups? What do you think generally, as an owner of the company? And as the person responsible for communications, how will we spin this?"

"That's a lot to respond to." He leaned back in his chair. "Is this the kind of discussion you used to have with Rick?"

Maura nodded. "In the twelve years I've been here, Rick's been involved in every reduction in force we've had. As Vince reminded me, Rick doesn't like them. But Rick's good at wrestling with the implications. We've never gone forward until he agreed.

Sometimes I made proposals he didn't like, but generally he followed my advice."

"What would Rick do this time?"

"Based on the state of the business, he'd do it. We need more discussion on whether to cut ten percent in each division or whether to vary the cuts. But unless we have a miracle on revenue, I think Rick would conclude we need to reduce headcount, however painful it might be."

Kevin was quiet for a moment, then said, "I agree. You can tell Vince we've talked. I don't know how I'd cut Marketing and Communications, but you have my support to take the planning to the next level. And if we have good reasons for what we're doing, I think we can sell it to the employees who remain."

"Thanks, Kevin." Why couldn't all the officers be so rational? Maura dashed back to her office to pack up her briefcase and head to the airport.

$$\$\,\$\,\$$

It was Friday evening, the end of the second work week since Rick's accident. Kevin sat in Rick's hospital room with Vince and Paige. The doctors now insisted the family make other plans for Rick's care.

"They say we need to move Rick by the end of next week," Paige said. Her voice was low, but Kevin didn't think she sounded as teary as when the neurologist first raised the issue. Maybe she was getting used to the idea. "I went to visit the long-term care facility this afternoon. It's not much different than the hospital. Maybe it will be all right."

"I don't see why we can't give him more time here," Vince said. "It could take a while for him to get better."

"We can't keep putting our heads in the sand." Kevin knew his words were harsh, but he had to get through to Vince. "Rick's not going to get better any time soon. We need to deal with it."

Paige gasped softly at Kevin's bluntness, but nodded. "You're right, Kevin." Her voice was firmer than Kevin expected. "I'll call the long-term care place Monday. Start arranging for them to take Rick."

"Do you want me to do it?" Kevin asked.

"No. I will."

Vince stared at the floor as Paige and Kevin talked. "What about PlayLand?" he asked. "Does that mean we have to name someone to replace Rick there?"

"I think so," Kevin said. "You know it's getting harder without a CEO. The officers all have their own ideas about what to do."

"I don't want it." Vince's voice was flat.

"Don't want what? The job?" Paige asked.

Vince nodded.

"It wouldn't be permanent," Kevin said. "I think we should name an interim CEO. Let's give Rick a few more weeks before we work on a longer term solution."

"I know it isn't my call," Paige said, pushing her hair back from her face. "But Dewayne said we should all agree. If not you, Vince, then who?"

"I don't know." Vince jumped up and paced the small hospital room. Kevin looked at him in surprise. Vince didn't usually get so agitated; he usually turned morose.

"All I know," Vince continued, "is I have more than I can do now. Launching the action figure line. Alex hounding me about costs. Dealing with Ben and Jennifer. They're still fighting about how to market the frigging characters. Leo pushing for concessions for Toy Mart and other chains. Talking to Grant about how to get production back on schedule without overtime. If I had Rick's responsibilities, too, how could I do it?" His voice broke.

"Okay, Vince. It doesn't have to be you," Paige said. "What about one of the others? Alex? Dewayne? Maura did say if it wasn't you, it shouldn't be Leo or Grant."

Vince snorted. "Well, she's right. Leo would be awful. He'd give the entire first run of action figures to Toy Mart at cost."

"Grant could do it. Or Alex or Dewayne. If you're sure you don't want it," Kevin said to Vince.

"Why not you?" Paige asked Kevin.

"I don't want to step ahead of Vince. Besides, I'm not sure Leo would listen to me either."

"Alex knows the business, doesn't he?" Paige asked.

"Yes," Kevin replied. "He knows more than Dewayne. But Leo'll run all over Alex, too."

"What about Grant?"

Kevin was surprised at Paige's persistence. Why did she want Rick's replacement named right now?

He shrugged, looking at Vince. "What do you think?"

Vince shrugged also. "I don't care. As long as it isn't me."

"Will you care what people outside the family think?" Paige asked, touching Vince's arm.

"They'll think what they think. It's not like we're doing anything permanent. Rick'll wake up."

"He might, but it could be a long time," Kevin said. "What do you want people saying in the meantime? Do you want them to think Grant is Rick's long-term successor?"

Vince lifted one shoulder. "I suppose it would look more like an interim move if we named Alex or Dewayne."

"Probably." Paige nodded. "Which one would you choose, Vince? It's really up to you and Dewayne. Kevin and I will back you up, won't we?" She turned to Kevin.

He nodded. Paige was really pushing. Where had this woman been the last two weeks?

"If you say Leo would steamroll Alex, should it be Dewayne? After all, he's already a director with you," Paige said.

"Dewayne's as good as anyone." Vince was staring at the floor again.

"Kevin, is Dewayne all right with you?" Paige asked.

Kevin grinned. Paige had manipulated them into making the call, but that was okay with him. "Dewayne's fine."

"Well, then," Paige said, folding her arms across her chest. "Vince, will you talk to Dewayne, get him to put the papers together? Sounds like you and he sign whatever we need. But if he wants anything from Kevin or me, we'll sign, too. Right, Kevin?"

"You're the boss, Paige," Kevin said, chuckling.

CHAPTER 9: MONDAY, JANUARY 22

Maura was glad to leave home for the office Monday morning, even knowing she faced another officers' meeting. Kevin had called her over the weekend to tell her Vince would announce Dewayne as the interim CEO. Somehow, Paige had pulled it off.

The weekend with Liz and Estella had been a disaster. Liz had known exactly what kind of dress she wanted—a strapless gown in fire engine red. When Liz described her dream gown to Estella, the older woman told Liz no dress without straps was proper for a quinceañera. Liz countered by describing for her grandmother what her friend had worn last year. Estella called Liz's friend a "puta," which even Maura knew meant "whore." Or at least "floozy."

Liz dissolved into tears, and she and her grandmother scarcely spoke at all. Maura tried to make peace, but neither her daughter nor her mother-in-law listened. Liz tried on several dresses sullenly, but Estella soundly rejected the only dress Liz liked.

Finally Estella threatened to make Liz a dress. Even as a toddler, Liz had refused to wear Estella's handsewn clothes. By the end of the shopping trip, Estella was also in tears, and Maura nearly so.

Saturday night, after everyone was in bed, Maura described the day to Carlos.

"Did Liz look like a puta in the dress she liked?" he asked.

"Of course not." Maura smiled, remembering. "She looked lovely." The dress was more burgundy than red, and set off Liz's dark hair and eyes. "It was strapless, but she could wear a shawl during Mass." Maura justified the style in her own mind. "Seed pearls sewn all over the bodice. We could give her a pearl necklace and earrings. She'd be gorgeous. Like red and white roses. She even started talking about a red and white rose theme for the party. So much more sophisticated than the princess themes her friends have had."

Even now, driving to work, Maura had a lump in her throat as she thought about her daughter. "She's growing up so fast," she'd told Carlos.

"Buy her the dress she likes," he said. "I'll deal with Mama."

That was easy for him to say. Whatever happened, Estella would blame her, not Carlos. Carlos could do no wrong in Estella's eyes, whereas Maura was the gringa daughter-in-law who'd seduced her son. Maura swallowed hard and pulled into the PlayLand parking lot.

$ $ $

Over the weekend Vince had talked to Dewayne. "I'd be honored to act as interim CEO," Dewayne said.

"You won't have to do much," Vince told him. "We'll each still run our own divisions. But you can chair the staff meetings. I don't need that thankless task. And be our referee."

Dewayne brought a document appointing himself as interim CEO to Vince's office first thing Monday. They signed it, then the two of them walked into the officer staff meeting together. Vince motioned Dewayne toward the head of the table. The other officers looked at Dewayne in surprise.

"Kevin and I have asked Dewayne to serve as interim CEO while Rick is incapacitated," Vince announced, looking down the table at his peers. A red flush rose from Leo's neck to his cheeks. Alex dropped his pencil. Grant scowled.

"Why?" Leo exploded.

"We need someone to be in charge. Dewayne and I have been directors of PlayLand along with Rick. I'm too busy with the product launch, so Kevin and I asked Dewayne to step up. He'll chair our meetings and sign corporate papers until Rick is back." Vince wanted to downplay the importance of Dewayne's role. He needed the group to back Dewayne so the pressure was off him.

"Rick's wife Paige and I were involved in the decision," Kevin added. "It's important for us to show the rest of the company and the business community we're together on this."

Leo's face remained red, but he didn't say anything more.

"Shall we get started?" Dewayne said, leaning back in Rick's chair.

$ $ $

Alex followed Maura out of the officers' meeting, practically stepping on her heels. "We need to talk," he said.

"I've got fifteen minutes," she said, glancing at her watch when they arrived at her office.

"What was all that about?" Alex asked as he shut the door.

"What was all what about?" Maura thought she knew, but she wanted Alex to spell it out.

"Dewayne. Why is he the interim CEO?"

"He was already a director."

"Yeah, but so's Vince."

"Vince is too busy," Maura said, "Or at least that's what he said."

"Why Dewayne? Why not me?"

Maura was silent.

"After all," Alex continued, "I'm the one dealing with our cost structure. That's our biggest problem. Shouldn't I be the one in charge?"

"You think so?"

Alex snorted. "It makes more sense than Dewayne." He leaned toward her. "Or Leo or Grant. They lead major divisions. Dewayne's just our lawyer."

"I wasn't there when Vince and Kevin made the call," Maura said. "I don't know what they talked about." Literally, this was true. But she suspected Paige had followed through on her promise to get the brothers to make a rational choice. Now, would the rest of the company support that choice?

$ $ $

Kevin sat at his desk with his head in his hands. He was tired. He'd spent most of the weekend at the hospital with Rick and talking with Vince and Paige about next steps in Rick's care.

The officer meeting that morning hadn't gone well. Kevin had hoped naming Dewayne as interim CEO would force the group to work together, but it hadn't played out that way. Dewayne made them follow the agenda, but they hadn't done any better resolving conflicts than last week. Alex fixated on reducing costs, while Leo and Grant resisted. Grant pushed for new equipment to meet production quotas, despite the cash flow problems. Leo leaned on Vince and Kevin to decide on the action figure marketing, saying he needed to get back to Toy Mart.

"Hey, Kevin," a quiet voice from his doorway caused him to glance up. Jennifer. Too bad her boots and calf-length skirt hid her legs, but she still looked fantastic.

"Hey, yourself." Kevin smiled, trying not to ogle her like Ben did. "What's going on?"

"How's Rick?"

Kevin shook his head. "No change. I'm pretty bummed out. You have any good news?"

"Sorry. I'm here to vent again. Got a minute?"

"Sure." Kevin gestured at the seat across from him.

"It's Ben." Kevin heard the frustration in her voice. "He's lying about Gus. Last week Ben said all he'd promised Gus was a transfer out of Games. But Gus says Ben told him he could help develop the action figures. Legal says the company has to pay Gus so we own the figures outright, but Gus won't sign anything unless we promise him he can work on the line. I don't know how to handle Ben."

"You're doing all right. No one else even surfaced the issue with Ben. At least now it's out in the open." Kevin wondered if his words made Vince look bad. Vince should have known what Ben was doing.

"Ben's such a sleaze. Why does PlayLand put up with him?" Jennifer hesitated. "I've heard he was Rick's college roommate. Is that true?"

"Yes."

"So that's how this company operates? Nepotism?" Jennifer stopped, a blush rising on her cheeks.

Kevin grinned. Been a long time since he saw a girl blush.

"I guess I shouldn't say that," she said. "I don't mean to say you got your job through nepotism."

"Why not? It's true. My dad built this company. Nothing I can do to change that. But I happen to like what I do."

Jennifer let her hair swing forward, hiding her face for a moment, then shook it back and faced Kevin directly. "Sorry. I feel

116

I can talk to you, but I'm probably overstepping my bounds."

"Not many people feel they can talk openly with me. I'm glad you do."

"So, how do I handle Ben? If he's Rick's friend, does it matter what the rest of us think?"

"Just keep doing what you're doing. People know you have integrity and he doesn't."

"What good does that do?"

"Well, you're impressing me, for one thing. Does that matter?"

Jennifer ducked her head, a small smile on her lips. "Yeah. Thanks." She stood.

Kevin watched her walk to the door. "Hey," he said.

She halted in his doorway and turned back to him.

"Are you free Friday night?" he asked.

Jennifer eyed him skeptically. "I think so, but I'll have to check."

"I have tickets to a play. The company has season tickets we circulate among the officers. No one else can go Friday night. I wasn't planning to go either, because of Rick. But someone ought to put in an appearance for PlayLand. How 'bout it?"

Jennifer pushed a lock of hair behind her ear. She started to speak, then hesitated.

"What is it?" asked Kevin.

"I don't date people at work. It's a bad idea."

"I agree." Kevin smiled. "But I really should go to the play. I'd like some company, and I enjoy yours. Let's not call it a date. Simply two friends having dinner and seeing a play."

"Nothing more?"

"Nothing more."

Jennifer took a deep breath. "Okay."

"Shall I pick you up at seven?"

"It's probably a mistake, but okay." She smiled, which took the sting out of her grudging acceptance.

After Jennifer left, Kevin sat frowning at his office door. Now why had he done that? Like she said, it was probably a mistake. But he did want to see her.

Kevin was still scowling at his door when Maura stopped by.

"I'd like to talk, Kevin, but this doesn't look like a good time."

"Just thinking." Kevin shook his head as much to clear it as to deny what Maura had said. "What's up?"

Maura came in and sat. "What'd you think of the reactions to Dewayne's appointment this morning?" she asked.

Kevin shrugged. "Not a ringing endorsement."

"What'd you expect?"

"I guess I hoped the rest of the officers would welcome it. What are you hearing?"

Maura shook her head. "Alex came to talk to me. He was stunned. Had lots of questions. Why wasn't it Vince? Why Dewayne, not Alex? He's so focused on cost reductions he can't see anything else. If other people don't agree with him, he thinks they're incompetent."

"Which is why Alex wasn't a good choice," Kevin said. "Can't see the big picture. Heard anything from Leo or Grant? I'm more worried about them."

"No," Maura said. "But I'm sure you noticed Leo couldn't say anything civil the whole meeting. He stormed out at the end. Grant was pretty quiet. I don't know what he thinks."

$ $ $

When Maura got back to her office after talking with Kevin, her assistant Kay handed her a note. Alex wanted to meet about the headcount reduction. Maura sighed and found her file on her desk. She wanted coffee, but headed straight to Alex's office.

"Hello, Alex." She sat without an invitation.

Alex turned away from the spreadsheet open on his monitor and grimaced. "Where are we on the payroll cost reductions? I should have asked earlier." No comment about his emotional response to Dewayne's appointment.

Maura put on her reading glasses and opened her notes. "It's about what I expected. Grant doesn't like it, and will probably fight us. But he'd prefer to cut headcount than reduce pay and benefits. Leo will fight any cuts in Sales tooth and nail. Vince wouldn't give me an opinion. Kevin will support it, but doesn't like it. Dewayne's mostly worried about the potential for adverse impact."

She looked at Alex over her glasses. "Unless we think we can save the company by reducing headcount in only Finance and HR, we still have a lot of work ahead."

"Damn. We need every penny of the ten percent payroll

reduction to get to a cost structure the bankers will accept. Where do we go from here?"

"Without Rick, I don't know." Maura pushed her glasses up on top of her head. "In the past, I've always had Rick behind me when we downsized. I don't know if Dewayne can cajole us into agreement, particularly when he doesn't like the headcount reduction himself. Can we propose the cuts to the bankers and get them to force our hand with the rest of the officers?"

Alex raised an eyebrow. "Oh, they'll force our hand all right. Whatever we propose they'll take as a given. They might require additional cost-cutting measures as well. That's why we can't put anything on the table if we're not sure it'll fly. We need Vince and Kevin behind us. And Dewayne."

"Vince won't get off the fence unless he has to." Maura shook her head. "He hasn't made one decision since Rick's accident. Not on headcount. Not on the marketing program. He let Ben Thornton get away with lying about ownership of the action figures. He wouldn't take the interim CEO role. I'm sick of it."

Alex stared at her. "What's this about the ownership of the action figures?"

"Haven't you heard?" Maura was surprised. She thought the rumors about Ben and Gus would have made it through the grapevine by now. But maybe Alex was too tied up in his numbers to listen to anything about product. "Turns out Gus developed the characters during college. Ben presented them to Vince as PlayLand's creations. That's the genesis of our new action figure line."

Alex bolted out of his chair, crossed his office, and slammed his door shut. Maura had never seen him move so fast. "Holy crap!" he yelled at her, his usual crisp diction gone, and his Brooklyn upbringing rising to the surface. "We're telling the banks the action figure line will save the company. Without new product, we'll never get our credit line extended. Cost cuts alone won't sway them. We need revenue. Forget us buying time. We're screwed without new product."

"Dewayne's working on it." Maura put on her most soothing HR voice. "He had Vince give Gus a contract to buy him off. We're going to have to pay Gus to get the rights. Gus wants to get an attorney, so we don't know yet how much he'll demand. I'm assuming he has a price. We just don't know how high."

Alex turned to his phone and punched in numbers. After a couple of rings, Vince answered.

"Vince, it's Alex. Maura told me Ben misled you about the source of the action figures."

"Now, that's an overstatement," Vince began.

Alex interrupted. "Do we have the rights to the action figures or not?"

"Ben swears Gus will sign over the rights."

Alex frowned and shook his head at Maura. "Vince, we need it nailed down today. You and I are meeting with the banks next week. There can't be any doubt about us delivering on the new product line."

"I talked to Gus on Friday. I'll follow up today. He wanted time to talk to his lawyer."

"And another thing," Alex continued. "I'll ask Dewayne to go with us to the bank meeting, but I think we should take Maura, too. I'd like for her to present our headcount reduction. That okay?" Alex looked at Maura with a question in his eyes and mouthed, "Can you go?"

She nodded.

"Well," Vince said slowly, "You know how badly the employees will react if we downsize."

"I don't care what employees think." Alex's mouth narrowed into a thin line below his neat mustache. "Without a new line of credit we won't have any cash to pay them. We have to get the line extended, or we're doomed."

"Are you saying we don't have a choice?" Vince sounded weary.

"That's what I've been saying all month." By now, Alex's accent sounded like he had never been west of the Hudson.

"Then why ask me what I think?" Vince's voice was thinner, as if he had turned away from the phone.

Maura spoke up. "Vince, we need the family's support. And Dewayne's. Alex and I can make the case to the bankers. But we need Dewayne to make the division heads fall in line, like Rick would have. And we need you to represent the family. Otherwise, we won't get the cuts implemented."

Vince was silent. Finally, he said, "Let's take this one step at a time. We'll talk to the bankers about headcount. I'll support you next week. But I don't want any internal rumors. Let's wait before we force anything with the division heads."

Maura pressed the point. "Then I can talk with the bankers next week about a ten percent headcount cut? But we won't declare specifically which group will cut what."

Vince hesitated again. "Yeah, okay. If Dewayne agrees. But we'll work out the details with the division heads before we announce anything."

"Thanks, Vince," Alex said. "Maura and I will talk to Dewayne and brainstorm what to say next week. We'll get with you next Monday to finalize the agenda. Be ready to talk about the action figure line. And you'd better have the ownership clear."

Maura noticed when Alex got upset, he ordered everyone around, even the Players brothers. Maybe more people should be firm with Vince. Maybe Alex wouldn't have been such a bad choice as interim CEO.

"Sure. Whatever," Vince said. And he hung up.

Alex shook his head. "Well, that tells us a lot. You know, in Finance Vince is known as the CBO."

"What's that?" Maura asked.

"Chief Brother Officer. His only strength is being Rick's brother."

Maura smirked, though she knew she shouldn't. "Don't count on him to say much about action figures next week." She tapped her glasses on her file. "We'd better have a good story on the cost reduction."

$ $ $

On Monday afternoon, Kevin went to Vince's office to lean on his brother to get PlayLand's rights in the action figures settled. Unfortunately, Ben was in Vince's office when Kevin got there. They were already talking about the action figures.

"Do we have the situation with Gus resolved yet?" Kevin asked. "We have to get on with the marketing plan if we're going ahead with the line."

Ben spoke up. "Oh, we're going ahead with it. Gus'll go along. I'm just trying to persuade Vince to drop Jennifer's comic books.

Gus'll have less to complain about with a product giveaway than if we use his original comic book stories."

Kevin shook his head. "But the comic books are more creative. The 'buy one, get one free' approach is stale. Besides, doesn't Gus have rights in the characters themselves, even without the comic books?"

Vince pressed his hand to his stomach as he nodded. "Dewayne says there's a risk regardless, because the action figures are based on Gus's characters. But the risk is greater if we use comic books, because that's the character format Gus developed before he came to PlayLand."

"Then it all boils down to whether Gus will sell us the rights?" Kevin sat next to Ben. "Ben, I thought you said he'd fall in line."

"He will. I had things under control, until Dewayne made Vince talk to him. Now Gus has dollar figures in his eyes. Let me talk to him. I'll beat him down."

Kevin shook his head. "No can do, Ben. It's your fault we're in this mess. If you'd been up front when you proposed the action figures, we'd have it worked out by now. We'll do it Dewayne's way." Kevin turned to Vince. "Have you talked to Gus again?"

"He said he needs to see a lawyer before signing anything." Vince belched and grimaced. "I haven't heard back from him yet."

"What did you tell him?" Kevin leaned toward his brother. He wished Ben weren't there, so he could really push Vince.

"I gave him the name of someone Dewayne recommended. A lawyer Dewayne says is fair and fast." Vince burped again, covering his mouth. "I told Gus we needed an answer soon. But I don't know what kind of leverage we have to make him get back with us quickly."

Ben said again, "Let me talk to him."

"No," Vince said. "Dewayne said you weren't to go anywhere near Gus. We can't look like we're pressuring him."

At least Vince's being direct with Ben, Kevin thought.

"But we are pressuring him. We have to," Ben argued. "He's our employee, we can talk to him. We need this product to save our hide. I'm the one who can get this done."

"Ben, you are not to talk to Gus," Vince said quietly, rubbing his forehead. "You can't do anything Legal says we shouldn't."

"Well, then, I'm not asking." Ben stood up to leave. "I'll get this fixed." He stormed out of the office.

Kevin watched Ben leave. The situation was escalating. Ben would screw with Gus's head, and then Gus wouldn't sign a deal. "Don't you have Ben under better control than that?" he asked his brother.

"Than what?" Vince responded wearily. "I told him not to talk to Gus."

"He's not listening."

"What more can I do? You want me to fire him? I can't, not without Rick's okay."

Kevin shrugged. "Seems we'll have to fire him at some point. With or without Rick. He's a loose cannon, and he's going to keep hurting the company until he's gone."

Vince sighed.

Kevin looked directly at his brother. "Are you going to use Jennifer's comic books or let Ben do what he wants?"

Vince shook his head. "I don't know. I've told Jennifer to go ahead with the comics, assuming we can get Gus to agree. But if he doesn't agree, we'll have to use Ben's approach and take the risk on the ownership of the characters. We have to have the new product. I can't alienate Ben too much while this is pending."

"Why not? My group could handle a traditional promotion at the drop of a hat. We don't need Ben."

Vince just shrugged.

Kevin stood to leave. "You know, Vince, you're head of Product Development. You need to make the call. Decide between Ben and Jennifer. But if you want my opinion, go with Jennifer."

Vince stared at his fingertips without saying anything.

As Kevin left, he wondered whether pushing Vince had done any good.

$ $ $

On Monday evening Kevin was in Rick's hospital room again. Alone this time. Paige had been there with the twins awhile, then left. Vince hadn't shown up.

Kevin took a deep breath and leaned back in the plastic chair by Rick's head. "Well, big brother," he said out loud, "The company's falling apart without you. Your pal Ben is as underhanded as ever.

He stole ideas from Gus Powell, and tried passing them off as New Ventures creations. He's wrecking our chances of getting the action figure line to market in time to do any good this year."

The machines whirred, the only sign Rick was alive.

"Alex is fretting over what to tell the bankers. Toy Mart wants our hide. Maura wants to cut headcount. The officers are lining up and taking sides. I don't know what Vince will do. Brother Vince isn't stepping up the way we need. Dewayne's now our temporary CEO, but he's not helping."

Had anything gone well since Rick's accident? Kevin wondered. "The only nice thing since your accident," he said, continuing his monologue, "has been working with Jennifer. Where's she been hiding? We should get her out of Dolls. She could run circles around Vince and Ben both. She's smart and creative. And damned attractive as well."

"I asked her out," he confessed. "Probably stupid of me. You always said not to date PlayLand employees. But I haven't met anyone like her in a long time."

Kevin stopped talking and watched his brother. Rick hadn't moved at all that evening.

Kevin leaned over the bed and said into Rick's ear. "If you're in there, it's time to come out. Time to stop hiding. We need you. If you don't come back, I don't think PlayLand will survive." Kevin paused again. "And Paige and your boys need you, too."

He sat back in his chair, listening to the monitors continue their rhythmic pulsing until he dozed.

Sometime later, Kevin awoke. Rick was stirring. Kevin buzzed the nurse's station, and a nurse came to check on Rick.

"He's still unconscious, sir," she said.

"Can he hear me?" Kevin asked.

"We don't know."

Kevin leaned over his brother again. "Last chance, buddy. We need you."

CHAPTER 10: FRIDAY, JANUARY 26

When Vince walked into his office Friday morning, Dewayne was waiting for him.

"Where are you with Gus?" Dewayne asked.

Damn it, he should never have agreed to make Dewayne interim CEO, Vince thought. Dewayne had been breathing down Vince's neck all week. "No word since Monday. I gave him the lawyer's name you gave me."

"Well, I just got a call from that guy. Says he's representing Gus now. He seems to think PlayLand should pay big bucks for the rights to the characters. Maybe I should have given Gus the name of someone less aggressive."

"How much?"

"Two hundred thousand."

Vince's gut clenched. "That's three times what Gus makes in a year!" he said in a panic. "If other employees find out Gus's getting a windfall, they'll quit. Lots of people have developed stuff for us over the years. They didn't get a penny extra."

"Doesn't matter. That's what the lawyer told Gus his stuff is worth. That's what Gus wants."

"Is it really worth that much?"

"What's it worth to PlayLand is the question? We've got shit without the action figures." Dewayne's voice reverberated in Vince's head.

"How strong is Gus's case?" Vince asked.

"It's a close call," Dewayne said. "Our copyright lawyer thinks Gus probably owns the stories. Unless we've made substantial changes in how the characters look, he probably owns those as well. All it takes to prove copyright infringement is access and similarity."

"What does that mean?"

"If PlayLand had access to the drawings Gus developed before he started working here, which we did because Gus gave the drawings to Ben, and if PlayLand's designs look similar to Gus's, which it sure as hell sounds like they do, since they were based on Gus's drawings, then the courts can infer copying and we lose. In fact, what Ben did is probably direct evidence of copying."

Vince rubbed his forehead. "Couldn't we fight Gus? How original were his drawings anyway?"

"Maybe. But it would take years. We need that product line for Toy Fair."

Shit, thought Vince. He was trapped. "Then we have to pay?"

"Got to pay something. Why don't you see what you can talk Gus into? But don't let this fester. Get it done."

Vince's head pounded. "I want Gus to keep it quiet if we pay him. We can't let other employees find out. Can we get a confidentiality agreement?"

"We can write it in the agreement," Dewayne said, "But I can't promise a judge would enforce it. What do we do if Gus talks? Fire him? We need him."

"Let's face that when it happens. I want him to think he can't talk."

$ $ $

Vince stewed about how to approach Gus. Dewayne had put him in a no-win situation. He had to get results. And fast. He'd have to pay Gus whatever it took. But two hundred thousand?

He rubbed his stomach. It hurt like hell. He belched, then walked to the Games department to find Gus.

When he got to Gus's cubicle, he said, "Where are those famous drawings we've been talking about?" His voice sounded unnaturally jovial even to himself.

Gus startled as he turned away from his computer and looked at Vince. "I gave most of them to Jennifer," he replied. "But here's one I kept."

He gestured at a ruled notebook page tacked on his bulletin board. "I did this my sophomore year. For my first story. It's Beowulf, with the slasher arms. He can kill anything, yet keep his distance from his prey."

Vince looked at it. Just a sketch. Was this what all the fuss was about? Why did this nerd have PlayLand over a barrel? "I hear you have an attorney now." Vince tried to keep any judgment out of his voice.

"Yeah, I wanted to know what my drawings are worth." Gus pushed his horn-rimmed glasses up on his nose and peered at Vince from under his hair. "You said I could talk to someone."

"What's he say?"

Gus stood to look over the walls of his cubicle, then sat and whispered, "He says he asked you for two hundred thousand."

Vince sat in the flimsy plastic chair Gus had for visitors. "Seems like a lot. What'd it cost you to do the drawings?"

"I was in college. Didn't cost me anything. What's that have to do with it?"

"Wouldn't the two hundred grand more than pay for your whole education?"

"My lawyer says the drawings are worth a lot to PlayLand."

"What happened to the ten thousand offer I made you earlier in the week?"

"My lawyer says I should get more." Gus set his jaw, but he didn't meet Vince's eyes.

No doubt about it, Gus was nervous. Probably as nervous as Vince was. He took a deep breath. It was time to earn his executive pay. "Gus, I want to be fair. But if we had put you on these drawings full-time at your current salary, you wouldn't have made anywhere near two hundred K in the time it took to develop them."

"Yeah, but my lawyer says PlayLand will get a lot more than two hundred thousand out of them."

"We don't know that, Gus. The new product line could be a dud."

Gus's voice rose as he stood again. Vince was afraid Gus might come across the desk at him. "My guys are great! No one else has anything like them. I mean, have you ever heard of anyone like Delphi with the bionic brain? And they're mine. I have lots of stories already developed. My lawyer says I should get oversight of the whole product line because they're my ideas."

"Gus, our Marketing and Product Development groups know a whole lot more about selling these characters than you do. You said before that you hadn't been able to sell them outside of PlayLand."

"But they're mine." Gus's jaw jutted forward.

The pain in Vince's gut rose to his throat. He had to get a deal with Gus; Dewayne and Alex had told him so. "What if I promise you can be involved on the marketing team?" Vince hoped his voice didn't sound too anxious.

Gus settled back in his chair. "Will I have final say-so?"

Vince shook his head slowly, watching Gus. "I can't give you that much. I have to keep the whole team happy. But I can have you work for Jennifer on the comic books and do the first drafts of the story lines. You'll have to let her make the final calls. Can you live with that?"

"I don't know." Gus stared down at his hands. "I guess so. Jennifer's nice." Without raising his head, he mumbled, "But there's still the money."

"Gus, we need a decision. I'm going to make you a take it or leave it offer." Vince paused and gulped. He hadn't run this by anyone. Dewayne and Alex might think he was stupid. But they'd told him to get the character rights. He had to do something, and there was nobody around to ask.

"As I s-s-said," Vince stammered, "you can work on the marketing team with Jennifer. And you can have fifty thousand up front. If the action figures are in our line next January, you'll get fifty K more. And another fifty each year we keep the characters in our product line. You'll get at least fifty grand now. You could get more than two hundred K, if the line is successful. But you have to sign a contract with Legal today."

Gus was silent. Then he looked up and thrust his chin out again. "I need to talk to my lawyer." Vince didn't know if it was stubbornness or stupidity. He figured he and Gus were in the same boat. Neither of them knew what they were doing.

"Call him. You have until the end of the day to accept my offer and sign whatever Legal says we need. Call me when you've made up your mind."

Vince left Gus's cubicle. When he got to his office, he slammed the door behind him, and sat in his chair shaking. He belched, then left messages for Alex and Dewayne telling them what he'd done. Hell, I own this company, don't I? he fumed. What can they do if they don't like it?

As Vince hung up, there was a knock on his door. "Come in," he yelled. He knew he sounded surly, but he couldn't help it. Why wouldn't people leave him alone?

The door opened. It was Jennifer. "Can I talk to you?"

Vince sighed. More problems.

"I need a decision on the action figure marketing." Jennifer sounded nervous.

"What's the problem? I told you to go ahead on the comic books."

"We're about to start spending money. Procurement needs to get the printing contract lined up. Sales has to negotiate space in the stores. Chains like Toy Mart will want sales guarantees. And I haven't pushed Gus for the story lines while you're negotiating with him. Toy Fair is only a month away, and we need samples by then."

"I told you to go ahead. And we should have word from Gus by the end of the day." Vince's head throbbed almost as much as his stomach.

"Is the comic book cost built into the current budget?" Jennifer asked. "I know you're meeting with the banks next week, and they won't want any surprises after the fact."

"You told me the cost for the comic books would be about the same as the promotional marketing. That was built into the budget." Vince didn't want to spend time rehashing the same issues.

"Yes, but Ben's starting to spend money also. You told us both to go ahead. So we both have expenses. You said we should limit our spending, but we can't move forward without some costs."

"Go ahead with the comic books. I'll talk to Ben." Vince rubbed his forehead. Shit. He couldn't put that decision off any longer either.

"And Gus? When can I approach him?"

"Jennifer, give me time." Vince's voice was sharper than it should be, but he just wanted to be left alone. "I should hear back from Gus today. Wait until Monday to talk to him. I'll let you know what happens." Then Vince tried calm down. "I did tell Gus you'd use him on the comic books, but I told him he couldn't control the scripts. You get final approval on the story lines. But you have to work with him."

"Okay, I can handle Gus. Thanks, Vince. But please let me know if I have to cut back on the marketing costs. Otherwise, I'll assume I have the same budget that's in the original plan."

$ $ $

Jennifer smiled as she headed back to her office. She'd won. Vince had given her the action figures. And the comic books.

She scowled, wondering what Ben might try to pull next. He wouldn't let it go easily.

But tonight she was going out with Kevin. Her smile returned. Probably stupid of her, but she was looking forward to it.

$ $ $

Maura's office phone rang. It was Dewayne. "We need to talk about the Atlanta case," he announced.

Dewayne had become more dictatorial now that he was the acting CEO, which irritated Maura. Technically, he was her boss, so she tried to shrug it off. "What about it?" she asked.

"Legal isn't getting enough support from HR. I told you we needed the personnel files of everyone involved in the Sales reorganization last year. The court's initial disclosure meeting is coming up soon. We still haven't seen the files."

"Sorry, Dewayne. I'll make it a priority."

Maura paused. She didn't want to tell Dewayne how to do his job, particularly now that he was in charge of the whole company. But sometimes he was too gung-ho. "You know, Steve Williams, the plaintiff, could raise disability discrimination as well as race and sex," she said. "I'm concerned he may say PlayLand didn't do everything we needed to do to accommodate his mental illness."

"I'm comfortable taking our chances," Dewayne said. "As best as I can tell, the Sales group had good reasons for reorganizing. This guy Williams simply didn't—or couldn't—do the new job. We can defend it."

"Okay. I just wanted to be sure you knew my perspective. I'll get you the files. But this case worries me."

"The headcount reduction worries me more," Dewayne said. "Where are you and Alex on that?"

"I've pulled together materials for us to use with the banks next week. Are you going to that meeting?"

"That's the plan," he said. "Send me what you're going to present. I want to make sure we're not setting ourselves up for an adverse impact claim."

Maura thought Dewayne's focus was too narrow, only seeing the legal issues. He should be taking a CEO's perspective. What did he think about the company's cost structure? "Do you agree we need to cut headcount?" she asked.

"I'm not entirely convinced. There are a lot of risks."

"What's our alternative?" she asked. "We need to reduce payroll."

"I want to be sure we're doing it right," he said. "Send me your presentation."

No doubt about it. Dewayne was more dictatorial. "Will do," she said.

$$\$ \$ \$$$

It was Friday afternoon. Vince wanted to go home. But he'd told Gus to get back to him that day, so he needed to wait. He'd wait until five, he told himself. That's the close of business. Gus had better call before then.

At four forty-five, he started packing his briefcase. Gus could call him on his cell.

His phone rang.

"It's Gus."

"What's your decision?"

"I get to work on the action figure line?"

"I told you, yes. But Jennifer runs it."

"Okay."

"Okay what?"

"Okay, I'll take your deal."

"I'll get Legal to send you a contract tonight."

Vince smiled, rubbed the back of his neck, and called Dewayne.

$$\$ \$ \$$$

Rick Players watched the light wavering in the distance. It had been so real when he first saw it, the most beautiful thing he'd ever seen. But now the light was far away. It had receded, grown dimmer, as Kevin had spoken to him.

"Last chance, buddy. We need you," Kevin had said.

Rick's sense of time was warped, but he must have been watching the light for hours now, maybe days. Watching the light retract, while Kevin's words echoed in his head.

Rick was sad because he knew the light would not return.

"We need you, buddy," he heard again.

The hands he had seen before waved dimly in the distance. This time they were waving farewell. He felt a faint touch on his shoulder, but it was gently pushing him away. The light was gone, not even a pinprick left.

He opened his eyes. He was in a hospital bed. The fluorescent lights were bright, but they weren't welcoming like the light he had seen in his dreams. He was awake.

Chapter 11: Wednesday, February 21

Rick Players sat in his den at home on Wednesday morning, February 21, waiting for Dewayne and Alex to arrive. Rick had regained consciousness three and a half weeks ago, and had felt trapped ever since, first in the hospital, then in rehab, and now at home.

Rick remembered nothing from the time he and his sons left the house with the snowmobiles on the day of the accident until he woke up in the hospital. For the first few days after Rick came out of the coma, his doctors poked and prodded and put him through MRIs and CT scans. They gave him crutches, and had him hobbling as much as his woozy brain permitted. His head spun and he couldn't concentrate. The words he wanted to say didn't come to him.

But every day his symptoms diminished. "You don't need to be here," the neurologist told him when the tests were over. "A couple of weeks in a rehab center would do you more good than sitting in a hospital bed. Focus on physical and occupational therapy."

"Are you sure?" Paige asked, with a worried look.

"Get me out of here," Rick said.

In the rehab center, he had daily physical therapy for his broken leg and to help his balance. Speech therapy helped the words come back, and within days he was conversing normally.

"No visitors, other than family," Paige told him. "PlayLand can wait." She'd become more forceful since his accident, he thought. But he let her manage him.

In between therapy sessions, Rick spent most of his time in the rehab center's bright solarium with a view of the Rockies. He sat there for hours, watching the changing light on the mountains, so peaceful and lovely. He wished he could get outside in the snow.

But after a week in rehab, he said to Paige, "Get me out of here."

"You still need crutches," she protested.

"I can use crutches at home." He could put some weight on his leg now, he didn't need the rehab center.

"But the stairs—"

"I'll manage." It was time for him to assert himself.

Back home, Rick fluctuated between worry and boredom. He enjoyed the extra time with Paige during the day, and he liked seeing his boys each afternoon when they got home from school. But after a few minutes of family conversation, his thoughts turned to PlayLand.

There were no views from his home in a gated community in Lakeview to distract him, nothing to watch but the early robins pecking at the still snow-covered ground. He was trapped inside by his house and his mind.

"I should get back to work," he told Paige the Friday before Presidents' Day weekend. He didn't really want to delve back into PlayLand's problems, but he knew he had to. Soon.

"Give it another week," she said.

"I'm bored sitting at home."

"Are you sure you're not depressed?" Paige asked. "The doctor said people often are after traumatic brain injuries."

"I'm not depressed," Rick said irritably. But it was easier to acquiesce with Paige's request to wait a week than to argue with her.

The twins were home most of the holiday weekend, slamming doors as they went in and out. Rick watched them, wishing he had their youth and mobility. But his crutches kept him on the couch.

Yesterday, the Tuesday after he had fretted over the long weekend, he called Mary, his assistant at PlayLand. He told her to schedule his staff members to visit him and brief him on PlayLand's status.

"I thought you weren't working this week," Paige said when he told her.

"I can't put it off forever," Rick said. "I'll stay home for the rest of the week. But I need to get ready for whatever's facing me in the office."

He had seen his brothers Vince and Kevin, of course. They had visited regularly since he had regained consciousness. They told him they had visited while he was unconscious, and he had a vague sense they had been present in his dreams.

After he woke up, Vince and Kevin brought Rick up to date on many of the developments at PlayLand. "I'm glad you're back," Vince told him, soon after he came out of the coma. "It's been a shitty start to the year. Finances are the worst of it. Alex carps about cash flow every time I see him. And I've been up to my eyeballs in the action figure launch."

"How is the new product line?" Rick asked. He would see it soon enough, but he wanted to show some interest in Vince's problems.

"All right, I guess," Vince said, sighing. "But your pal Ben and Jennifer Scott fought over control the whole time."

"You need to manage your staff better." Rick had told Vince that for years. Vince should have stepped up while Rick was out, but it didn't sound like he had.

"Dewayne wouldn't get involved either." Vince frowned and rubbed his forehead. "Don't know why we bothered to appoint him interim CEO."

"Why did you?" Rick asked. He had been peeved when he first heard of Dewayne's appointment, wondering why Vince had dodged the responsibility. "Why not you, Vince?" Rick asked.

"I told you, I had enough to do with the product launch." Vince sounded put upon.

Paige and Kevin told him they had approved of Dewayne also. "No one was taking charge," Paige told him. "Maura said Dewayne would be the best choice in the short run."

"Maura?" Rick said. "Why did she get involved?"

"We asked her," Paige said.

"We needed a figurehead," Kevin said. "Dewayne merely signed papers and ran meetings. We held things together until you could get back. We need you back at work, Rick."

Someone had told Rick they needed him before, over and over. But he couldn't remember when. "I'll be ready soon," he said.

And now he was ready.

$ $ $

Dewayne and Alex arrived midmorning on Wednesday. Both

men had insisted they needed to see Rick as soon as possible, so Mary scheduled them together as early in the day as Paige would permit visitors.

Paige ushered the two men into the den.

"How are you?" Dewayne asked, pumping Rick's hand.

Rick mumbled something appropriate while they sat.

Alex immediately handed Rick a spreadsheet and started talking. "The banks wouldn't increase our line of credit. You have to get involved. At the rate we're bleeding, we'll draw down the entire line by the end of June. And revenue from the action figures won't start until August, even assuming the line launches on time. We'll be in a real bind by summer."

"Why wouldn't we launch on time?" Rick asked. "Are there production problems?"

"Grant says we're on schedule," Dewayne said.

"We still have a gap of a couple of months." Alex's voice rose to a nasal squeak. "We don't have any assurances from the banks we can get more cash. No guarantees when we met with them last month, though they said they'd talk again in March."

"The bankers wouldn't listen to anything we said," Dewayne added. "Once they heard you were conscious, they wanted to hear from you. They want your estimates on new product sales. And your promises on cost reductions. That's what it will take to get the line of credit increased."

"Is there a meeting date?" Rick asked.

"Not yet." Alex shook his head. "We didn't know when you'd be up to it."

Rick sighed. "Set it for mid-March. Surely I can travel by then."

"We need a cost cutting plan in place first," Alex said. "Maura and I are working on headcount reductions, but the other divisions aren't cooperating."

Rick raised an eyebrow at Dewayne, who nodded. "Not a lot of support," Dewayne said in a neutral tone.

"We have to reduce payroll costs," Alex said. "It's the only way to save PlayLand."

"What's your plan?" Rick asked, grimacing as he lifted his injured leg onto a leather ottoman.

"You and I should spend some time going through it. With

Maura. She knows the workforce better than I do," Alex responded.

Paige appeared in the doorway and tapped her watch. "Time for Rick's therapy."

"Before we go," Dewayne said, "you should hear what Ben Thornton did."

Rick waved Paige away. "Give us a few more minutes," he said. He had a vague recollection of hearing about a problem with Ben. "Vince told me something," he said. "But I don't remember the details."

Dewayne raised an eyebrow. "You don't remember? Ben came damn close to getting us sued for copyright infringement."

"Explain it to me again."

"Do you know Gus Powell in Games?"

"I think so," Rick said, frowning. "Short guy, thick glasses? Long hair?"

Dewayne nodded. "That's him. Apparently, the action figure line was originally his idea. As we've pieced it together, when he was in college, Gus developed a series of characters with bionic properties. Seems Ben told Gus he should give his characters to PlayLand, because he'd never be able to market them on his own. But Ben never told anyone the characters were Gus's."

"He did what?" Rick leaned forward in alarm, but his leg cramped and he had to sit back.

"Gus even had story lines for his characters," Dewayne continued. "A lot like the comic books we came up with. Even when Jennifer suggested we use comic books to sell the action figures, Ben didn't say anything. We only learned about it when Gus told Jennifer."

"So what did we do?" Rick asked, massaging his thigh.

"Vince negotiated a deal with Gus. We have to pay Gus fifty thousand a year as long the action figures are in our line. Plus let Gus work on the line, though Vince got him to agree PlayLand has creative control." Dewayne hesitated, then continued. "Vince did a decent job of mitigating the disaster, once he got on the ball."

Rick shook his head. "Fifty grand a year. Shit! That's a lot of money on top of his salary."

"A hell of a lot of money," Alex chimed in.

Dewayne folded his arms across his broad chest. "We don't have much choice. Legally—and this is attorney/client privilege now, I wouldn't say this publicly—Gus has a strong claim he owns the characters. We're over a barrel. We're selling the product already, our customers like it, and we don't have anything else."

"What does Ben say?"

Dewayne shrugged. "He says he and Gus had a deal. But he didn't get anything in writing from Gus, and hadn't paid him a nickel. Ben simply told Gus he'd get him transferred out of Games. There's no evidence of any legally binding deal." Dewayne looked at Rick over steepled fingers. "Rick, I know you and Ben go way back, but as your General Counsel, I have to tell you Ben screwed up. You need to deal with this."

"I'll talk to him." Rick clenched his jaw as he tried to digest what Dewayne had told him. "I wonder what made him do it."

"Talk to Vince, too," Dewayne urged. "Product Development is all bollixed up. Not only did Ben claim credit for Gus's work, but he doesn't have anything else in the New Ventures pipeline. Plus, Ben and Jennifer sparred over the marketing plans for the line. Frankly, Vince hasn't shown much leadership. Though he ultimately got the deal made with Gus. That was good work."

$ $ $

When Rick returned from his physical therapy appointment in midafternoon, he had a message from Alex. "Can Maura and I stop by after work?" Alex's recorded voice bleated. "We'll be there at five o'clock unless we hear from you."

Promptly at five, the doorbell rang. Paige ushered Alex into the den. Maura arrived a few minutes later. Rick sat on the couch, his aching leg propped up on an ottoman. Therapy had been a killer today.

Maura asked about Rick's rehab, but Alex interrupted. "Can we get on with why we're here?" Alex asked.

"Why the rush?" Rick asked.

"I told you this morning," Alex said. "If we don't get moving on the cost reductions, PlayLand is doomed."

"Doomed?" Rick asked, raising an eyebrow.

"We'll be out of cash."

"Okay," Rick sighed. "What's the plan?"

"Payroll is our fastest growing budget item. The bankers

specifically asked how we could cut payroll," Alex said. "But they didn't like the reduction in force plan we presented in January."

"I think they knew we weren't committed to it," Maura chimed in. "So my staff looked at our org charts again after the meeting. We've analyzed in more detail which positions could be cut in each division. But HR can't do any more without your go-ahead. The other VPs are balking."

She and Alex laid out their spreadsheets for Rick and walked him through the proposal. As they finished the review of each division, Alex stacked the pages for that division in a separate pile on the couch beside Rick. Soon the couch was covered.

"Which officers are balking?" Rick asked when they had gone through the numbers on every division.

"Leo is the worst," Maura said. "But Grant is pushing back hard in Operations."

"The smaller divisions can't cut enough to make up the difference, if Operations and Sales don't play," Alex said. "It'll take your order to make them move."

"Is your proposal on the agenda for our staff meeting next Monday?" Rick asked.

Maura nodded.

"Leave me the file. We'll talk about it then." Rick sighed as he leaned over to pick up the spreadsheets strewn across the couch. Now he was depressed.

Chapter 12: Monday, February 26

At six thirty in the morning on the last Monday in February, snow lay on the streets of Lakeview. A heavy winter sky hung over the Rocky Mountains beyond town.

Rick was returning to the office for the first time since his accident. He couldn't put it off any longer. He had to position the business for the bank meeting, now set for March 15. He had to oversee the product launch. He had no choice; PlayLand needed him.

As Rick clipped his cell phone to his belt, a sense of dread overtook him. He wasn't looking forward to the Monday morning officers' meeting. He had postponed it until nine thirty, not wanting to cope with rush hour on his first day back.

Rick drove to work, arriving at nine. He maneuvered himself out of his car. He moved slowly into the building, still using one crutch for support.

He greeted the guard, who welcomed him effusively, took the elevator to the third floor, and hobbled toward his office. As he passed, voices called out in greeting. He smiled and waved as people wished him well. He shook several hands, clapped several backs, and everyone was hearty. He was exhausted by the time he reached his office.

Its mahogany furniture hadn't changed. Some stacks of files had disappeared. New mail sat in his inbox. Thankfully, the pile wasn't too high; his assistant Mary had sent him correspondence to review at home.

Mary walked in with a cup of black coffee, as she had every day before his accident. He'd stopped drinking coffee in the hospital, but he didn't want to hurt her feelings. "Thanks," he said, and put the cup down on his desk. He turned on his laptop and stared out the window while it booted up.

Mary handed him his staff meeting file, the agenda neatly clipped to the front of the folder. "I know you usually set the agenda for these meetings," she said, "But Dewayne sent this over Friday. The information for each topic is in there. Sorry you didn't get a chance to review it ahead of time."

"I'll wing it. It won't be the first time."

Mary left, and Rick went through the file quickly. Nothing new, except a unionization attempt in one of the plants. Yes, he could wing it.

Rick picked up the file in his free hand, took his crutch with the other, and headed to the conference room, leaving the coffee cup behind. Again, cheery voices followed him down the hall, signaling employees' recognition the boss was back. Rick wondered whether people were asking whether he was ready to be back. He didn't know the answer himself.

Most of the officers were already in the conference room when Rick arrived. The vice presidents said in chorus, "Rick, welcome back!" "Glad to see you made it!" "Didn't think you'd be late to your first meeting back. Is this a new Rick?"

He took the greetings and ribbing in good humor, then sat. "Let's get started, shall we?" he said immediately. "Alex, you're up first. Cash flow."

Alex passed out the same spreadsheets he had shown Rick the week before, and went through them in the same droning tones. The officers squabbled when Alex finished, and Rick sighed and looked out the window. A shadow passed over the mountains.

"Okay," Rick said. "We have the meeting with the banks set for the fifteenth. Let's move on." He looked at his agenda. "Vince and Leo, what are our sales projections after Toy Fair?"

"Retailers were all charged up about the new product line," Leo said. "Bionics are big this year, and we've tapped into the craze. We'll meet projections. Once the new product is in the stores, we'll get more traffic through our aisles. That'll increase sales of existing product lines, maybe by five percent." Rick almost tuned Leo's puffery out, until he heard, "Except for board games. Board games are dead. Don't see how we can save that crap. Everyone's moving to video games and phone apps."

Rick decided to ignore Leo's comments about board games. He didn't have the energy to take on another topic. "Vince, do you agree with Leo's projections on the action figures?" he asked.

"Sounds about right." Vince's tone was noncommittal.

Kevin spoke up. "Our Marketing polls are in line with what Leo says on action figures. But I'm not as optimistic about existing product sales. A three percent increase is all we can expect. We can't count on kids buying our old products when we have something new." Then Kevin took the same tangent Leo had. "But I do agree about board games. We need to get that line revamped. And move into video games."

Rick didn't want to deal with Kevin either. "What else did we learn at Toy Fair?"

"I talked to the CEO of Toy Mart," Leo said. "They still want exclusivity on the action figures. Even if it's just one SKU that only they can sell, or a special comic book. Or at least advance delivery of the line. They won't budge. They want something they can promote to consumers as exclusive."

"What about price concessions?" Vince asked.

"They want that, too," Leo said. "They've been firm on both exclusivity and price since January. I can't get them to back down."

"Vince, Kevin, what do we have to offer?" Rick asked, looking at his brothers.

"We're having enough trouble delivering the first few characters in time for the summer promotion," Vince said. "I don't think we can get any unique SKUs for Toy Mart."

"That kind of defeatist attitude won't fly." Leo's face turned red as he spoke, waving his hand with the diamond ring. "I have to give them something."

"How much lead time would Toy Mart want?" Grant asked. At least Grant was calm. "We could deliver the first action figures to Toy Mart two weeks before they're available to other customers."

"Maybe." Leo sat back and relaxed. "What if I offer two weeks advance time on the first character, and a five percent price reduction?"

"Five percent!" Alex slammed his pencil on the table. "Toy Mart is ten percent of our sales, so right there you're giving up half a point on action figure revenue. That wrecks all my cash flow projections. We'll go bankrupt!"

"What if we offered Toy Mart a special comic book?" Kevin suggested. "I know they want both price and product concessions. But if we make our exclusivity offer strong enough, would they give on pricing? Or what about delayed payment terms, rather than a decrease in price? That way we get the money, but Toy Mart wins, too. They don't have to pay as quickly."

"Delayed payment still hurts cash flow. But it's better than not getting the money at all." Alex tipped his head from side to side, as if weighing the options. "We might make it if we don't push back their payment date by more than three months." He nodded. "If Rick gets our credit line increased, I can figure out how to handle the delay."

"I'll talk to Toy Mart," Leo said, folding his hands in front of him. "No guarantees how they'll react. But at least this gives me something to offer."

Rick sat back. "Then we have a plan?"

"It's something," Leo repeated.

"Assuming the banks go along," Alex added.

"What's next?" Rick asked, glancing at the agenda.

"Headcount reduction," Maura said. "We need to make a call." She, too, passed out papers to the other officers, and went through her material. Nothing new from what Rick had seen the week before, so he watched the other officers' reactions.

Leo was the first to explode. As Maura had talked, he had jumped up and strode to the buffet to get another cup of coffee. When she finished, he turned back to the table and shook his finger. "Maura, I told you. Every Sales employee we have is busting their buns. We need them all. I can't handle the distraction of a layoff and sell a new product line at the same time. No cuts in Sales."

"It's also a terrible time for cutting in the plants," Grant added. His face was stern, but his voice was measured. "Until we get the kinks worked out of the action figure production process, I need flexibility to staff up or work overtime. I can't cut some folks while forcing others to work overtime. That'll bring on the unions for sure!"

Rick's head ached. Maybe he should have stayed home another week. "Speaking of unions," he interrupted. "What's this about New Mexico?"

Grant responded, "Alice Sorenson, the plant manager in New Mexico, called on Friday. She said employees got some weird calls at home last week, asking how they felt about PlayLand and about our compensation and scheduling practices. One of the supervisors also found a union button in the restroom."

Dewayne spoke up for the first time all morning. "I hope you told the managers not to ask employees whether they received union calls. Do we need to get Legal and HR down there for some management training?"

"I had Timothy Baylor, the HR Director who works with Operations, on a plane to Albuquerque on Saturday," Maura said. "He spent Sunday with Alice, and he's in the plant today. Tim used to be a supervisor in Manufacturing. He won't get us into legal trouble. I'll let you know as soon as I get an update from him."

"Stay on top of it," Rick told Maura and Grant. "Okay, back to headcount." He rubbed his aching leg.

"The union issue complicates any layoff." Grant frowned. "I don't think the timing is right to cut employees."

"I agree," Dewayne said. "Fighting a union election would distract the entire New Mexico plant and half of headquarters. We haven't had a plant go union yet, and it's always been our goal to stay union free. Do we still believe that?"

"We do," Rick stated. Since his first days at PlayLand, his father had drilled into him it was better to work directly with employees than to have a union in the middle of management decisions. "We've worked hard to keep employees at PlayLand satisfied. We aren't changing our approach now."

"Well, damn it, Rick," Grant said, "How can people be happy if we cut their jobs?"

"We haven't had union problems during earlier headcount reductions," Maura said with conviction. "It's all in how we explain it. Our folks are smart. They'll understand the need to cut costs. And we've always paid fair severance. I don't like layoffs, but we have to keep our business needs top of mind. If we plan carefully, we can handle the reduction. But we do need to understand what's driving the New Mexico union contacts."

"With our cash problems, we have a good case for the reduction in force." Kevin nodded in response to Maura's comments. "No one likes to cut jobs, but I don't feel bad telling employees the truth."

"I don't want my people tied up in HR meetings. They need to be on the road selling." Leo returned to the table, sat, and leaned across at Maura. "Any time spent on a layoff takes away from the business."

Alex spoke up, tapping his pencil for emphasis. "This year our business is to cut costs. We can't complete the product launch with the cash we have. We can't get more funding without a plan to cut costs. Maura's headcount reduction is the only idea I've heard that reduces our costs significantly."

"Okay," said Rick. This debate would go on all day if he didn't stop it. "I want everyone to send Maura their best stab at reducing budgets by ten percent. That's what we need, isn't it, Alex?"

Alex nodded.

"Send your proposal to Maura by end of day Wednesday," Rick continued. "If you can do it without payroll cuts, fine, but I want ten percent out of your budget." He turned to the CFO. "Meanwhile, Alex, put together our best proposal for the banks. You and I need to talk by the end of the week. Managing cash flow is critical."

They had covered the agenda. Rick gathered up his papers to leave. "As Kevin said, no one likes to reduce headcount. But Kevin and Maura are right. We've weathered staff reductions in the past. Meeting adjourned."

$$\$ \, \$ \, \$$

Maura and Grant left the staff meeting together. As they walked down the hall, Grant said, "I know you're doing what you think best on the headcount reductions. I hope you know why I'm pushing back."

Maura nodded. "Operations has a tough year ahead. No hard feelings on my part. You're always straight with me. I appreciate that."

"If Rick decides on staff cuts, I'll do it. I merely want to be sure it's necessary. So I'll fight you as long as I can. When Rick makes the call, I'll back his decision one hundred percent, whichever way it goes."

They stopped at the entrance to the HR Department. Grant's office was downstairs. "What's really happening in New Mexico?" Maura asked. "Is there a union behind this, or just some disgruntled employee?"

"Don't know," Grant replied. "Alice isn't a strong plant manager. She should have known about the union button. Her staff isn't talking to her like they should. We may need some management changes."

"The last thing we need is union interference." Maura frowned as she asked, "How did Rick seem to you?"

Grant grimaced. "Distracted and irritable. I suppose that's normal after what he's been through. Why?"

Maura shook her head. "He seemed off to me, too. Preoccupied. Staring out the window. We can't let him push himself too hard. He can't have a relapse. Too many decisions only Rick can make. The rest of us can't keep fighting because he can't—or won't—make the calls."

"Agreed. I'll keep an eye on him." With a mock salute, Grant headed down the stairs toward his office.

$ $ $

Later Monday morning Maura looked up from a phone call to see Dewayne in her doorway. She gestured to him to come in her office, whispering, "It's Tim Baylor in New Mexico." Then she said into the phone, "Tim, Dewayne Jefferson just walked in. I'll put you on speaker."

"What's going on?" Dewayne asked when Tim's voice came through the speaker.

"It's pretty sketchy," Tim said. "A union button was left in a women's restroom last Tuesday. Teamsters, though I don't know why the Teamsters would want to organize us. A first-line supervisor picked it up, but she didn't tell anyone. I've read her the riot act. She won't make that mistake again."

"Better be sure she doesn't," Dewayne said. If Maura hadn't known Dewayne better, his deep voice would have felt threatening.

Tim didn't seem bothered by Dewayne's tone. He continued, "On Wednesday employees started getting calls at home. We didn't hear until Friday, from the plant manager's secretary. Her son got a call Thursday night, someone saying they were doing a survey. Asked whether he liked PlayLand, whether it was a safe working environment, what he was paid, who his friends in the plant were. Typical union stuff. He didn't think anything of it, until he went to work Friday, and learned his buddies had had similar calls."

"How do we know all this?" Maura asked.

"The kid had lunch with his mom Friday, and told her. She's been around long enough to know to tell her boss. Alice called me, as she should have. But we're behind on this. We should have heard Tuesday about the button, not Friday afternoon. We have some training to do."

"Careful," Dewayne said. "I don't want any unfair labor practice complaints."

"Don't worry," Tim said. "I've only talked to supervisors so far. I've told them all not to question employees. The good news is the hourly folks are volunteering information to their supervisors. At least to some of them. We're getting a good picture of what's happening."

"What about the plant manager? How's she handling this?" Maura asked.

"She's a basket case," Tim said. "Alice is basically a good person. Knows a lot about manufacturing. But she's an engineer by training. Never managed a large group before, let alone in an operating environment. Never dealt with a union."

"Why didn't the HR person down there let us know?" Dewayne asked.

"There isn't one," Tim said. "It's a small plant. The office manager handles occasional HR and benefits questions. Spends most of his time on local procurement stuff, payroll, and cost accounting. I fly down when there's a personnel problem. I think I should stay for a few days. Assess how serious the threat is."

"Okay," Maura said. "I want updates every day." She hung up. "Feel better?" she asked Dewayne.

"Not really. Tim's a good man, but this could blow up."

"Or fade away. I'm not downplaying the possibilities," Maura said as Dewayne shook his head at her. "But let's see what Tim learns."

"Okay." Dewayne paused. "Another subject. Did you think Rick acted subdued this morning?"

"I wondered. What did you think?" Being candid with Grant was one thing; Grant wouldn't use it against her. Maura didn't know about Dewayne.

"He wasn't as sharp as he usually is. Seemed unfocused."

"Well, that's natural, after being out for so long. Don't you think?" she asked. "He's still catching up."

Dewayne pursed his lips and shrugged. "I guess. But let's watch him. You're in HR, can you think of an excuse to ask him how he's doing?"

"I don't need an excuse. I care about Rick. I'll stop by his office later."

$$\$ \ \$ \ \$$

In midafternoon Maura walked to Rick's corner office. She smiled at Mary. "I'm sure everybody's been to see him today, but does he have a moment?"

Mary nodded her head at Rick's door. "Go on in."

Maura cracked the door, peeked her head in, and asked, "Are you free?"

"For you, Maura, any time." Rick swiveled his chair away from the window to face her as she walked in. At least he was smiling.

She sat on the edge of his guest chair. "I don't want to be a pest, Rick. Just doing my HR thing. How're you doing?"

Rick grimaced. "People been asking all day. I'm fine."

"Okay. Pace yourself. We're better off if you don't try to come back too fast."

Rick turned to the window. "Leo says there's a tough negotiation coming with Toy Mart. Alex says we have to get the banks to increase our credit. You say we need to cut heads, and unions are breathing down our necks. And you want me to take it easy?"

"I didn't say take it easy, I said pace yourself. We need you, Rick. Don't get yourself sent back to the hospital."

"I get it." Rick sounded testy. "But if it wasn't you, Maura, I would have thrown you out when you opened your mouth. I don't have time to pace myself. Thanks for stopping by."

Rick's irritation didn't bother Maura. Her teenagers could be surlier. "I got an update from Tim Baylor in New Mexico," she said, as she stood. "He's still talking to folks. Doesn't know yet if the union threat is serious. I'll keep you posted. Thanks for the time."

Maura walked out, shutting the door behind her. She stopped at Mary's desk. "He's pretty cantankerous. Has he been this way all day?"

Mary smiled discretely. "Oh, you know Rick. His bad moods blow over. Don't worry. He's probably unhappy about being out of the loop so long."

Maura laughed. "Thanks, Mary. I don't want to get you in trouble with our mutual boss, but if you see him having any problems, would you let me know? I'll keep it quiet, but we need to be sure he isn't hurting himself."

"Will do." But Maura wasn't sure if Mary would tell her anything. Mary protected Rick at all costs.

Before heading back to HR, Maura walked down the hall to see Kevin. She knocked on his open door, and he turned around from his computer. "Well, hello, Maura!"

"You're chipper this afternoon." She smiled. "What has you so upbeat?"

"Glad to be alive. What brings you here? No one unionizing Marketing, I hope."

Maura sat. "It's about Rick." She hesitated. "I hope you don't mind me talking about him."

"What's up?" Kevin raised his eyebrows.

"He was pretty testy with me just now. How's he been at home?"

"I haven't been around him much in the last couple of weeks. Paige kept a tight rein on visitors. She'd know better than I do. Or maybe Vince. Have you talked to Vince?"

"No. Vince is preoccupied with the product launch. I thought you might know how Rick's really feeling."

Kevin shook his head. "Right after he regained consciousness, he seemed out of touch. Vince and I both noticed. But I think he's okay now. Do you want me to talk to Vince? Or Paige?"

"Would you? If your family thinks he's okay, we'll give him time to get back into the job. If not, then you, Vince, and I should talk."

$ $ $

By the end of Monday, Kevin had heard from Maura, Grant, Alex, and Dewayne, all asking whether Rick was all right. He told each of them to give Rick time, but privately he had the same worries they did. Kevin had dropped by Rick's office three times that day, and found Rick staring out the window each time.

On the third occasion he joked, "What's out there that wasn't there earlier?"

Rick answered him gravely, "Have you ever watched the light on the mountains? Yellow in the morning. Bright white at noon. Now in late afternoon, the mountains are blue, almost black against the graying sky. I've never noticed before."

Kevin said something about Rick turning into an artist instead of a skier, and Rick smiled. Not like his take-charge older brother, Kevin thought.

After most employees had left for the day, Kevin set out toward the executive suite. His office was half the length of the building away from Rick's and Vince's offices. He wasn't sure which brother he wanted to see. He'd start with whomever he saw first. When he reached the soft carpeting of the executive suite, Rick's office was dark. Vince was packing his briefcase.

"Headed home?" Kevin asked.

"As soon as I can," Vince said.

"Can we talk for a minute?"

"Want to get a beer?" Vince asked.

"Not tonight. This'll only take a minute."

"All right." Vince gestured for Kevin to sit.

Kevin closed the door behind him, sat, and leaned back in the chair. "Great view. Have you ever watched the light change on the mountains?" he asked.

"Never look at them." Vince rubbed his head. "By this time of day, all I want is a drink. Or nine holes of golf in the summer."

"Rick was talking about light on the mountains earlier today."

Vince snorted. "Rick? Since when did he look at anything but his inbox?"

"That's why I'm here. Several people told me Rick has been totally distracted all day. I've seen some of it myself."

"Who've you talked to?"

"Maura. And Alex. And Grant. And Dewayne."

Vince grunted and rubbed his head again. "Well, you can discount Maura. HR types are overly sensitive."

"Yeah, but you can't call Alex or Dewayne sensitive. Alex says

Rick doesn't seem interested in the bank meeting. He's leaving the presentation up to Alex. Dewayne said something similar, though he did say Rick agreed to talk to Ben about Gus."

"Well, that's something. If I were Rick, I'd let Alex mess with the numbers, too."

"Yeah, but that isn't Rick's style. He always wants the financial details."

"So? Maybe he's turning over a new leaf in his old age. Don't worry. It's only been one day."

"Yeah, but Grant said Rick wasn't even concerned about the union in New Mexico."

"Rick seemed okay at the staff meeting this morning." Vince shook his head. "You're blowing things out of proportion."

"Rick blew up at Maura today. That's not like him. He has a lot of respect for her."

"Yeah, well, he's probably just having a bad day. Maybe his leg hurts. Or his head." Vince rubbed his own head.

"What if Rick isn't up to running the business?"

"Christ, Kevin, you're as bad as all the pissers working for me." Vince stood and paced his cramped office. "What do you want me to do? I have enough on my mind. The launch costs are creeping up. I have to hound Jennifer constantly to keep them in control."

"Maybe you and I should sit down with Rick. Get him to let us take on some of his responsibilities for a while."

"I just said my plate's full. I can't handle what I've got. We need Rick. The bankers and the top customers won't listen to anyone else, now he's back."

"But that's just it, Vince. What if he isn't really back?"

"You said he told Maura he's fine. Do we accuse him of lying?"

"No, but we need to do something." Kevin stood up and stepped in front of his brother's pacing. "Aren't you concerned about Rick?"

Vince's face was red, and he shouted, "I'm concerned about the product launch. I'm concerned about my staff. I'm concerned about Toy Mart. I can't be concerned about anything more. Rick's a big boy. We don't need to babysit him. Let Maura watch him. That's what we pay her for."

"He's our brother." Kevin dropped his voice to counter Vince's yelling.

"Do whatever you want, Kevin. I'm leaving it alone. And I'm going to get a drink now. You coming?" Vince picked up his briefcase and opened the door of his office.

"Not tonight, Vince. Thanks anyway."

Kevin strode angrily back toward the Marketing Department. His steps slowed as he approached the main hallway. He didn't want employees who were still around to think there'd been an argument in the executive suite. Rumors were easy to start and hard to stop.

Back in his office, Kevin slumped in his chair. Where'd Vince get off punting on Rick's condition? Kevin was working as hard as Vince. If Vince was so concerned about his workload, he should want Rick fully engaged. His whole life Kevin had had to push Vince, even though Vince was a lot older. Going outside to make snowmen, taking the car for ice cream, getting Mom's Christmas present before she died. He was sick of managing Vince.

But one more time, Kevin would have to step up. Kevin would sit down with Rick himself. Alone, since Vince didn't have the time.

CHAPTER 13: THURSDAY, MARCH 1

On Thursday morning, his fourth day back at work, Rick dragged himself out of bed early. Before his accident, he always tried to get to the office ahead of most other employees. He needed to get that habit back. He could get more done without interruptions.

When his father ran the business, it seemed Richard controlled Rick's schedule. Since becoming CEO himself, Rick had wondered why he didn't have the same control. He was the boss, wasn't he? How come everyone else managed his schedule?

He listened to voice mail on his cell phone as he drove. His day began with several problems, as usual.

"Rick, it's Kevin. Need your approval for a small increase in the marketing budget for Games. Sunday ad prices in California are going up."

"Rick, it's Leo. The buyer for Toys Galore is in this afternoon. We'll get a big order out of them for action figures, so I want the guy to spend a few minutes with you. I'll have Mary put the time on your calendar."

"Rick, Grant here. We had a plastics spill in the main plant last night. Nothing serious. No one hurt. Only minor damage. But we have to file an EPA report."

Rick used to like these little crises. They kept him close to the business. Today they seemed petty.

He responded to problems he could handle as he drove, and forwarded other calls to Mary or his staff. As he entered the parking lot, he ran his finger around his cashmere turtleneck collar. Already it felt like a noose.

Rick pulled into his reserved parking spot near the main

entrance and hobbled his way into the building. Only the security guard was there. "Good morning, Mr. Players."

"Morning, Bob. How's the family?" Rick smiled. Bob was usually on duty when Rick arrived.

"Doing well, Mr. Players. Doing well. Daughter got a volleyball scholarship to Arizona."

Rick stopped at the elevator and turned to the guard. "That's great, Bob. You and Martha must be proud."

"Yes, sir." Bob grinned. "Makes up for the times I took her to the ER with a busted ankle or twisted knee."

Rick laughed. "Kids are a lot of trouble, aren't they? But we wouldn't have it any other way." The elevator opened and he headed to his third floor office.

As Rick approached the executive suite, Alex darted out of the Finance Department. He must have been hovering, waiting for Rick.

"Hey, Rick, can we talk?" The CFO carried a thick folder. He wore a dark suit and red tie; Alex's bankers' suit, they called it.

"What's up, Alex? Meeting with the banks today? Or trying to match Dewayne's sartorial splendor?"

"No meeting. Cash flow projections are worse than I thought." Alex stayed at his heel as Rick slowly made his way down the hall. "We need to talk now." Alex sat, not giving Rick an opportunity to delay the discussion.

Mary followed them, bearing two coffee mugs. Rick grimaced. Only four days back and he was drinking the swill again. "Thanks," he said, as she left the office.

He glanced out the window. The mountains were grey in early morning, the sky barely distinguishable from the land. He slumped in his chair. "Shoot," he said.

Alex opened his folder and spread several pages over Rick's desk. "On Monday I said we had cash to carry us into early summer, right?"

Rick looked at Alex's numbers and nodded.

"But expenses for January and early February were higher than last year. Petroleum prices shot up, which raises product and transportation costs. And non-product costs are going up, too. Unanticipated marketing expenses. Outside legal fees are higher than Dewayne budgeted, with that new lawsuit in Atlanta. Yesterday I got rough figures through the end of February. We're bleeding, Rick."

"That's what you said Monday."

"But more than I thought. At this rate, we'll run out of cash in April, not June. We need more credit simply to pay our bills."

"The bank meeting is in two weeks."

"We need to move it up to next week. We can't wait two weeks." Alex tapped his mechanical pencil rapidly on the papers in front of him. His leg twitched to the same rhythm as the pencil.

Rick shook his head. "Won't they think we're desperate?"

"Well, we are. They'll know as soon as they see our numbers."

Rick sighed. "Alex, we can't look like we can't manage the business. I'm not going to change the meeting date." Was he being petulant? Rick wondered.

"But if we stick to our current timeline, we won't have time to react before we're out of money in April. Today's March first. The officers still aren't on board with the cost reductions. Have you talked to Leo and Grant?"

"No. These are the first new numbers I've seen since Monday. Have you and Maura talked? Are you getting what you need from the rest of the group?"

"We received recommendations from everyone but Leo yesterday. Grant wasn't happy about cutting Operations, but he delivered what you asked. He did good work. Leo hasn't given us squat. I left him a message late yesterday. He never responded. He won't respond until you make him."

"Can't you call him again?"

"Sure. But what leverage do I have? I'm only the CFO. You're his boss."

"Tell him you and I talked, and I told you to get the information from him."

Alex shook his head dubiously. "Okay. But you know Leo. He's a master. He's our chief negotiator, for God's sake. He plays with the big boys at the customers, and stonewalls everyone here."

"Just do it, Alex."

"What about moving the meeting with the banks up to next week?" Alex was being bullheaded.

"No." Rick drummed his fingers on the desk. He wasn't ready yet. It would be a difficult meeting.

"You think we can cut costs significantly by April if we don't meet with the banks until mid-March?" Alex raised his eyebrows. "Respectfully, that's bullshit. This is serious. The old Rick would have been all over it. 'Cash is king.' How often have you said that?"

Rick gave Alex credit for not backing off. Alex was stubborn. That's why Alex could birddog Leo.

Alex continued, "We need money to fund severance payments this year. We need a solid plan to reduce long-term costs, or the banks won't give us anything. We need good prospects for increasing revenues, so the action figure marketing has to look really strong. All these things cost money. We can't wait."

Rick's leg throbbed, and it wasn't even eight o'clock. Alex was right. PlayLand needed cash. He'd have to play his role as CEO, whether he wanted to or not. "All right, Alex. I'll talk to Leo. You reschedule the meeting." Rick glanced at his online calendar. "Anytime next Wednesday through Friday. No earlier. We need all the time we can to get our act together."

Alex stood up. "Thanks, Rick. It's good to see you haven't lost your game." Alex gave a jaunty salute and bounced out of the office.

Rick turned and gazed out the window. Now, the rising sun reflected off the snowy mountains so brightly it hurt his eyes. He shut them, but still saw the brilliance against his eyelids. Again he thought of the piercing light he saw in his coma, beckoning him to leave his life behind.

He'd been required to talk with a psychologist at the rehab center before they let him go home. The shrink had asked Rick what he recalled from the coma, what sights and sounds and impressions. Rick had been vague at first, but as he grew comfortable with the doctor, he talked about the light and the voices.

"That's not unusual," the psychologist assured him. "Lots of people report visions of light or of people they've known, both living and dead. Were you attracted to what you saw?"

Rick nodded. "It was hard to turn away."

Again, the psychologist reassured Rick, but cautioned him to call about any feelings of depression.

Staring out the window now, Rick wondered if he was depressed. Did his lack of engagement with PlayLand, and even with Paige and the boys, mean he wanted die? No. He was glad to be alive. Glad to see the mountains, to watch his sons, to greet people like Bob this morning who had joy in their lives.

But there's no joy in my life, he thought. So many problems, and they all landed on his desk. Vince and Kevin weren't ready to step up. Vince wasn't interested, and Kevin was untested.

He was lonely. As CEO, he had no peers. But the business needed him. He couldn't sit out his melancholy until he felt better.

Rick sighed and turned to his computer. He typed a quick email to Leo, copying Alex, telling Leo to get the cost reduction information to Alex and Maura pronto.

Then he looked out at the Rockies again. The sunlight was softer, but still reflected off the snow. Rick watched for several minutes as the light changed moment by moment. Damn it, he thought. He just wanted his problems to go away.

He picked up his phone and rang his secretary. "Mary, would you set up a meeting with Maura as soon as you can?"

$ $ $

Maura rushed down the hall toward her office at eight thirty Thursday morning. She was late. Carlos was traveling and she had taken the kids to school, which always put her behind for the day.

The neck of her jade green wool dress itched. Some days she wanted the extra authority that business attire gave her, but it came at the price of comfort. Carlos said this dress set off her blond hair and blue-green eyes. She tried to tell herself looking attractive and professional was worth it, and resisted the urge to scratch.

Dewayne called out as she walked past the Legal Department. "Maura, got a moment? I heard from local counsel in Atlanta."

Maura turned into Dewayne's office, which reminded her of a funeral parlor—heavy chairs upholstered in dark maroon fabric. "Right," she said, remembering. "Plaintiff's deposition was yesterday. How'd it go?"

"Local counsel says this Steve fellow was a total fruitcake. Why'd we ever hire him, anyhow?"

Maura shrugged. "Sometimes we make mistakes. What'd he say?"

Dewayne gave a bass chuckle. "Claims he has post-traumatic stress disorder from service during the first Gulf War. Says he can't go outside, has agoraphobia from the PTSD. The nightly news reports on the current wars in Iraq and Afghanistan give him flashbacks, so he's getting worse. Says our change in his job duties pushed him over the edge. Couldn't make the sales calls we started requiring."

"How much of what he says is true?"

Dewayne's wide shoulders lifted and fell. "His attorney produced medical records. Steve's been talking to his shrink for the last couple of years about flashbacks. But there's no documentation he can't work. Looks like our defense will hold up. He didn't do his job. But he might get some shrink to testify he was disabled."

Maura leaned against Dewayne's door jamb. "So the PTSD is real?" she asked. "He isn't faking that?"

"Doesn't look like it."

"What will a jury think about us firing a Gulf War veteran with a mental illness?"

"Don't be so defensive." Dewayne crossed his arms across his ponderous chest. "We can win. The guy didn't do his job. Even if his shrink says he was disabled, Steve never told his boss. No reason we had to accommodate a mental disability without some notice from the employee. Our termination was legal. And he didn't even include a disability claim in his EEOC complaint."

"I know the disability laws, Dewayne. But we have an ex-employee who probably had a mental illness. Why didn't this come up before we fired him?" Maura shook her head. "How can we say we're employee advocates if we know so little about our people? I'm disappointed in his manager, and in my staff as well."

"Water under the bridge, Maura." Dewayne's tone mirrored his condescending smile as he waggled his forefinger at her. "Managers aren't required to know everything. In fact, the laws are designed to let employees keep information about their medical condition private, unless they want an accommodation. Steve clearly didn't want us to know because he never asked for an accommodation."

"So he got himself fired instead." Maura smiled wryly. "What's the old saying? The law is an ass?"

"An ass it might be, but we're not liable."

Maura stepped into Dewayne's office from the doorway. "What could we settle for?"

"Settle? Why would we settle? I told you we can win."

"How much would our legal fees be? And how much time will it take from Sales and HR? Is it right for us to throw Steve out on the street, when we changed the rules of the game on him?"

"Maura, you're usually tougher than this. Are you going soft? Maybe you should have worn pants today instead of that pretty green dress."

"Back off, Dewayne. Or you'll be named in a discrimination case yourself." She smiled as she spoke, but she hated when Dewayne tried to intimidate her.

Dewayne held his hands out, palms toward Maura, in a conciliatory gesture. "Now, Maura, we both know PlayLand can't afford to throw money at a case like Steve's."

"I merely asked what we could settle for. Is it less than the cost of defense?"

Dewayne shrugged. "Maybe. But we can win."

"Talk to local counsel and see what he says. This isn't simply a guy who wouldn't do his job. He may have been wacky, but we should have known about it."

"Okay, I'll ask. But I won't settle until we've talked again."

"Sounds good."

As Maura turned to leave, Dewayne asked, "Any update on the union issue?"

"Not yet," Maura called over her shoulder. "I'm about to phone Tim Baylor now."

Maura got to her office, dropped her briefcase beside her desk, and picked up her phone as she sat. She needed to call Tim, but first she dialed Grant. When Grant picked up, she asked, "Heard anything from New Mexico?"

"I was about to call the plant manager. Come on down, and we'll call together."

"On my way."

Grant had both Tim Baylor and Alice Sorenson, the Albuquerque plant manager, on the phone when Maura reached his office.

"What's going on?" she asked. "I'll need to brief Rick later. How serious is the threat?"

"We're overreacting," Alice said. "A few employees were called at home about how they like their jobs. Could be a political survey, for all we know. City elections coming up, and there's a living wage ordinance on the ballot."

"Do you agree, Tim?" Maura asked.

"It's possible," Tim said slowly. "But I think it's more than that. I've talked to every supervisor in the plant now. Only hourly employees got the calls. Three managers have hourly workers living in their households—a spouse or a kid. In every case, the caller asked for the hourly employee, not the manager. Sounds like a union to me."

"Who've you talked to?" Maura asked.

"Only the managers," Tim said. "In one case, the manager tried to take a message for his son, but the caller said he'd call back later when the son was home. And he did."

"Any risk of unfair labor practice charges?" Maura pressed. "Did these managers grill their family members about the calls?"

"I've told them all to avoid interrogation or threats. But this one manager did question his son about the call."

"Make sure every supervisor knows how cautious we have to be," Grant said. "We can lose a campaign, simply because of some stupid remark by a manager. Even to his kid."

"I know," Tim responded. "But how do you tell a father not to ask his son about late-night calls?"

"Just emphasize the point every chance you get, Tim," Maura said. "How's the management team holding up?"

"We're fine," Alice said. "We know what to do. I'm trying to keep production up. It's hard with managers in meetings with Tim all the time. We need push employees to keep making product."

"It's important to meet production quotas," Grant said. "But your most important job right now is to keep the union from taking this any further. Tim, I know we can't inquire, but do we know what the callers asked employees?"

"We know the gist. Several employees volunteered the details to their supervisors. There were at least two callers, a man and a woman. The male caller tended to call our male employees, and the female caller called the women, though they weren't precise. Some of the employees with names like Chris and Sandy got mixed up. Sounds like the callers were working off a list of names. Employees were asked whether they were paid fairly, how well they liked their supervisor, what changes they wanted in the workplace, like scheduling. I'm pretty sure it's union reps."

Alice interrupted, "You don't know that, Tim."

"Not for a fact. But it's pretty standard practice. They're feeling our folks out to see if they'd support an election campaign."

"Okay," Maura said. "Take it seriously. Keep it low key, but let's put out our own feelers. See what the gripes in the plant are."

"I'm pretty close to my employees. I know what the issues are," Alice said.

"What are the top three problems in the plant?" Maura asked, rolling her eyes at Grant. She didn't think Alice was close to the employees at all.

"I didn't say we had problems," Alice said. "I said issues. Everyone wants more money. Wage rates are an issue, but that's an issue in any workplace. The amount of overtime we've been working is an issue. But we've assigned the overtime fairly, and we can't get the work done without the extra hours. And third would probably be supervisor turnover. People get used to one manager, then we move them around. But I have managers on special projects. One supervisor just had a heart attack and is on medical leave. I can't help that."

"Don't transfer supervisors unless you have to," Grant said. "Slow down all projects not directly related to increasing productivity. Overtime is likely to get worse in coming weeks, but make sure folks get at least one day a week off. Can we do that?"

"Sure," Alice said. "I'll let you know if I can't make quota with those limitations."

Tim said, "I'll work out a plant manager meeting schedule. Give all employees a chance to talk with Alice directly in small groups. I'll attend some of the meetings before I leave, and then have at least a couple of managers attend each one with Alice. Anything else?"

"That's a start," Maura said. "Thanks, Tim."

They hung up, and Maura turned to Grant. "Alice isn't taking this seriously."

"I'll talk to her again," Grant said. "She's new at the job and very focused on production. She doesn't understand our union avoidance philosophy like she should."

"Make sure she's dealing with employee relations. And I'm worried about the rest of the managers in the plant. Do you want me to keep Tim there awhile longer?"

"Let's see where we are tomorrow afternoon. If he has the schedule set up, he can leave and go back in a couple of weeks. Now you see why I don't want to cut people in Operations? Employees are already upset about overtime. We'll need to work more overtime if we reduce headcount."

Maura smiled ruefully. "I wish we didn't have to cut. But I don't see what else to do. But thanks for your Operations proposal. That's more than some of our colleagues have done."

"Still nothing from Leo?"

"How'd you know? I'm hoping we get his input today. He missed yesterday's deadline."

$ $ $

By noon Kevin was hungry and wandered down the hall toward the vending machines located near the Dolls Department. He caught himself looking for excuses to go to Dolls frequently these days. The latest figures on the comic book and action figure orders after Toy Fair seemed to be a good reason to congratulate Jennifer. Besides, he was really hungry.

Kevin poked his head in Jennifer's office. "Hey," he said, "Did you see the orders for comics this week? You really wowed them at Toy Fair. It's our biggest promotional offering in years." He grinned, then sobered at her harried expression.

Jennifer sat at a small worktable covered with papers and production prototypes of various action figures. Stacks of papers were also piled on her desk, and sticky notes framed her computer monitor. She wore dark horn-rimmed glasses instead of her usual contact lenses.

Kevin looked at Jennifer more closely. No make-up. The tail of her blouse untucked and wrinkled. It wasn't like Jennifer to look unkempt, particularly when it was only midday. "Bad day?" Kevin

162

asked.

"Busy. At a turning point in the launch. Orders for the comic books are in, and we're starting to get orders for the action figures themselves. But production in the plants is slower than anticipated, I'm still waiting for final approval on the last comic book before we print, and I don't know where Gus is."

"Have you had lunch?"

"Who eats lunch these days?" Jennifer riffled through her stacks of papers without looking up. Kevin had the impression she wished he would go away, but he plowed ahead.

"I planned to grab peanuts out of the machine, but I'm hungrier than that," Kevin said. "Want to join me? Just the cafeteria downstairs. It won't take long."

Jennifer stared at him through her glasses. At least she realized he was there. "I don't have time, Kevin. Sorry."

"Did you eat breakfast this morning?"

She looked back at the chart in front of her. "An apple."

"Come on. You can take thirty minutes. If you don't, you'll need to stop for coffee and a doughnut at three. That's what happens to me if I skip lunch."

Jennifer frowned. Kevin couldn't read her eyes through her glasses. Her mouth was set in a thin line. Then she smiled. "You win," she said. "I am hungry."

She stood and he let her precede him down the stairs to the employee cafeteria on the second floor. They grabbed some food, paid for it, and sat at a table near the windows.

"Admit it," Kevin said, biting into his sandwich. "The view of the Rockies is a lot better than the mounds of paper in your office." The cafeteria shared the same view as Rick's office a floor above them.

"Yeah, but those mounds of paper will be there as long as the mountains, if I don't put in some serious hours." Jennifer picked at her salad.

"You're working long hours as it is. If your office light is any indication."

Jennifer sat back sharply, her eyes wide. Whoops, Kevin thought. Did she think he'd been watching her? Well, what if he had? "I've been here late myself a lot of evenings," he added. But her office wasn't in his regular path of travel. "And the Dolls group has the best coffee in the building," he continued. Was he digging himself out of the hole or in deeper?

"That's because we clean the pot more than once a month, unlike you Marketing apes." Whatever she thought, she wasn't going to call him on it.

Kevin changed the subject back to the action figure launch. "What's your biggest hurdle now?" he asked. Jennifer's shoulders relaxed. If he wanted her to talk, he'd have to keep it work-related.

"Getting the comic books printed and shipped to stores," she said. "To promote the characters. And we need consumer feedback. So we can increase production of the more popular figures."

"You've thought this out pretty well," Kevin said.

Jennifer lifted one shoulder. "No different than marketing dolls. The comics are actually a great promotional tool." She smiled. "They're working well. We might even start an online fan club. So we could need some of your people's support, along with IT."

"You should be proud."

She nodded. "I am. And Gus gets a lot of credit for creativity. Sometimes he gets spacey, but his characters and story lines are good." This time she gave Kevin a full grin. "So I guess he knows preadolescent boys better than I do."

Kevin smiled. "Try asking the rest of us guys sometimes. Gus doesn't have to be your only resource."

"But he's safe. All he cares about are his characters. Not about scoring."

"You mean, unlike Ben?" Kevin said, scowling.

"Unlike a lot of guys." Jennifer shrugged with a wry smile. "You'd be surprised."

Kevin was silent, chewing on his sandwich. He had tickets to another community benefit. Should he ask her to go? He'd had to cancel the last time, because it was the day Rick had come out of the coma. Kevin had only seen Jennifer at work and at a couple of PlayLand get-togethers. He wanted to get to know her better, but she seemed so suspicious of men at PlayLand.

"Are you going to eat that salad or pick at it?" he asked to keep the conversation going.

"Sorry I'm bad company."

That was his opening. "You're not bad company. In fact, I'd like more of it. How 'bout another attempt at dinner? I have another charity affair tomorrow. It's short notice, but could you go? I felt bad about canceling last time."

"Well, you had a good excuse." She gave him a full smile. "We were all glad Rick was better."

"Then how about tomorrow?"

Her glance skewered him. "Same deal? Business dinner?"

"If that's how you want it."

Did he imagine it, or did Jennifer seem disappointed at his response? She shrugged. "Sure. What time?"

$ $ $

Except for a few minutes talking with Leo and the Toys Galore buyer, Rick spent Thursday in his office. He alternated between bursts of concentration on the paperwork on his desk and staring out the window at the massive mountains.

He hadn't had any time outside since his accident. Paige wouldn't even let him sit on the porch on sunny days, saying she was afraid he would take cold or slip on ice. She made sure she or one of the twins was no farther away than the next room. He had more privacy at work than at home.

He hadn't been skiing since Christmas. No snowmobiling or snowshoeing since the accident. He hadn't felt the sharp winter air on his face other than when limping from parking lot to building entrance. He needed space. He needed to run, though his leg wouldn't let him yet. Rick gazed at the mountains, wishing he could slalom down them, away from computers and spreadsheets.

There was a sharp knock on his door. Mary stuck her head in, "Will you talk to Leo?"

"Sure," Rick said, sighing.

Leo sat and slapped a file down on Rick's desk. "Thanks for talking to Toys Galore. Now we need to talk about Toy Mart. I just talked to their head buyer."

Rick was silent. Couldn't Leo have handled this via email or a phone call? But he simply nodded.

"I made a tentative offer along the lines of what we discussed in staff on Monday. Exclusive comic book. Great idea, by the way. And advance shipping before other customers get the action figures. Didn't go far enough. I know Alex doesn't want us to offer price reductions, but I raised the concept of delayed payment. At least he didn't hang up on me. But we may need to offer some type of terms."

"How far was he willing to go?"

Leo shrugged. "Didn't talk details. No timeline on how long they'd get an exclusive, nor how long they could defer paying us. I wanted to see if these parameters made sense before Alex and I crunch the numbers."

"Where do you think they are?" Was this all Leo had to report? Why hadn't he just called Rick?

"Not sure. They'll talk to their finance guys and get back with me. I said I'd talk to Alex about specifics."

"Then we don't know any more than before?" Rick said sharply.

"Well, we know they'll consider it." Leo smiled. He probably thought this was progress.

"But you don't know what we'll have to concede on terms or on product?"

"Nope. Should I go ahead and meet with Alex?"

"Sounds like you already said you would." Rick turned toward his computer, hoping to signal the end of the conversation.

"Okay." Leo started to get up. Then out of the corner of his eye, Rick saw him sit back down. "Something else," Leo said.

Rick raised an eyebrow. Now he'd find out the real reason Leo stopped by.

"I was on the phone with my district managers this morning," Leo said. "You know, my usual weekly call. By the way, our sales last week looked good. Except board games, of course. I asked my guys about their staffing levels. To a man—or I guess I should say man and woman—they say they're already short-staffed."

Leo opened the file he'd thrown on Rick's desk. "Here's what they said. I took notes." He read, "The New York manager says 'I have stores we can't call on now.' Florida says, 'We could use three more reps.'" And the manager in Texas says, and I quote, 'Hell, with the turnover we've had in Dallas, all my experienced reps are babysitting newbies.'"

Rick interrupted. His voice was louder than it needed to be, but he was pissed. "Leo, I told you not to spread rumors about the reduction in force. I don't want employees talking about staff cuts until we make the call."

"Hold on, Rick." Leo put out a hand, his ring flashing. "I just wanted to be sure I wasn't out of sync with my people when I told you we couldn't cut anyone. I didn't tell them anything. I swear. I only asked whether they were understaffed. I could give you more quotes. They all agree. Sales can't cut any more positions."

"When was the last time any manager admitted to being overstaffed? Particularly in Sales. You guys negotiate everything." Rick grimaced, rubbing his leg. "Don't talk to them again. Got it?"

"Sure, boss. But can I tell Maura? She should hear how the field is feeling."

"Keep it to Maura. No more caucusing. And get your headcount reduction proposal to Alex."

"Thanks, Rick. I'll work something up. And I'll talk to Alex about Toy Mart, then brief you again." Leo grinned as he left Rick's office.

Rick turned back to the mountains and sighed.

$ $ $

By late afternoon, Rick admitted to himself he'd put off dealing with Ben. He hadn't even talked to Vince yet. He didn't feel strong enough.

Why had Ben cut corners on the action figure line? Ben knew how important new product was. Ben would have some tale to tell; he'd always been able to talk himself out of trouble. Ever since freshman year.

Rick had never understood why, but Ben had stuck to him like chiggers since they'd met. Rick smiled, remembering the countless times Ben had saved Rick's butt with a tackle. Off the field, he'd paved Rick's way, too. Rick had the money, but Ben had the easy grin that got them girls.

Until Rick married Paige and Ben married Nicole. That was a weird situation, Ben marrying her so quickly. Maybe Ben had saved Rick's butt then, too, though Rick would never know. It was never the same between them after that.

Rick sighed. He needed to talk to Vince. Then Ben.

Rick headed to Vince's office. It was close enough he left his crutch behind. "Got a minute?" he asked his brother.

Vince glanced up, but said nothing. Rick sat in his brother's over-furnished office. "We need to talk. About Ben and Gus."

"I think we worked it out," Vince said. "It's okay."

Rick frowned. "I need to know what happened."

"Oh, Ben was a little zealous in pushing the action figures." Vince leaned back in his chair, rubbing the back of his neck. He didn't meet Rick's eye. "He should have given Gus more credit for developing the line."

"Dewayne says Ben let everyone think New Ventures developed the action figures, when they were based on work Gus did in college."

"Well, that's the way it seems. But, as I said, I think it's smoothed over with Gus."

Rick snorted. "For fifty thou a year, according to Dewayne."

"Yeah, but Gus's lawyer wanted two hundred." Vince sounded defensive. "I talked Gus down to fifty a year. Might cost us more in the long run, but only if the line's successful. That's not so bad. Dewayne said it was okay."

"But it shouldn't have happened." Rick stood up, walked to the window, and stared at the mountains. Vince didn't have quite the panoramic view Rick had, but it was still beautiful as the sun set behind the jagged peaks. "Why does Ben say he did it?"

"Something about wanting a successful new line. You know Ben. He can talk at you a long time. You're never sure what he said when he shuts up, but it sounds good while he's talking."

Rick was silent. Vince's assessment of Ben was accurate. "I need to talk to him. Does he know he screwed up?"

"I think he knows we're not happy." Vince belched and rubbed his stomach. "It wasn't a pleasant conversation."

"Sorry you had to deal with Ben without me."

Vince shrugged. "I guess that's why you made me a vice president."

Rick went back to his own office. He didn't sit down, though he saw Mary had left a stack of new mail on his desk. As he had in Vince's office, he stood by the windows behind the desk. By now the Rockies were silhouetted in shadow, the sun low behind them. No dazzling light like he had seen in his dreams in the hospital. He still wanted to return to that light. Rick stared at the mountains for a long time, avoiding the paperwork on his desk.

$ $ $

That evening after Rick and his family had eaten, the doorbell rang. Paige tried to make conversation over dinner, but neither Rick nor the twins gave more than curt responses to her questions about their days.

Rick's first week back in the office was exhausting him, and he still had Friday to get through. He'd been jittery at home after he'd been released from the rehab center, anxious to get out of the house and away from Paige's hovering. But now that he was back at work, he felt like he was listening to everything from underwater.

Paige answered the door, her heels clicking on the marble foyer floor. Why she wore heels at home Rick had never understood. She said it was to make her seem taller, but he and the boys knew how petite she was, and there wasn't anyone else to impress.

"Why, Ben," Rick heard her say. "Rick will be so glad to see you. Come in."

Rick sighed. He was too tired to talk to Ben now. But Paige ushered Ben into the dining room.

"Look who's here, Rick." Her voice was bright and brittle. When they dated, her high soprano tones had appealed to him, but tonight she sounded shrill.

"Hi, Ben." Rick rose to shake his ex-roommate's hand. "What brings you out tonight?"

Ben clapped Rick on the back. "Just wanted to welcome you back to the land of the living. I've tried to catch you at the office all week, but kept missing you. Thought I could brief you on developments in New Ventures."

Ben hadn't been to see Rick at PlayLand; Mary would have told him. "Let's go in the den." Rick gestured to the den across the hall.

"Shall I make coffee?" Paige's smile included both Rick and Ben.

"That would be great, Paige. Thanks." Ben answered before Rick could decline. Damn, Rick thought, that meant Ben planned to stay awhile.

They went into the den, and Ben closed the door. Rick sat behind his desk, rather than on one of the leather club chairs or sofa. He wanted some formality tonight with his old roommate. Ben was trying to take charge, and Rick couldn't let him do it. Not if he was going to talk to Ben about stealing Gus's ideas.

"What's up?" Rick asked.

"We're off to a great start on the action figure launch. Did Vince tell you?" Ben picked up a paperweight from Rick's desk.

"That's what I hear." Rick was noncommittal. He wanted to hear what Ben had to say.

"What else have you heard?" Ben asked. He glanced at Rick through half-lowered eyelids. "I'll bet everyone's pounding down your door. That's another reason I came tonight. So we won't be interrupted."

"Yeah, I've had a lot to catch up on." Again, Rick waited. The silence dragged on a bit too long. Usually Ben kept a glib patter going.

Ben shifted the paperweight from hand to hand with small tosses. Finally, he said, "Comic book prototypes look really good. You know Gus Powell from Games is working with us. And Vince let Jennifer work with me on the launch."

"Way I hear it, Jennifer's running the launch." Rick fiddled with his pencil. "You're lucky to have her."

Ben leered like he had during frat parties. "In more ways than one. She's pretty hot." Ben's grin faded when Rick didn't respond, and he shrugged. "She's not a bad product director either."

Paige brought in the coffee, and Ben jumped to his feet to help her. When she had left, Ben asked, "What do you think of Gus?"

"Don't really know him." Rick picked up his coffee cup, but didn't drink, just held it to warm his hands.

"He's one spacey dude."

"How so, spacey?"

"Says one thing one day, something else the next. You know, like that maniac freshman in the house our junior year, the one who never came back after Christmas break." Ben put his cup down on Rick's desk.

"That guy was psycho. You don't mean Gus is mental?" Was that how Ben was going to play it? Rick wondered.

"No, not really." Ben paused. "But I think he could be. We should watch him. And be careful what we tell him. I wouldn't want him sneaking off to a competitor with our trade secrets." Ben picked up the paperweight again and pretended to examine it, all the while scrutinizing Rick through a veil of eyelashes.

"You think Gus would do that?" Rick stared at Ben over his coffee mug.

"I'm not saying he would. I'm only saying we should watch him."

"Why?" Rick tried to keep his voice level, though he was impatient with Ben's insinuations.

"He claims he had these really elaborate story lines for the characters completely developed when he was in college. But when he came to me several months ago, all he showed me were doodles." Ben tossed the paperweight in the air and caught it. "I told him no one would buy his chicken scratchings, but I'd see what our creative folks could do. Told him not to get his hopes up. I paid a freelance designer a few hundred bucks for some color mock-ups. Then I showed them to Gus. He went apeshit on me. Said I'd stolen his ideas. But the difference between what he'd done and what the freelancer did was night and day. That's what I'm talking about."

"But Gus created the action figures, right?" Rick didn't trust Ben's wide-eyed expression. It was the same face Ben used when he'd sworn to one girl another girl had spent the night on the frat house couch. But Rick had been the one on the couch, while Ben and his latest squeeze had at it in the room the two boys shared.

"Oh, sure. Gus created them. But he couldn't do anything with them. When he complained, I promised him I'd let him work on the line for New Ventures. Get him out of the Games backwater. We have to do something about board games. They're sucking the life out of the whole Games group. To be frank, Vince isn't doing anything about it."

Rick didn't want to get off track, talking about Games. "Let's stick to Gus. What'd you promise him? I need to understand what we've agreed to."

"Well, I'm glad I stopped by then. Vince and Dewayne are blowing this all out of proportion." Ben dropped all pretense of nonchalance, leaning forward. "You know Vince agreed to pay Ben fifty grand a year?"

Rick nodded.

"That's ludicrous. I had Gus working on the line for nothing. Just the promise of another job. Vince's throwing money away, and

Dewayne told him to."

"Dewayne's concerned Gus would sue later, if we don't buy the rights."

Ben shifted in his seat. "See, that's what I mean. What kind of idiot would sue his employer over a few college drawings? I mean, what could Gus really do to PlayLand?"

"Dewayne says he could sue for all our profits on the line. Even if PlayLand won, we don't want the publicity of an infringement case."

Ben smiled narrowly. "You're right. I guess you need to be sure Gus is locked up tight. But it really galls me. Doesn't it make you mad when someone does something so stupid?"

Rick grimaced at the irony of Ben's statement. "Sure does."

After a few more minutes of small talk, Rick told Ben he was tired. After he escorted Ben out, Rick leaned back against his solid oak front door and sighed. What was he going to do about Ben?

CHAPTER 14: FRIDAY, MARCH 2

Around nine Friday morning, Rick got a call from Leo, who launched into his pitch even as Rick said hello. "Are you really going through with this headcount reduction? I tell you, it's a mistake to cut employees in Sales. Axe the whole Games group instead. They aren't contributing a dime to profits."

Rick rubbed his forehead. "Did you send your cost-cutting proposal to Alex and Maura?"

"Not yet. I wanted to touch base with you one more time. How can I sell the bejesus out of action figures if my people are worried about their jobs?"

"Sales isn't any different than any other division. I told you to get your proposal done yesterday."

"We're on the front line," Leo said. "You can buy crap through Procurement instead of making it in Manufacturing, so cut a plant or two in Operations. We're almost done with the launch now, so axe the Marketing staff. Or outsource support groups like HR and Finance and IT. But how can you get action figures into stores without Sales?"

Rick looked out his window. God, how he wished he were skiing. "Get your proposal in. Everyone has to play by the rules. Give me ten percent, like the other divisions have. Then I'll make the call."

"You're the boss, Rick, but I don't see how Sales can cut."

"Just do it." Rick hung up.

A few minutes later his computer beeped. Incoming email from Leo to Rick, Alex, and Maura. Rick read it—full of the same self-serving palaver Leo had given him on the phone.

He opened the attachment. Leo had submitted what Rick asked for, but no more. No creativity, simply a flat ten percent cut in each of the Sales budgets. Who knew what Leo would do if his budget was cut? Even if Alex, Maura, and Rick changed Leo's proposal, who knew what he'd do? Unless Rick gave him a direct order, Leo would do what he damn well pleased. Rick didn't have time to micromanage Sales. He was already bucking up Vince in Product Development. And spending hours with Alex on the cash flow crisis.

$$$

Maura's phone rang as she worked through the cost reduction figures for her meeting with Alex that afternoon. She let her assistant answer the call, but Kay said, "Tim Baylor in New Mexico. Can you take it? He's heading home this evening, but wants to talk to you first."

Damn. She had meant to call Tim that morning. Maura picked up the phone. "Hi, Tim. How's it going?"

Tim launched into a description of all of the interviews he had conducted over the last couple of days.

This could take an hour! she groaned to herself. "Tim, I'm trying to get ready for a meeting. What's the bottom line?"

"I'm not seeing a serious threat at the moment. A couple of employees talked to a union rep, but there doesn't seem to be any support for a union among the other employees."

"Then you don't think the union will take this any further?"

"Not now. The supervisors are holding coffees with the rank and file. No problems surfacing in the initial employee sessions."

"You're coming back to Lakeview?"

"Nothing more to do here. I'll stay in touch with the plant from headquarters."

"I want them sending you daily email recaps of the employee sessions."

"You got it."

"Isn't there anything more we can do? How about talking with other employers in town?"

"I've called several companies in the area, and I've asked the plant manager to contact others. No other employers have had any suspicious activity. The union shops have good relationships with their locals. Albuquerque isn't a union hotbed. Best I can tell, we just have a couple of disgruntled employees."

"All right. Let's talk next week. See if we can figure out what our employees' concerns are."

"Yeah, I have some ideas on that. There's this one guy who—"

"Tim," Maura interrupted, "I need to go. Call me when you get here. I want to talk in detail. Assess whether there's anything more we should do."

She hung up and went back to her spreadsheets.

$ $ $

Jennifer bounced into Kevin's office midmorning on Friday. "Hot off the press," she announced. "The first comic book production—issues one and two. Thought you might want a look."

Kevin turned around from his computer screen. Jennifer beamed and her tawny hair swung around her shoulders as she tossed two comic books on his desk. Kevin grinned back. "Congratulations," he said, picking up the books.

Kevin hadn't read many comics since he was twelve, but these looked pretty good. "Wow," he said. "Those colors really pop. Who's that guy? Camero? What's his shtick? Oh, the vision thing."

"Aren't they great?" Jennifer said. Kevin wanted to invite her to sit, but the way she skipped from foot to foot he didn't think she'd be able to stay still. Giddy as a kindergartener. She came around his desk to stand behind him and pointed. "Look. See Adolpho. He's the hero. The artist got his character down pat. And the bad guy. Look on page five." She turned the page. "Have you ever seen anything so evil?"

Kevin tried to stifle his smile. "Awesome," he said. Her citrusy perfume wafted past his nose.

"The discount coupons we talked about are on the back page. Buy one action figure, get the second for half price. Kids'll buy the comic book for the coupon."

"This is great." Kevin leaned back in his chair and cocked an eyebrow. "Are you always this excited about a product launch?"

"Not since my first doll launch." Jennifer chuckled as she went back around his desk and sat. "Most of the time they're pretty routine now. But this line was a new challenge. New consumer segment. And all the problems with Ben and Gus. The comic books were my baby. It's so great to finally see them in print."

"When do they ship?"

"First run goes out to stores tomorrow. Then it's full steam ahead. Nothing can stop the product launch once the promotional materials are out there." Jennifer sprung out of the chair. "I need to check on the publisher. Make sure they're ready to ship. And start on the exclusive for Toy Mart. Vince told me that's a go."

Kevin smiled after her as she left. Then she turned her head back into his office. "Thanks, Kevin. I know I'm acting like a kid myself. Sorry to be so unprofessional, but I'm really pumped."

"No problem, Jennifer. We'll talk more tonight. We're still on, right?"

"Wouldn't miss it." She waltzed out of his office as bubbly as when she waltzed in.

$ $ $

Grant wanted to empty his email inbox so he could leave early Friday afternoon. He and Linda had dinner plans.

His Manufacturing Director, Martin Cunningham, burst into Grant's office. "Huge fucking problem," he said. "Shitty equipment. Shut down the goddamn molding machine. Completely shot. Can't stay on schedule."

"What the hell's wrong?" Grant asked.

"Don't know. Melt temperature's too fucking hot. Scorches product. Leaves gas bubbles. Had to throw out an hour's production on Delphi. Looked like crap. We let the machine cool down, started it up again. Same fucking thing. Need a full maintenance check. It'll take all weekend."

"Jesus! And the schedule?" Grant jumped to his feet.

"Today's numbers shot to hell. By Monday morning, we'll be behind pace. We were already planning weekend overtime. We need this machine 24/7 for the next two weeks to stay on schedule."

"Can we step up production on the other machines?"

"We're already running them into the ground. Can't risk the newer equipment breaking down, too. Then we'd really be screwed."

"Christ, Martin! What are our options?"

"Mechanics working around the clock. Hope to fix it. It's a piece of shit, but our best bet is to get it back online."

"What's the contingency plan?"

176

"Outside production."

"You want us to find a vendor to make new product in the next two weeks?" Grant's eyebrows shot up. "That'll take a miracle."

"Yeah, well, I can only make what my machines can make. If they're broken, you'll have to go outside. I won't know more until Monday. Procurement needs to source some options over the weekend."

"You know what you're asking?" Grant shouted. "You want a vendor to commit to an emergency job over a weekend? You know what that'll cost?"

"Don't have a clue. That's Karen's job. I just know my machines. We're at full capacity. Doing my fucking best to get that piece of shit back online, but I can't tell you more until after the maintenance check."

"What about moving production to one of our other plastics plants?" Grant asked. "I'll have to tell Rick about this. Christ, it'll put him back in the hospital."

"I told you, we're in overtime already. All the plants are at full capacity."

Grant swore again. Then he strode to his office door and called to his secretary, "Get Karen Heintz here. Pronto."

Karen rushed in moments later and looked from Grant to Martin. "Uh, oh. The two of you together on Friday afternoon. What's up?"

Grant sat. "One of the plastics machines is down," he said. "It's causing product defects. Martin's trying to fix it, but we won't know the status until Monday. No other internal production capacity."

"The only plastics work in queue is action figures," Martin added. "It's all time critical."

"How soon can we get emergency capacity at a vendor?" Grant asked.

"Geez." Karen slumped in the chair next to Martin. "Domestic, right? No time for Asia?"

Grant shook his head. "Nope. We need all the components done in the next two weeks to get them assembled and distributed on time."

"Air freight?" Karen asked. "Expensive, but that might buy us more time."

"Maybe," Grant said. "Which costs more, Asia with air freight or domestic?"

Karen shrugged. "Won't know until I get the bids."

"Don't forget we have to get the molds to the vendor," Martin said. "I can overnight them anywhere, but I've got to know where to ship them."

"What can you have for me on Monday morning?" Grant asked Karen.

"Monday?" Karen's voice was shrill. "It's four thirty Friday now. Saturday in Asia already."

Grant looked at her without comment.

"I'm on it." Karen rose to leave.

"Martin, go with Karen," Grant ordered. "Tell her what we need and when. Shift the least essential components to the vendor. Keep our own equipment full blast on the most critical pieces. We can't let quality suffer."

Martin and Karen left, and Grant slouched in his chair. Christ! He didn't need this crap. Not on a critical product launch. Hell! He needed to call Rick. And Alex. Alex would yell about the cost. Grant picked up his phone.

$ $ $

Maura and Alex spent the afternoon holed up in his office with all the division cost reduction proposals. They argued over what changes to recommend to Rick. When they finished, Maura took a copy of what they hashed out to give to Rick. Rick would make further changes, but she and Alex had a strong plan to reduce labor costs by ten percent.

She was also ready to talk to Rick about the New Mexico union effort and the Atlanta lawsuit. She planned to push Rick to settle the Atlanta case, if Dewayne got a reasonable offer. The more she thought about it, the less she wanted a trial against a mentally ill former employee.

She wondered why Rick had asked to meet with her. Was it one of the topics she had prepared for? Something else? She had no idea. Usually, Mary gave Maura a topic when Rick wanted to meet.

The meeting was scheduled for five thirty. Mary was shutting down her computer when Maura arrived. "He's waiting for you,"

Mary said.

"Know what he wants?"

Mary shook her head. "I assumed you knew."

Maura knocked, then entered Rick's office. He motioned her toward a table in the corner. Rick took the chair facing the windows. Maura sat across from him, her back to the mountain view.

She set her files on the table. "I have the numbers Alex and I pulled together this afternoon. I also have updates on the union and Atlanta issues. Where would you like to start?"

"You decide," Rick said. He sounded remote, even nervous, as he stared out the window.

"Some quick updates first. We're pretty sure there's a union behind the phone calls in New Mexico. Tim Baylor was there all week working with our supervisors. I'm concerned the plant manager isn't taking this seriously, so I've asked Grant to follow up with her."

"Okay."

"Any other information you'd like on this topic?"

"I'm sure you and Grant are on top of it."

Maura tried not to frown. Rick usually cared more about union threats. "On the Atlanta lawsuit, Dewayne's convinced we can win at trial, but I don't like it. Our former employee is a veteran from the first Gulf War with PTSD. I think a jury would find him sympathetic. PlayLand changed his job requirements, and he couldn't cope. He didn't ask for an accommodation, so we may not have legal liability, but I don't want to treat a disabled employee that way."

"What do you want to do?" Rick glanced at her, but his gaze quickly went back to the window. Maura found it disconcerting to talk to his blank stare.

"I told Dewayne to see what it would take to settle the case."

"You think we should settle?" Rick's eyebrows went up as he turned to her. It was the first expression Maura had seen from him since she sat down.

"I don't like to pay off former employees, but I also don't want to go through a courtroom battle."

"You and Dewayne decide."

"Dewayne doesn't want to settle."

"Can you two come to some joint recommendation?"

"Don't know yet. We'll have to see what the plaintiff wants."

"Keep me posted." Rick's eyes wandered back to the window.

Had what she said even registered with him? "Then we can get a settlement demand?" she asked.

"Sure." Rick looked at her, but she wondered whether he was listening. His voice was monotone.

Maura moved her litigation and union files to the bottom of the stack and opened her reduction in force file. "The big item to discuss is the headcount reduction. The bank meeting is scheduled for the fifteenth. We need to decide what cuts to recommend and get all the divisions ready. We might even want to make some announcements before the meeting. Alex says we need to show we're serious about getting PlayLand's costs in line."

"Okay." Rick rubbed his hand over his chin.

"Alex and I have a proposal. I can walk you through it."

"Okay."

Maura gave Rick a spreadsheet and pulled out a copy for herself. She put on her reading glasses and looked at Rick over the frames. "The bottom line is we can cut payroll by ten percent. But Alex and I don't want to make the same cuts in every division. We should cut the support groups—HR, Finance, IT, and Marketing—deeper. Not cut as much in Operations and Sales. At least now. Next year we can come back to those groups, after the product launch."

Maura paused, waiting for Rick to react. He didn't.

"We'd cut Product Development ten percent now," she continued, "but we should look at them more strategically over the next twelve months. We have to make a call on what to do with Games. And New Ventures isn't delivering much. Maybe the other Product groups could take over new product development. But we can't get those issues resolved in a week."

"Why not cut Operations and Sales now?" Rick asked.

At least he was paying attention, Maura thought. "We should cut some. But Grant and Leo made a good case they need resources to get the action figures produced and into stores. That's our top priority this year."

"You're not just letting Leo get his way? He pissed me off, not getting his recommendation in on time. And he did a shitty job."

Maura laughed. "He pissed Alex and me off, too. His analysis was a piece of crap." She pointed at the Sales section of her spreadsheet. "Here's Leo's proposal. What Alex and I came up with is in the next column. We got an eight percent reduction in Sales, but not line by line. We gave it some thought."

Rick examined the spreadsheet, and marked a few numbers with his pen as she spoke.

Maura continued, "Alex and I decided Sales should keep almost all the front-line sales positions, plus the employees dedicated to our top five accounts. But they can cut half the district managers and half the dedicated sales reps at the smaller accounts. And significantly reduce travel and in-store service this year."

Rick glanced up. "They just added service resources in last year's reorganization."

"I know." Maura nodded. "That's the problem. They'd have to undo some of what they did last year. Talk to Leo before you make the call. But the bottom line is we need eight percent out of Sales to make this work. The support groups aren't big enough to take the pressure off Sales and Operations."

Rick examined the spreadsheet at length, while Maura sat silently. Finally he looked up. "Okay, talk about Operations."

Maura tapped the bottom line in the Operations budget. "Nine percent out of Operations. They're our largest cost center, so we need to get close to ten percent to meet the company-wide target. Alex and I suggest five percent out of action figure production and purchasing costs. Grant will have his work cut out for him to get there. Then they have to cut close to fifteen percent elsewhere to average nine percent total."

"How can they cut fifteen percent?" Rick frowned as he spoke.

"Close the South Carolina plant. Grant proposed downsizing it by fifty percent, but if we outsource Games production offshore, we save the cost of that facility entirely. We've talked about closing that plant for three years. Now's the time."

"Have you talked to Grant?"

"Alex and I haven't talked to anyone yet. We need your okay."

Rick sighed deeply and gazed out the window again. "Are you and Alex committed to taking twelve percent out of your groups?"

"We have to be to make this proposal credible."

"Is this all necessary?" Rick whispered. Maura wasn't sure if he was talking to himself or to her. She didn't respond.

Rick turned to her with a piercing stare. "We have to do this to get through the year, don't we?"

She nodded. "Nobody likes to reduce headcount, particularly HR, but we have to."

Rick sighed. "Are you and Alex ready to review this with the rest of the group?"

"With your backing. We could tweak it here and there, but we need your support on the framework, or the rest of the officers won't take it seriously." Maura wanted Rick on the hook when she and Alex went public with their recommendation. It would be attacked from all angles.

"Bring it to the staff meeting Monday." Rick turned back to his window.

Maura stayed seated. Surely Rick had something more to discuss, or he wouldn't have set up this meeting.

Rick stared out the window. Maura watched the silhouette of the Rockies darken. Should she leave? Finally, she asked, "Rick, how're you doing?"

He turned toward her. His gaze was sad. "It's rougher than I thought."

"How so?"

"I don't seem to care about anything. About any of the problems we have." He sighed. "I know what we're dealing with is serious. Everyone's looking to me for decisions. I know what to do, how to make the calls. I simply don't have any interest in playing the game."

"Did this start with your accident?"

Rick shrugged. "It's worse now. At home the last couple of weeks, I dreaded coming back. But honestly? It's been building for months."

"Lots of people get burned out," Maura said. "At all levels."

Rick stood. He didn't face her as he said, "It's not a short-term thing. I want out."

Stunned, Maura tried to understand. Rick had always been in control. Charging ahead. He wanted out? How could he want out?

Rick paced his office.

What the hell should she say now? Maura panicked. How could PlayLand survive without Rick? How could she survive? She felt like she had when she heard about Rick's injury.

"What do you want to do?" she asked.

Rick stopped pacing, his eyes pleading. "I don't know. Never done this before. What's a CEO do when he's had enough?"

"What did you and your dad do?" Maura tried to approach the problem clinically. "You were Chief Operating Officer when I got here. It was obvious you were going to take over from him."

"Yeah." Rick sat down. "His health was bad. Already had signs of dementia. We worked together for a year or two before he retired. Then I became CEO. But I haven't planned for a successor. I always assumed it would be Vince."

Vince! Maura thought. God, no. She had to get Rick off that track. How? Had Paige told Rick about their discussion while he was unconscious? "While you were out," she said slowly, "Linda and I worked on a succession plan. In case you didn't come back."

Rick smiled wryly. He didn't seem upset. "Then we have a start."

"I almost pitched my notes after you woke up," she admitted. "I didn't want someone finding the file and thinking the wrong thing."

"Who'd you decide should replace me?" Rick asked. His tone was lighter and he grinned. "I'm exceedingly curious."

Not yet, she thought. She needed to think about how to sell him on Grant. "Depends on what you want. How long you want to take. Whether we go inside or outside."

His eyebrows shot up. "Outside?"

"That's one option. My notes are pretty rough," she said. "Let me clean them up. I'll get you the file on Monday. There's no ideal candidate. Pros and cons to lots of people."

Rick sighed. "I know. No one's perfect. That's why this is so hard. Okay, let's talk next week." His eyes turned stern. Almost scary. "Not a word of this. Not to anyone."

"Of course, Rick." She was surprised at his vehemence. Didn't he trust her? But she understood. None of this could get out. He couldn't become a lame duck.

"I haven't told Paige yet," he said. "Or Vince or Kevin. This is just between us."

$ $ $

Maura drove the long way home, winding through the foothills, to give herself time to think. After Rick's bombshell, she was too keyed up to deal with family.

She had never dreamed Rick would want to leave. Rick had hired her. He was the only boss she had had at PlayLand. Rick *was* PlayLand. If he left, everything would change. Her job would change; it wouldn't be the same working for someone else.

Rick couldn't pick Vince. Such a namby-pamby. Paige saw it; why couldn't Rick? How could Maura get Rick to choose Grant? A non-family member.

She should have been more proactive about succession planning before Rick's accident. Linda had pushed for it often enough. But I thought we had time, Maura moaned to herself as she pulled into her driveway.

The kids were at a basketball game, so only Maura and Carlos were home. She greeted Carlos with a kiss. "I'm going up to change," she said.

She went upstairs, but detoured to her home office and powered up her laptop. She opened the succession document and started editing.

She didn't know how much later it was when Carlos called, "Maura, dinner's ready." She kicked her heels off, so it looked like she'd at least started to change, and went downstairs.

Carlos scowled when he saw her still in her work clothes. "Glad you could join me," he said.

Great, now he was pissed. Maura sighed. She made an effort at conversation, asking Carlos about his day. She didn't volunteer anything about PlayLand.

While they ate, Maura mulled over the pros and cons of various vice presidents replacing Rick. Grant was by far the best candidate. Vince was too indecisive. Leo was a bastard despite his strong relationships with customers. Alex was too narrowly focused on numbers, no passion for product.

Carlos waved a hand in front of her face. "Are you there?" he asked. "What's going on?"

She couldn't tell Carlos, even though she usually told him

everything. She had promised Rick. "Just a problem with a manager."

$ $ $

That evening after dinner, Rick sat in his den staring at the fire, the only light in the room. He was worried. Worried about the production problem Grant had called about. Worried more about the conversation with Maura.

What had he done? He groaned, dropping his head into his hands. Would Maura keep it quiet? If his intentions got out, PlayLand would suffer. As would Paige, who cared so much about being the CEO's wife. He would have to tell her. Soon.

But he was relieved, Rick admitted secretly. Everything he told Maura was true. He'd wanted out even before the accident. Everyone wanted a piece of him, and he couldn't take it. There had to be more to life than crunching numbers and refereeing his staff's squabbles.

Chapter 15: Monday, March 5

Kevin whistled as he drove to work Monday morning. He'd been whistling all weekend. His good mood started when he picked Jennifer up on Friday evening. She lived in a small Tudor house in a neighborhood of young families. Kevin doubted there were many single people living near her. After she settled into his SUV, he asked her why she'd chosen her house.

"I like to garden," she said. "I have a little patio. My first spring I planted perennials. This year I'm adding impatiens. I can eat outside in summer. Or sit and read."

"Flowers?" Kevin grinned. "Flowers and dolls? I guess that makes sense."

She scowled at his teasing.

The hospital benefit dinner was at a downtown hotel. On the way Kevin explained the hospital was recognizing PlayLand for its contributions to the Pediatrics Department.

"We donate toys for the kids every year," he said. "It's a good cause and good PR for the company. Paige said the dinner was too much for Rick, so I said I'd go."

At the hotel, Kevin handed his keys to the valet. Jennifer was already out of the car when he got to the passenger side. He followed her into the lobby.

She wore a black dress under an electric blue jacket. The skirt was short and her legs were long. Flashy earrings looked expensive, hair piled loosely on her head. What would it take for it to tumble down? he wondered.

Over dinner, Kevin quizzed Jennifer about the comic books. They shared what they'd heard about the production problem. They could have been at a business meeting for all the personal information they shared.

When the after-dinner program began, Kevin found himself watching Jennifer rather than the speakers. He clapped when everyone else did, but his attention focused on her neck. He smelled her perfume when she moved. Honey-blond wisps escaped the loose knot of her hair and brushed her skin as she turned to smile at him, applauding. Then he realized the room was watching him. It was time to accept the award for PlayLand. He knew he spoke, but couldn't remember what he said. When he looked out at the audience, the only person he saw was Jennifer.

The program ended, and the band started playing. Jennifer swayed slightly in time with the music. "Dance?" he asked.

She scrutinized him the same way she had when he asked her to dinner, then lifted one shoulder. "Sure."

She felt good in his arms. Nice height. He was careful not to pull her too close. He wasn't sure how to dance with a co-worker. Maybe this was why Rick told him not to date employees. But Jennifer didn't work for him, so it wasn't against policy. And it wasn't a date. Just a community dinner where they both represented PlayLand.

They danced. They drank. They talked. Too soon it was midnight, and the band played its last song.

Kevin drove Jennifer home and walked her to her door. "Thanks," he said. "I enjoyed it."

"Me, too."

He hesitated, then leaned over to kiss her cheek. She turned her head and met his lips with hers. "Good night. See you Monday."

Now it was Monday, and Kevin was whistling.

$ $ $

Monday morning, Rick walked into his office pretending more vigor than he felt. His mind ticked off the work for the day. Get his staff committed to the headcount cuts. Conference call with Leo and Toy Mart. Follow up on the production problem. And he still needed to talk to Paige. He'd avoided that discussion over the weekend.

He glanced out the window. Overcast skies, no sunshine reflecting off the slopes. A grey day to suit his mood.

A few minutes before the morning staff meeting, Alex came to

Rick's office with spreadsheets showing the budget and headcount reductions.

"Leo's not going to like this," Alex warned Rick, as they walked together to the conference room.

"None of us like it," Rick responded. "But we have to do it to keep the business going."

Rick began the meeting by asking Grant for an update on the production problem.

Grant's face was grim. "The oldest injection mold machine in the plastics line broke down midday Friday. Manufacturing got it back up, but it overheated again. It's causing burns and bubbles in the product. The maintenance guys ran full diagnostics over the weekend."

"What'd we learn?" Rick asked.

"Needs a couple replacement parts," Grant said. "We've called the supplier. Hope to overnight the parts today and install them tomorrow. Then we pray nothing else goes wrong. We're living on borrowed time with that piece of crap. It should have been retired five years ago."

"Why are we using it?" Leo asked, examining his fingernails.

Grant shrugged. "We don't use it much. Don't need it when production is low. But for the next several weeks we need all the capacity we can get. We have six action figures and their accessories to manufacture. All on a short timeframe."

"If we're up and running by the end of the day tomorrow, how does our production schedule look?" Rick asked.

"We'll be four to five days behind on this machine. We've moved the more complicated work to other equipment. We'll only use this machine on easier components. If we get it going. But some small pieces will fall behind schedule. A couple of detachable weapons." Grant rubbed his chin and grimaced. "That means assembly and packaging will be about a week late. We can make up a day or two by putting extra people on the assembly lines, but we'll probably ship a few days late."

"Does that include the Toy Mart shipments?" Leo asked. "We promised them two full weeks of exclusivity."

Grant shook his head. "We can ship overnight to Toy Mart. It'll cost a bundle, but we don't have any other choice."

"What about outside sourcing?" Rick asked.

"We considered it. But we hope to have the machine fixed by the time we could get specifications to a vendor. Karen Heintz is talking to our best domestic injection mold vendor just in case. But outside production is definitely Plan B."

Rick looked around the room. "Any other ideas? Vince, what's the Product Development perspective?"

"We've already shipped the comic books. They all went out last week, except the Toy Mart exclusive, which we're designing now," Vince replied. "Jennifer doesn't think we can delay the promotions or timelines we've already advertised. Kids expect the action figures in mid-June, like we promised. If we don't have product in the stores, we'll have a marketing fiasco. We could send the figures out without accessories, but the packaging all shows weapons and such. We need it all to go out on time."

"Do you agree, Kevin?" Rick asked.

Kevin leaned back with a sigh. "Yep. No way to communicate with consumers. No good way to explain the delays. I hadn't thought about simplifying the accessories and changing the packaging. But that sounds expensive."

"No." Alex shook his head emphatically, pounding his pencil on the table. "We can't afford new packaging. Cash is so tight now any overruns will make the banks balk. With extra production costs and overnight shipping to Toy Mart, I'm going to have to revise our financial statements for the bank meeting next Thursday as it is. Don't throw any more money at this problem."

"Get going on the new numbers," Rick told Alex. "I want a draft by end of the day. Grant, work with Alex to make sure we have good estimates on production costs."

Grant and Alex both nodded.

"Okay," Rick said, "Let's talk about the reduction in force. We need a plan before the bank meeting."

Alex passed out his spreadsheets. "These pages show each division's current budget, the proposals you each sent Maura and me, and the changes Rick, Maura, and I've made," he explained. As the vice presidents reviewed the spreadsheets, Alex droned on, going through each division in detail.

When Alex finished, Rick said, "You'll see I didn't keep everyone to a flat ten percent." He emphasized his involvement in the plan. "I've cut where it makes most sense for PlayLand overall."

Nevertheless, Leo looked at Alex rather than Rick as he exploded, "What's this crap about axing half my district managers? And travel costs, too? How the hell can I manage Sales without travel dollars? How can the piddly few managers remaining manage their territories? Revenue will plummet, just when we need it the most."

"It's my call, Leo," Rick responded. "Get your folks focused on our top accounts. I didn't cut anyone dedicated to those accounts."

"But you're cutting all my service dollars, even at those accounts. I can't meet my sales goals with these cuts." Now Leo was whining, not yelling. With Leo, that was progress, Rick thought.

"Anyone else have any comments?" Rick asked.

"You've cut Marketing by twelve percent," Kevin said. "But only eight percent in Sales and nine percent in Operations. What's your rationale?" Kevin raised an eyebrow at Leo as he emphasized the lower reductions in Sales and Operations. Good boy, Rick thought, Kevin was trying to help.

"We need to focus on action figures," Rick said. "Operations has to deliver the product, and Sales has to sell it to our major accounts. The smaller chains will buy if the big stores have the line on their shelves. We'll have to reduce marketing costs on other product lines until the action figures are launched."

"We'll take another look at Operations and Sales later this year, after the launch," Alex added.

"Another load of shit," Leo muttered, so low Rick barely heard. "Every reorganization in Sales means six months of lost revenue. Takes that long for my people to get back in stride. We're asking for trouble."

Rick sighed. If he didn't confront Leo now, he'd be dealing with his crap for weeks. "What was that, Leo?" he asked.

Leo shrugged. "I think you're being short-sighted, that's all."

Rick tried to assess the others' reactions. Grant had his pencil and calculator out. "Grant, any concerns?" Rick asked.

"Trying to get my head around it," Grant said. "Operations has a nine percent reduction, like Kevin said. But we still have to cut action figure costs by five percent. And fifteen percent on other product lines." Grant shook his head. "How do you seeing us getting there?"

Maura answered, "I don't know how you're going to get the five percent on the action figures. You and Vince'll have to sort that one out. You can get your fifteen percent elsewhere by closing the South Carolina plant."

Grant stared at her. "You want me to close South Carolina in the middle of a unionizing attempt in New Mexico?"

"What choice do we have, Grant?" Maura said. "We've talked about closing South Carolina for three years. Now's the time. It would have been easier last year, but it's not going to get any better. The plant loses money. You recommended downsizing it yourself. We're better off closing it altogether and selling the building. We can downsize board games and make them offshore."

"Board games have been in our product line for decades," Vince said. "I hate to axe them."

"I'm the one who started the line, remember?" Rick said. "We're not axing Games. At least not yet. But the line needs revising. It can't limp along much longer without a new face. Much as I hate to admit it."

Grant looked at Rick. "Do you agree with closing South Carolina? We'll be at the mercy of foreign vendors on Games."

Rick sighed. "It's a tough call. But yes, I agree. I trust Procurement to come up with good outsourcing options. We can get good quality paper and cardboard production in either Asia or Mexico."

Grant punched some figures into his calculator quickly, then glanced across the table at Vince and Kevin. "If we reduce marketing expenses and make a few modifications on the specs to reuse some of the molds, I think we can get our five percent. Can we talk later today?"

Kevin nodded. Vince shrugged.

"Any other discussion?" Rick asked. A few more questions, but nothing serious. His staff realized he was committed, Rick decided. They wouldn't push back at the moment. But he wasn't sure yet how committed they were to the cuts.

"Are we all together now?" Rick asked the group. "When we leave this room, I don't want any more debate. Just execution. If any problems develop, bring them directly to me. Alex and Maura started this work, but I'm directing it. This is our battle plan. Am I clear?"

Most of the officers nodded. Leo stared down at his notepad, pen in hand. Rick called him out. "Leo, do you support this?"

Leo looked up. "You're the boss."

Not a ringing endorsement, Rick thought, but it was all he was likely to get. "Okay. This is what we'll show the banks next Thursday. Start implementing now. Work with Maura and Dewayne on scheduling staff cuts. And Kevin on outside communications. Get estimates of the short-term costs to Alex by Tuesday. When we ask for an increase in our line of credit, we need to know when we'll need the cash."

Rick gathered up his files to signal the meeting was over. As people started to leave the room, he said to Leo, "Let's talk about Toy Mart."

Leo sauntered toward Rick's end of the table and slumped in the chair next to Rick, his jaw set in a challenge. "What's to talk about?" he asked. "We know what we need to offer Toy Mart."

"I need you on board with me," Rick said. "You're one of the senior officers. The others look up to you. You were damn near insubordinate this morning."

Leo pounded a fist on the table. "Rick, you've never understood Sales or how we bust our tails for this company. The product groups create this crappy merchandise, and we're expected to sell it. We put our asses on the line every time we go to into a store, and now you're cutting my budget. We just reorganized. We're doing everything we can to keep expenses down, but it costs money to keep customers happy." Leo waved at the spreadsheet Alex had given him. "With this new shit, I can't even send my people on the road. We'll only see half our customers once a quarter. Customer relationships will go to hell. It's going to hurt sales. Just you wait."

"Every time we change anything in Sales you get bent out of shape," Rick said. "When we cut last year, you complained. But you made it work. I've watched you make corporate directives work ever since I started at PlayLand. I worked for you as a sales rep once. Remember? You've always managed to get the job done. For PlayLand and for our customers. You can do it again."

"It's not about whether I can make it work. It's about whether I should have to. And about whether I want to." Leo shook his head. "I'd only say this to you, Rick, but some days I get so damn tired. Putting up with this bullshit for thirty years. I'm sick of it. I could walk out of here tomorrow. There are days that's all I want to do."

Me, too, buddy, Rick thought. Me, too. "Some days we all get sick of it," was all he said.

Leo frowned. "Not you, Rick. It's in your blood."

Rick stood up to leave. "I need you on this one, Leo. I can't have you badmouthing my decisions. Not this time." He clapped Leo on the shoulder. "Now let's go call Toy Mart."

They walked back to Rick's office. Rick placed his speakerphone between them, and Leo dialed the Toy Mart buyer.

Rick listened. After the usual back-and-forth banter between Leo and the buyer, the call turned serious.

"This is what we can offer," Leo said. "One exclusive comic book. That's in addition to the five promotional books everyone gets. Two weeks early shipment on the action figures. Delayed billing for three months."

"We had hoped for an exclusive action figure, as well as preferred pricing," the Toy Mart buyer said.

Leo started his usual pitch about how he had done what he could for Toy Mart and PlayLand valued their business.

Rick didn't have time for this. He interrupted. "No exclusive characters this year," he stated. "We need a cohesive presentation of the product in all accounts in our launch year. As for reduced pricing, unless you have a competitive offer to show us, I can't offer you anything more."

"No harm in asking," the buyer said. "We value the PlayLand relationship also. You can count on the Toy Mart order."

After a few more minutes of Leo schmoozing, the call ended. Rick leaned back and smiled. "Congratulations, Leo, you got the sale."

Leo grinned. "Never doubted it."

$ $ $

Ben walked into the crowded restaurant just after noon and looked around. The family diner wasn't his usual lunch fare, but it was far enough from PlayLand he shouldn't meet anyone he knew.

Except for Gus. Gus had called Ben that morning and demanded to see him immediately, and Ben suggested they meet here for lunch.

Gus was already seated and waved wildly at Ben.

Ben hurried over to Gus's booth. "Don't make a spectacle of yourself," he said. Ben tried to keep his tone jovial. No need to piss him off, he thought. Not until he found out what Gus wanted.

"Hi yourself, asshole," Gus responded.

Ben grimaced. Not going to be a good lunch. The waitress came to their table, and Ben ordered calmly, "Roast beef sandwich, please. On rye—no, make that pumpernickel. Hold the lettuce."

Gus ordered a hamburger. His voice grew increasingly loud as he answered the waitress' questions about condiments. Ben sensed the conversations at tables around them stop. "Sorry. He's a little stressed today." Ben apologized to the waitress for Gus, and gave her a smile that promised a big tip.

"Quiet down, Gus," Ben said, when they were alone. "People are staring. What's the big deal?"

"You know what the big deal is," Gus replied. Gus spoke quietly now, but he still sounded hysterical. "You stole my drawings."

Ben leaned forward, keeping his voice low. "We've been over this. I used your drawings to get the action figure line approved. That's all. You've made your deal with Vince. You're going to get paid."

Gus's eyes were wild. "No, the comics. I saw them. One of the stories is mine. Exactly what I drew in college. You took it. You must have. You worked with the freelancer on it. You stole it."

Ben sat back in the booth, wondering if Gus was merely speculating, or if he knew something. "Quit screwing with me, Gus. This is old news. You gave me the drawings."

"I didn't give you these drawings. But they're missing. I thought I lost them. Or threw them out. But you stole them. Because you used my story line." Gus was wilder than Ben had ever seen him.

"Calm down," Ben said, leaning across the table. He had to keep his cool. Couldn't let Gus have it here in the restaurant. But he'd make Gus pay later. "I found some drawings in the trash when we moved offices last year. I rescued them. I thought we might need them for the line."

"But you never said." Gus pounded his fist on the table.

"Why should I? You'd given me enough to get started. We didn't need them until Jennifer wanted comic books. We all did some of the stories. You. Me. Jennifer. So I used your old drawings. What of it?"

"But you didn't tell anyone they were mine." Gus pounded again, so hard the silverware jumped on the table.

"Calm down," Ben said again, grabbing Gus's wrist. "Your stories'll get published, won't they? And Vince promised you a promotion. Exactly like I said he would. Plus you're getting fifty grand a year for your crap." Gus's windfall still pissed Ben off.

"But you lied about my work again." Gus went on and on about how he developed the fucking stories as an undergrad. Let him rant, Ben thought. As long as he's quiet. No scenes in the restaurant.

Their food arrived. As Ben picked up his sandwich, Gus said, "I'm going to tell Vince and Rick. And Legal. No way will they keep you around when they find out you stole my drawings."

"How can I make sure you get promoted if I'm fired?" Ben let a little anger show in his voice. Gus was going to fuck up everything Ben had planned. Ben sure as hell couldn't keep the line fresh by himself. He needed Gus to replenish the characters and story lines. He couldn't have Gus talking about how Ben screwed him. "We're a team," he told Gus.

Gus shook his head. "I don't need you. Vince and Dewayne know the characters are mine. I don't trust you. You're a real asshole. I'll tell them to get you off my action figure line."

Christ, now he believes it's his line, Ben thought, stunned. Nothing would have happened without Ben. He'd made the line happen. Ben took a deep breath to keep his temper in check, but his fist clenched under the table. "Gus, you had a great idea, but you couldn't sell it. The line would never have been this far along if I hadn't pushed it. You know that."

"Jennifer would have got it to market," Gus muttered.

"Jennifer's just a pretty face and tits. I did it," Ben insisted. "Don't try to cut me out now."

"Or what?" Gus asked. "What can you do to me now? Vince promised me the money and the promotion. He'll believe me when I tell him you stole the story lines."

"Why would he believe you? You don't have any proof. You don't have the drawings."

"But you told me you took them out of the trash."

"Did I say that?" Ben backpedaled with a grin. "You must be mistaken. Why would I take them? Who knew a year ago we'd need the fucking stories, for God's sake? You threw your sketches out, and no one's seen them since."

"But it was my story line." Gus was getting loud again.

Ben saw red. He pushed his plate away and shook his finger at Gus. "If you tell anyone I stole the fucking drawings, you'll regret it. You'll never go anywhere at PlayLand, and I'll make sure your action figures fail. They'll never see a second season of production. And you won't get any more money from Vince."

Gus's face turned white. "But they're my characters. You can't kill them."

Ben stood up. "Try me. Finish your lunch. And don't try anything back at the office." Ben strode toward the door and paid cash at the front desk. He smiled and made sure the waitress got her big tip. Ben glanced back at Gus, who sat staring at his hamburger.

Ben was still pissed as he got into his Jaguar. I should blow his fucking head off, he thought with a smile. He opened the glove compartment and ran his hand over the handgun inside. Don't be stupid, he told himself.

He knew he needed to be in control when he returned to work, so he drove around town awhile. Who knew what Gus would do next? He could tell anyone—Vince, Jennifer, Dewayne . . . maybe even Rick—anything was possible. Rick was the only one who mattered. If Ben stayed on Rick's good side, made sure Rick remembered what he owed Ben, all his problems would go away.

When Ben was breathing steadily again, he drove back to PlayLand. As he parked his Jaguar, he saw Gus walking across the lot toward Vince near the entrance to the building. Damn, what was Gus doing now? Ben had to force himself to leave his pistol in the car.

$$$

Vince pulled into his parking spot at PlayLand after lunch and got out of his car. As he pulled his briefcase out of the back seat,

Gus rushed toward him. A pain lanced through Vince's gut. Gus had complained about one thing or another for weeks. Didn't like how the action figures looked in the comic books. Wanted changes even after the books were printed. The kid had no concept of cost control, and Vince was tired of dealing with him. How had Gus become Vince's responsibility anyway?

Gus's face was red, his hair more disheveled than usual, and his glasses askew. "Ben," Gus gasped. "Stole my drawings. He told me so."

Vince sighed. "We know that, Gus. I thought we worked all that out. We have a deal."

"But he took more than I thought." Gus caught his breath, and words poured out. "I had drawn whole stories for the characters. They disappeared last year. When we changed offices. My original drafts for comic books. I didn't give those to Ben. I thought I'd thrown the file out. But Ben took it."

"What difference does it make?" Vince asked, as he walked toward the building entrance. "I told you we'd pay you for your ideas. You'll get the first check when the comic books ship. That's next week."

Gus trotted behind Vince. "But he took my story line and submitted it as his. Ben did a couple of the comic book stories. I was too busy to do them all. He was supposed to develop his own ideas, but he used mine."

"How do you know?" Vince said over his shoulder, stepping through the revolving door into the building.

Gus caught up to him. "He told me. We just had lunch. He told me he took the file out of my trash. But I think he went through my office. He stole the file, plain and simple."

They were the only two people on the elevator to the third floor. Vince didn't know whether to be glad no one else heard Gus or whether it'd be better to have a witness. Gus was unpredictable, but surely he was harmless. "We can't stop the comics now, Gus. They're printed. Shipping tomorrow. You'll get your fee next week, just like we promised."

"This isn't about the money. It's about Ben. He's stealing. You need to stop him. If you don't, I'll talk to Dewayne. Or Rick. Or the cops. Or someone. Ben's stealing from me."

The elevator stopped. Christ, I don't want him following me, Vince thought. "Okay, Gus. I'll talk to Ben. I'll see what he says."

"Will you let me know? I need to know if he lies to you." Gus continued to tail Vince down the hall.

Vince turned around to finish the conversation in the hall away from his office. "All right. I'll get back to you. But it might be next week. I don't know when I'll have a chance to talk to him. Now get back to work."

Gus shambled off toward his cubicle. Vince watched him a moment, shaking his head. Gus was getting weirder every day. Vince wouldn't put it past Ben to have stolen from Gus, but he didn't know what good it would do to talk to Ben. PlayLand was already paying Gus. What difference did more drawings make? Vince sighed, rubbing his stomach. One more goddamn thing for him to do.

$$\$\,\$\,\$$

Rick met with Maura midafternoon Monday to review her succession plan. He read the profiles on his staff, glancing up at Maura occasionally as he read. She was nervous, he realized, which wasn't like her.

When he reached the end of the document, he understood why. Grant! He tossed the papers down on his desk. "You think Grant's the best candidate?"

"Yes." Maura ticked off Grant's strong points on her fingers as she spoke. "He has a strong operational background, and Operations is our largest division. He's never managed Product Development, but he has a good feel for product. He understands the financial issues, though he doesn't know the nuances. And he's a good manager of people."

Rick was silent. How would he explain to his family if he didn't choose Vince? Vince always got the short end of the stick. From their father. Now working in Rick's shadow. "What about Vince?"

"Vince has managed Product Development. He has a long history with the company, of course. He knows something about Operations, and he's worked with some big retailers over the years," Maura said slowly. Rick caught the hesitation in her voice. "On paper, he's qualified. But he has a reputation for being slow to make decisions."

"Give me some examples." Rick picked up his pen and toyed with it, still watching Maura.

"While you were out, the brunt of the action figure launch fell on Vince. Or should have. He didn't handle it well. Ben and Jennifer bickered constantly. He let them both think they were running the show for far too long." Maura paused. "People thought he couldn't decide anything without you."

"He seems to have dealt with Gus pretty well." Rick continued to play with his pen. He knew Vince worried too much. He was deliberate, that's all, Rick told himself. He couldn't fault Vince for wanting to make the right calls.

"Yes, but Ben was screwing up worse every day. Vince gets credit for stepping in with the offer to Gus." She hesitated again. "Once pressed, he came up with a creative proposal. But Dewayne had to force the issue."

"Would you work for Vince?" Rick asked bluntly.

Her eyes widened, and she stammered. "Th-there isn't anything wrong with Vince. As a person. He's very nice. Treats people well. I don't have any objections to working with him. Or for him. But he's not the best person to replace you."

"I have family to consider."

"That's why Vince is a candidate," Maura said. "I know you have to consider him. He is family. And he's the head of Product Development. Which is an important role. But you asked for my opinion. If it were my call, I'd pick Grant." Maura's words were defensive, but her voice was level. It was her honest assessment, which Rick respected.

"Grant's the best people manager on my staff," Rick said, thinking out loud. "Runs Operations like clockwork. Always on top of production and vendor problems. Most of his staff is competent, too. He hires good people."

Rick sat silently. What would he tell Vince? And even Kevin? His father had created this business. How could Rick hand it off to someone else?

Rick waved at Maura's write-up. "You have Leo and Alex on the list also."

Maura nodded. "They each have good skills, but I don't see them as frontrunners. Leo knows our customers inside and out. But he has a lousy temper and resists change. He doesn't respect his peers, and they don't like him. He's not a good leader."

"And Alex?"

"Alex understands the business. All the details. But he's never managed outside of Finance. He's a wizard at numbers, but has no personality. No vision."

Rick mulled over Maura's comments.

She continued, "I also have Kevin on the list. You should think about where his career is going long-term. If you give Kevin the right exposure, in another five years he'd far outshine Vince as a CEO candidate. Kevin's smart. He's well-liked. He's had good exposure in the company, and we can get him good experience if we plan carefully. He's doing well in his current job, but he could handle more responsibility. I think he should run Product Development as his next assignment."

"What about Dewayne? He's not on your list."

Maura shook her head. "When I drafted this proposal in January, we hadn't appointed Dewayne as the interim CEO yet. I didn't even know he was a director. Frankly, he didn't do anything during his weeks in charge to make me consider him as a permanent CEO. A great legal mind, but not a strong leader. Like Alex—no vision."

After a pause, Maura continued, "We could also look for an external candidate. But there are viable candidates internally. Grant's the strongest. Vince is the logical family member. Unless you want to make your departure public, we're better off staying inside. Vince wouldn't like it any better if you went outside than if you promoted Grant."

Rick remained silent, stewing. He hadn't thought about going outside PlayLand. If he didn't pick Vince, Maura was right—Grant was the best internal candidate. He wouldn't find anyone better on the outside. But how could he pass over Vince?

Maura echoed his thoughts. "Your choice boils down to Grant or Vince. Kevin doesn't have the experience yet, and the others are too narrowly focused."

Rick blew out a deep breath, then picked up Maura's document. "You've given me a lot to think about," he said. "To be honest, I'm leaning toward Vince. I can back him up. Like I have in Product.

But I won't decide now. I have time to plan."

"You're sure you want to step down?" Maura asked. "It would be easier if you stayed even another year or two as CEO. Then make the call. We could watch Vince and Grant more closely. Maybe even tell them they're candidates to replace you."

Rick looked at her sharply. He'd told her this was confidential. "Do they know I'm thinking about leaving?"

Maura shook her head. "I haven't said a word. But while you were in the hospital, the topic did come up. Linda's been pushing me for a couple of years to work on a succession plan with you. And I kicked myself that it wasn't in place before your accident. So at the time, I talked to Grant. Just to see if he wanted to be a candidate. Because of the conflict if Linda was involved in the planning. He loves Operations, but I think he'd be interested in becoming CEO. He'd be a fool if he wasn't."

"What about Vince?" Rick asked.

"Vince asked me whether we had a succession plan. Before Dewayne was appointed as the interim CEO. I told him I couldn't talk to him, as long as there was a chance you'd be back. Because he'd clearly be a candidate to replace you. I didn't know how the corporate governance worked. But obviously, he was the senior family member in your absence."

Rick said quietly, almost to himself, "So Vince knows he's a candidate." That almost clinched it. How could he tell Vince he was being passed over?

"Yes," Maura said. "And so does Kevin. After Vince came to talk to me, I felt I had to let Kevin know also. Because I didn't know the family dynamics or decision process. I told them both they'd have to sort it out within your family. That's when I went to Dewayne."

Rick sighed. No way could he avoid talking to both Vince and Kevin about wanting to leave. What a mess! And the easiest way to minimize the mess was to make Vince his successor.

He looked at Maura. "Okay. You gave me what I asked for. Let me think about it. And remember, keep it quiet."

Maura did not move to leave. "There's one more thing," she said. "If Grant's your choice, we have to decide what happens to Linda."

Rick was surprised. Linda? But Maura was right. The CEO's spouse couldn't work at PlayLand, particularly not in a sensitive

Human Resources role.

"Our anti-nepotism policy says we can't have one spouse reporting in the other's chain of command," Maura said. "If Grant is CEO, Linda can't work here at all. I don't want to lose her, but if you want Grant, I'll have to replace her."

"Maybe that's one more reason to name Vince."

Maura stood up. "Well, be careful, Rick. If we don't handle it with delicacy, Grant could get ticked off, and they could both leave. Linda knows my opinion, so they'll want to know why Grant doesn't get the job. I'll support you whatever you decide, but let's talk first."

After Maura left, Rick leaned back in his chair and turned toward the mountains. No matter what he did, it wouldn't be easy. The family would be upset if he didn't choose Vince; Grant might leave if he did.

Maybe he should stay, he thought. At least until the end of the year. Get through the action figure launch. Cut costs. Get the business back on track. But how could he come into work every day and perform a job he didn't want?

He'd talked to his personal attorney and tax advisor. It would take about six months to get the legal paperwork and accounts in place for the charitable foundation. He could stay at PlayLand until that work was done. But he'd rather not. He'd rather start the charitable work now. And take some time off. Enjoy the outdoors. Play with his boys. He couldn't do any of that as long as he was CEO.

The sunshine broke out on the mountains to the west. Rick smiled to himself at their beauty.

CHAPTER 16: WEDNESDAY, MARCH 7

Vince parked his car in the PlayLand lot at eight Wednesday morning. Already he had shooting pains in his stomach. He'd thought his work on the action figure launch was done, until Grant called Tuesday afternoon. "Are there any simplifications we can make to get back on schedule?" Grant asked Vince.

Vince didn't want to reengineer the line. Hell, he didn't know how they could cut at this late date. Maybe Jennifer would have some ideas. Or Ben. Technically, Ben was still in charge of the action figure line, even though Jennifer had done all the work on the launch.

Then Vince remembered he had told Gus he'd talk to Ben about the drawings. He'd forgotten. It was a lose-lose conversation for Vince. What the hell would he do if Ben admitted stealing the drawings? Only Rick could fire Ben, even though Ben reported to Vince. And what would he do if Ben denied the theft? PlayLand needed Gus to keep the action figures updated over the next year or two, so Vince couldn't let Gus get pissed off. Why couldn't his staff all play nice together?

Vince got out of his car. In a repeat of Monday's incident, he heard Gus calling him. Vince groaned. Gus had parked as close to Vince's reserved parking spot as possible.

"I've been waiting for you," Gus said. "Have you talked to Ben yet?" Gus sounded hysterical.

"No. I told you I probably wouldn't have a chance for a few days."

"Good," Gus said, surprising Vince. "I have evidence." Gus waved several loose papers, then thrust them at Vince. "I found them."

"The drawings? Then Ben didn't steal them?" Vince sighed in relief.

"They were in Ben's office." Gus's eyes bulged behind his thick lenses. "He went through my office, so I went through his. Last night after everyone was gone. He had a huge file of my drawings. I didn't take them all. I don't want him to suspect anything's missing. But I took enough to show you. Look." Gus pointed. "I drew these years ago, but they're exactly like the story Ben wrote. Practically identical. Here, take them."

Vince took the papers Gus shoved at him. He thumbed through them, but he didn't remember the comic books well enough to know how close the drawings were to Ben's submission. "I don't know if this'll prove anything. They aren't signed or dated. How will these prove you came up with the story before Ben did?"

"Look at them, Vince. They're my work. Anyone can see that." Gus's voice got louder. "Talk to Ben. See what he has to say."

"All right, Gus, calm down. I said I'd talk to him, and I will." Vince tried to shake Gus off.

Gus shadowed Vince into the building, a repeat of Monday. "I haven't given you everything I took," Gus whispered. "I kept some. In a hidden file. And I made copies of these. He's going to lie, so I'm keeping my own evidence. To make my case against him. Will you let me know what he says?"

"I said I'd get back to you." Vince strode toward the elevator.

"If I don't hear from you by tonight," Gus said, "I'm going to my lawyer. I have rights. Ben can't steal my work. Neither can PlayLand."

Gus continued his rant as they rode the elevator up to the third floor. As they got off, Vince turned to Gus. "No one's going to let Ben steal from you. I'll let you know what happens."

Vince's stomach was roiling when he reached his office. He called Jennifer and asked about the action figures.

"I don't know how we can cut back on production," she said. "The comics are already on their way to stores. We need to come out with all six action figures. So we deliver what we're promising in the comic books."

"What if we're late?" Vince asked.

"Major communications problem. With retailers and consumers.

Think of the disappointed kids."

$ $ $

Maura sat in her office, still fretting about her conversation with Rick. Couldn't he see making Vince CEO would destroy PlayLand? As she considered how to convince Rick to pick Grant, Tim Baylor stopped in her doorway. "Can we talk about New Mexico, or do you want a written report?" he asked.

"Come on in."

"Here's the deal," Tim said as he sat. "I'm pretty sure only a couple of employees talked to a union rep. One woman complained to her supervisor about some recent scheduling changes. She has problems arranging day care with the new schedule. That's the only issue I heard about the whole time I was there." He shrugged. "Well, employees aren't too fond of Alice Sorenson, the plant manager. But the scheduling change is the only complaint they have about PlayLand."

"What's your assessment of Alice?" Maura asked.

"Not the best plant manager. She tries, but she's trying too hard. Employees think she's faking it. Then when she changed the schedule without notice, employees decided she didn't care about them. Fortunately, we have a good supervisor where the scheduling complaint came up. In the Packaging Department."

"How'd this get out of hand?"

Tim shook his head. "The supervisor in Packaging was on vacation when the new schedule was announced. The employee complains to a couple of co-workers. Gets them riled up. Their supervisor's gone, so there's no one they trust to talk to. So they go to someone's husband, he's a union steward at another company. Of course, the steward promises he can fix everything."

Maura frowned. "How'd you find out all this out? You didn't talk with any of the hourly employees, did you?"

"Nope. Just managers. When the Packaging supervisor returned, he made the rounds. Did the usual 'how's it going' routine. He said employees were more than eager to tell him what they thought about the schedule change."

"You're comfortable with how we got our information?" Maura trusted Tim's instincts, but wanted to make sure they hadn't pushed too hard in their eagerness to manage the unionization attempt.

"Yes. The only way not to have heard this information would have been if the manager told his employees not to talk to him. Labor laws don't require that. He handled it fine." Tim sounded confident.

Maura relaxed. "Okay. So what's with the schedule change?"

"As I said, it caused a few people problems with day care. I told Alice to put the change on hold while we discuss other options. She didn't like it, but agreed to talk to Martin and Grant this week. And she'll tell folks the revised schedule isn't a done deal."

"Would you follow up with Martin and Grant?" Maura asked.

"Sure," Tim said. "Part of the problem is employees didn't get much notice. It's a bad time. Maybe we can wait until summer to implement the change. The extra time would help people find day care. But I don't know what Operations needs to do to maintain productivity, so I don't know whether that'll work."

"Find out what Martin and Grant say. We'll consider the New Mexico situation to be under control."

Tim promised he would and left Maura's office.

As Tim left, Maura's phone rang. It was Dewayne, wanting to talk about the Atlanta lawsuit. "The plaintiff has amended his complaint," Dewayne said. "He's adding a federal Americans with Disabilities Act claim and a similar claim under Georgia law."

Maura slumped in her chair. "What'd I tell you? I knew we were vulnerable."

"I still think we can beat the guy at trial. But this raises the stakes. Now we'll have to face the accommodation issue. You're sure he never asked to be accommodated?"

"That's what I was told. But he'll probably say his managers should have known he was disabled. Do you have a settlement demand?"

"Not yet," Dewayne answered. "I told local counsel to ask. But plaintiff's counsel wouldn't talk settlement until he served the amended complaint. He wants to raise the price. It won't work. An employee has to ask for an accommodation before we have to do anything."

"Well, we thought he would add the disability claim all along." Maura had never felt good about this case, and now it was going downhill. She wanted to get rid of it. "Please get a settlement demand out of them."

"You're the client," Dewayne said. "If the demand is less than the cost of defense, we can settle."

$ $ $

Vince had had his secretary Deanna set up a lunch meeting on Wednesday with Ben. In hindsight, he wished he hadn't made it lunch. Now he couldn't leave if Ben got angry. He shouldn't be so worried. After all, Ben worked for him. But Ben always made Vince nervous. Maybe because Ben got along better with Rick than Vince did.

Vince arrived at the restaurant first and took a table. Ben strolled in a few minutes later, perfectly groomed in an expensive camel hair blazer, open-necked dress shirt, and grey trousers. Vince felt rumpled in comparison. A pain went through his gut, and he ordered a beer to wash it away.

They ordered, and made small talk. PlayLand was all they had in common.

When their food arrived, Ben asked, "What's up? Must be some reason you wanted to meet. Something more important than how bad Games is doing."

Ben's pushiness was one reason Vince hated him. He gulped his beer and felt the alcohol hit his gut. It didn't sooth his digestion the way he'd hoped. "It's Gus," he said.

Ben lifted an eyebrow. "Jesus, I thought we took care of him. You promised him a shitload of money. Isn't that enough? I'm sorry I ever saw his fucking drawings. Should have left them in the garbage can."

Vince took another sip, glancing over his glass at Ben. "The way Gus tells it, you're milking his ideas. He says you stole more drawings."

"Now, wait a second. I never stole anything. He gave me those drawings. To sell you on the action figure line. I told you that weeks ago." Ben's face turned red.

Something was bothering him, Vince thought. Ben didn't usually let on when he was riled. "Other drawings. Not what he gave you. He says you used his drawings to develop your story line in the comic books."

"That's what he says, huh?" Ben stabbed his pasta, gripping the fork so tightly his knuckles were white. And he chewed hard and fast. He was nervous, all right. Or angry.

Vince felt a little better. Ben wanted him to talk, so he would keep quiet.

Ben took another bite, and chewed some more, glaring first at Vince, then at his plate.

Vince couldn't wait him out. "He says you took a folder of drawings out of his office last year. He showed me one."

Ben's eyes narrowed. "If I stole the drawings, how'd he show them to you?"

"He says he took them back last night."

Ben pointed his fork at Vince. "You let him get away with that? He admits he took them. Out of my office. You didn't fire him?"

"He's made serious charges about you. I need your side of the story. Did you take anything out of his office or not?" Vince couldn't eat any more; his stomach churned.

"No, I didn't take anything out of his office. Now, what are you going to do about him? He's getting weirder every day." Ben leaned back in his seat.

"How did you come up with your story line?"

"Jesus, I don't know. Where do any ideas come from?" Ben picked up his glass. "We met. Several times. Me, Gus, Jennifer, a couple of product managers, the freelance artists. Sometimes some of us. Sometimes all of us. Gus threw out ideas. Jennifer, too. We all did. We agreed on who'd do what, and went from there. I worked with one of the artists, because God knows I can't draw."

Vince saw a way to reconcile what Gus and Ben were saying. "Could you have taken an idea Gus mentioned? Maybe an idea based on one of his earlier drawings?"

Ben took a sip, then smiled. "Anything's possible. All I know is I didn't steal anything. Not from Gus. Not from anyone. He's a loony-tune, and you know it."

"He showed me a sketch. Where'd he get it?"

"Do you have it?" Ben asked. "Can I see it?"

Vince pulled the drawing Gus had given him out of his jacket pocket and handed it to Ben.

Ben snorted. "Never seen it before." His hand trembled. "He

probably had it all along. He didn't give me everything last year. At the time I only wanted descriptions of the action figures. Not story lines. We didn't need those until Jennifer came up with the fucking comic books." Ben pointed a finger at Vince. "Say, how come Gus hasn't accused Jennifer of ripping him off? He was going to do comic books. Did she steal from him? Or maybe he just likes her because she's got great tits."

Vince sighed and reached for the sketch. Ben seemed reluctant, but did let Vince take the drawing back. "I have to take Gus's complaint seriously."

"Yeah, well, how do you think I feel? The freak accuses me of stealing every time I turn around. He doesn't have any proof, and you know it."

"All right. I'll talk to him again." Vince put the drawing back in his coat pocket, finished his beer, winced as it landed on top of his meal, and excused himself.

Back in his office, Vince looked at the drawing again. Only a sketch. How could it cause so much fuss? He opened one of the comic books on his desk, and flipped through its pages. On page twelve was a more professional version of the sketch he held in his hand. The balloon words were almost identical. Maybe Ben could have dreamed up the story without Gus's sketch, but not likely.

Another sharp pain shot through Vince's gut, and he pulled out antacid tablets from his desk drawer. He picked up the phone and called Rick.

$$$

At home Wednesday evening, Rick was silent during dinner. He had to talk to Paige about his plans, but he didn't know how she would react.

When the twins left the table, he asked Paige to come into the den with him. Her eyebrows lifted. Rick generally kept the room for his use only. He brought PlayLand files home and wanted to be able to spread his work out without disclosing anything confidential.

Paige followed him quietly and sat on the couch facing the fireplace. Rick took his time lighting the fire, then sat beside her.

Rick wasn't sure how to start this conversation, so he eased into it. "I've been thinking about making some changes at work," he began, watching his wife's face. He knew she didn't have a clue what he was about to say. "This has been coming on since before my accident, but I've been thinking about it more in the last couple of weeks. I want to do it."

Paige frowned. "Do what?"

"Step down as CEO."

"What?" Her eyes widened. "Why?"

"I have to fight myself every morning to go to the office. The work doesn't mean anything. It should, because PlayLand's at a critical point now. But it's not what I want to do."

"But you've wanted to be CEO of PlayLand all your life."

"No," Rick said, pushing a strand of her hair behind her ear. "It's what my father wanted. And I did it. For him. For the employees. For the kids who buy our toys. But there's more I want out of life. If I don't do it now, I never will."

"Is that why you've been drinking more?"

Rick shrugged. "This isn't about me drinking. I haven't been drinking more. This is about what I want to do with the rest of my life."

"What about our family?" Paige had tears in her eyes.

"We have money. We'll still have money. I don't need to work."

She looked away from him. "But the position. Doesn't it mean anything to you?"

"Being CEO?" He shook his head. "Not really. What matters is whether I feel good about getting up each day. I haven't for a long time."

"What do you want to do instead?" After she spoke her lips pressed together into a thin line. Was she angry? Hurt? Or merely surprised?

"Establish a foundation. Dad planned to give away a portion of his wealth to charity when he died. I want to set it up now. Head it myself. See what I can do for children in the community." Rick leaned forward. This part of his dream excited him, and he hoped it would excite Paige also. "Give back from PlayLand's toy business to children. Maybe focus on health care. Maybe education. I don't have the details yet. But I can make a difference in kids' lives. Create some successes I can see. Just think what we can do!"

"But what about PlayLand? You can't just leave. Who's going to run it?" Paige seemed puzzled. Well, he'd never talked to her like this before. She didn't know much about the business.

"Not sure yet. Probably Vince."

"Vince? Is he ready?" She looked skeptical.

"Why? Don't you think he's ready?"

"Maura and I talked while you were in the hospital. About who should replace you. She didn't want Vince."

"She still doesn't. But this is my call."

Paige hesitated, then put her hand on Rick's arm. "You know," she began, then paused. "Vince wasn't much help after your accident. I asked him and Kevin what to do. He kept putting things off. Kevin pushed him, too, though you know how nice Kevin is."

"You don't see what Vince does at work."

"No. But what Maura said about Vince matched what I saw."

Rick stood and stepped to the fireplace. "Damn it, Paige, I can't pass over Vince. We won't have a decent Thanksgiving dinner the rest of our lives."

"Can he do it, Rick?"

Rick shrugged. "I'll have to help him. But I'd have to help anyone. Like Dad helped me."

"How much time will you get back for yourself if Vince succeeds you?" Paige asked.

"At least half, I'd say."

"Ideally, how much time do you want to spend on the foundation?"

"Within a few months, probably most of my time."

"For the long run, who's the best candidate?" Her voice was quiet, but firm.

Paige was cross-examining him, Rick thought in surprise. Like Dewayne did. "Other people are quicker at making decisions. Grant. Leo. Dewayne."

"Who's the best leader you have?" She was really pushing.

"Grant. Leo's strong in Sales, but not otherwise. Maura does a good job in HR."

"Where does Vince excel?"

Excel? That was a tough question. "He's led Product Development for several years now." Rick sounded defensive, even to himself.

"And what's Product done since he took over?"

Rick looked at Paige sharply. She sure had a good handle on PlayLand's problems, he thought. "Where'd you come up with all these questions?"

"I'm not stupid, Rick. I listen."

"I never thought you were stupid. But you never seemed to care."

She shrugged. "Maybe that's because you cared enough for both of us. Or seemed to." She paused. "Do you care now, Rick? Do you care what PlayLand will be in eight or ten years when our boys are ready to work there?"

He hadn't thought about the twins. He'd been too concerned about himself. "You don't think Vince can do it?" he asked.

Paige shook her head.

"Kevin?"

"Not now," she said. "Maybe in a few years."

"Then I have to go with Grant."

"I'm not telling you what to do, Rick."

"Like hell you aren't!" But he grinned.

"You're the one who wants to leave. You could keep running the company. None of this has to happen." She stood and moved next to him.

Rick left her and sat on the couch she had vacated. "Paige, what do you want me to do? Give up my life to this business?"

"Your father did."

"Dad loved the company. He didn't have any other interests. No hobbies, no causes. He only wanted the foundation for tax reasons."

Paige sat beside him. "And what's your commitment to it? What have you ever done except some charity golf tournaments?"

"That's just it, Paige." He leaned toward her. "Do you know what it felt like to lie in the rehab center and realize I didn't have anything to show for my fifty-some years on the planet? There was a reason I didn't die this winter. I need to figure out what that reason is. I need more than maintaining the company my father built. I want a cause of my own."

She stared at him. He must sound odd, he thought. He wasn't usually idealistic. But, damn it, this was important. He needed to change his life, even if Paige didn't like it. She could come along on the ride or not. He wanted her with him, he realized. But he would make the change regardless.

Her mouth was a narrow line. "You're set on this, aren't you?"

He nodded.

Her lips softened. She shifted forward and touched his arm. "You know I want you to be happy, don't you?"

"Well, you haven't said so."

"I do," she said, tears in her eyes. "I know you've been unhappy this winter. I've been worried. I thought it was the business, all the financial pressures." She took a deep breath. "You surprised me tonight, that's all."

"Then you're okay with this?" Rick asked, cupping her cheek gently.

"It's not mine to be okay with." She fit herself under his arm and put her hands on his shoulders. "So who's it going to be?" she asked.

"I guess it has to be Grant."

"If you say so." She smiled.

Chapter 17: Thursday, March 8

Maura got a call from Rick late Thursday afternoon. "We need to talk," he said, so she headed for his office. Rick, Vince, and Dewayne were there when she arrived.

As Maura sat, Rick said, "It's Ben and Gus." He turned to Vince. "Tell them."

"I've had a couple of conversations with Gus and Ben over the last week," Vince began. He paused and rubbed his stomach. Dewayne raised an eyebrow at Maura. Not good if Vince was already hesitating, she thought.

"Gus said Ben took some drawings from him. He was really agitated. Flailing his arms and shouting. As bad as Gus's ever been."

"Shouting?" Maura asked. "Did he threaten you?"

Vince shook his head. "No. Not me. Just Ben. I told him we'd already dealt with Ben. That we knew Gus created the characters. That we'd already agreed to pay him. In fact, the first check's being cut now. But Gus says he has proof. Says Ben used his ideas in the comic books."

"Did he show you any evidence?" Dewayne asked, leaning back and steepling his fingers.

Vince rubbed his stomach again. "Gus says Ben stole a file from him last year. Out of his office. He showed me something. Looked like Gus's other sketches, so I didn't think much of it. I told him I'd talk to Ben. Just to get rid of him. Otherwise, he'd still be following me around the damn building."

"What does Ben say?" Maura asked. "I assume he denied everything."

Rick looked at her sharply. "Let's hear Vince out."

Vince sighed. "Yes, Ben denies it. Says he didn't steal anything. Says he only took what Gus gave him. What's more, Gus admits he took a file from Ben's office. That's where Gus got the drawing he gave me."

"Gus admits taking Ben's file?" Maura asked. "And Ben denies he took anything from Gus."

"That's about it," Vince said.

"Our policy says employees can't take things from other people's offices without permission. Gus admits he violated that policy. And we don't have anything on Ben." Maura pursed her lips. Damn, she thought. She wanted a reason to get rid of Ben, but she hadn't heard it yet.

"Yeah, but here's the kicker." Vince laid a sketch on the table. "This is what Gus gave me." He opened one of the newly published comics and laid it next to the drawing. "Here's a page from the story Ben developed with a freelancer. Practically identical."

Dewayne picked up the two pages and looked at them closely. "Could be a copyright violation," he said. "Clear similarities. If Gus can prove Ben had access, we have a problem."

"Who do you believe, Vince?" Maura asked.

Vince hesitated. "Gus," he said, staring at his hands as he spoke.

"Why?" Dewayne asked.

"Don't trust Ben. Gus may be wacky, but he's honest." Vince grimaced, as if in pain. "I don't know what to do." He picked at his thumbnail.

"That's why I wanted to talk," Rick said. "Vince—as the division head—HR and Legal all need to agree. Whatever we decide. Ben's a good friend. A longtime friend. But I can't have a senior leader here passing off other people's ideas as his own. How do we get to the bottom of this?"

"In other employee situations, HR would investigate," Maura said. "Talk to both employees. We need someone outside the chain of command. Want me to do it?"

Rick and Dewayne both nodded.

"Did Gus say whether he has any more drawings?" Dewayne asked. "We need all the facts."

Vince shrugged. "Says he does. But he only showed me this one. I don't know what he has."

"What's Ted think?" Maura asked, referring to Gus's direct supervisor, who reported to Vince.

"I haven't talked to him," Vince said. "I wanted to know what Rick thought."

"We need him involved, before we take action against Gus," Dewayne said.

"We don't know what we'll do yet," Rick said. "Let's see what Maura comes up with."

"Okay," Maura said. "Let's talk about outcomes. What if Ben did take the file? What if he has passed off Gus's work as his own? What then?"

"Vince, you're the division head. What would you do?" Rick asked.

Vince looked at Rick. "I don't know. He's been here a long time?" He spoke as if asking Rick for the answer.

"If it were any other employee," Maura said, "we'd fire him. Without a second thought. We'd better be prepared to fire Ben."

Rick frowned at her, then turned to Dewayne. "What do you think?"

"Maura's right," Dewayne said. "It's tough to fire a company director. But we can't have managers acting this way. Copyright violation is against the law and bad business judgment."

Rick looked at Vince. "Vince?"

Vince shrugged. "Are you okay with firing him, Rick?"

"I won't decide now," Rick said. "We need to investigate. Get the facts. But I can't let people steal from other employees. Not even my friends. I'll fire Ben if the facts support Gus's version."

"Then I'm on board, too," Vince said.

"What about Gus?" Maura asked. "He's admitted taking the file from Ben's office."

"If Ben took the file from Gus, wasn't Gus justified in taking it back?" Dewayne asked, though his voice didn't sound like there was any question about it. "It was Gus's personal property. Drawings from before he started at PlayLand."

"But Gus should have reported it," Maura said. "Not just taken it out of Ben's office."

Dewayne grunted. "That may be HR policy, but no jury would think Gus did anything wrong."

"Okay," Rick said. "Maura, I hear you. But if Ben took the file from Gus, I'm not going to get stuck on policy if Gus took it back."

"What if we can't prove Ben took the file?" Maura said. "I want to be sure we're thinking this through."

"Maybe we reprimand Gus," Rick said. "But we still need him on the action figure line."

"He's not as important as he was earlier," Vince said. "Jennifer has it pretty well in hand. She'd like to have him around, but I don't think he's essential."

"But it's his creation," Dewayne said. "We think we've got a deal now, but it could go sour if Gus gets unhappy with what how we use his characters."

"We'll try not to rock the boat with Gus," Rick said. "Maura, you talk with Gus and Ben. Then we'll regroup."

"What do I tell them?" Vince asked. "I told Gus I'd let him know."

"Tell him you're still investigating." Rick said, standing. "Maura, get on it quickly. In the meantime, Vince, don't say anything to Ted. Not unless we have to fire Gus. Ben is Ted's peer. I don't want Ted involved while we investigate Ben."

Maura and the others got up to leave. She glanced back at Rick. He stared out the window, his hands clasped tightly behind his back. "Anything else, Rick?" she asked.

He turned to face her. "Stay," he said.

She sat back down as Dewayne and Vince left. Rick closed his office door behind them and sat across from her.

"I've decided on Grant," he said in clipped tones.

"Are you sure?" Maura asked.

He nodded. "Paige convinced me it's best. I guess she's right." He sighed. "But telling people is going to be damn difficult. I need to talk to Vince first." He looked at Maura. "Don't rush me."

"It's your show, Rick. You call the shots."

CHAPTER 18: MONDAY, MARCH 12

At the weekly officer staff meeting, Rick turned to Maura. "Are we set on the headcount reduction?"

She nodded. "The HR directors are working with each vice president to confirm the best positions to eliminate. We're analyzing workforce demographics to be sure there isn't any statistical evidence of discrimination."

"My staff is drafting severance agreements and waivers of liability," Dewayne said. "We should be ready to talk to employees early next week. But remember, it will be a couple of months before people leave the payroll. It'll take that long to make sure the waivers are valid."

Rick looked around the room. "We need to keep this reduction confidential. I can't emphasize that enough. Maura's and Dewayne's staffs and this room are the only people who've been involved. You've each made the decisions on your group. Don't tell other managers yet. The employees losing their jobs deserve to hear directly from us next week. Not through rumors or the media. Most are good employees. They've contributed a lot to this company. We can't afford to keep our current overhead. It's not their fault."

He waited for the group to nod in acknowledgement.

"We'll have to present the full headcount reduction to the banks Thursday," Alex said. "I'd hoped to hold back a little in reserve, in case Maura and Dewayne found any issues. But we can't. Particularly after the production cost overruns."

Rick adjourned the meeting.

$ $ $

Late Monday Rick walked down the hall to Vince's office, his heart pounding. He hadn't expected to be afraid of telling Vince; he'd rehearsed this meeting in his mind all weekend. Gone over it a thousand times in his head.

All he had to do was tell Vince he was leaving and say Vince wouldn't succeed him. But he didn't know how Vince would react. Would he cuss at Rick? Admit he wasn't CEO material? Plead for a chance at the job?

Rick cared how Vince would react. He'd been Vince's big brother longer than he'd been Vince's boss. He'd protected Vince as a kid. Hell, he'd taught Vince to swing a golf club, then Vince had worked so hard to get better than Rick. And he was. Vince hadn't been worth shit as a football player—too skinny—but he could swing a club better than Rick by the time he started high school.

Rick had been proud of Vince when he tried to make it on the pro circuit. Vince had been the only Players brother with guts enough to walk away from their father. Rick had rooted for him to make it, maybe more than Vince rooted for himself. But he hadn't made it. He hadn't given the game all he had.

And he hadn't given PlayLand all he had either. Vince only went through the motions, looking to Rick to tell him what to do.

Now it's my turn, Rick thought. His shot at doing something outside of PlayLand. And he couldn't leave the company in Vince's hands. So he had to tell Vince he was being passed over. It would be the toughest thing he'd ever done.

He got to Vince's office. "How 'bout a drink?" Rick heard the hearty falseness in his voice, and wondered if Vince heard it, too.

"Heading home for a quick sandwich," Vince said. "My gut hurts like crazy. I should see someone about it, but I hate doctors."

"Come on," Rick said. "We need to talk. We could have a quick one at your place."

Vince shrugged, and gathered up his belongings.

Rick drove behind Vince to his townhouse. Once inside, Vince opened the refrigerator. "Beer?" he asked.

"Sure." Rick took the Coors Vince handed him. The brothers sat in the living room, staring out the picture window at the snow-covered golf course.

"Won't be long before I'm driving off that tee," Vince said.

"That'll be good." Rick gulped his beer. "I have some news. I wanted to tell you first," he said in a rush. "I'm stepping down as CEO."

"You're what?" Vince's voice cracked.

"I don't want to work at PlayLand anymore."

"Jesus!" Vince slammed his bottle down on the coffee table. "We spent three goddamn weeks muddling along while you were out of it. Now you're walking away?"

"I can't do it."

"Why the hell not?"

"I don't care. Not like I used to. It doesn't feel important."

"You don't care." Vince got up and paced the room. He turned to Rick. "You don't care. Well, what about all the people who rely on you? Don't you care about them? We need you."

Rick sighed. "That's what makes it hard. I've given this a lot of thought."

"A lot of thought? Hell, you've only been back two weeks." Vince's face turned brick red.

"I wanted to leave even before the accident. Who knows? Maybe that's why I got hurt. Trying to find a way out of being trapped."

"Trapped? Don't go all psycho on me. No wussy shrinko stuff. Tough it out. It's just some midlife crisis or something. You don't need to leave."

Rick looked at his brother, who still paced the room. "I do need to leave. And I'm going to."

"Well, who the hell's going to run PlayLand?" Vince shouted.

"Grant. That's what I wanted to tell you."

As Rick spoke, he watched Vince crumple into an old man. His face went from red to white, his mouth etched into a thin line. He sagged into his paunch and lost two inches in height. "Grant." Vince's voice was flat. "You don't want me?"

"We never said you would succeed me."

"No. But I always assumed. Someday."

"And maybe you'd be ready someday, Vince. But today Grant has more experience."

"He's only been at PlayLand for what? Eight or nine years?"

"Something like that."

"What's he have that I don't?"

"He's done a great job in Operations. His people love him. He's decisive."

"And I'm not?"

Rick shook his head.

"I dealt with Gus."

"Yes. And did a good job."

"Grant's not family."

"I know that," Rick said. "Believe me, I've thought about family. This isn't easy."

"You're passing me over for Grant."

Rick nodded.

"Can't you stay and teach me?"

"Is that really what you want, Vince?"

Vince shrugged. "I don't know. I always thought someday . . . ."

Rick sighed. "I'm getting out now. For my own sanity. But I'll give you time before we announce anything."

"Goddamn. I never thought it would end like this."

"End?"

Vince waved his hand. "The family. Running PlayLand."

"The family isn't ending. We still own PlayLand. You'll still run Product Development, and I'll stick around as Chairman."

"It won't be the same," Vince said.

$ $ $

Rick left, and Vince stared out the window. The fairway was in deep shadows now. He could barely see the trees against the snow. His stomach churned. Forget about a sandwich.

It was over. Rick was walking away from PlayLand, leaving Vince behind. Who the hell did Rick think he was? Abandoning the family like that. Christ, Vince thought. He'd tried to get away from PlayLand. Been sucked back in by Rick and their father. Now Rick was leaving? Not fair.

What the hell would happen without Rick? Rick had kept them all together. Through their father's decline. Through the crappy business downturn. How could PlayLand survive?

Grant to replace Rick. And not a damn thing Vince could do about it. Rick controlled most of PlayLand's shares. If Vince didn't go along, Rick could dump him as a director. Appoint someone else who'd elect Grant. Making a stink wouldn't change anything.

Vince drank another beer and stewed about the mess Rick had

dumped on him. He had no choice. He had to go along. But he didn't have to like it. He didn't have to feel good about being passed over by his own brother.

As Vince thought, he realized his stomach had relaxed. In fact, he might be hungry. He didn't have to worry about replacing Rick. Rick had taken that decision out of Vince's hands.

He made himself a sandwich and turned his mind to more pressing problems. Gus and Ben. He'd probably have to fire Ben, Vince thought. He'd never fired anyone before. He'd been able to transfer problem employees out of his department before they had to be fired. But he hadn't been able to transfer Ben. Rick hadn't let him.

What did he have to show for his years at PlayLand? A wrecked marriage, a daughter lost to him, an ulcer at age forty-six. As he ate his sandwich, Vince worked himself into a serious case of self-pity that only another drink could help.

The doorbell rang as he mixed a gin and tonic. He opened the door. "Ben," he said. "What are you doing here?" Vince held the door in his left hand, his right hand braced on the frame.

Ben stepped forward, forcing Vince to step back from the doorway. "I was in the neighborhood. Wanted to follow up on our conversation," Ben said entering the foyer. "It really got to me. I can't believe Gus's claiming I stole from him. I can't let it rest. Can we talk?"

Vince hesitated. He was still keyed up after Rick's bombshell, and he didn't want to talk to Ben. But it would be churlish to refuse. "Okay. Want a gin and tonic? Or a beer?"

"Gin's fine." Ben followed Vince into the living room and sat on the couch while Vince fixed the drink. "Great view. Do you watch the pro tournament from your deck?"

"I had a group over last summer," Vince said.

Ben sat with his arm along the back of the couch and seemed ready to make small talk all evening. Cool as always.

After handing Ben the gin, Vince sat in a chair across from the couch with his own drink. "What can I do about Gus tonight?" he asked.

Ben's eyebrows were furrowed, his mouth practically pouting. "I feel like the victim," he said. "I'm asking you, as my boss, what can

I do? You showed me one drawing. What else did Gus tell you? What's he accusing me of? Do I need a lawyer?"

Vince started to speak, but Ben interrupted. "I'm not upset at you or PlayLand. You gotta do what you gotta do. But Gus is pissing me off, and I want to know my rights. I'm thinking of filing a grievance against Gus."

Vince shook his head. "Just let it play out, Ben."

"Are you saying I have nothing to worry about?"

Vince squinted at Ben. Did the guy want a commitment? "I can't tell you anything, Ben. These things take time."

"I don't have time, Vince." Ben leaned forward, elbows on knees, and shook the ice in his glass. "The comic books are out. Action figures in production. I don't want a cloud hanging over my head. This should be the highest point in New Ventures history. I have a winner, and Gus is stealing the credit."

Vince stared at Ben in amazement. "You think you should get credit for the action figures?"

Ben sat back smiling. "I'm the one who saw its potential. Sure, Gus dreamed up the characters, but I'm the one who ran with it."

"And Jennifer?"

"This was a New Ventures project. Jennifer horned in at the last minute. I'm not saying she didn't contribute, but I led the charge."

Vince stared into his glass. "Some people don't see it that way."

Ben stood up. "See, that's what I mean," he said, gesturing with his glass. "What are people saying? Who thinks I don't deserve credit?" Ben loomed over Vince, making him feel uncomfortable in his own home.

"Well, Gus, obviously," Vince said. "And Dewayne."

"Where does Rick stand?"

Vince looked back at his glass. "You and Rick go back a long way. He wants to be sure you get a fair shake."

Ben snorted. "Well, praised be small favors. What does that mean?"

"We need to know how far you took this thing with Gus," Vince said hesitantly.

"What do you mean, how far I took it?"

"Did you take his drawings for your story line or not?"

Ben slammed his glass on the coffee table. Now the table would be dented, Vince thought. "Hell! I told you I didn't take his fucking file. Do you believe me or that paranoid twerp?"

Vince shrunk back in his chair. "I compared the story you did with Gus's drawing. They're very similar."

Ben strode across the room and looked out the window. "I told you I didn't copy Gus's drawing. Maybe I saw it, but I didn't have it when I worked with the freelancer." Ben walked back and sat on the couch, visibly trying to stay in control, but his hand shook, like it had at lunch. "What else does Gus have on me? Don't I deserve to know the whole story? Were there other drawings?"

Vince paused. How much should he tell Ben? Then he nodded.

"Can I see them?" Ben asked.

Vince went to his briefcase and pulled out the file Gus had given him. He handed it to Ben.

Ben thumbed through it, then looked up. "Would you believe me if I said I'd never seen these before?" His voice was taut.

Vince shrugged. "I don't know what to believe."

Ben picked up his drink, took a slug, and set the glass down. "Has Rick seen this?"

Vince shook his head.

"Are you going to show it to him?"

"If he asks."

"Is this everything?" Ben seemed calm, but the tremor in his hand was enough to shake the papers he held.

"Everything Gus gave me," Vince said. "I don't know what else he has."

Ben stood, still holding the file. "Can I take it? I want to compare it to what the freelancer drew. You'll get it back tomorrow."

Vince stood also. "I can't let you take it, Ben." He held out his hand for the file.

Ben ignored him, and headed for the door. "I said I'd give it back, and I will," he said over his shoulder.

Vince lunged, grabbing for the file. "Give it to me, Ben, or this is the last straw."

Ben shoved him, and Vince fell. Vince seized Ben's ankle and pulled him to the floor as well. The papers in the file spewed across the room.

Vince was taller and younger, but Ben was in better shape. Vince wasn't a brawler, and Ben had been an offensive lineman. They struggled and punched, grappling on the floor.

Vince kneed Ben in the groin. Ben threw a right hook into Vince's jaw. Vince saw stars. He broke away from Ben and struggled to his feet. Ben came after him and punched him in the gut. Vince doubled over. Ben threw him against the fireplace.

Vince's head hit the mantle. He went down.

$ $ $

Vince didn't move. Ben slapped his face—hard. "Wake up, Vince." No response.

He checked for a pulse. None.

He listened to see if Vince was breathing. Nothing.

Ben worked over Vince, slapping him. No response.

Dead.

Ben sat back heavily on the carpet. Jesus, he hadn't meant to hurt Vince. All he ever wanted was to fit in, to be part of Rick's world. That's all.

Now here he was on Vince's living room floor, and Vince was dead. Furniture and papers everywhere.

What should he do? This wasn't his fault, Ben screamed to himself. He'd been pissed at Gus and Vince, but he hadn't meant to hurt anyone. Christ, he'd left his gun in the car. That showed he hadn't planned to hurt anyone. He'd only hit Vince a few times. Vince came after him first.

Ben picked up his drink off the coffee table and downed the contents.

He stood slowly, looking at the glass in his hand. He took it to the bar, poured some gin straight, and drank it down. Then he washed the glass, dried it with paper towels, and, holding the glass with the paper towels, returned it to the shelf above the bar with others like it. He wiped down the gin bottle as well.

Ben gathered the drawings on the floor and put them back in the file Vince had handed him. With more paper towels, he wiped everything he thought he'd touched. He stuffed the towels in his pocket and took the file. He walked out the front door, wiped the inside and outside knobs with a towel, and got in his car.

He glanced back at Vince's house, then drove off. This wasn't his fault.

CHAPTER 19: TUESDAY, MARCH 13

Tuesday morning Kevin gave himself permission to stop for a tall mocha latte—after all, he'd been to the gym Monday evening. Now he sipped the infusion of caffeine and sugar on the drive to work. And caught himself smiling as he recalled his date the week before with Jennifer. If it had been a date.

Still smiling, he strode into the building. After he settled into his office, he sorted through his inbox. He started to whistle, but stopped himself with a glance at his open office door. No need for people to wonder why he was so happy.

Around nine his assistant Robin stuck her head in his office and said, "I just had a call from Deanna, Vince's assistant. Vince hasn't shown up. Doesn't answer his phone. And his schedule's full today."

"I don't know where he is," Kevin said. "I haven't talked to him since yesterday."

"Deanna wants to know what to do."

Kevin shrugged. "Vince is a big boy. Give him a while." He turned back to his paperwork.

At eleven thirty Robin and Deanna both appeared in Kevin's doorway. "Hate to bother you," Deanna said, "But Vince still isn't here. Can't get him on his home or cell phone. Rick's busy, so I came to you."

Kevin frowned. Even if he was sick, Vince should have called. "Okay," he said. "I'll take an early lunch and swing by his house. But if he's not there, I don't know what I can do."

When Kevin got to Vince's townhouse, he rang the bell. No answer. He tried the knob. Locked. He smiled, remembering Mom telling them to keep a spare key hidden. He searched, found

Vince's spare in a flowerpot on the front porch, and opened the door.

"Vince?" No answer. He walked through the entry and into the living room.

Vince was sprawled on the floor by the fireplace. Kevin rushed to his brother and shook him. "Vince," he said, "Wake up."

Vince's body was cold, but Kevin shook him again. There was blood by Vince's head, but surely not enough to hurt him. Maybe he was knocked out. In a coma, like Rick had been.

Kevin dialed 911.

Then he called Rick, told Mary to interrupt Rick's meeting. "Get over to Vince's house," Kevin told Rick. "Something's wrong." He wouldn't tell Rick any more. If he said more, it might make it true.

Within a few minutes, paramedics and police arrived, sirens blaring. "He's been dead for several hours," the paramedic said.

Dead? Vince was dead? Kevin heard a roaring in his head, felt a fist in his gut. He sat. Vaguely, he heard voices talking about abrasions on Vince's face and hands and chest. "Looks like a fight," someone said. "Know anything about that?"

Kevin shook his head. Fight? Vince never fought.

The police outlined Vince's body with yellow masking tape. About that time Rick arrived.

The police banished Rick and Kevin to the kitchen and questioned them about when they had last seen Vince. "Last night. I was here with him last night," Rick said, looking as bad as Kevin felt. Kevin wondered what his brothers had talked about.

They watched and listened as the police searched the house and dusted for fingerprints. "Does anything look out of place?" a policeman asked.

The townhouse looked like no one spent much time in it; only Vince ever did. One of the bedrooms at Vince's house was furnished for his eight-year-old daughter, but she didn't visit her dad often. Now she never would, Kevin realized.

One officer brought a piece of paper over to Kevin and Rick. "Recognize this?" he asked. "I found it behind a chair."

"It's a drawing of one of PlayLand's new products," Kevin said.

"Have you seen it before?"

"Can't say. I've seen so many of them."

"Who has access to these drawings?"

"Lots of people. Me," Kevin said. "Jennifer Scott. Gus Powell. Ben Thornton. Several other product managers. The freelance artists who worked with us."

"Who might have seen this drawing?"

"Any of them. We all saw lots of drawings. Jennifer, Gus or Ben might know more." Kevin gave their titles and phone numbers to the officer. "Can I take the drawing back to PlayLand?" he asked. "Someone might need it."

"No, sir. It's evidence. You can come to the station for a copy."

Rick said very little while Kevin talked to the police. He responded only when asked a direct question. Because of their age difference, the three brothers were not close friends. But Kevin could tell Rick was taking Vince's death hard. Maybe it was Vince's violent end. Maybe it was Rick's own recent near death.

Kevin had thought nothing could be as bad as Rick's coma, but this was worse. He'd lost a brother.

$ $ $

Maura's office phone rang midafternoon Tuesday. "Vince is dead," the caller said.

The words were so unexpected that for a moment she couldn't place the voice. Then her mind kicked in as her stomach rose to her throat. "Kevin? Is this Kevin? Oh, my God. Your brother Vince?"

"Yes." Kevin's voice sounded far away. "The police say he was beaten to death."

"Beaten? You're kidding."

Kevin was silent.

Maura closed her eyes as she realized what she had said. How stupid! "Sorry. Oh, my God, I'm so sorry. You wouldn't kid about this. What happened?"

"Don't know. Happened last night. He didn't show up for work today. I went to his house around noon. I found him. Dead. By the fireplace." Kevin took in a long, shuddering breath and expelled it slowly. "I'm still at his house."

"Oh, Kevin, how awful! Any idea who did it?"

"No."

"Does Rick know?"

"Yes. He was here, too. I called him. He just left to go tell Vince's ex-wife and daughter. Tina's only eight. Rick's pretty shaken up himself. I don't know how he's going to tell Tina."

"You must be upset, too. Anyone would be. How awful for the little girl. And for Rick." Maura closed her eyes, remembering when she had had to tell Liz and Rafe about her father's death. "What can I do?" she asked Kevin.

"Can you tell people in the office? Vince's staff. And spread the word. I don't know what's best. I'm not thinking straight."

"Okay. I'll meet with the officers and Vince's staff. And get something out to employees."

"I don't know what to tell them. Quite the communications guy, huh?" Kevin's laugh sounded like a sob. "Watch the TV news, so we can tell employees at least what's public knowledge."

"Kevin, don't worry about it. Just take care of yourself and Rick. I'll deal with folks here." She made sure he had her cell phone number and told him to stay in touch.

Maura hung up and dropped her head to her hands. Déjà vu, like the day of Rick's accident, but so much worse. She hadn't had much use for Vince as a colleague, but he didn't deserve to be killed in his own living room.

She walked over to Vince's office and first talked to Vince's assistant. Deanna burst into tears, and Maura sent her home.

Then she told Rick's assistant. "Mary," Maura asked, "would you keep an eye on Vince's and Rick's offices? And call an emergency officers' meeting in fifteen minutes. I'll tell Vince's staff right after that."

For the next ten minutes, Maura sat at her computer writing a statement to discuss with the officers and to read to Vince's staff. She had her assistant Kay call the Employee Assistance Program to get a counselor at PlayLand by four o'clock to meet with employees.

Printed copies of her statement in hand, Maura rushed to the executive conference room. Only Alex and Dewayne showed up. "Grant's in the plant," she heard. "Don't know about Leo."

Her hands shook as she told them Vince had been murdered. The local news had reported a death in Vince's condominium complex, but the name of the victim had not yet been released. Her peers reacted with shock.

"I'll cancel the bank meeting Thursday," Alex said. "Rick'll need time."

"I hadn't thought about that," Maura said. "I doubt Rick or Kevin have either."

She gave copies of her notes to her colleagues, and asked them to tell their staffs in half an hour. "I need to meet with Vince's staff before you say anything," she told them.

By the time Maura got to the Product Development conference room, rumors of Vince's death had spread. She could tell by the hush as she walked down the hall. Maura had never had to report a murder of an employee before. She didn't know how Vince's staff would react.

They took it hard. Jennifer dropped into a chair, her face turning white. Even Ben looked shaken. Maura asked them to read her statement to their departments as quickly as possible, and offered herself and her staff to talk to the employees. "And the Employee Assistance Program will be here at four. Encourage people to attend the EAP session, or send them home if they prefer."

Maura wandered through Product Development after the meeting. As word spread, there were sounds of weeping throughout the division. Vince had not been a strong leader, but employees thought he was a nice guy. Violence so close to home was hard to accept. Most people chose to stay at work, to be with others who had known Vince. Enough employees attended the EAP session to fill the largest conference room in the building.

Maura had her assistant keep an eye on the news to see what was reported. All that was public was Vince died of a blow to his head, there were no signs of a break-in, and the police were not saying whether they had any suspects.

$ $ $

Grant was at the Lakeview plant Tuesday afternoon to inspect the injection mold production line. "How's our old machine, Martin?" he asked the plant manager.

"Limping along. Not enough speed to meet production quotas. But it's not overheating. And no more defects." Martin shook his head. "That's all we can hope for."

Back in Martin's office, Grant asked, "How can we get back on track with production?"

"Can't do it with this piece of crap," Martin replied. "I need a new machine. Any money for that?"

Grant shrugged. "I doubt it." His cell phone rang.

It was Karen Heintz. "Have you heard? Vince Players is dead," she said.

"Dead? What are you talking about?"

"It's all over the news. Killed at home. Maybe a robbery, but the cops aren't saying. Maura met with Vince's staff. Jennifer told me. Maura sent an email. Didn't say any more than what's on the Internet."

Grant hung up and turned to Martin. "See what's in your email about Vince."

"Christ, Grant! He's dead," Martin said. He read Maura's message to Grant.

Within fifteen minutes, Martin's assistant had a bulletin on the plant communications monitors. Grant and Martin returned to the production floor. The pall over the workforce was tangible. Employees gave them nervous glances. What more could go wrong at PlayLand?

$ $ $

At the end of the day, Maura called Kevin. He and Rick were at Rick's house, with Paige and Rick's twins. Rick had returned home after talking to Vince's ex-wife and daughter. "We don't know if Tina really understands," Kevin said about Vince's little girl. He asked Maura to stop by on her way home.

When she arrived, Maura saw evidence of tears on everyone's face. The police had questioned Rick, Kevin, and Vince's ex-wife. Kevin told Maura the police were likely to question some of Vince's staff at work the next day. Maura agreed to find a conference room for the interviews and schedule employees to meet with the authorities.

Kevin gave Maura a copy of a drawing. "This was found at Vince's house," he said. "The police don't know if it means anything. They've kept the original for evidence. Would you give it to Jennifer? Someone might need it for the product launch."

Rick motioned Maura into his den as she was leaving.

"Alex postponed the bank meeting," she told him.

He nodded, but seemed distracted. "Don't do anything about the plans we've been discussing," he said. "I don't know what to do. I need to think."

"Of course, Rick," Maura said. She'd wondered what impact Vince's death would have on Rick. Would he change his mind about leaving? Had he talked to Vince? How had Vince reacted? Did it matter, now that Vince was dead?

$ $ $

Rick was alone in his den after everyone had gone. He lit the gas fireplace and poured himself a Scotch. He sat on the couch and gazed into the flames. He sipped his drink slowly and shivered. The fire and the whiskey couldn't warm him.

What had he done? He might have been the last person to talk to Vince. Maybe the last thing Vince had heard was he wasn't good enough. Rick couldn't take back that conversation. No way to tell Vince he was sorry.

Rick heard soft footsteps behind him.

"Come to bed, Rick," Paige said. "It's been a hard day."

"I told him."

"What do you mean?"

"Vince. I told him last night. That he wouldn't be CEO."

"Oh, Rick." She put her arms around him. She was warm.

"He was devastated." Rick exhaled heavily. "Did I do the wrong thing?"

She touched her forehead to his. He felt her shake her head. "No," she said. "You did the right thing. It just feels wrong now."

"I'll never be able to tell him I'm sorry."

"Are you sorry?"

He sighed. "I don't know."

Chapter 20: Wednesday, March 14

Maura delivered the drawing to Jennifer Wednesday morning. "I don't recall seeing it before," Jennifer said, "But it looks like a page from one of the comic books. I'll see if anyone else recognizes it."

"The police will be talking to employees today. People Vince worked with." Maura said. "Is anything strange happening? Anything that might shed light on Vince's death?"

"Other than the whole Ben and Gus thing, no. By the way," Jennifer added, "Gus wasn't at work yesterday."

"Why not?"

"Don't know. Gus reports to Ted. He might have called him. But Gus and I were supposed to meet, and he didn't show up. I assumed he was upset about Vince. Want me to call him?"

"Please," Maura said. "And ask Ted if he's heard from Gus. Was Ben here yesterday?"

"Yes. I try to avoid him." Jennifer shuddered. "But remember? He was there when you told us about Vince's death. That was midafternoon, wasn't it?"

Maura nodded, remembering. After the meeting Ben had asked her if he could help by checking Vince's mail or sorting his files. He'd been more unctuous than usual. Others on Vince's staff had needed to speak with her, so she'd brushed him off.

"Find out what you can about the drawing, and let me know," Maura told Jennifer. "Kevin says it was found at Vince's home."

$ $ $

Jennifer searched for Gus, but the light in his cubicle was off. Ted, Gus's boss, hadn't heard from him. Other employees told her Gus hadn't been around yesterday or today. She called Gus's cell phone. No answer, so she left a message. Thirty minutes later, Gus called her back.

"Where've you been?" she asked. "Have you heard about Vince?"

"I saw it on the police wires. That's why I didn't come to work."

"What?" Jennifer asked. Gus sounded more paranoid than ever. Why was he listening to police wires?

Gus lowered his voice to a whisper. "Ben did this, you know."

"Why on earth would you say that?" Jennifer asked. Gus didn't sound rational.

"To cover up. He stole my drawings."

"What?"

"He took a file from my office. Used my drawings for his story line."

"How do you know that?" Jennifer rolled her eyes. The conversation was getting weirder.

"I thought I lost my file. But Ben admitted he took it. And his story was exactly like my drawings."

"Where's the file now?"

"I gave part to Vince. I've got the rest."

"Can you describe the drawings you gave Vince?" Jennifer picked up the sketch Maura had given her. Gus described several scenes. One sounded like what she held in her hand. "Tell me more," she asked. Even the details matched.

"So which story do you think Ben copied from you?" she asked.

"The third one," Gus said. She pulled a sample comic from a stack on her desk and compared the drawing and the printed version. Very similar.

"Why are you asking?" Gus asked.

"A drawing like what you're describing was found at Vince's house."

"You see," Gus crowed, "Ben did it."

"But you gave the drawing to Vince. That must be why it was at his house."

"Where's the rest of the file?" Gus asked. "Why wasn't this drawing with the others? Ben stole the file before. I'll bet he stole it again. From Vince. And if Vince had it, Ben would kill Vince for it."

"You're jumping to conclusions." He sounded odd, even for Gus. "You'd better get to work. The police are coming to talk to people at PlayLand today. You can tell them whatever you want."

"Is Ben there?"

"I don't know. He was here yesterday."

"Was he acting normal?"

"Nothing's normal, Gus. Vince is dead."

"Did Ben act like he was trying to cover it up?"

"I try not to spend much time with Ben."

"I'm not coming in until the coast is clear," Gus said. "Call me if Ben's gone."

"I'd really like for you to look at this drawing. Just come to work."

"Call me." Gus hung up.

Later that morning, the police interviewed a number of PlayLand employees. Jennifer told them about her conversation with Gus, including his suspicion Ben killed Vince. "But Gus is paranoid," she added.

The two officers exchanged glances. They asked her more about Ben and about Gus.

$$ \$ \, \$ \, \$ $$

Grant worried about the action figure production quotas. The news of Vince's death had slowed work in Operations even more than Rick's accident had.

Vince had worked in Operations early in his career, and was remembered as a wishy-washy supervisor, more concerned about how he looked than about the people who worked for him. Still, there was respect for the Players family and horror at the violent nature of Vince's death. Employees spent their time talking, rather than pushing plastic parts through the machinery.

On Wednesday morning, Grant drove to the main plant to get an update from Martin. "Where are we after revising the production schedule?" Grant asked.

Martin grunted. "Can't get more than eighty percent capacity out of this blasted machine," he said. "Got to run it slower than it's rated for, or it heats up. That and the lost time while it was down mean we'll be hard pressed to stay on schedule. If anyone takes five minutes more on break than planned, we're cooked."

"We can't handle six more weeks like this," Grant said. "Murphy's law says something else will go wrong."

"Then you'd better work with Procurement on other options. I'm doing the best I can." Martin's chin thrust out, and he sounded defensive.

"You're doing wonders," Grant said, frowning. "You fixed the problem, and we're almost back on schedule. But we need some flexibility."

Martin nodded. "I know. I'll tell folks they're doing great."

"No," Grant said. "I'll tell them. I'll walk the floor before I go back to headquarters. I want to see how they're feeling about Vince, too."

"It's a shock." Martin's face was somber. "I never liked the guy, but no one deserves to get beat up in their own living room."

"No kidding." Grant was quiet a moment, then said, "I'll talk to Karen about putting a vendor on standby. Build in some slack."

"Can we send some of the work outside?" Martin asked. "I hate giving work to suppliers, but we've pushed our group as hard as we can. Spring breaks are coming up. I'd like to offer a little vacation time. Current schedule doesn't permit any time off until May."

"You're right." Grant nodded. "It will cost us more to go outside. But I'll take the heat with Finance."

"Besides," Martin said, "I worry about our productivity. While Rick sorts out what happens after Vince's death."

"What do you mean?" Grant asked.

Martin sounded sheepish as he spoke. "People are already asking who'll lead Product Development. Not the line employees. They don't give a shit who's in charge of Product. But the supervisors care. Big changes in Product Development can make our lives hell. Will priorities stay the same? What product quality standards will new management set? How much will they interfere with Operations? The managers here are asking questions I can't answer."

"Well, I don't know either," Grant said, as he stood to leave. "Nothing will change right away. Everyone's focused on the action figure launch. That won't change. But I don't know what comes next."

"I have to tell them something," Martin said.

Grant shook his head. "I'll ask Rick. Or Maura. If they know. But keep folks concentrating on production. Don't let them worry about corporate politics."

After his plant walk-through, Grant headed back to headquarters. When he returned, he called Rick. "So sorry about Vince," Grant began, "What an awful thing. The Operations folks are thinking about you and your family."

"Thanks. We're still working with police. Don't know yet when his body will be released. Probably by the end of the week, after the autopsy." Rick seemed to struggle with the word "autopsy."

"Any word on who did it?"

"Not that the cops are saying. They talked to the family. They're interviewing his staff today. I can't believe anyone at PlayLand would hurt Vince."

"We'll get production back on schedule. We'll have to use outside capacity. Costs'll go up, but we can do it. The plant folks are pulling together."

"Good to hear, Grant. Thanks. Make sure Alex knows the cost implications. We were scheduled to meet with the banks tomorrow, but that's been pushed back to next week."

"Understand, Rick. You need to focus on your family."

"I can't believe how much energy this takes. Sorting through Vince's affairs. Dealing with our feelings. And the authorities keep coming up with more questions. I wonder how we'll get through it."

"I hate to put more problems on your shoulders, Rick, but people are asking who will lead Product Development next."

"Shit, Grant," Rick said. "Are they lining up for Vince's office already?" Rick paused, then continued in a calmer voice. "Sorry. I haven't thought about replacing him yet. His staff will have to hold things together for a while. I'll talk to Maura soon. Tell your folks to hold their frigging horses."

"Sorry. I don't mean to pressure you. I'll tell people it'll take some time."

"Thanks, Grant. And keep Alex updated about costs."

Grant called Alex and gave him rough estimates on production expenses if they sent work out to vendors. Alex was not happy, but conceded the cost overruns could have been worse.

Grant left a message for Karen to offload ten percent of the action figure production for the next six weeks to a vendor, and to send him final cost numbers by the end of the day.

Then he sat at his desk reflecting on the morning. On a whim, Grant walked up to Maura's office. She was in. "Is Rick doing okay?" he asked.

"What do you mean?" Maura sounded cagey.

"I just talked to him. I know this has to be a horrible time. But I was around when he had to hire full-time nursing help for his dad. Even then, he didn't snap at me like he did today."

"Give him time." Maura's eyes softened. "This was his brother. A younger brother. No one expects someone in their forties to die. And murdered. In his own home."

Grant nodded. "I'm getting questions from my managers about who's going to take over Product Development. Ghoulish, I know. Vince only died two days ago. But that's the way people think. They worry about what it means for them. Rick bit my head off when I mentioned it. But we shouldn't let it go too long."

Maura's smile was a thin line. "If you think Operations has questions, you should hear Product Development." She shrugged. "It's natural. But I don't think Rick is ready to talk yet." She gave Grant a piercing look. "What are your thoughts on Vince's replacement?"

"Well, it's not for me to say." Grant was surprised. Maura had never asked him about officer moves in the past.

"You've been around a long time, and Operations works closely with Product Development. Who's ready for the job?"

Grant scowled, thinking. He hadn't expected the question, but he did have opinions. "Of Vince's staff, I'd most like to see Jennifer get the job. Others have been around longer, but she shows the most promise."

He paused and ran through other possibilities beyond Vince's direct reports. "Rick should consider Kevin. He can handle more than his current job. With Vince gone, Rick needs to think about who will succeed him. Kevin could be ready, if Rick takes a few years to groom him."

Maura smiled. "We talked earlier in the year about you being Rick's successor."

Grant dismissed the idea with a wave. "He was in a coma then. Now he has time to decide. Kevin could be a good CEO, with the right experience. Frankly, Kevin would be better than Vince ever would have been."

"Back to Vince's replacement. Anyone other than Jennifer and Kevin?"

"I imagine Rick will have Ben on his list, because of their friendship. But Ben gets no respect from Operations. He'd be a tough sell to everyone but Rick."

Maura lifted an eyebrow without comment.

Grant was suddenly worried. "Are you going to pass what I've said along to Rick?"

"Only if he asks," she replied. "Don't worry. My thoughts are similar to yours. I'd thought of Kevin also. And Jennifer. And I agree with you about Ben."

$ $ $

By four o'clock Wednesday afternoon, Rick wasn't thinking straight. He should go home. Vince's death had walloped him. Not only had he lost a brother, but their last conversation about succession wracked him with guilt.

Rick didn't know what to do. Should he continue with his plans to leave PlayLand and name Grant CEO? Should he stay to get the company through the shock of Vince's death? It felt like he should do penance for hurting his brother right before he died.

Despite Rick's remorse, Vince's death made him realize how uncertain life was. He could be disabled at any time—physically as he had been after his accident, or mentally as his father was. He could die unexpectedly, like Vince. If he wanted to work for the community, now might be his only chance.

He still yearned for some reason to live beyond PlayLand. How much did he owe Vince? The rest of his family? The employees at PlayLand?

As Rick stood staring out at the mountains, someone knocked. Ben entered, crossed the office, and wrapped Rick in a bear hug. "How are you, Rick?"

This was the old friend Rick knew. "It's rough," Rick said, dropping into a chair by the table next to the window. "I keep remembering Vince as a little boy, following me everywhere, like a puppy. He made me so mad. Now all I see is the goofy grin plastered on his face as he trailed behind me."

Ben sat across from Rick. "Damn, Rick. I wish this hadn't

happened."

"Thanks."

"What was Vince working on when he died?" Ben asked. "Anything I can help with?"

Rick shook his head. "Jennifer says the action figure line is under control. Grant has issues with production, but says he can cope. Not much you can do there."

"What about Gus? Has he been found?"

"What do you mean?" Rick didn't know Gus was gone.

"No one has seen him since Vince's death. Maybe he had something to do with it. I saw them together in the parking lot last week. Gus seemed pretty upset."

"Vince told me he'd talked with Gus. He said Gus told him you'd stolen some drawings." Rick looked at Ben more sharply. "Did Vince talk to you?"

Ben looked surprised, but his voice was even as he spoke. "Yeah. At lunch last Wednesday. I told him I hadn't stolen a damn thing. I never saw Gus's damn file." Ben squinted at Rick. "What else did Vince tell you?"

"That's all. Said he would follow up with you. Did he?"

Ben shook his head. "We never talked again after that lunch." Ben paused, then rose. "Well, if there's nothing I can do . . . ."

Rick sighed. He didn't want to deal with Ben now. Sooner or later he would have to decide whether to believe Ben or Gus and whether to keep Ben at PlayLand. But not today. "No, Ben. Thanks for stopping by."

$ $ $

Why that weasel Vince, Ben thought as he left Rick's office. Vince hadn't said he told Rick about Gus's accusations. Whom else had Vince told? Without Vince around, there was no way for Ben to know.

It wasn't his fault Vince had died. It had been an accident. He couldn't let Vince's death bother him now. He had to stay close to Rick, make sure Rick believed him.

He'd have to deal with Gus. Last year he'd decided Gus was his ticket to success. He'd needed a new product line, and Gus's characters were it.

But now Gus was a problem. Gus was fixated on his characters.

Ben couldn't let a nobody like Gus stop him. Not when he was so close to proving himself.

CHAPTER 21: TUESDAY, MARCH 20

The following Tuesday dawned bright and cold. It had snowed over the weekend, and now the ground bore a messy slush that froze at night into a treacherous glaze. Maura went to work early, wanting to beat rush hour traffic and get a few hours of work in before the midmorning funeral for Vince. She wore a navy pantsuit with small gold earrings, conservative attire to show respect for Vince and the Players family. Half the company would probably attend the funeral.

It had been an odd week since Vince's death, probably the oddest of her career. Human Resources managers got jaded at the things they learned about employees. But she'd never dealt with an employee's murder. Once she'd handled a domestic dispute that became work-related when an irate husband came to his wife's office and brandished a pistol. But no one was hurt, and the incident soon was forgotten.

Vince had not been killed at work, and it still wasn't clear whether his death had anything to do with PlayLand. But because he was a Players, everything about Vince was connected to work.

Gus had still not returned. He had called Jennifer a couple of times, but no one had seen him. Jennifer tried to get him to come to work, but he refused. The police had not yet interviewed him, and they, too, were looking for him. The lead detective said he was a "person of interest." If he showed up, his managers were to call the police immediately.

The police interviews of other employees had not raised any connections between Vince's murder and PlayLand, at least not that the detectives had told anyone about. Nevertheless, rumors abounded. Some employees believed Gus had killed Vince. Their only evidence was Gus was such an odd duck. Another camp suspected Ben, but only because they disliked him, not because they had proof. A third group thought it was simply a home robbery. Maura and her staff dealt with the speculation the same way they dealt with other workplace gossip. They told employees to report suspicions through official channels and otherwise keep their mouths shut—advice the employees generally disregarded.

While coaching her staff on how to deal with rumors, Maura had prepared to implement the headcount reduction. She scheduled her HR staff meeting for Tuesday morning before the funeral.

"Are we ready to proceed with the employee conversations tomorrow?" Maura asked.

Petra Terrell, the HR Director coordinating the reduction in force across the company, responded, "As ready as we'll ever be. Got all the documentation from Legal. Coached division heads on how to talk to displaced employees."

"Has Legal signed off on the adverse impact analysis?" Maura asked.

"No race or sex discrimination in any of the divisions," Petra said. "Operations has a potential age discrimination issue. They're terminating proportionally more older workers, but that's because the South Carolina plant has an older population than the other plants. It's all explainable."

"Legal isn't worried?"

Tim Baylor spoke up. "I talked to Dewayne. He's okay with it. As long as we can explain why we're closing the South Carolina plant."

"We're clear on that, aren't we?" Maura asked. "It's the least productive plant."

Tim nodded. "We're fine. Grant and I are headed there tomorrow to handle the closing ourselves. It'll be brutal."

"Any concerns in the other divisions?" Maura asked.

"Leo is still grousing. I'll get him through it," Heather Eaton, who worked with Sales, said.

"Product Development is a problem, because there's no vice president," Sara Matthews, who supported that division, told Maura. "We have the names Vince gave us before he died, but you and I will need to get the Product Directors on board. They still don't know what's happening."

"Set up time with the Product Directors for this afternoon," Maura told Sara. "We should have done the employee communications last week, but we held off because of Vince. Now, it needs to go like clockwork to stay on schedule. The bank meeting is in two days."

"It's a good thing the New Mexico unionization attempt fizzled," Tim said. "We couldn't have handled both that and the headcount reduction."

"You're right." Maura sighed. "Vince's death has been more than enough distraction. The workforce is fragile right now. The next few weeks won't be pretty. Not while employees digest the layoff on top of everything else."

$ $ $

As she expected, the church was full for Vince's funeral. Maura watched the Players family walk in just before the service began. Rick had made no effort to talk to her about leaving PlayLand since the day Vince died. She assumed he planned to stay on as CEO, at least for the time being. She hoped so, employees didn't need another curveball thrown at them.

After the church service, many employees and managers went to the graveside, despite the chilly temperature and muddy cemetery. Maura was surprised to see two of the investigating officers at the funeral and burial services. They wore dark suits and overcoats, and were inconspicuous, except to the few employees who had talked to them.

Maura greeted them and asked why they were there.

"Standard operating procedure," they said.

Toward the end of the graveside service, Maura saw Gus at the fringes of the crowd. She eased over to the police officers and pointed Gus out. The officers moved quickly toward Gus and escorted him away. He went quietly, without any disturbance.

$ $ $

Right after lunch, Maura had a call from Gus. "You turned me in," he said.

"I told the cops who you were," she replied. "What's going on? You haven't been at work for over a week. Do you want to get fired? Ted asked me yesterday whether he should."

"It's too dangerous. Ben's after me."

"Oh, come on." Maura threw her pen on her desk, venting her frustration. A little irritation in her voice might let Gus know how serious the situation was. "What's Ben going to do?"

"He killed Vince," Gus whispered.

"How do you know?"

"The drawings. Vince had my file. Now it's gone."

"So?" Maura asked.

"Those drawings wouldn't mean anything to anyone but Ben. He killed Vince for them."

"Did you tell the police?"

"Of course," Gus answered. "They said they'd talk to him again. That's why I can't come to work. Not until Ben's behind bars."

"Then the police let you go?"

"They don't have anything on me. Ben's the one who did it."

"Gus, I don't want to fire you. But you have to call Ted today. And Jennifer. She needs to talk to you, too. And you need to be back at work by next week. Until then, your time off counts against your vacation. I'm sure you have time saved up."

"Yeah."

"Do you hear me? Will you call Ted? I'll check with him."

"Okay. Ted and Jennifer have always been square with me. It's only Ben I can't trust."

"Just get back here."

Maura hung up and shook her head. Was Gus that valuable to the action figure line, or could they do without him? She would ask Ted and Jennifer. If they didn't need Gus, PlayLand should fire him for abandoning his job. He was no different than the guy suing them in Atlanta.

Maura left Ted and Jennifer a voicemail message. "Let me know when you hear from him. And think about how much you need him. Is he important, or can we fire him?"

$ $ $

On Tuesday afternoon Maura and Sara Matthews met individually with the Product Development Directors, explaining to each that they would need to implement a reduction in force in their groups the following day. "I hate to spring this on you, right after Vince's funeral. But we're meeting with our lenders Thursday.

245

We need to have the headcount reductions underway."

"How were the employees picked?" the directors asked.

"Vince picked them," Maura said. "Legal reviewed his plan."

"Don't we get any say?" Jennifer asked during her meeting.

"Would you have made different choices?"

"No. He knew people's performance better than I thought. But I wish I'd been involved."

Maura nodded. "Vince was under strict instructions to work only with HR. In the other divisions, the VPs will be having the conversations with employees. But you and Sara will have to work together in Product Development."

"Why didn't you tell me about this last week?" Ben asked. "I told you I'd help with whatever Vince had going."

"If I'd asked any one of Vince's staff to handle this, the others would have been upset," Maura told him. "Let's just get it done."

After the meetings with the Product Directors, Maura went to see Alex about the bank meeting.

"I got updated cost figures from Grant," Alex said when she walked into his office. "There's been a five percent cost overrun on two items. We've held to plan on the rest. Not as bad as I thought."

"What about the production schedule?" Maura asked.

"The banks won't care about that, but Grant has an outside vendor who'll take the pressure off Manufacturing."

"We should be okay on headcount as well," Maura said. "We're ready for the conversations tomorrow. It'll be hard, but we'll get through it."

Alex sat back. "If nothing else goes wrong, we can handle Thursday's meeting. We should get the cash we need."

$ $ $

Maura went home late Tuesday night. After meeting with Alex, she had fielded calls from several division heads with questions about their upcoming meetings with employees. Heather told Maura one of the Sales employees to be terminated was on vacation. They agreed Leo and Heather would call that employee Wednesday afternoon.

"I hate to spoil her vacation," Maura said, "But it's important to let her know where she stands."

When Maura got home, she went upstairs to her bedroom and

threw herself on the bed. Carlos was reading in a chair across the room.

"Bad day?" he asked.

"We're implementing the headcount reduction tomorrow. That's why I'm late."

"Rafe's doing homework. Liz said she'd get a ride home from practice."

"I'll say good-night to Rafe." Maura didn't move. "Thanks for handling things here."

"How was the funeral?"

"God. I'd forgotten. That was only this morning." She threw an arm over her face. "The church was packed. Gus Powell was there. So were the cops. They took him in for questioning."

"Still no word on who killed Vince?"

Maura shook her head. "I wonder if we'll ever know."

CHAPTER 22: THURSDAY, MARCH 22

The next two days passed in a blur for Maura. On Wednesday, each vice president and HR director had a full schedule of meetings with individual employees left without positions in the downsized organization.

Late Wednesday afternoon, they held group meetings with employees who would remain at PlayLand. By the end of the day, all headquarters employees knew of the reduction in force. Morale was as dead as Vince Players.

"This never would have happened if old Richard was still here," Maura heard more than once as she roamed the halls.

Early Thursday morning, Rick, Alex, and Maura boarded a leased jet and flew to Chicago for the meeting with their bankers, postponed because of Vince's death. Rick began their presentation with an overview of PlayLand's marketing.

"We developed a sharp new action figure line," he said. "Aimed squarely at preteen boys, and we're getting huge orders. Kids are buying the comic books off the shelves as we speak. Oprah says we're presenting a positive product for boys."

"What kind of staying power will the line have?" one bank executive asked.

"Too early to say," Rick responded. "But there are already orders on eBay for the figures. Collectors are offering above-market prices, even though the first character isn't in the stores yet. Somebody thinks they'll do well."

Alex described PlayLand's finances. "Right now, our revenue is flat to last year, without the action figures. But with current orders, revenue will climb this summer and continue at double digit increases through the rest of the year." He pointed his laser at the

PowerPoint slide. "Not only will we get a bang from the action figures, but we don't see much cannibalization. Increased traffic in the toy stores should yield higher sales of existing product also. Revenue should stay at the higher levels through the middle of next year."

"But you're asking for a long-term commitment from our bank. What's your long-range revenue projected to be?"

"We're planning new characters in the action figure line next year," Rick said. "And more comic books. We can keep the line fresh for several years."

"If consumers keep buying it." The lender scratched his nose. "What about your other products? Board Games have been declining."

"We're working on it," Rick said. "Once the first action figures are in the stores, that's my top priority."

"What about cost overruns? You can't save your way to prosperity, but your costs have been too high this past year."

"You're right," Alex said. "We've made major strides in holding down production costs, even with retooling equipment for the action figures. But the big thing is our focus on payroll. Maura?"

Maura described the headcount reduction in detail. "Here's a graph showing the percentage reduction in each of our divisions," she said. "Both headcount and payroll dollars. It totals ten percent of payroll. We announced the cuts at headquarters yesterday. Impacted employees will be off the payroll by mid-May. Today, our VP of Operations is in South Carolina announcing our plant there will close in three months. By midyear, this reduction will be fully implemented."

"What about severance costs?" One of the bankers had his calculator out. "You won't see the savings until the end of the year at best."

"You're right," Maura said. "But you asked about long-term plans. Long term, this is the best thing we could do for the health of the business."

"Let me give you the cash flow projections for the rest of the year," Alex said. He talked through a slide demonstrating the short-term need for cash, and the long-term benefit of reducing PlayLand's cost structure. "And that's why we need the increase in our line of credit," he concluded.

At the end of the meeting, the banks agreed to increase PlayLand's line of credit to thirty million. The interest rate was a quarter point higher than they had hoped for, but "We can afford it," Alex said on the flight home. The trip back to Lakeview was much more relaxed than the morning trip to Chicago.

Rick was silent for most of the return trip. He drank his Scotch quietly, while she and Alex debriefed the meeting. It was nearly dark when they landed, and Maura looked forward to relaxing at home.

"Come have a drink with me, Maura," Rick asked, and she nodded.

Maura drove behind Rick to a small bar near the airport. Over their drinks—another Scotch for Rick and a glass of Chardonnay for Maura—they rehashed the bank meeting again.

"It went better than I expected," Maura said. "They seemed pleased by our cost cutting. And I think they like the new product line."

Rick nodded, toying with his glass. "I hope so. We need their funding." He blew out a deep breath. "I want to proceed."

"Proceed with what?"

"Naming a successor. I've been thinking since Vince was killed." He shook his ice, then gulped his drink. "You know, I talked to him."

Maura hadn't known. "How did he take it?" she asked.

"Hurt. It was the last conversation we had before he died. I'll never forget it." Rick grimaced, then looked Maura straight in the eye. "My head isn't in the game," he said. "Vince dying didn't change anything. I hated being at the meeting today. I hate driving to work each morning. The company needs a CEO who's fully engaged. I can't do it."

Maura sighed. "I'd hoped you'd think differently. Are you sure?" she asked, frowning at Rick. "Once you go public, you can't go back. Even as a family member, it'd be hard to change your mind."

"I know."

"You still want Grant to be your successor?" Maura asked.

"You still think he's the best candidate?"

She nodded. "He knows the company. He's a strong leader. He'll need some help, but I think the staff will support him."

"Who's the weakest link among the other officers?" Rick asked.

"Leo," Maura said without hesitating. "He's so negative, and Sales has always pushed back on Operations. Leo and Grant see the world very differently."

"Any other concerns?"

"You need to decide who will succeed Vince in Product Development, and Grant in Operations. And you need to decide what to do about Ben. It's not fair to make Grant or Vince's successor clean up the mess Ben has made."

"Who should run Operations and Product?"

"Move Kevin to Product Development."

Rick raised an eyebrow. "Why? He's doing great where he is."

"Yes. But you should prepare him to follow Grant as CEO. Kevin has great potential, he just needs experience. With you and Grant to groom him, he could be ready when Grant leaves." Maura looked at Rick. "You're still planning to be Chairman?"

Rick nodded. "I can't let the business get too far away from the family. I might bring in some outside directors also. We could benefit from external perspectives." He was silent, staring down at his glass. When he looked back at Maura, he said, "Okay, let's play with Kevin at Product. What about Marketing and Communications?"

Maura lifted one shoulder. "That's less important than Product. The more important question is what you intend to do with Ben."

Rick sighed. "Ben's lost all credibility, hasn't he?"

"Frankly, yes. And you'll lose credibility, too, if you keep him." She tapped her finger on the table for emphasis. "And you'd give Kevin a lion he can't control if Ben reports to him. At the very least, Ben will keep coming to you, instead of working through Kevin. And worst case, Ben's lack of ethics will get this company into hot water. We're damn lucky we worked out a deal with Gus." She paused. "You know Gus thinks Ben killed Vince?"

"He doesn't have any proof!" Rick slammed his glass down.

"No. But half our employees think so poorly of Ben they're willing to believe he did it." Maura smiled wryly. "The other half think Gus probably killed Vince."

Rick sat silently, so Maura did, too. When a group of men at the bar shouted, Rick glanced at the basketball game on television. Then he looked at Maura. "Okay." He took a deep breath. "How do we get rid of Ben?"

Part of Maura wanted to tell Rick to kick Ben's ass out on the street, but she was afraid Rick would balk at treating his old friend that way. "Shall I put together a severance package for us to discuss?"

Rick shrugged. "Do what you think is right."

"Can I talk to Dewayne? I'd like his perspective on how much trouble Ben has caused. That'll make a difference on how generous we should be."

"Okay. But don't talk to anyone other than Dewayne. Keep it quiet."

Maura nodded. "All right. What about a successor in Operations?"

Rick shook his head. "I've had enough. I'll get Grant's input after I talk to him. But I'm not ready yet."

$ $ $

Grant and Tim spent Thursday at the plant in South Carolina. The small cardboard manufacturing facility was off I-26 between Columbia and Greenville, an area long known for lumbering and paper mills. PlayLand had bought the plant twenty years earlier. At the time, the Board Games line was growing, and PlayLand needed all the printing capacity it could find. Now Board Games were passé, and Asian companies could print product more cheaply. PlayLand could no longer afford domestic printing.

Grant and Tim had chartered a plane to South Carolina and met with the plant manager, Sam Dixon, Wednesday evening. Sam was stunned to hear his plant would close in ninety days. "We have two hundred fifty people here. And their families. What are we going to tell them? There aren't any other jobs in the community. Not that pay good money."

"I know, Sam." Grant said. "I hate it. But we can't afford the plant. We might have a few jobs available at our other locations, but they'll have to move to New Mexico or Colorado. And it'll be new work. We're not going to make games in the U.S. anymore."

"What about severance?"

"One week's pay per year of service and continued health

benefits for the same time. Two weeks per year of service for the managers. Some on-site outplacement for everyone over the next few months until we turn off the lights. That's what PlayLand has done in other situations."

"Does Rick Players know about this?"

Grant nodded. "He approved it." Grant didn't tell Sam he had fought the decision, and had only acquiesced when Rick declared it necessary. Now he had to support the company without wavering.

Just like Sam supported the company Thursday morning. When Grant and Tim told the first shift employees the plant would close, Sam stood by Grant stiffly and silently with tears in his eyes. Sam's determination to be a good corporate citizen almost brought Grant to tears as well.

Grant and Tim met with small groups of employees throughout the day. Repeatedly, Grant was asked, "Why is PlayLand doing this to us?"

"It's business," Grant said. "For the company to survive, we need to produce our toys and games at the lowest cost possible. This plant is no longer the lowest cost producer."

"Then you're sending our jobs to China?" someone asked.

"If the Chinese can make a quality product for less money, that's what we have to do. Even with shipping costs, Asian companies are cheaper. Our suppliers are doing the same thing to us. And Toy Mart and other retailers are squeezing us every day."

It was a good thing the South Carolina plant didn't make action figures, because not much product got made that day. Emotions were too raw.

Tim planned to stay through Friday to answer questions and line up outplacement services. Grant stayed for the start of the night shift. The South Carolina plant only ran two shifts, which was one reason it was unprofitable—the equipment sat unused for eight hours a day and two days a week.

Once he made the announcement to the night shift, Grant went to the airport and flew through the dark back to Lakeview. He drank a stiff Scotch on the plane, then another.

Grant remembered his own job loss ten years earlier when the company where he'd worked had been bought out. No role for him in the new organization. Shortly thereafter his first wife was diagnosed with cancer. The roughest year of his life. He understood how the employees in South Carolina felt. All PlayLand could do was try to help them through the transition.

He arrived home well after midnight, dropped his clothes on the closet floor, and crawled into bed next to Linda's warmth.

$$$

Rick found Paige when he got home. "I'm going ahead with it."

"With leaving PlayLand?"

"Stepping down, yes. I told Maura."

Paige sighed and touched his cheek. "What's next?"

"I need to talk to Kevin. Before anyone else. I want the family together on this, if possible."

"You'd better be convinced this is right for you. Whatever Kevin says. If you're not sure, don't do it."

CHAPTER 23: FRIDAY, MARCH 23

On Friday morning, Rick called an impromptu meeting of his staff. "Tell us about the plant closing," he asked Grant.

Grant gave a brief summary, ending with, "It was brutal. One of the worst things I've ever done as a manager."

"You did what needed to be done," Rick said. "Managing in tough times is hard." He looked around the room. "You're all doing a great job." Rick seemed at ease; Maura didn't notice any of the angst he had shown in the bar on Thursday evening.

Rick continued, "Now here's a recap of our meeting with the banks. Thanks to Alex and Maura—really, to all of you—we had a great story to tell. The analysts were impressed with the product launch and our cost reductions. We got the expanded line of credit. That gives us some breathing room. But the next several months won't be easy. We have to hold the line on costs. And make sure the action figures sell."

"And morale is miserable after the downsizing," Maura said. "Grant told you about South Carolina. The rest of the company is reacting the same way. The employees who lost their jobs will be around for the next few weeks. Be sensitive to how they're feeling. And we need to keep the other employees engaged. That means lots of communication. Let them know how important their work is."

"Everything comes back to communication for you HR types," Leo said. "Aren't we ever done talking?"

"No," Maura said. "Employees need to hear from their managers. No matter what. They only know what they hear from their supervisors. And supervisors only know what we tell them."

"We need every employee focused," Alex said. "Our financial

problems aren't fixed. The credit line is a Band-Aid. Now we have a little cash to draw on. But it's expensive cash. Our interest is one hundred fifty basis points above prime. Make sure we need each nickel before we spend it. And I want to pay down the line as quickly as we can. Otherwise, the interest expense will kill us."

"Let's get through the product launch," Rick said. "Consumer polls on the comics are great. Wonderful feedback. Kids are clamoring for our action figures now. So get those suckers into stores on schedule."

It sounded like Rick's head was still in the game. Maybe he'd change his mind. Or at least delay his departure. Maura smiled. Or maybe that was wishful thinking on her part.

"We're on schedule now," Grant said. "I have a vendor helping, and internal production is set through spring. We'll ship product by the first of June."

Rick thanked his staff for their support through Vince's death. "I know people want to know how I'll replace Vince. I'm working on it. When I've made a decision, you'll be the first to know. In the meantime, just keep making toys. We're turning the business around, but we're not done yet."

As the officers left the meeting, Maura heard Rick ask Kevin to meet him that evening. Rick stopped Maura as she walked out. "I'm going to talk to Kevin and Grant soon," he said. "Would you put together salary increases for them? Kevin for Product and Grant for my role."

Maura mentally kicked herself. "Sorry. I should have thought of that. How high are you willing to go?" she asked.

"Whatever you think is fair."

"Can I talk to Ed Horton on my staff? He has our executive compensation salary surveys."

"No. No one else involved. Give me your best estimate."

"I'd do a better job with Ed's input."

"This has to stay quiet until I'm ready to go public."

"Okay." Maura paused. "And what about your pay?"

Rick smiled. "That's fair. Do one for me as Chairman, too. We sure as hell don't need to pay two CEOs around here."

$ $ $

Maura met with Dewayne later on Thursday, behind closed

doors in Dewayne's office. As usual, Dewayne's office was pristine—no papers on his desk, no files on the credenza. Maura wondered how he got anything done without visible paperwork.

"I've talked with Rick about Ben," she said. "I don't see how we can keep him here. No one supports him. It's difficult for Rick, but we have to help him get rid of Ben. I think Rick'll agree to let Ben go, if we offer him some severance."

"You've heard the rumors Ben killed Vince, haven't you?" Dewayne asked.

Maura smiled, glad to know Dewayne could gossip like everyone else. "Yes, but there's no proof. The cops aren't saying anything. No indication they even suspect him. They must not have any evidence other than what Gus says."

"They met with Ben for a long time last week."

"Yeah, but there's been no follow-up. Have you talked with the investigating officers?"

Dewayne nodded, leaning back in his chair and crossing his arms across his belly like a ponderous Buddha. "I asked earlier this week whether Ben was a suspect. They wouldn't say."

"Before we pay him to leave, can you call again? They'll probably say more to a lawyer than to me. Obviously, if he killed Vince, we don't want to pay him severance."

"I'll call the prosecuting attorney, not the cops. I know him from some bar activities." Dewayne shook his head. "Hard to believe Ben would have killed his golden goose. But I'm with you. I don't want to pay him off, then find out he murdered Vince."

"I'm thinking of a pretty minimal severance offer," Maura said. "But I don't know how Rick will react if we lowball it. Ben's his friend."

"Maybe you give Rick a range. Let him decide," Dewayne suggested. "Show him the minimum—though it still sticks in my craw to pay him anything—up to what we offered the downsized employees."

Maura thought about Dewayne's proposal. "We've been more generous to director-level employees in the past," she said. "But I think we can persuade Rick it wouldn't be right to pay Ben more than what we're paying good employees whom we just laid off."

Dewayne said, "Okay. Tell Rick I say no higher than the

downsizing package, and better if we keep it lower. We can defend any legal claims Ben might try. He admitted he took Gus's drawings initially, even if he's denying Gus's latest accusations." Dewayne paused. "Say, do you know how Rick's going to replace Vince?"

"I don't think he's decided yet," Maura said. Rick had specifically said not say anything to anyone.

"You're sure he hasn't thought of offering Ben the job?" Dewayne asked, leaning forward. "We don't want a paper trail showing Rick wanted to promote Ben, but we fired him."

"Rick would have told me if he wanted Ben for Product," Maura said. "He knows we're talking about firing Ben."

Dewayne sat back. "Well, that's a relief." He tore off the page of notes he had taken during their conversation and stuck it in his folder. "Got time for another topic?"

"Sure," Maura said, picking up her file on Ben.

"I'm hearing more rumors from New Mexico. About the union."

"What rumors?" Maura asked.

"An anonymous letter sent to Legal today. It says employees are still talking to the union rep. Faxed from a New Mexico phone number."

Maura sniffed. "What credence can you put in an anonymous letter?"

Dewayne shrugged. "Just wanted you to know. It mentions yesterday's South Carolina plant closing. Whoever wrote it knew about that closing already."

"Send me a copy. I'll get Tim to look into it."

"Sure." Dewayne wrote himself a note.

"Does Grant know?" Maura asked. "He'll say he was right about the plant closing increasing union activity."

"Not yet, but I'll tell him. I don't have much faith in that plant manager down there. What's her name?"

"Alice Sorenson. I don't have much faith in her either," Maura said, "particularly if the situation escalates. Tim's in South Carolina now, coming home tonight. Let me talk to him, and see if he can get to New Mexico next week."

$ $ $

Before she left for the day, Maura looked up Vince's salary as

Vice President of Product Development and calculated a pay increase for Kevin that split the difference between his pay as Vice President of Marketing and Communications and Vince's final pay.

The increase for Grant was more complex. She really needed a market survey of CEO salaries at companies of PlayLand's size, but she didn't have any recent surveys. Grant shouldn't make as much starting out as CEO as Rick made after several years in the role. She looked up Rick's salary history. She aged his starting CEO figure for inflation, compared it to Grant's current salary, and developed a range she thought was appropriate. Let Rick decide.

She called Rick. "Here's what I have. Take Kevin's base pay up ten to fifteen percent. That's a hefty increase. We'll adjust his pay again during the next salary review cycle."

"And Grant?"

"That's tougher. There's a pretty wide range you could consider. He'll be playing at a whole new level, so I'd say start at the low end. I suggest a twenty percent increase in base pay. But his incentive pay is what I'm most concerned about."

"Why's that?"

"Well, we haven't worried about your incentive plan, because you get more income from dividends than incentive. But Grant won't have that. I'm assuming you don't want to issue him stock. If you do, we'll need Dewayne's involvement on the legal issues."

"No stock. Why can't we continue his current incentive plan for the rest of this year?"

"CEOs get a bigger percent of pay in incentives than VPs. And don't you want Grant measured on the whole company's performance, rather than Operations?"

"Yes."

"Then we need to come up with new metrics. And we should take the target value of his incentive up by at least twenty percent. Probably thirty."

"Seems steep."

"As I said, I'd like to talk to Ed. But this is my best guess. Honestly, if anything, I think you'll be low."

$ $ $

When Kevin arrived at Rick's house for dinner Friday evening, Paige and the boys made a big show of greeting him. He'd always been a favorite of the twins. At thirty-five, Kevin was twenty years older than the boys, but eighteen years younger than their father. He bridged the gap between Rick and his sons. Kevin enjoyed the pranks he and his nephews played on Rick as much as the boys did.

Paige seemed subdued during dinner, but the boys' rambunctious conversation made up for it. Sometimes they still acted like ten year olds, and Kevin egged them on. After dinner, the boys headed off to a party.

"Let's go in my office," Rick said.

Kevin was surprised; typically Kevin and Rick sat with Paige in the living room. He looked at her.

"Go on," she said. "I have a movie to watch upstairs."

Kevin sat by the fireplace, and Rick poured cognac for the two of them. "This must be serious," Kevin said, "You're giving me the good stuff."

Rick sat across from Kevin. "It is serious. I have something to tell you. I've been thinking about this since my accident, long before Vince died. But now my plans are gelling."

"Plans for what?"

"Leaving PlayLand."

Kevin stared at his brother. Maybe he had heard wrong. "You said you're leaving PlayLand?"

Rick nodded.

"Why?"

"There are other things I want to do with my life. That's all I think about," Rick said quietly. "I resent being at work, dealing with the company's problems. I can't spend time with my family. I can't do volunteer work. I can't ski, even when my leg gets back to normal. I can't do any of the things that matter to me."

"Doesn't the company matter to you?"

"Yes." Rick held stared into the glass in his hand, swishing the cognac. "That's why I feel so bad. But my head's not in the game. I can't stay."

"But you can't leave. A lot of people depend on you, Rick. What's going to happen to us?"

"I'm trying to do this right. At this point, only you, Paige and Maura know."

"So what's going to happen?"

"I want Grant to become CEO. But I want you and me to agree before I talk to him."

Kevin frowned at the fire. "Who else did you consider?"

"Vince, before he died. You. Maybe Alex or Leo."

Kevin looked at his brother. "Thanks, but I'm not ready."

Rick's face relaxed. "I'm glad you said that. I agree. That's why I want Grant."

"Grant's good. Well-respected."

Rick nodded. "He's a strong leader. Not a real visionary, but a good operator."

"Leo will be pissed." Kevin grinned at the thought.

Rick sighed. "Leo worries me. He could do a lot of damage with customers if he wanted to. We need him. Grant doesn't have any relationships with retailers."

"What are you going to do?" Kevin took a drink, feeling the cognac warm its way down his throat.

"I'll call myself Chairman of the Board. I'll stay available, at least for a while. But I want to start Dad's foundation now. There's no reason to wait until he dies. I have his power of attorney."

Kevin nodded. "I'd like to work with you on that."

"I'd like that." Rick looked at Kevin. "But what do you want to do at PlayLand? Do you ever see yourself as CEO?"

Kevin shrugged. "I've thought about it. Who in the family hasn't? But I didn't think it would happen for a long time. Maybe never. I figured you'd be around for years, and I'd only take over when you were old and decrepit. Like you did for Dad."

"If I'm going to be around for years, I don't want to spend them as CEO," Rick said. "My accident taught me that. But Grant won't work forever. He's in his late fifties now, so seven or eight years, max. You could be ready to be CEO by then. Maybe sooner."

Kevin sat back. "I haven't thought about timing. But my gut tells me not to rule it out."

"Then we'll work on it. We'll make Grant CEO now. And he and I will coach you." Rick looked at Kevin. "I'd like to start by having you lead Product Development now."

Kevin stared at Rick, almost as stunned as at Rick's decision to step down. "Product. Now? That's a huge job."

"Yes. Knowing Product is a big part of running the company. Grant has some knowledge, but probably not as much as he needs. You've worked at PlayLand for almost fifteen years. Longer than Grant. You can help him, even though you haven't run a big division before."

"But I've only been in Marketing for two years."

"Yeah, but you're doing great. You're ready to prove you can do more. And you can learn from Grant at the same time."

Kevin watched the fire a minute.

"There's a pay increase," Rick said.

Kevin waved his hand. "I don't care about pay," he said. "It's a lot of responsibility." Could he handle it? You know you want it, he told himself. "I want it," he said out loud, looking at Rick. "I want the job. But I hope you were serious about staying close by for a while."

Rick laughed. "Oh, I imagine you'll see more of me than you want, little brother."

"Wow," Kevin said, leaning back in his chair and running a hand through his hair. His mind raced through changes Product Development needed. Board Games. Better marketing of existing lines. Get next year's action figures developed. And Grant as CEO. Working with Grant would be a blast.

"There's so much to do," he said to himself as much as to Rick. "What will we do about Operations? Who will take over Marketing?" He ticked through the implications of the changes. "Wow," he said again, more quietly this time.

"You're asking the right questions, kid." Rick's eyes gleamed. "You'll get the hang of it."

The brothers worked together through the evening, and again on Saturday and Sunday. By Sunday afternoon, they had a plan. Rick would talk to Grant on Monday. Assuming Grant agreed, Kevin would take over Product Development and keep the Marketing part of his existing role. They would ask Jennifer to lead Marketing, reporting to Kevin.

They didn't have a good plan for the Communications function, but maybe Leo could take it on. Maybe expanding his responsibilities would mollify Leo when he learned of Grant's promotion.

On Sunday afternoon, Kevin mentioned Ben. "I won't keep Ben in Product Development. You can fire him before I take over or move him someplace not reporting to me. But if he's in Product Development when I take over, I'll fire him the first day. He's created too much havoc."

"Maura and I have already talked," Rick said. "She and Dewayne are working up a severance package for Ben now. I'll handle it."

"One last point I need to raise," Kevin said. "You know, I've been interested in Jennifer."

Rick looked puzzled. "Yeah, she's good. Throw everything you can at her. See how far she can take it. She'll get good experience managing Marketing. Maybe she should have New Ventures, too."

"No. I mean I'm interested in her," Kevin repeated. "Personally. We've seen each other socially a few times."

Rick raised an eyebrow. "Oh," he said, "You mean you've dated her. Seriously?"

Kevin shrugged. "Dunno. Maybe. We didn't get that far. We didn't even call it dating. She says she doesn't date guys at work, so it was just PlayLand things. I took her to a couple of community dinners. I can handle it. But I don't want it to affect her career."

Rick leaned back in his chair. "Well, you can't date someone who's working for you. Even if you aren't calling it dating."

Kevin nodded. "I said I can handle it."

CHAPTER 24: MONDAY, MARCH 26

On Monday morning, Maura and Dewayne met in the Legal Department conference room to discuss a severance package for Ben. The walls were lined with law books, so heavy the shelves sagged. Maura wondered who could know everything in those books.

"I talked with Rick this morning," she told Dewayne. "He wants to pay Ben near the high end of the range we talked about. He thinks that'll help Ben leave quietly."

"Ben doesn't deserve a nickel, you know."

Maura smiled, thinking of all the times Dewayne had urged her to pay a problem employee to leave. "That's supposed to be my line," she said.

"Ben's already cost this company far more than he ever contributed. Gus is merely the latest fiasco. You know we paid off two employees who complained about him—one for sexual harassment and another for race discrimination. I'm surprised we haven't had more harassment complaints, given how he talks."

"You tell Rick," Maura said. "I've already tried. He has a soft spot for Ben. Dates back to college."

"I'll bet Ben was using Rick even then," Dewayne grumbled. "But I suppose we have to be professional. Got to get rid of him. I guess it's worth it. And Rick's okay with it?"

"He was okay with the high end. He said you and I should decide how to negotiate with Ben. He didn't give me specifics about where to start. Here's what I'm thinking," Maura said, putting on her reading glasses and glancing at her notes. "We offered the employees in the reduction in force two weeks per year of service. Rick agrees we shouldn't give Ben any more."

"Where do we start?" Dewayne asked.

"Let's begin by offering Ben one week per year of service, but give him health insurance twice that long. He worked here a few years right after college, then left for a few years, then rejoined PlayLand twenty years ago. Under our seniority guidelines, he has twenty years of service. So that would be twenty weeks of pay—call it five months—and ten months on insurance."

Dewayne's mouth narrowed. "Not a bad deal for the SOB, but he'll think he's worth more. I don't think he'll leave quietly for five months' pay."

"I don't either. But it's enough money to say we're serious. And it leaves Rick room to be the good guy. If Rick later offers two weeks per year of service, he can be Ben's friend, and we look like the heavies. I think Rick would appreciate us positioning him like that."

"Will Rick stick to two weeks?"

"He says he will." Maura shrugged. "It's his money."

"Okay." Dewayne sat back. "I'll have one of the staff attorneys draft this up and get it to you by noon. Tell Rick I support it. Assuming we get all the standard waivers from Ben—non-compete, non-disparagement, a full release of legal claims against the company or its officers, etc."

"Ben will want PlayLand to release him from any claims by Gus or anyone else. Can we do that?" Maura asked.

"We can agree to anything," Dewayne said. "But I don't recommend it. We don't know what shit Ben might have said or done over the years. Gus keeps raising new allegations against Ben. I don't have a clue what's real and what's only Gus's imagination. But I wouldn't put anything past Ben."

"Then what do I tell Rick about PlayLand releasing Ben?"

"Tell him I'm against any kind of release. PlayLand might technically be liable for anything Ben did as a manager at PlayLand, but I don't want to let Ben off the hook."

"Okay. But Rick might call you."

"I'll be ready."

Maura started to leave, but Dewayne motioned her to stay. "Got a settlement demand in the Atlanta case."

"I'd almost forgotten," Maura said. "We've had so much going on here at headquarters. How much?"

"Twenty-five grand."

"That's all? That sounds pretty reasonable, given what we'd have to pay local counsel in Atlanta."

"It's the right ballpark." Dewayne leaned forward, squinting at Maura over his half glasses. "But we can talk them down to ten to fifteen. This guy wasn't even trying to do the job."

Maura sighed. The plaintiff in this case was so much more sympathetic than Ben. "Given what we're going to have to pay Ben, I don't feel like playing hardball with Steve Williams."

Dewayne sat back, his bulk filling his large plush chair. "I know. And we do have some risk, given the disability claim. I'll authorize local counsel to go up to twenty thousand, but I'll tell him we'd prefer ten to fifteen. Let's see what he can do."

"Sounds good. And thanks. I know you wanted to fight this one."

Dewayne grinned, pushing his glasses up on his head. "I want to fight them all. But we have to be reasonable. This is one we should settle."

"Will you call Leo? He'll be pissed. He never wants to settle a claim from a Sales employee."

"Yeah, I'll call him. I'll tell him I support it. As a nuisance settlement."

Maura said, "While we're talking about legal issues, Grant hadn't heard about the latest unionization rumblings in New Mexico. I talked to Tim this weekend. Poor guy was wiped out after South Carolina, but he's headed to Albuquerque this afternoon."

$ $ $

When Maura returned to her office, Jennifer Scott and Sara Matthews, the HR Director supporting Product Development, were waiting for her. "What's the problem?" Maura asked, dropping her notebook on her desk and motioning Jennifer and Sara to sit down.

"Gus. He's here," Jennifer said. "He still says Ben stole documents and killed Vince. He's telling everyone who'll listen. The whole division's in an uproar."

Maura sighed. "We'll probably have to send him home. Why do I feel that's exactly what he wants us to do?"

"He says he isn't safe at work and he isn't safe at home," Sara said. "I don't think he'll go home. I think he'll disappear again."

"Tell him to check in every morning and talk personally to one of the two of you. Or Ted. Make sure he has your phone numbers, cells included. And tell him he has to call one of the psychologists in our Employee Assistance Program."

"Can we do that?" Jennifer asked.

"If we think he isn't capable of working, we can," Maura said. "He certainly doesn't sound like he can work this morning. And he's been AWOL for over a week. I want a psychologist to tell us whether he can work or not. And if he comes back, he has to agree not to gossip about Ben or anyone else."

"What if he's right?" Sara asked. "Could he sue us? If we tell him not to talk about what he thinks happened to Vince?"

Maura looked at Sara quizzically. "Are you buying into what Gus's saying? Call Legal, talk to them. But employees at private companies don't have free speech rights. We can't have one employee accusing another of murder." Maura rubbed her forehead. It was too early in the day for a headache, but a big one was on the way. "In any event, I want Gus out of here now. Do it quietly. I don't want him claiming we damaged his reputation. And I don't want him spreading any more rumors. Tell him we'll pay him for today, so he's not out anything. Ask Legal how long we should give him to get his act together."

"Okay, boss," Sara said.

Maura heard the doubt in Sara's voice. Sara wasn't typically sarcastic or skeptical. "Do you think Ben had something to do with Vince's death?"

Sara lifted a shoulder and pursed her lips. "I don't know. You know Ben's reputation. He's evil. But Gus's pretty loony. Neither of them has any credibility."

"Just get Gus out of here. And where's Ben?"

"Trying to play it cool. In his office," Jennifer said. "Everyone's avoiding him. I don't know what will happen if he and Gus see each other."

"Then don't let them see each other. I don't want a confrontation in the workplace." Maura sighed. If either Gus or Ben threatened the other, she'd have to enforce the company policy against workplace violence. One or both would get fired. Ben was going anyway, though few people knew it yet. But Gus might be salvageable. If he was worth salvaging. She wasn't sure.

$$$

Midafternoon Monday, Maura had a call from Tim Baylor in Albuquerque. "What's happening?" she asked.

"I've only been here an hour, but seems like a couple of employees are stirring up trouble again," he said. "They're still not happy with the shift schedule changes. Even though we delayed implementation, they're still badmouthing Alice and some other supervisors. They're advocating work slowdowns. If management can close a plant, then they say they can decide not to work."

"Is it only a couple of guys or the whole plant? What's the general mood?" Maura asked.

"Supervisors say most of the employees want to work. The problem is two employees. Both have complained about several issues in the last year or two. I'm told their co-workers don't like them. The bulk of the employees aren't crazy about Alice, but they want to keep their jobs. They won't slow down production."

"How'd you learn all this?"

"Relax, Maura." She could see Tim's grin through the phone line. "You've trained me well. I got a cup of coffee in the break room first thing after I arrived. Some of the guys remembered me from my last trip. They spilled their guts. Our two problem folks have been pretty vocal. Most of the employees think they're troublemakers. My coffee pals were happy to volunteer what they knew. I didn't ask a single question."

"What about the women who had day care problems before?"

"They're not complaining now. The delayed schedule change was enough, they just needed to get through the school year. They know we can't keep the schedule the same forever. They'll go with the flow."

"What do you recommend now, Tim?"

"Wait for these guys to make a mistake, then fire their asses. They'll screw up. Everyone knows they've been talking about a sick-out. I'll bet the two of them start calling in sick soon. Or monkey with their equipment. Or do something else equally stupid."

"It's risky," Maura said slowly. "What if they don't? Or what if they convince others to join them? We could have an unfair labor practices claim on our hands."

"We'll have a claim from them at some point no matter what we do," Tim said. "I'd rather fight them after they're fired than while they're still working here."

"What about Alice? And the other supervisors? They seem to be part of the employee relations problem."

"Tell Grant to move Alice. Isn't there some nice job at headquarters she could do? One of the department managers here is a really great gal. If she gets promoted to plant manager, the troops will line up behind her in a heartbeat. Or someone from headquarters who's a good manager. Or even take Sam Dixon from South Carolina. I liked him."

"I'll talk to Grant. Make sure all the supervisors know not to take any action on our two malcontents unless they call you or me first. I don't trust Alice to use good judgment, and this is risky. We've had enough legal issues recently."

$ $ $

Rick sat in his office late Monday afternoon. He stared at the Rockies, dark and foreboding with the sun low behind them. The meeting with Ben and Maura was the last thing on his calendar that day.

Ben arrived right on schedule. "You wanted to see me? What's up?"

"We need to talk. Let's go next door." Rick stood and intercepted Ben before he got comfortable. Maura was already in the conference room. Rick sat next to Maura and gestured to Ben to sit across the table.

"Whoa!" Ben said. "Got the big guns in. Why's Maura here? Am I being fired?" His tone was casual, despite his words.

Ben wouldn't make it easy, Rick thought. He took a deep breath and said, "You've caused a lot of trouble over the last few months, Ben. It's hurting the company. I can't let it continue."

"What do you mean?" Ben's brows furrowed, but he still didn't sound worried.

"This business about taking drawings from Gus and not giving him credit for his creations."

"Come on, that's old news. Vince worked all that out with Gus."

"But it hasn't stopped. Gus claims you took more drawings. I can't have a director in this company—particularly in New Ventures—accused of stealing from other employees. You're supposed to create new product, not copy other people's work."

"Yeah, I hear Gus's spouting off again. You know he says I killed Vince? That's bullshit. I'll sue him for defamation. I've known Vince since he was a kid. Remember him hanging around the frat house? You don't believe I killed him, do you?"

"This isn't about Vince. This is about your work."

"Well, fuck." Ben leaned across the table. "How did Gus get to you? We go back too far for you to believe him over me."

"It isn't just Gus," Rick said. "You don't have any credibility in the Product group. Or anywhere at PlayLand. No one trusts you. I need to make some changes in the division, because of Vince's death. You can't stay." Rick swallowed hard. He and Ben did go back a long way. He had to do this for PlayLand, but it hurt. "You asked if you were being fired. The answer is yes. Maura will tell you what we'll do to help you transition. But you can't stay."

Ben looked stunned. Rick had never seen Ben shocked into silence before.

Then Ben's eyes narrowed. "After all I've done for you," he said.

"I can't overlook what's happening, Ben."

"Well, what if I had overlooked the mess you got yourself into with Nicole?"

Rick stared. What was Ben talking about? What did Nicole have to do with Ben's job? "She doesn't have anything to do with this."

"Nicole has everything to do with this. You slept with her, remember? Just before your fucking wedding. I got you out of hot water with Paige, by marrying Nicole." Ben stood and loomed over the table toward Rick. "And you want to fire me? After I saved your ass. Big time."

Rick felt like he'd been sucker punched. He glanced at Maura. Shit! What was she thinking? Her face was blank—good HR blandness, gave nothing away. He'd have to explain to her. Later. Right now, he had to get rid of Ben. "I never asked you to help. Whatever you did you did on your own."

"Sure," Ben sneered. "I slept with Nicole, all on my own. When she turned up pregnant, I married her, all on my own, so you didn't have to tell Paige. I bailed you out." Ben ran a hand over his face, as if wiping away his anger. But it came right back as he stared at Rick. "Are you sure you want to fire me?"

"Are you threatening me, Ben?"

"What happens to your nice marriage and your nice-guy reputation when I tell everyone you fucked your fiancée's best friend the week before your wedding?"

"Paige knows. She's the only one I care about."

"People will talk. You can't fire me—I saved your ass."

"Whatever you think you have on me doesn't matter. Not as much as PlayLand's future." Rick stood up. "Maura will talk to you about your severance. I'm sorry it's ending this way, Ben."

Rick turned to leave, as he and Maura had agreed. His legs shook. He had never dreamed Ben would bring up Nicole.

Ben's next words struck Rick like a knife. "This isn't the end, Rick. I promise you."

$ $ $

Maura saw Rick stiffen and stumble at Ben's threat. But he didn't turn back. She stood, shut the door behind Rick, and turned to face Ben.

Ben said with venom in his voice, "Well, that was pretty. How'd you talk him into firing me? More of your reduction in force? Getting rid of everyone Rick relies on? Did you know he was such a prick?"

"Ben, I'm not here to talk to you about why this is happening. I simply want to go over your severance package."

"This is bullshit. I saved this company with the action figures, and no one gives a fuck." Ben leaned toward her, his linebacker size a threat. "You'll pay for your part in this, Maura."

A shiver went down her spine, but she tried not to show it. "Ben, let's be adults. Let me go over the agreement with you." She went through the terms PlayLand was offering.

When she said the company would pay him five months' severance pay—slightly more than a week per year of service—Ben jumped up. "Bullshit," he said. "You'll hear from my lawyers. Rick owes me more than that."

"You should consult an attorney," Maura said. "That's your right. Have your lawyer call Dewayne. His business card is in the packet

271

I'm giving you."

Ben grabbed the papers from her.

"Call me with any questions," she said. "Or your attorney can call Dewayne. You need to leave the building now. We'll arrange to get your personal belongings to you. Your security access will be terminated this afternoon. You won't be allowed back in the building unescorted. Standard operating procedure."

Ben looked at her. She couldn't read his eyes, but they weren't friendly. "What about Gus? He admitted he took a file out of my office. Is he getting fired, too? And he claims I killed Vince. My lawyer will hear about all of it. I'll sue Gus and PlayLand. And Rick personally."

"We'll wait to hear from you or your lawyer. I need an answer on the severance agreement soon. If you don't sign it, you won't get paid for any time after today."

"Fuck you, Maura." Ben stormed out of the conference room. He went to his office, grabbed his coat and keys, and headed down the stairs to the main entrance.

After watching Ben leave, Maura called Security. Then she braced herself before heading to Rick's office. They had agreed to debrief after she reviewed the severance terms with Ben.

But Christ! She didn't want to talk to Rick now. She didn't want to know about his affair with Nicole, whoever she was. Rick was her boss, for God's sake! HR managers were like priests, always hearing people's confessions. She hated this part of the job.

Rick was staring out the window when Maura arrived at his office. "I'm glad I don't do that every day," she said, dropping into a chair across from him. He didn't move. "How are you doing?" she asked with more solicitude in her voice.

Rick didn't look at her. "I've known Ben since the first week of freshman football practice. I never thought I'd be firing him."

Maura was silent.

Rick turned, his expression somber. "I'm sorry you had to hear all that."

Maura shrugged. "Comes with the territory. HR people hear a lot of things."

"I never knew he thought he was doing it for me. Marrying Nicole. I could have dealt with her." Rick sighed and looked out the window away from Maura. "Most of it's true, you know."

Maura closed her eyes. "Do you really want to tell me?" Please, no, she thought.

"I was engaged to Paige," Rick said, as if Maura hadn't spoken. "Nicole was her best friend. I slept with her one night. Just before Paige and I were married. I knew immediately I'd made the biggest mistake of my life. Then I made another mistake. I told Ben."

None of this should matter to PlayLand. But Maura hated knowing Rick had screwed up so royally. How would she feel if Carlos slept with someone else? How had Paige felt when she found out? Damn Rick. "You said Paige knows."

Rick nodded. "Ben said not to tell Paige before our wedding. That it would blow over. We got married and went on our honeymoon. When we returned, Nicole was seeing Ben. They were married about a month later. Ben didn't tell me why they married so quickly." Rick dropped his head into his hands. "Then Nicole announced she was pregnant. I wondered about the timing, but didn't ask."

Maura waited.

Rick continued, "Nicole lost the baby a couple of months later. She and Ben got divorced. Then Nicole told Paige everything. How the baby could have been mine. It was rough between Paige and me. I talked to Ben." Rick paused. "He said he'd married her to keep her quiet. In case it was mine. But I never asked him to."

He turned to look at Maura. "Paige and I managed to patch things up. I've never played around on her since. It was before we were married."

Maura sighed. Too much information, she thought. "She'll still be hurt if Ben says anything now. And I assume your sons don't know anything."

Rick turned back to the window and shook his head.

"Well," Maura said, "We'll have to see what happens."

Rick was silent.

Maura stood to leave. "I need to have IT turn off Ben's computer and building access codes. And I think I'll call Gus, to tell him to watch out for Ben."

Rick winced. "Do we have to? Gus will tell everyone Ben was fired."

"All right. I'll wait. But let's not leave it too long." Maura sighed. "I need to go. It's been a long day."

$ $ $

The tires of Ben's Jaguar squealed as he cut off traffic rushing out of the PlayLand parking lot. That bitch Maura! She must have convinced Rick to fire him. Rick wouldn't do it on his own. Not after everything Ben had done for him.

Who else could have got to Rick? Maybe Gus. But why would Rick believe Gus over Ben? Rick needed him, always had. Ben had protected him since freshman year. Made sure Rick knew he was his best friend.

Because Ben needed Rick, too. His contacts. His money. His name.

Now Rick was firing him with a shitty five months' pay. Ben would never get another job as good as at PlayLand. Not in five months. Not in five years. Someone was going to pay. He'd get a lawyer. Damn straight.

But first, Ben had to find out what happened. He knew where Powell lived.

Ben headed to Gus's house, and stormed out of his car to pound on the front door. No answer.

He went next door and rang the doorbell. A matronly woman in a bathrobe answered. Ben put on his most charming grin. "Have you seen Gus Powell recently?"

She smiled. "He asked me to take care of his cats for a few days. Said he's staying with a friend."

"I really need to see him," Ben said. "It's his birthday, and I have a present for him. A surprise." He flashed another grin. "Do you have his cell phone number?"

She nodded.

"Would you mind calling him to ask where he's staying? Tell him there's a delivery from work and they need to get it to him tonight. Remember, it's a surprise."

She called Gus, wrote down an address, and gave it to Ben.

Ben waved at the woman as he started his car. He drove slowly until he was around the corner, then he sent his Jaguar screaming.

Gus was at a weekly hotel for business travelers, a place with adequate security, but anonymous. Ben wondered if Gus was paying for the suite, or if the bastard had convinced PlayLand to pay. Didn't matter. Ben had him now.

Ben took his handgun out of the glove compartment and put it in his jacket pocket. He walked into the lobby and found a house phone. He called the operator. "Gus Powell, please."

The operator made the connection. The fucking idiot had checked in under his own name.

"Hello?" Gus said.

"Gus Powell?" Ben asked, deepening his voice.

"Yes?"

"Front desk. Delivery for you. From PlayLand. Do you want to come to the lobby? Or I can have someone bring it up."

"What is it?" Gus's voice was suspicious.

"An envelope. A woman dropped it off about ten minutes ago." Ben described Jennifer Scott. "She didn't stay. Just asked us to get it to you."

"Someone can bring it up."

"What's the room number?" Ben held his breath. A hotel employee wouldn't have to ask. But Gus rattled off a number. One more indication how stupid he was.

"I'll have it brought up in a few minutes." Ben hung up, went to the guest computer in the lobby, and folded a piece of printer paper into envelope size. Two minutes later, he headed to Gus's room.

He knocked, then hung back out of sight of the door. He needn't have bothered. Gus immediately pulled the door open, and Ben sprang into the room.

"You fucking bastard." Ben snarled, grabbing Gus's throat as he shoved the gun in Gus's face. "You got me fired. Because you couldn't keep your fucking mouth shut."

"Don't hurt me, Ben. They'll know it was you." Gus's voice squeaked. Ben wouldn't be surprised if the moron had already pissed his pants. "I've told everyone you killed Vince. It was you, wasn't it? They'll know you did it if I get hurt."

"Why would I kill Vince?" Ben said. "I've been living off the Players family for years. Vince couldn't do a damn thing about it. You're the one who spoiled everything. We could have milked those fucking drawings of yours for years. The Players paid you a bundle for them, but if you'd stuck with me, you could have gotten more."

Gus's eyes widened. "What do you mean, more?"

"Those action figures are going to save Rick's fucking company. He would have paid us anything. But you've kissed it all goodbye."

Ben's hand tightened further around Gus's throat and he slammed him against the wall, the gun digging into Gus's temple. "And now you're going to pay. I want a cut of what they gave you. For all the trouble you've caused me."

"I don't have it yet." Gus's voice wavered.

"You're lying. Your first check was due this week. And if there's one thing I know about Rick, it's that he pays his bills on time. Where's the check?" Gus pushed the gun harder against Gus's head.

"On the desk. Over there. But you can't have it."

Ben pulled Gus over to the desk. "Sign it over. It's not like fifty grand will get me very far, but that's my price for not killing you now. You think I killed Vince? Then you don't think I'd mind killing a piss-ant like you, do you?"

"There'll be a paper trail from the check."

"No one can do a damn thing unless they find me. There won't be any proof I did anything other than take your fucking drawings. The check will have your endorsement on it."

Gus pleaded. "Don't do this, Ben."

"Sign it, asshole."

Gus ripped the check in two and threw it on the ground. "There's your check, you bastard. That's what Adolpho would have done. Now what are you going to do?" He was shaking, but his chin jutted out.

Ben sneered. "You think you're a fucking hero, do you? You just tore up your only hope of getting out of this alive. You're coming with me." He shoved Gus toward the door, grabbing the folded paper he had handed to Gus as he entered. He didn't think he had touched anything else in the room. Other than Gus.

Ben pulled Gus down the stairwell, the gun still at Gus's head. The stairwell was empty, but when they reached the exit at the bottom, Ben looked out the window and saw several people in the parking lot. He moved the gun down to Gus's side. "A gut wound would still probably kill you at this range," he said. "Don't try anything."

Ben walked Gus toward his Jaguar. He didn't know what he was going to do next, but Gus was the only insurance he had. His career was over. The piddling severance wasn't enough. What would Rick pay to ransom Gus?

As they crossed the parking lot, a van pulled in front of the main hotel entrance. Several men piled out, all talking loudly.

Gus veered suddenly toward the van, trying to shove Ben away. "Help!" Gus yelled.

One of the conventioneers shouted, "You guys here for the convention? Join us in the bar."

"Sure!" Gus tried again to pull away from Ben. Gus was sweating, but continued to struggle.

Ben grabbed him tighter. Gus was much smaller than Ben, and Ben still had a gun in Gus's ribs, but Gus didn't seem to care. Gus shook himself free and careened toward the van.

"If I'm going to die," Gus shouted, "I'm going to die like Adolpho!"

Fuck! He couldn't shoot Gus. Too many fucking witnesses. Ben ran to his Jaguar, started it, and peeled out of the parking lot. As he glanced back, he saw Gus gesticulating wildly as he talked to the van passengers. Christ, the cops would be after him now.

Ben drove aimlessly for a few minutes. Where could he go? The cops would go straight to his house. The cabin!

He headed out of town.

CHAPTER 25: TUESDAY, MARCH 27

Jennifer walked into Maura's office Tuesday morning. "I just had the weirdest phone call from Gus. The weirdest yet."

Maura turned from her computer, taking her glasses off. "What did he say?"

Jennifer shook her head. "He says Ben kidnapped him last night. Or tried to."

"You're kidding." Maura dropped her glasses on her desk. Even for Gus, this was far-fetched.

Jennifer nodded. "Gus says Ben tried to take his fifty thousand dollar check from PlayLand. Then took him at gun point out of his hotel. Gus says he only escaped because some other hotel guests saw them. He's already talked to the cops."

"Where is Gus now?"

"I don't know. I said we needed to talk to him. As a follow-up to our last conversation. I didn't know what else to do. But I don't know where he is."

"Good thinking. Has he seen a shrink yet?"

"I didn't ask. He agreed to meet me here at one o'clock. Can you be there?"

Maura checked her online calendar. "Okay," she said, then turned to her phone. "First, let's call the cops. See what they say."

Maura dialed the number of the lead detective investigating Vince's murder. She identified herself and hit the speaker button so Jennifer could hear the conversation. "Detective Palmer, I have Jennifer Scott, one of our Product Development Directors, here with me. She had a strange report from an employee, Gus Powell. He apparently had some incident with another employee last night."

The officer laughed. "You mean the abduction?"

"Then it really happened?" Maura asked.

"Here's what I know," Detective Palmer said. "There was a 911 call from the Executive Suites Hotel near the airport. Caller alleged attempted theft and abduction. When the officers responded, your guy—what's his name? Powell?—alleged that one Ben Thornton came to his hotel room, pulled a gun on him. Then Thornton allegedly took Powell outside at gun point. Thornton was allegedly going to drive off with Powell. No word where."

"Were there any witnesses?" Maura asked.

"The responding officers took statements. Witnesses said Powell and another man were stumbling around. Witnesses thought the two were drunk. They admitted drinking themselves. They described the man with Powell as big, but they didn't get a good look at him. Or else they were in no condition to notice. No one other than Powell mentioned a gun. They did see the other man drive off in a sports car."

"Do you believe Gus?"

"All I know is what's in the police report. We're still trying to find Thornton. If he shows up at work, we'd appreciate a call."

"Then you don't know if what Gus said is true?"

"Hell, Ms. Ramirez," Detective Palmer said, "all I can tell you is what's in the report. We have an APB out on Thornton now, but there's no sign of him."

"Thank you, Detective. Both Gus Powell and Ben Thornton are our employees. If you learn anything further, I'd appreciate a call from you, too."

Maura hung up and looked at Jennifer. They both started laughing. "What do you think? Is Gus being paranoid, or did Ben really kidnap him? This shouldn't be funny, but it is." Maura chuckled. "Okay, let's see what Gus tells us. I don't know what to do with him."

"What about Ben?" Jennifer asked.

Maura sobered quickly. "You aren't hearing it from me, but his days were numbered anyway. Let me worry about Ben. When Gus gets here, bring him to the HR conference room. I'll get Sara and Ted there also."

$ $ $

After Jennifer left, Maura called Rick. "I want to cancel the severance offer we made Ben," she told him. She described her conversations with Jennifer and Detective Palmer.

"But we haven't heard Ben's side," Rick said.

"No," Maura admitted. "But we shouldn't offer Ben anything until we sort out what happened. We can always put the agreement back on the table later."

"Won't pulling the offer make Ben madder?"

"Maybe. But he's already mad. He threatened us yesterday. Now he may have pulled a gun on Gus."

"Will Ben go public with what he talked about yesterday?"

"I don't know. If that worries you, then we'll leave the severance offer alone."

Rick sighed. "If Ben had threatened anyone other than me, you wouldn't have let them have a say, would you?"

"No."

"Then pull the severance. I'll deal with it. I'll talk to Paige tonight." Rick paused. "And Maura?"

"Yes?"

"I'm going to make the offer to Grant tonight."

Maura shook her head as she hung up. Rick had too much on his plate, poor guy. A long-time friend threatening to go public with a humiliating story from his past. His brother's unresolved murder. His decision to step down as CEO.

If Ben's threats and Rick leaving the CEO job were ever linked, Rick would look like he was hiding something, trying to avoid publicity and humiliation. Maura wondered if Rick had thought of that.

She called Dewayne. "Rick and I fired Ben last night. I presented him with the severance terms you and I discussed. But now Rick and I want to pull it off the table. Can we do that?"

"What happened?"

Maura described the conversation with Ben, leaving out what Ben had revealed about Nicole. Someday Dewayne might need to know, but not now. "It ended with Ben threatening Rick. And he was pissed at the severance amount."

"Why pull the offer now?"

"Because Gus says Ben tried to kidnap him last night."

"What?" Dewayne's voice boomed through the speaker. It sounded like he had leaped out of his chair, though Dewayne couldn't leap very far.

"I don't know whether to believe Gus," she said. "But the police have an APB out on Ben. I don't want to pay Ben anything if he's breaking the law and threatening another employee. It's one thing to threaten Rick and me in the heat of the moment. It's another to go after a PlayLand employee with a gun."

"Does Rick agree?"

"Yes."

"All right. I'll send Ben a certified letter this morning. And hand deliver a copy to his house. We can't be sure he'll get it. Sounds like he's nowhere near his house, if the cops can't find him."

$ $ $

Shortly after one o'clock, Jennifer and Gus walked into the HR conference room, where Maura, Sara and Ted waited. "Hello, Gus," Maura said, rising to shake his hand. She wanted to impress Gus with the seriousness of the conversation. He mumbled a greeting and sat, not looking anyone in the eye.

"We told you last week you could have a few days to get your problems under control and to contact our Employee Assistance Program. What progress have you made?" Maura asked.

Gus glanced around wildly. "Did Jennifer tell you?" he asked. "About Ben? He tried to kidnap me."

"Okay," Maura said, "Let's start there. Tell us what happened."

Gus recounted how he had let Ben into his hotel room. Ben wanted the check. Gus tore up the check. "Can I get another check from PlayLand?" Gus asked. "I should have gone straight to the bank."

"We'll get you another check," Maura said. "What happened after you tore up the first one?"

Gus described how Ben took him at gun point to his car and how he had escaped. "I just kept thinking what Adolpho would have done. And that's what I did," Gus said. "Adolpho saved me this time!"

If she hadn't heard about the police report, she'd think Gus lived in a fantasy world, Maura thought. But the witnesses confirmed something happened, so she couldn't discount Gus's story totally.

"Okay. What next?" she asked.

"He'll be after me again. You know he will. He threatened to kill me. I probably shouldn't be here today. But I had to let you know how dangerous he is. That's what Adolpho would do."

Gus's leg twitched as he spoke. His pupils were dilated, his eyes wide. He looked like he was about to bolt. But then, Gus often looked that way. "You think Ben is still after you?" she asked.

"Yes, Ben. Who else?" Gus's voice was impatient. Maura wondered how much longer she could keep him there.

Maura looked at the others in the room. What did they think? Sara sat impassively, but her lips were pursed as if she were trying not to laugh. Jennifer rolled her eyes at Maura. Ted was frowning, but silent.

"Let's talk about the criteria I set last week," Maura said to Gus. "Can you come back to work? Is your personal life under control?"

"That's up to Ben. He's who's making things out of control. If he's gone, I'm okay. But how do I know he's gone? I think he'll be back."

"Have you called the Employee Assistance Program?" Maura asked.

"No."

"Why not?"

"I have to stay in hiding. I'm nervous enough being here now."

Maura decided to play along with Gus's paranoia. "Ben has probably skipped town. The cops can't find him. I think you should be safe for a while. What if you and Sara call the Employee Assistance Program hotline together? Make you an appointment with one of the counselors? Sara can drive you there in a car Ben's never seen. But we need you to talk to an EAP counselor before you return to work. And we'd like to get you back to work as quickly as possible."

Gus resisted, but finally agreed. Gus and Sara left to call the EAP.

Maura turned to Jennifer and Ted. "How important is Gus to the next phase of the action figures and comic books?"

Jennifer shrugged. "He's been thinking about the characters for years, while the rest of us are new to them. He has their whole world in his head. But if we had to, we could do it without him."

Ted nodded. "I don't need him back. If he weren't working with Jennifer, I'd add him to the headcount reduction in Games."

"How has he been to work with?"

Jennifer smiled ruefully. "Difficult, but not impossible. He and I get along fine, and most of the team is okay with him. Other than Ben, of course. Gus doesn't trust Ben, and Ben acts like Gus is dirt. I don't know how Ben ever talked Gus into giving him the drawings in the first place."

"Ted?" Maura turned to him.

Ted shrugged. "He was okay in Games before all this started. Never close to his co-workers, but he did his job. Now, rumors are all over the place. People think he's odd. I don't know what would happen if we brought him back. I assumed he'd move to Jennifer's team."

"Do you want him on the team or not?" Maura asked Jennifer.

Jennifer tossed her hair over her shoulder. "Frankly, I'd rather work without him. He's too weird. And once he has an idea, he won't back off. These characters are his babies. He doesn't compromise. But I didn't think I had a choice. These are his creations, after all. So I can work with him if I have to."

Maura sighed. Her gut told her that in the long run Gus would be a problem. Maybe it was better to deal with him now. "Let me talk to Dewayne about our options. And we need to hear what the EAP says about his fitness to work."

$ $ $

Rick met Grant at the Lakeview Tennis Club for a drink after work Tuesday evening. As he drove to the club, Rick worried about Ben's threats and the reports about Ben and Gus. Got to tell Paige, he thought. Shit, he'd thought PlayLand's financial problems were bad, but this was worse. He'd fired his best friend, and now he didn't know what Ben would do to the company ... or to Rick's family. Everything he'd worked for all his life could go up in flames. Just when he thought he was moving toward a better life.

First, Grant. Rick was burning his bridges, but he was on the right path. For himself. For his family. To get his life the way he wanted.

Rick hoped Grant would accept the job. But what about Linda? How would she take it? Grant didn't have an easy decision to make.

"Good work on handling production this year," Rick told Grant when their drinks arrived. "We could've had a real mess. Your folks got us through."

"I have a great team."

"And you lead them well." Here goes, Rick thought. Dive in. "I'd like you to take on a bigger role at PlayLand. Have you thought about that?"

"I'm happy running Operations. It's what I know. What I do best. What do you have in mind?"

"I want you to replace me as CEO."

Grant's glass hit the table hard, sloshing Scotch over the side. He stared at Rick. "Holy shit. That's not what I expected. I thought you might want me to replace Vince."

"You could run Product. But I want you as CEO."

"Why? Are you having health problems after your accident?"

Rick shook his head. "No. Just don't want the job." Why did he have to explain himself? Better get used to it. "Maybe the accident threw me a curve. I have other things I want to do."

"Is this about Vince dying? Maybe it's too soon. Don't do anything you might regret."

"I've been thinking about this a long time. Since the accident, at least, maybe before. I'm sure." Rick eyed Grant closely. "No need to be modest. Maura said she talked to you about the CEO job in January. You told her you wanted it."

"You were in a coma, for God's sake. I never thought you'd step down now. You're younger than I am." Grant ran a hand over his face. He looked at Rick, frowning. "You're really serious?"

"Never more so." Was he getting through?

"Jesus." Grant sat back, his eyebrows still furrowed.

Rick saw in Grant's eyes when he thought of Linda. His frown deepened. "What about Linda?" Grant asked. "Can she stay at PlayLand if I take the job?"

Rick sighed. "Maura and I talked. Can't have one spouse reporting to the other. Particularly not in HR. Too much potential for conflict. The appearance of favoritism. I'm sorry. If you're CEO, Linda can't work anywhere at PlayLand."

Grant rubbed his chin. "Even in a family run company? Where

you worked for your dad and your brother works for you?"

"We don't live in the same households. I know it's hard. But it's a typical policy."

Grant sighed. "I know. Linda and I talked in January. She said then she'd leave if I was offered the job. I think she'll be fine. But I need to talk to her. I can't commit until I talk to her."

Rick nodded. "I understand. I won't hold you to anything tonight. But I'd like an answer soon. And please make sure she keeps this quiet. I don't want anything said until we make a formal announcement."

"Of course."

"Tell her I'm sorry. We'll make it as easy as we can. No rush. She can take time to find a good position elsewhere. And Maura and I will give her glowing recommendations."

"She'll appreciate that."

"If she agrees, will you take it?"

Grant took a deep drink of Scotch. "Who else knows? Is Kevin on board?"

"Yes. I've told Kevin I want him to replace Vince. The only other people who know are Maura and my wife. I haven't made any decisions beyond Kevin. I want your input if you're going to be CEO."

Grant nodded. "Kevin in Product makes sense. Particularly if you see him as CEO someday." He raised an eyebrow as a question to Rick.

"I do. It'll be your job to get him ready."

Grant frowned in thought. "If I move, what about Martin Cunningham to head Operations?"

"I thought he'd be your leading candidate. I'm fine with him."

Rick and Grant talked on about the organization. Rick wished Grant had more knowledge about the company's finances and customers, but he asked good questions. He was the right guy for the job. Rick would be free. Assuming Linda would leave gracefully.

$ $ $

Grant sunk heavily into his Lexus SUV. Holy shit! CEO of PlayLand.

But what would Linda say? Damn! He hated to do this to her.

She'd be happy for him. Thrilled. But she loved working at PlayLand. Grant had told Rick Linda would be fine, but would she?

He started the engine, but didn't put the car in gear. Grant worried about telling Linda, but he also thought about his discussion with Rick. What a great opportunity! More than he ever hoped for. He'd been comfortable ending his career in Operations. But holy shit! CEO. He could put his stamp on the whole company. What a challenge!

He couldn't stay out of corporate politics now.

Grant hoped Rick would give him free rein, like he'd had in Operations. But being CEO was different. What would the Players family expect? On product? On finances?

What didn't he know? That's what worried Grant. He liked to know what he was getting into.

When he got home, Grant dropped his coat and briefcase and found Linda in the kitchen.

"Need a drink?" she offered.

"I'll fix it," he said, buying a few more minutes. He walked across the room to the wet bar. As he mixed his drink, Grant watched Linda, trying to gauge her mood as she chattered about her day.

He sat on a stool in the kitchen. "I had a drink with Rick tonight."

"How is he?" Linda asked, sitting on another stool beside him. "I haven't seen much of him since Vince's death. Is the family doing all right? Maura says Rick's been kind of remote."

"I think Vince's murder got to him more than he's admitting. Told me he's been under a lot of strain since his accident. Way before Vince died." Grant paused. He couldn't put it off. "He asked me to meet with him because he wanted to talk about my career."

Linda turned to Grant, an eyebrow raised.

"He wants me to be CEO."

Both eyebrows shot into her bangs. "CEO? But that's his job."

"He says he wants to step down. And he wants me to replace him."

Linda's eyes were bright as she hugged him. "Grant, that's wonderful! You know I thought you should take over when Rick was out. But I had no idea he'd leave now."

"He and Maura have been talking about it. You didn't know?"

Linda shook her head. "Maura shouldn't have told me, and I'm glad she didn't." She leaned over and kissed Grant. "This calls for something more than meatloaf, but that's what I have. How about champagne to go with it?"

He smiled. "No, thanks. I'm still in shock myself." He paused again. That was the easy part, he thought. "Rick and I also talked about you."

She stilled.

"Rick said you can't stay at PlayLand if I'm CEO."

"And what did you say?" she asked, her eyes narrowing slightly.

"I said I understood. That you and I had talked about it back in January, and I thought you understood as well." But did she?

"What's Maura's position?" Her voice was calm, with little inflection.

"Rick says Maura will be sorry to lose you. But they can't have an exception to the anti-nepotism policy in HR."

"Do you agree?" Linda asked, getting off the stool. But she didn't move back to the stove. She stood watching him.

"Yes. I hate what it does to you, but I agree with the policy. If this is a sticking point for you, I need to know now. I'll turn down the CEO job if you can't live with it." And he meant it, he thought, surprising himself. "I've been happy in Operations. I can stay happy there for several more years. Or I can leave PlayLand and be happy somewhere else. But I can't be happy without you."

Linda's eyes filled with tears. "I needed to hear you say that," she said, sitting back beside him. "I'll leave PlayLand. It'll hurt, but I can do it. For you and for the company. You're the best person to replace Rick. I just needed to know we're in it together." She leaned her head against his shoulder.

Grant pulled her close. It would be all right. "Linda, there's no contest. Between you and PlayLand, I'd pick you any day."

She cried while he held her. It would be all right.

$ $ $

Rick found Paige in their bedroom. "I fired Ben yesterday," he told her.

She looked at him in surprise. "After all these years? Why?"

"He's been passing off another employee's ideas as his own. Maura and I talked to him. Then today we heard he might have

287

gone after the other employee with a gun."

"Ben? With a gun? Has he ever done anything like that before?"

"Not with a gun. He used to get into bar fights."

Paige shook her head.

"There's more," Rick said. "He brought up Nicole. In front of Maura."

"What's Nicole got to do with this?" Paige asked sharply. "I thought that was over years ago."

"She has nothing to do with anything. But Ben thinks I owe him something. He's threatening to go public."

"The boys!" Paige said. "You can't let Ben do that to us."

"I can't keep him at PlayLand."

"But what will we tell the boys?"

"I don't know. Nothing, I hope. But I don't know." Rick sighed.

CHAPTER 26: WEDNESDAY, MARCH 28

Leo stormed into Maura's office Wednesday morning as she was going through her mail. "What's this I hear about settling the Williams case?"

"Did you talk with Dewayne?"

"That's why I'm here. He says you pushed him into it. Says we could've won this one, but instead we're paying the bastard twenty grand."

Maura wished Dewayne hadn't punted this one to her. "We might have won," Maura said calmly, taking off her reading glasses so she could see Leo. "But I didn't think it was the right thing to do."

"This Williams guy wasn't doing his job. He wasn't doing anything!"

"This Williams guy, as you call him, was mentally ill. Steve Williams is a sympathetic plaintiff. And it would have cost far more than twenty thousand to try the case. Dewayne didn't disagree with me on that. We could have settled more cheaply if we'd done our homework. HR didn't investigate it closely enough. So blame this one on me."

"Damn straight, I blame you."

"But let's not spend our time fighting Williams. It doesn't look good in the papers or to other employees."

"Damn it, I hate to settle these things. Why didn't you talk to me sooner?" At least he wasn't yelling any longer.

"You're right, Leo. I should've talked to you. But you always fly off the handle like this. It's pretty hard to have a civil conversation with you about any employee claim."

"Are there any other Sales guys you want to pay off?" Leo didn't bother to hide his disdain, even though she'd apologized. She wasn't surprised; he was always hard to work with.

"He's the only Sales employee suing us at the moment," she said mildly. "Unless you know of any others. Do we need to talk about it more, or are you done?"

Leo plopped down in a chair across from her, as if suddenly deflated, his anger spent. "Christ, these employee lawsuits piss me off. We always end up paying people who don't give a damn about their jobs."

"If I really thought this guy didn't give a damn about his job, I wouldn't want to settle either. But I don't think he was capable of doing the job. Not the way we needed. Maybe we had the right to change the job, but I still don't feel good about it."

Leo shook his head. "If we had the right to change it and he couldn't do it, we shouldn't have to pay. We need to run our business the best we can."

"Do you have a better rep in the territory now than Steve was?"

Leo grinned and waved his hand, diamond ring flashing. "Yeah. The new guy is dynamite. Setting records. Probably because Williams hadn't done anything for so long."

"Well, then PlayLand is better off. Think of the twenty thousand as a cost of doing business. I bet the new guy racked up more than twenty grand in increased sales in his first six months."

Leo nodded. "That's about right."

"Then every dollar now is pure gravy. Feel good about that, instead of beating us up for settling. Sonia Freeman is a good Sales Manager. She doesn't need a lawsuit hanging over her head."

Leo snorted. He stood and strode toward the door. As he walked out, he turned and shook his finger at Maura. "You'll never convince me this is right. And that's what I'll tell my folks. But I'll also tell them to keep selling as much damn product as they can."

"Attaboy," Maura muttered as Leo left her office.

$ $ $

Rick kept his back to the window as he worked in his office Wednesday afternoon. The clouds were threatening over the Rockies, which had been in shadows all day. No one had heard anything about Ben since Maura had talked to the police on Tuesday. No one had been at Ben's house when Dewayne's letter was delivered. Rick didn't want to think about Ben, so he tried to think about other things.

Leo sauntered up to Rick's doorway. "I was in the neighborhood, and I thought you'd want some good news," he said with a grin.

"Yeah, I could use it."

"First report's in on wholesale bookings for the action figures," Leo said. "Last week we started selling to smaller customers, below our top ten. First time these guys have seen the product since Toy Fair. They love it. Orders ahead of pace. It's looking good."

"Best news I've had in days, Leo." Rick went around his desk and clapped Leo on the back, shaking his hand.

"I got a letter for you to send out to the sales force. Thanking them for their work." Leo handed Rick a piece of paper with handwritten notes scrawled across the page. "Okay?"

"Good idea. Get it to Kevin, and have his communications team go over it." Rick gave the page back without reading it. "While you're at it, ask him what other groups I should congratulate, too."

"Hell, Rick, I did this for the Sales force." Leo's voice was petulant. "My guys are busting their buns out there. They need kudos from headquarters. Why spoil that with copycat notes to those clowns in Product and Operations?"

Rick sighed. "Talk to Kevin. We'll differentiate the letters. I'm not taking anything away from Sales, but lots of groups contributed."

Leo opened his mouth as if to complain further, but he didn't say anything for a moment. Then he asked, "Can I raise another issue?"

"What's that?" Here came the real reason Leo had dropped by, Rick thought.

"Maura and Dewayne have settled this frigging disability case in Atlanta. Did you know about that?"

"Dewayne mentioned it. Made sense financially."

"No one ever discussed it with me." Leo shook his head. "My people fired that SOB for good reason. He wasn't doing his job."

Rick sighed. He should have known Leo would come to him directly. "It doesn't make sense to keep fighting," Rick said. "Not when we can settle for less than we would pay outside counsel."

"If we take that approach on every case, sooner or later we'll be paying every damn employee we fire." Leo leaned over Rick's desk. "I don't want any more settlements in Sales."

"Your concern is noted. But we can't pay lawyers all over the country. Not when we can get rid of a case cheaply. I'm sorry you weren't told sooner."

Leo was cussing when he left Rick's office. Rick wondered how Leo would react when he found out Grant would be the next CEO. Rick would be having another discussion with Leo that day for sure. No soft starts to the conversation about sales results then; Leo would come in steaming and leave fighting.

Late in the afternoon, Kevin came to Rick's office and plopped down, saying, "Long day."

"Yeah," said Rick. "Did Leo come to see you?"

Kevin nodded, pulling Leo's handwritten page out of a file. "Gave me this maudlin letter. Wants you to send it to the field reps. Great work on the action figure line. Yadda, yadda. Calls them 'marketplace gladiators.'"

Rick grinned. "That's why I sent him to you. I knew you'd clean it up."

"His draft was pretty bad. But we'll come up with something. It is great news about the sales forecast. We really need a shot in the arm."

"You're telling me," Rick said. "I spent the last two hours with Alex. We have enough cash for the next several weeks, thanks to the bank deal. If sales come through, we'll be all right. But if we can't pay down the debt later this year, we'll be in worse shape than we were in January."

"No wonder you want to abandon ship."

Rick sighed. "I hate leaving PlayLand in a mess. We still have a hard slog ahead. But the turnaround is likely to take a while. Longer than I want to give. I need to make the change now."

"Did you talk to Grant?"

Rick nodded. "He's on board. He seemed surprised."

"He's not the only one. Have you set an announcement date?"

"Not yet. Maybe June. After the action figures are out in the market."

"Aren't you afraid of leaks if we wait?"

"Yes, but I want to be sure we roll out the announcement

effectively. You and I should sit down with Grant and Maura. Maybe next week. We need to start planning soon."

$ $ $

At the end of the day Maura was catching up on paperwork. Linda Mason came into Maura's office and shut the door. "Can we talk?" Linda asked.

"Sure." Maura put down her pen, took off her glasses, and faced Linda with her hands folded on her desk. She thought she knew what was coming; it wouldn't be fun.

Linda handed Maura a handwritten page. "This is my letter of resignation," she said. "Grant and I talked last night. He told me you and Rick say I have to leave. I understand. I won't stand in Grant's or Rick's way."

Tears came to Maura's eyes. "Linda, I am so sorry. I feel terrible about you leaving. I want Grant to be Rick's successor, but I hate what it does to you."

"I'm sorry, too. I've loved working for PlayLand. And for you. But it's the right thing for Grant. And for PlayLand."

"You don't have to go right away. We're probably several weeks away from an announcement. Rick says you don't even have to leave before the announcement. Take your time to decide what you want to do next."

"I will. There's no effective date in my letter. It only says you and I will work it out. But I wanted to tell you today. So you and I are clear."

"I appreciate that." Maura smiled. "HR has done a lot of good things over the last several years. You've been a big part of it. See what you did, though, by pushing me on the succession plan?"

Linda laughed. "Don't blame this on me. I wanted the plan when Rick was incapacitated. I never thought he'd choose to leave. I was shocked when Grant told me."

Maura nodded. "You and everyone else. Even Kevin. But maybe you should take a page from Rick's book and think about what you want next out of life. You have an opportunity to do that now. I'll be a reference for anything you want to pursue."

"Thanks." Linda lifted her shoulders then slowly lowered them. "I don't know yet what I want. Maybe consulting. Or I may not work for a while."

"That's hard to believe, Linda. You've been as career-minded as me for as long as I've known you."

"Well, maybe now's the time to stop. At least for a bit."

"Whatever you decide, I hope we'll stay in touch." Maura went around her desk as Linda stood to leave. She hugged Linda. "HR people don't hug much, but I want you to know I've always considered you a friend as well as a colleague."

Linda returned the embrace. "Me, too. You've been a great friend and a great boss."

$ $ $

At home that evening, Maura dealt with dinner and the usual conversation about Liz's quinceañera. Maura had reserved the hotel ballroom; now Liz was fixated on food. What could the kids eat that wouldn't be too messy when they were all dressed up?

When Maura had told Liz she could get the dress she wanted, Liz had smiled brighter than she had since she last believed in Santa Claus. She'd thrown her arms around Maura and Carlos and gushed about getting flowers to match the dress. Maura wished her life was as simple as Liz's—a new dress and roses to make life perfect.

After the kids had gone to their rooms, Maura poured herself a glass of wine and sat next to Carlos in the family room. She stared at the gas fire warming the room on the cool March evening.

Carlos put an arm around her and asked, "What's up? Must be something big because you haven't said a word all night."

"It's been a freaky week," she said, turning sideways on the couch toward him. "And it's only Wednesday. Monday we fired Ben. Tuesday we learned Ben kidnapped Gus. Or so Gus says. He's certifiably paranoid. I don't know what to believe."

Carlos laughed. "You know what they say," he said. "Even paranoids might be right when they think someone's out to get them."

"That's what's so weird. He's the oddest duck, but he's been more right about Ben than anyone else. Him and Jennifer."

"How so?" Carlos shifted away and took one of Maura's feet into his hands. He stripped off her sock and massaged her foot.

"Mmm," she said. "Feels good." She leaned back on the opposite arm of the couch and put both feet in his lap. "Jennifer always said

Ben was bad news. Borderline sexual harassment. Dissing her in front of their peers. Things like that. Now Gus's accusing him of theft and plagiarism and even murder."

"Murder?" Carlos's fingers stopped moving. "What murder?"

"Vince. Gus claims Ben killed him. There's no proof. Or none I've heard. But Gus says some drawing found in Vince's house means Ben was there that night. I don't follow it myself."

"Have you stepped up security at PlayLand?" Carlos's hands felt very possessive on her foot.

"Ben's not going to hurt anyone at PlayLand," Maura said. "All we know for sure is he yelled at Gus. Witnesses at the hotel confirmed that."

"Be careful. You know how I'd feel if anything happened to you." Carlos kissed her toes and moved on to the other foot.

Maura rubbed the newly massaged foot on his thigh. "Why don't you show me?"

Later in bed, she said, "I didn't tell you the other reason it's been a difficult week. Linda's leaving."

"Why?" Carlos asked, toying with a strand of her hair. "I thought you liked Linda."

"I do," Maura said with a sigh. "She's great. I'm sick she's leaving. But . . . you have to swear to keep this confidential?"

"You know I don't repeat anything you tell me."

"This is big, Carlos." Maura rose on her elbow and leaned over him. "I'm serious."

"Okay. What's so big?"

"Rick's going to step down, and Grant's going to replace him."

"Whew!" Carlos whistled. "That is big. Why?"

"Rick wants to do other things. Family stuff. I hate him going."

"So why does Linda have to leave?"

"Policy. One spouse can't work anywhere in the other spouse's chain of command. If Grant is CEO, Linda can't work anywhere at PlayLand."

"That doesn't seem fair."

"It isn't. But it's a common practice. And it's a good thing from an HR perspective. Saves a lot of arguments about favoritism. I can't make an exception in HR. We'd lose all credibility with employees about our policies, if we pick and choose when to enforce them."

"So you're throwing Linda out?"

"Not me personally. But PlayLand, yes." Maura tried to distance herself from the decision emotionally.

"But you're the heavy?" Carlos always cut through to the heart of the matter. That's why he was a good sounding board.

"I suppose so. Me and Rick. And Grant." She wanted to spread the responsibility around. But in the end, she was Linda's boss. Other than Grant, she was the one who knew how much this hurt Linda. Maura leaned back on the pillows. "God, it makes me sick to lose her. But that's what I have to do."

$ $ $

Grant came home late Tuesday evening after spending time with the second shift in the Lakeview plant. He found Linda crying in their bedroom. "What's wrong?"

Linda wiped her eyes. "I didn't hear you come in."

Grant sat on the bed beside her. "What's the matter?"

"I didn't want you to see me crying."

Grant just waited.

"I talked to Maura this afternoon. Told her I'd leave. I'm going to miss PlayLand."

Grant sighed. "That's what I was afraid of." He walked across the room and took off his cashmere blazer, hanging it on the teak valet. "This isn't a done deal, you know. I don't have to be CEO, and you don't have to leave."

"I know," Linda said. "But it's the best thing."

"Not for you."

"Yes, even for me. I want you to be CEO. You'll be great. But it still hurts."

Grant sat back down beside her. "Your call," he said. "I won't do it if you can't live with the result. But the longer we let it ride, the harder it will be to change our minds. So be very sure if you want me to take my name out of the hat."

She dried her eyes. "I want you to take the job. I won't let on at PlayLand how hard this is. But don't be surprised if you find me crying at home again."

CHAPTER 27: MONDAY, APRIL 2

At the officers' staff meeting Monday morning, Leo reported that comic books were flying off the shelves.

"It's all Jennifer's doing," Kevin said. "She came up with the idea. The comics are creating great hype for the action figures and paying for themselves. They're our top sellers for preteen boys. Kids are coming into the stores in droves. And spending money. All our boy products are up over last year. And we have reorders on the action figures before they're even in the stores."

"Yeah, Toy Mart increased its order by twenty percent," Leo announced. The room applauded. "All top retailers have increased sales. All because my guys are tramping the streets, talking to buyers."

"I think the product has something to do with it," Kevin said.

"Can Operations keep up with demand?" Leo asked.

Grant shrugged. "It'll be tight. We're on schedule with initial production orders. But we'll have to start reruns as soon as the initial production is done. I'd hoped to give the plants a break, but I don't think we can. And I still need another injection mold machine. If we can't buy one, I'll be farming more work out to vendors."

"Which option costs more?" Alex asked.

"The equipment in the short-term. But over the long haul, we'd pay a premium to go outside."

"We can't commit any more cash this year," Alex insisted. "We need to pay down the credit line. We have the severance expense coming up, too."

"And we'd look crazy hiring people to run new equipment after laying people off," Maura said.

"But working the folks who are left so hard is a problem, too," Grant said. "Everyone's putting in overtime already. At some point, we'll have to staff back up. And in the meantime, morale is in the tank."

It was awkward, Maura thought. Some in the room knew of the changes, others didn't. Kevin was talking about product more than he used to. Soon Grant would be the one approving spending decisions—how would he manage Alex's penny pinching? Rick simply sat there smiling, letting everyone argue around him, like he was already out of the picture. Didn't anyone notice?

Or was it all her imagination?

$ $ $

After the meeting, Maura was back in her office. Her phone rang. "Hi, Maura. It's Tim Baylor. Listen, things are boiling in New Mexico. The plant manager just called. Maybe we can deal with the union sympathizers."

"What's going on?" Maura turned her back to the door so she could focus on what Tim was saying. They'd have to be careful, or they could end up with bigger problems than a couple of unhappy employees.

"The more vocal of the two employees has called in sick every day for the last two weeks," Tim said. "His supervisor asked him to fill out paperwork for a Family and Medical Leave Act absence after three days. Following policy by the book. But the guy hasn't turned it in, and says he won't. I think he's daring us to fire him."

"Is the FMLA paperwork due back yet?"

"No. He still has another week to get a doctor to approve him being off work. But he says he won't fill out the forms. Told his supervisor he hasn't been to the doctor, and says he isn't going. Says he doesn't feel well enough to work."

"That's all he says? Nothing else?" Usually absent employees did everything they could to keep their jobs, Maura thought. They gave some reason for not coming to work. Maybe a phony reason, but they said something. "What have we done to push the issue?"

"Well, you know how tricky FMLA is. We can't ask him about his medical condition. All we can ask for is the doctor's certification. No details about his health."

"Have you talked to Legal?"

"Yeah. They say it's risky to fire him now. They say we should wait until the FMLA filing time has expired. But what if the guy changes his mind and turns it in?"

Maura frowned. However big a problem this employee might be, it wasn't worth the risk of acting now. "Then he changes his mind. Don't jump the gun. But keep me posted. As soon as Legal says it's okay, I want him gone. And, Tim, stay close to this one. I don't trust the plant manager."

"Will do."

"What about the second employee?" Maura asked.

"Nothing happening there. But if the lead guy gets fired, the other one might settle down."

After Tim hung up, Maura picked up the crystal paperweight on her desk, fingering its bright facets. She gave Tim credit for aggressiveness, but she wondered if he was pushing the matter too hard. If there really was a union involved, they could be looking at a wrongful discharge lawsuit or unfair labor practices charge.

Or maybe she was gun-shy after Leo had yelled at her about settling the Atlanta case.

Sara Matthews walked into Maura's office. "I have the EAP counselor's report on Gus," Sara said.

"That was fast. When did they meet?"

"Last Wednesday, the day after Gus was in here. I asked Dr. Campbell to expedite his report."

"What's it say?" Maura took the copy Sara handed her. She put on her reading glasses, but looked over them at Sara. "I'll read it in detail, but give me the gist."

Sara flipped through her copy as she talked. "They met twice last week. Wednesday, then again Friday. Campbell says he hasn't done a full psychiatric evaluation. He only focused on 'fitness for duty.' Reading between the lines, Campbell thinks Gus has some mental issues, but isn't saying."

"What's he say about fitness for duty?"

"Bottom line, Gus can work. He's not very socially adept. I think that's how Dr. Campbell puts it. But he's competent to work."

Maura leaned back, scowling. "Damn."

"Yeah." Sara grimaced. "I haven't told Jennifer and Ted yet. They won't be pleased, but they'll take him back if we say they have to."

"What do you think we should do?" Maura asked.

"Well, we can't fire Gus based on this. I say we stay on his good side through the action figure launch." Sara hesitated, then continued. "What about this? Maybe we give Gus a choice. He can continue as an employee assigned to the action figure line, reporting to Jennifer. Or he can become a consultant. Then we should really try to sell him on consulting for us."

"Interesting," Maura said. "But why would he give up the security of a job?"

Sara sat forward, smiling. "You're thinking like Maura Ramirez. Think like Gus Powell. What you really like to do is draw cartoons. Live in your fantasy world. We tell him we'll use him as a consultant on the action figure line. And pay him about the same amount of money under contract as he gets in salary. But we don't have to deal with him day to day." She shrugged. "Maybe he'll go for it."

Sara's suggestion might work. But what about Ben? Would Gus come back in any capacity if Ben had not been found? "Has anyone seen or heard from Ben?" Maura asked.

"Not that I've heard," Sara said.

"He's just dropped off the face of the planet?"

"As far as I know."

Maura turned to her phone and dialed Detective Palmer. "Have you located Ben Thornton yet?" she asked.

"No, ma'am. We still have the APB out. And alerted the airlines. But we don't think he's left the area."

"Why not?" Maura asked.

"We've checked his credit card records. He stopped at a Wal-Mart on the outskirts of town the same day he allegedly pulled the gun on Powell. Nothing since then. He must be nearby. But we can't block all the roads, and we don't know where he went from Wal-Mart."

"You don't have a clue where he is?"

"Nope. My bet is he's holed up somewhere close. But that's only a guess. We won't know anything unless someone reports seeing his vehicle or he surfaces on his own."

Maura hung up. "Okay," she told Sara, "put together a

consulting deal for Gus. Work out the details with Jennifer and let me see it. Make sure you involve Legal, too. Then we'll talk to Gus again. We need to follow up soon, now that we have Dr. Campbell's report, so make it fast. And in the meantime, let's hope Ben turns up."

$ $ $

Rick, Kevin, Grant, and Maura met late Monday in Rick's office to discuss the rollout schedule. Maura was the last to arrive. "Sorry I'm late," she said, "Liz called me as I was leaving, upset about soccer practice. The coach yelled at her and she was in tears."

"Kids," Rick said, shaking his head. "Glad I didn't have girls. Okay," he continued. "It's April. What do we need to do before we can announce everything?"

"And what announcements should we make when?" Maura added. "You said you wanted your move effective about June 1. But we shouldn't leave the Product Development group in suspense about their new VP so long. The next few weeks are critical for the launch."

"It's only been three weeks since Vince died," Rick said.

"Yes, but we can't wait two more months," she responded.

"Do you think we should move the dates up?" Kevin asked.

Maura shook her head. "Not Rick's move. Let's separate the two announcements. Tell people now that Kevin's taking over Product. We don't have to say anything yet about Rick and Grant."

"That would work." Rick nodded. "It would also let Kevin be in the spotlight before we really shake the place up." He grinned at his brother. "Sounds good to me."

"Thanks, bro," Kevin said.

"What do you think, Grant?" Rick asked.

"Okay with me. Frankly, I'd like to concentrate on Operations until the action figures ship. Then we'll have our hands full managing reorders. And Rick, you and I need to talk about where I should focus my attention first in June."

"One issue at a time," Rick said. "What do we need to do to announce Kevin's move?"

"Not much," Kevin said. Maura made notes as Kevin ticked his points off on his fingers. "First, the standard internal announcement and a press release, like we always do. Second, a rollout schedule. Officers, then Product Development, then the rest of the company. Third, alert the local newspaper's business writer. A few hours' advance notice to him is plenty. Fax him a copy of the press release and offer to answer questions after the internal announcement. We don't want this in the paper before we tell employees."

"Can you and Maura handle it?" Rick asked.

"Sure," Maura said. "The only tricky part is the communication with Vince's former direct reports. They'll all have questions about where they fit into Kevin's organization. I'd suggest a group meeting, followed quickly with one-on-one meetings between each of them and Kevin. Kevin and I can plan that out."

"Maura and I can figure out who'll have what responsibilities in Product Development, as well as in Marketing and Communications," Kevin said. "We almost have it scoped out now."

"Make sure Grant and I see it before it's finalized," Rick ordered.

Kevin and Maura nodded.

"What's our target date for the Product announcement?" Rick asked.

"Can we plan for next week?" Maura asked. "Next Monday morning to the officers, then Tuesday to Product Development."

"Maybe Monday afternoon to the division instead," Kevin asked. "I don't want them to hear it through the grapevine."

"Are you suggesting our officers will leak it?" Grant asked. His voice was mocking. He was right, Maura thought. The rumor mill started at the top.

"That's pretty aggressive," Rick said, "But let's shoot for it. What about the CEO announcement?"

Grant rubbed the back of his neck. "If we're making the Product announcement next week, we shouldn't make the CEO announcement until at least May. Your June 1 plan isn't a bad target date."

"The delay will be hardest on you and Grant, Rick," Maura said. "You two will have to play your current roles without letting on that anything is going to change. And at the same time, you'll have to spend a lot more time together. Grant doesn't have to know everything on June 1, but the more time you two spend together, the easier the transition will be."

Kevin thumbed through his cell phone calendar. "It should be earlier than June 1. That's the week of Memorial Day. Lots of people on vacation. How about Monday, May 14? Get the shock out of the way before the holiday."

Rick nodded. "May 14 it is. We can always let the date slip, but we'll never be able to move it earlier than what we plan for."

Maura turned to Grant. "What we need most from you, Grant, is a plan for Operations. If Martin is going to take over as Vice President of Operations, who will replace him? What other moves are necessary? Should any of them happen before your announcement? You and I should discuss those issues."

Rick stood up. "Let's have weekly meetings of the four of us until the announcements are over. Starting with one more meeting before Kevin's announcement next Monday. How about Thursday afternoon?"

The others checked their calendars quickly, then nodded.

"By the way," Rick said, "I haven't told Mary about any of this, and I assume you've all kept your assistants in the dark, too. Let's talk on Thursday about who needs an early heads-up."

They gathered their files to leave. "Maura and Rick, can I talk to you both for a minute?" Kevin asked. Grant gave a mock salute, then left, shutting the door behind him.

"Rick and I talked about an issue with my move to Product," Kevin said to Maura. "It's a little delicate, but as head of HR, you should know about it. Jennifer and I have dated a couple of times. I'm going to tell her about my move tonight. There won't be a problem, but I can't keep seeing her if she's going to work for me."

Maura raised an eyebrow. "I had no idea, Kevin. Are the two of you serious?"

Kevin shook his head. "Too soon for that. But I don't want her hurt. She's important to PlayLand, and a really great person. She deserves to hear about it from me. I'd like to tell her about her promotion as well."

Maura glanced at Rick, who nodded. "Okay," Maura said. "She'll have to keep it confidential until next week, but make sure she knows how well she's thought of."

$ $ $

Kevin left Rick's office and walked through the rows of office cubicles in Product Development. Wow! he thought with a smile. In only a week, this whole group would report to him. Then he remembered Vince's death with a pang. His success had come at his brother's expense, which made it bittersweet.

Kevin found Jennifer in her office, files piled around her. "Have time for a drink?" he asked.

"I have some stuff to finish up. I can't leave yet," she said. She had a pencil behind one ear and her glasses on. She sat on one leg clad in dark tights, the other leg dangling to the floor beneath her short skirt. Even slightly disheveled, she had style.

"Bad day?" he asked.

"Just busy. Trying to help Operations decide which reruns of action figures to produce first. So I'm up to my eyeballs in schedules and costing."

"You need a break, and we need to talk," Kevin said.

She scrutinized him over her glasses. "Sounds serious," she said.

"Nothing bad. Got some news I need to share. Away from here." He didn't want to worry her, but he had to get her attention.

"Give me thirty minutes," she said. "Meet you at Gordon's down the street?"

"See you there."

Thirty minutes later, Kevin was in a booth in the back corner of Gordon's, facing the door. He ordered a Coors on tap. A few minutes later, Jennifer walked in. She'd put her contacts in. And combed her hair. Her long legs looked even better walking toward him than tucked under her.

Jennifer smiled when she saw him, walked to the booth, and sat across from him. The waitress came over, and Jennifer ordered a glass of Pinot Noir.

"So what's going on?" she asked after sipping her wine.

"Rick's decided who will replace Vince."

Jennifer frowned. "Why do I get the impression you don't think I'll like this?"

"He wants me to take over."

Jennifer's face lit up. "But that's great news, Kevin! You'll do a wonderful job. It'll be great working with you." As she said the last few words her smile slipped. She was getting the picture now, he thought.

"The announcement will be next Monday. I wanted you to hear it from me." He took her hand. "You know what this means, don't you?"

She withdrew her fingers from his and put both hands around her glass. "Will I report to you?"

"Yes."

"So we won't be able to see each other. Socially, I mean."

Kevin shook his head, watching her. What was she feeling?

Jennifer sighed deeply. "I knew it," she said, almost to herself.

"Knew what?"

"You're a Players. So there had to be bigger plans for you." She hunched her shoulders, then slowly relaxed. "I knew sooner or later I'd end up working for you."

"Then you have more foresight than I do."

"Did you think Rick would leave you running Marketing and Communications forever? Of course he wants you in a bigger role. Someday you'll probably replace him as CEO."

"Jennifer, I—"

She interrupted. "It's okay, Kevin. My heart isn't broken. I've enjoyed the time we've spent together, and it'll be great to work for you. I want a career at PlayLand, and I want the best people running the company. And you're one of the best." Her eyes brightened as she smiled at him. "I'd rather work for you than Ben any day. Or Vince for that matter. So congratulations."

Kevin frowned. Was he reading her right? She sounded too enthusiastic. Maybe a little brittle. But he told himself not to assume their time together had meant much to her. "Thanks," he said. "There's more."

She raised an eyebrow.

"Rick and I want you to take over the Marketing portion of what I'm doing now. You've done a great job with the action figure launch, and Marketing works on those types of promotions. Leo'll probably get Communications, but I see you taking that on in a year or so."

"What about Dolls? I really like managing that line."

"We'll have to talk about that. I want you to have New Ventures. You've shown you have a better feel for new product than anyone else. You can't do New Ventures, Marketing, and Dolls, too."

Jennifer was all business now. "So let me get this straight. I'd have marketing for all product lines, and development responsibility for new products? But someone else would take Dolls?" She paused, her brow furrowing. "What about action figures?"

"We'll leave them in New Ventures for now," Kevin said. "You'd have Marketing and New Ventures, including the action figures. What do you think?" He leaned forward, and his hand reached for hers. Nope, he shouldn't hold her hand. "I want you to have a job you can really sink your teeth into. You're one of our best directors. Rick and I both think so."

Jennifer nodded. "I want the job."

"Great!" Kevin said, lifting his glass.

She smiled and tapped her glass to his. "I appreciate your telling me," she said. She reached out and touched his cheek. "Strictly business from now on," she said in a prim voice that belied her gesture. "But I hope I can still pop into your office when I need encouragement."

Kevin smiled. "You bet."

"Thanks for the drink." She gathered her jacket and purse and walked out.

Kevin ordered another beer. He sat drinking until he couldn't smell Jennifer's perfume any longer. But he could still remember her legs as she had walked away. Damn! He couldn't think about her legs if he was going to be her boss.

$ $ $

Ben sat in the mountain cabin his first ex-wife owned, near a ski resort two hours from Lakeview. Thank God he'd kept the key after the divorce—he'd needed a place to crash often enough. But he couldn't hide out forever.

He'd been a fucking fool to go after Gus. Hadn't even managed to get Gus's fifty grand. Rick was the only one with dough enough to make a difference. Ben wondered if he'd scared Rick enough with his threat to go public about him banging Nicole. Nicole was a messed up junkie, but she wasn't a bad sort. Ben didn't really want to screw her over to get Rick.

But Rick didn't know that. Rick wouldn't want his old shit to hit the papers. He wouldn't want his sons to know how bad their old man had fucked up. Ben knew how to work Rick, he'd been doing it for over thirty years. He'd get something out of Rick.

After all, none of this was his fault.

CHAPTER 28: MONDAY, APRIL 9

On Monday, Maura arrived early for the eight thirty officer meeting. The announcement about Kevin would be made at the end of the meeting.

After everyone had gathered, Rick asked Alex for an update on cash flow.

"It's still rather grim," Alex said, his face mirroring his words. "Orders are strong, but we don't have the money yet. If customers pay on time, we'll be all right by June. But who knows?" Maura stifled a smile at Alex's pessimism.

"They'll come through," Leo said, grinning. "We sell to high-class retailers. Sales has saved our bacon once again."

"So far, so good," Rick said, then turned to Grant. "How are reruns going?"

"We've scheduled the forecasted reorders. We'll be okay unless customers order more replacement product than predicted. Might have to scramble then, but we have external vendors on standby. Good to go."

"And the headcount status?" Rick asked Maura.

She pulled out her notes. "Almost everyone who's leaving has signed their severance agreements. About twenty to go. They still have time. But it's looking good."

"Anyone who hasn't signed can still sue," Dewayne said. "We're not in the clear yet, but they're signing faster than I thought."

"And our marketing plans?" Rick asked.

"New comic books planned monthly for the next six months," Kevin said. "Each issue highlights a different character. We need Gus for the artwork."

"We're trying to get him back to work," Maura said, without

elaborating. This group didn't need to know Gus was being difficult.

Rick smiled after the reports. "Great work, everyone. Business is improving."

He took a deep breath, his face sobering. "It hurts that Vince isn't here to share our success. He was a large part of making it happen." Most of the faces around the table were blank. Maura bet her peers didn't think much of Vince's contributions, but they wouldn't contradict Rick.

"I want to announce Vince's successor as head of Product Development," Rick said. Leo's chair snapped forward. Alex looked up in surprise. Dewayne's face was impassive. Had Rick told him what was coming or not? Kevin tried to keep a straight face, but one corner of his mouth crept up in a boyish grin. "I've asked Kevin to take over," Rick continued, "and he agreed. Kevin worked closely with Product Development on the launch this year. Now he'll be responsible for all PlayLand's products in the years ahead. This decision is effective immediately."

Grant initiated a round of applause, and the others joined in. As Maura clapped, she saw Leo's mouth set in a grim line. He clapped, but he didn't look pleased. Alex shook his head, but smiled—seeming surprised, but not unhappy.

"Will you say a few words, Kevin?" Rick asked.

Kevin stood. "I was honored when Rick asked me to lead Product Development. My family has always believed in the importance of our company's products. It'll be hard to follow my dad and Rick and Vince, to fill their shoes. I'll need Rick's help, and help from all of you. We have work to do to take PlayLand to the next level, and I'm looking forward to my new role."

More polite applause.

"Any questions?" Rick asked.

"What about Marketing and Communications?" Leo asked immediately.

"That hasn't been finalized," Rick said. "Kevin will probably fold Marketing into Product Development. Communications is the wild card. We're still sorting that one out. More announcements to follow."

"What's the rollout schedule?" Alex asked.

Rick went through the plan, then adjourned the meeting.

About as expected, Maura thought. Kevin would do fine.

$ $ $

Rick called Leo aside as the others left. "You seem upset about the announcement," Rick said.

Leo waved his hand as if to dismiss Rick's comment. "Your call, Rick. But Kevin's pretty young to be handling all of Product Development. Hell, I was already working at PlayLand when he was born."

Rick grinned. "Yeah, and he was barely out of diapers when I started here. We're the old farts now, Leo."

Leo snorted. "Speak for yourself. I'm still kicking." He hesitated, not like his usual brusque manner. "I don't want to speak against Kevin." Leo paused again. "But how much experience does he really have with Product? Couple years as an entry-level Product Manager, and one stint as a Director?"

Rick shrugged. "Yeah. Maybe six years total. And the last three years in Marketing. He's done great in every assignment he's had. He can handle this."

"As I said, your call."

"Will he have your support, Leo?"

"Sure, Rick. We're all in this together." Leo's voice didn't sound as positive as his words.

Rick scowled at Leo. Was he on board or not? "Would you like to have the Communications group?" Rick asked. "I'd planned to talk to you later. But it might as well be now. A lot of the communications work is for Sales. There's a natural link. You'd have to spend more time on corporate stuff. But I'd like to see what you could do with it."

"What about pay?"

"That's why I wasn't planning to mention it. I haven't talk to Maura yet."

Leo's grim face eased. "Sure, Rick. Whatever you want. Should I talk to Kevin about the Communications bit?"

Rick clapped Leo on the back. "You're a valued member of the team," Rick said. "I'll be counting on you as one of our senior officers."

Leo relaxed even further. "As I said, we're all in this together."

$ $ $

Kevin and Maura had waited outside the conference room for Rick. Rick recapped his conversation with Leo. "I'll need a salary increase for Leo," he told Maura.

As the three of them walked to the Product Development department down the hall, they got a few curious glances from employees. Kevin overheard someone say, "Big guns are out." He wondered how they would react when they learned he was their new boss.

The Product Development directors sat in a conference room with Sara Matthews, their HR Director. The directors were silent as the three officers walked in. Jennifer smiled, but the rest looked uncertain.

Ben was not there. Dropped off the face of the earth, Kevin thought, after the hotel incident with Gus.

"I'm sure you're wondering why I asked you here this morning," Rick said. "I've decided on Kevin to replace Vince." Rick repeated the same speech he had made to the officers, but went into more detail on Kevin's background. "I hope you will help Kevin as so many of you helped me when I led this group years ago," he concluded.

Applause broke out, and someone cheered. That was a good sign, Kevin thought. He did worry about following Rick and Vince—he was the third Players brother to hold the job.

Kevin stepped forward, grinning. "I've always loved PlayLand's products. Like some of you, I played with them as a kid. Working on the launch this year has been great. We need more products like our new line to relevant for the 21st century. We need to build video games." Another cheer. "But we also need to keep our classic products fresh. Kids haven't changed that much. They still play with basic toys that foster their imagination. I'll need your help to get all this done."

"Will you be making any changes in the group?" one director asked.

"I haven't made any decisions yet," Kevin said. "I'll be meeting with each of you later today, and I'll want your input."

Sara passed out schedules to everyone.

"Sara has scheduled our one-on-one meetings. Please let me

know if you have a conflict, and I'll get with you some other time today or tomorrow. Our first priority is the action figure launch, so don't let my transition interfere with that. I'm excited about the projects we have underway, and I look forward to working with each of you."

"Sara has talking points for you to use with your employees," Maura said. "We'll have an email out to the whole company tomorrow, but let your folks know of Kevin's promotion today."

Kevin and Rick circulated, shaking hands with each of the Product directors. As Kevin spoke with Jennifer, her left hand covered their joined right hands for a moment. "Congratulations, Kevin," she said smiling, "I do look forward to working with you." Her hands were warm and soft and comfortable in his. He remembered her hand touching his cheek at the bar the week before and smiled back at her wistfully.

$ $ $

Monday afternoon Sara Matthews escorted Gus into the HR conference room. Maura and Jennifer were waiting. They had agreed Jennifer would explain the options to Gus.

"Gus, I'll be leading the action figure line going forward," she began.

"What happened to Ben?" Gus asked.

"He won't be working at PlayLand," Maura said.

"Did you fire him? Have you found him?" Gus asked.

"All you need to know is that he won't be working at PlayLand," Maura responded.

"So, as I was saying," Jennifer said, "I'll be leading the action figures, and I want you to work on the line. You have two options. First, you can continue as an employee of PlayLand, with your current title Assistant Product Manager. The other option is for you to become a consultant. You'd have more freedom to work on other things, but we'd still pay you for your work on the characters. We'd set an hourly rate that would give you about the same compensation. Your choice. Do you want to work as an employee in my group, or do you want to create your own stuff, with PlayLand as your first client?"

Gus squinted at Jennifer. "Are you trying to get rid of me?"

She shook her head. "I just said I want you to work on the action figure line."

"We're trying to give you choices," Maura said. "You don't seem comfortable working in a corporate environment. If you'd rather be your own boss, we can accommodate that."

"But I like PlayLand. It's Ben I don't like. If he's out of the picture . . . ."

"He is," Maura said.

Gus looked at his hands. "I could do what I want as a consultant?"

"Well, we'd have certain requirements for the projects you do for us," Jennifer said. "But when you aren't working for PlayLand, you can do whatever you want. We won't need you full-time."

"I wouldn't be full-time?" Gus asked, "What about benefits?"

Maura shook her head. "Consultants don't get benefits," she said. "We'd pay you a higher hourly rate as a consultant. But you'd need your own health insurance. You're young. I doubt it would be a problem."

Gus frowned. "My mom told me to always be sure I had a job with benefits. I couldn't have benefits as a consultant?"

"No, it doesn't work that way."

Gus looked back at his hands. "Then I guess I'd better stay an employee."

"And we'll be delighted to have you on the New Ventures team," Jennifer said, sighing.

$ $ $

At the end of the day, the executive suite was empty except for Rick and Kevin. Rick listened to Kevin recap his meetings with the Product Directors and the realignment of Product Development.

"You decide," Rick told his brother. "Talk to Maura and Grant. I don't need to be involved."

"Packing it in already?" Kevin asked with a grin.

Rick smiled. "Not quite. But I need to start distancing myself from decisions around here. You'll have to get used to handling things without me."

The door to Rick's office slammed open and Ben stormed in, his hair disheveled and his leather jacket open. "Tell me again you're firing me, you fucking bastard. If so, I'll go to the media about Nicole tonight."

Rick leaped up, his chair crashing against the window behind him. "How'd you get in?" he demanded. "We turned off your security access."

"No one stopped me," Ben said. "Did **you** authorize that piss-poor severance package? I'm worth a hell of a lot more. And I'm going to get it."

Shit! Ben was out of control. Rick had seen him like this before. Never ended well. "Calm down," he said, keeping his eyes on Ben. "Kevin, go find Maura so we can discuss Ben's severance." Kevin was smart enough to call Security.

Kevin moved toward the door, but Ben slammed it shut and blocked the exit. "Nobody's going anywhere. I want what's coming to me. I saved your ass with the action figures, Rick. Like I saved you with Nicole. You owe me."

"Nicole? What's this about Nicole?" Kevin asked, sitting back down.

Rick ignored Kevin. "All right, Ben. What do you want?"

"Just what's fair. You booted me out seven years before my pension kicks in. You need to make sure I get it."

"Seven years is a long time."

"You want to run this fucking place into the ground without me, that's your call. But you need to get me to retirement. After all I've done for you."

"I don't think HR will let me keep you on the payroll that long."

"You own the fucking company. You can do whatever you what," Ben shouted.

"I have to follow the law," Rick said. "Tell me what else might work."

"Then I need two million dollars."

Kevin snorted. "Ben, you haven't done a damn thing here except screw up. You're not entitled to a dime."

Ben pulled a handgun out of his jacket pocket and waved it at Kevin. "Maybe this makes me entitled. Let's see if the Players family wants to skip a generation. Vince is already dead. You want to join him?"

Rick felt an icy fury come over him. He'd suspected Ben killed Vince, he realized, but hadn't let himself voice the thought. "You killed him," Rick said, now needing to say it out loud to believe it.

"It was an accident."

Kevin leaped out of his chair. "You killed Vince!" he shouted. "You fucking bastard!"

Ben pointed the gun at Kevin's chest. "Back off. I'm only telling you once. He fell. Hit his head. Wasn't my fault." The pistol shook in his hand.

Christ! Rick thought. Got to calm him down. He reached for a notepad. "Okay, Ben," he said. "Name your terms. I'll write it down." He showed his hands. "I'm just getting a pen out of my pocket," he said, lowering both hands below the table. Don't let me screw this up, Rick prayed. He fumbled in his pocket and brought his right hand back up holding a pen. "Okay?"

"You can't be serious!" Kevin said. "Don't give him anything. He killed Vince."

Ben waved the gun at Kevin again. "Sit!"

Kevin sat.

Ben paced, his eyes shifting from Rick to Kevin.

Rick's left hand was still under the table. *Don't let him see!* He grappled with the cell phone on his belt. Dialed 911. At least he hoped that's what he dialed. Did it go through?

He heard static. Was there a voice there, too? Christ, he hoped Ben couldn't hear!

"All right," he said, "Tell me what you want."

As Ben talked, Rick told him repeatedly, "PlayLand will work this out with you, Ben. You said killing Vince was an accident." He used the company name and Vince's and Ben's names several times, hoping an operator heard him. If we die, he thought, I want them to know it was Ben.

Ben paced and talked about the money he needed, waving the gun around. His face glistened with sweat. He threw his coat on the table.

"Okay," Rick said, "Let me read this back—"

Two security guards burst into the office, weapons drawn. "Sir, we had a call—"

A shot reverberated in Rick's office. The first guard screamed and fell. *Bob! Shot!* Always greeted Rick in the morning. *Ben shot him!*

Ben pointed his gun at Rick. "Drop your weapon," he yelled at

315

the other guard. "Or I shoot Rick."

The guard dropped his gun and raised his hands. He walked backward toward Bob, who moaned in the corner, and knelt beside him. "He's hurt bad! Leg's bleeding."

"Kick his gun to me. Yours, too," Ben ordered.

The uninjured guard pushed the weapons toward Ben.

"Hands up." Ben waved his pistol at the guard. Then he turned to Rick and shouted, "What the fuck did you do? Did you call the fucking cops? You son of a bitch. I'll tell the fucking world about Nicole. Starting with Kevin. I'll bet he doesn't know."

Fuck Ben! Rick's mind screamed. Bob shot! In my office. No more. Not at PlayLand. He can't do this to me. And he can't mess with my people.

"You've taken this as far as you can." Rick heard a calm voice, distant as if coming through a tunnel. Was that him? Keep it together, he told himself. Ben had gone off the deep end, but Rick wouldn't go there with him. "The building's probably surrounded. Cops everywhere. You can't get out."

Ben looked out the window. "There's a dozen fucking cop cars in the parking lot. But I have you and Kevin. PlayLand can't afford to lose you. So get me out of here. With my money."

Ben backed toward the office door, pushed it shut and locked it. He was still sweating, even without his coat. He motioned from Kevin to the guard. "Tie him up. Use the phone cord." There was an extension phone on the table. "Make it tight."

Kevin complied.

The phone on Rick's desk rang. "Can I answer?" he asked.

"Take it slow," Ben said.

Rick moved to his desk. "Hello?"

"On the speaker. I want to hear," Ben said.

Rick pushed the speaker button.

"This is Detective Palmer. Lakeview Police. We had a call about a potential hostage situation. Your Security Department said guards responded to this number. Who's this?"

Rick looked at Ben. "You're in charge."

Ben glanced nervously at the phone. "You talk. But keep it simple."

"I'm Rick Players. I'm in my office with my brother Kevin, and

Ben Thornton, who's a manager here, and two PlayLand guards. One of the guards was shot. Ben has a gun."

"Will he talk to us?"

"There's nothing to talk about," Ben yelled. "I need two million. And a private jet to take me out of the country. If I get it within an hour, no one else gets hurt. Otherwise, I'll shoot the other guard. Then Kevin. Rick stays with me."

"Ben, be reasonable," Rick said. "I can't get that much cash in an hour."

"You can wire it. To my account in Bermuda," Ben said. "I've been involved in enough wire transfers around here to know it can be done."

Rick stalled. "I need Alex or someone in Finance to deal with the bank. I can't do it myself."

"Then get Alex up here. Now." Ben pointed the gun at the uninjured guard.

"Detective Palmer, where are the rest of the employees?" Rick asked.

"We're evacuating the building now. Moving people to the far end of the parking lot. Everyone's fine."

"Would you find Alex Draper, our CFO, please? I need to talk to him."

"What about the plane?" Ben asked.

"How will you get to the airport?" Rick asked. "Detective Palmer, what's the protocol here?"

The police officer turned the question back to Ben. "Mr. Thornton, what would you like to see happen?"

"I want an unmarked car to get to the airport," Ben said. "Rick stays with me. He can drive. No cops. Everyone needs to back off, or I'll shoot him."

"Okay, we'll see about the car and the jet," said Detective Palmer. He paused briefly. "Mr. Draper's here now."

"Rick? Kevin?" Alex's voice was strained. "What the hell's going on? Are you okay?"

"We're fine," Rick said. "I need you to work on a wire transfer. Ben wants money."

"You can't pay him," Alex said tersely.

"It's my money, Alex," Rick said, watching Ben. "If I want to give it to Ben, I can. What would it take to wire $2 million to an account in Bermuda?"

"We don't have that kind of cash! Not in the PlayLand accounts," Alex said. "We'd have to sell off some securities or draw on our line of credit. The banks are closed now. Can't do it until tomorrow. And I'll need an account number."

"Alex, I need you to do as much as you can as quickly as you can. Paige can access my personal accounts, so call her, too. And make sure she knows Kevin and I are okay. Let Detective Palmer know as soon as you find out what we can do tonight."

Rick turned to Ben. "You heard Alex. We're trying."

"You stay with me, Rick, until I have the money."

"All right. I stay with you," Rick said. "But you don't need the guards or Kevin. Why don't you let them go?"

"Not until I have the money and the plane." Ben gestured with the gun again. "Tie them up, Rick."

"No more phone cords. What should I use?"

"What do you have?"

"There's duct tape in Mary's desk. Shall I get it?"

Ben turned the gun on Kevin. "All right. But if you're not back in thirty seconds, I shoot Kevin."

Rick went out, leaving the door open. He rummaged in Mary's desk and saw a letter opener. Could Ben see him? He glanced toward his office. He couldn't see Ben. He grabbed the letter opener and shoved it in his sock. Then he got the duct tape and went back in his office waving the roll of tape. "Now what?"

"Tie 'em up."

Rick bound Kevin's hands and feet, squeezing his brother's shoulder as he finished.

He turned to Bob, whose face was grey. "Ben, do I have to tie him up? He's unconscious. Bleeding pretty badly. Can we call an ambulance? You don't want to add another murder to your problems, do you?"

"It wasn't murder, and don't tell me what I want. You've been telling me since freshman year. Now it's my turn."

"What if I ask Detective Palmer to have an ambulance on standby?"

Ben hesitated. "Okay. But no one comes in the building."

Rick turned toward the phone. "Detective Palmer, did you hear that?"

"We already have ambulances here, sir. Standard procedure in a hostage situation."

"Is that what this is?" Ben sneered. "A fucking hostage situation? I only want what's owed me." He yelled into the phone. "Where's my car? Where's my money?"

Detective Palmer's voice was calm. "We're working on it, Mr. Thornton. A car's on the way. Shall we get Mr. Draper back to talk to you?"

"You do that," Ben shouted.

"Is there anything else you need?" Detective Palmer asked. "How about food? Or medical supplies?"

Kevin spoke up from the floor next to the wounded guard. "We need bandages. Bob's leg's still bleeding."

"Mr. Thornton, can I send in some medical supplies?" Detective Palmer asked. His voice remained calm. "We can bring them to your floor and leave them by the elevator. We won't come any farther. You don't have to leave the office until we're gone."

Ben rubbed his forehead with the gun, but his eyes never left Rick. "All right. Send bandages. But no tricks. I'll start shooting if you try anything. And where's Draper?" he yelled.

"Right here," Alex said. "I can transfer a hundred thousand to you immediately, if you give me your account number. But the rest will have to wait until morning."

"I'm not leaving without two fucking million," Ben said. "We can stay here all night if we have to." He gave Alex the account number.

"The bandages and supplies are on their way in," Detective Palmer said. "We won't start up the elevator until you say so."

"Rick and I are going to the elevator," Ben said. "If you try anything, Rick gets it. So send those cops up, but they stay on the elevator. Otherwise, I'll shoot."

"All right, Mr. Thornton," Detective Palmer said. "They're starting up."

Ben poked the gun into Rick's ribs. "Let's go."

Rick walked down the hall ahead of Ben. They got to the elevator. It opened showing two police officers, one of whom shoved a box into the hallway. "Stay back!" Ben screamed, moving his gun from Rick to the officers. The elevator door started to close.

Now's my chance! Rick pulled the letter opener from his sock and stabbed Ben's back. The sharp point pierced Ben's shirt and flesh easily, like skewering steak.

Ben screamed and the gun went off. He fell, grabbing Rick's neck. Rick's bad leg gave way, and he went down with Ben. The gun spun across the floor. They both reached for it. They fought, Ben screaming again as he rolled on his back.

The elevator door opened, and the officers came out, guns drawn.

One of the officers kicked Ben's pistol away, shouting, "On the floor! On the floor! Freeze!" One officer cuffed Ben, the other Rick.

Ben yelled in pain, "You fucking son of a bitch!"

Rick stayed passive as the officers called for backup. Was it over?

One of the officers stood over him, gun still pointing at his chest. "Who are you?"

"Rick Players," he said. "That's Ben Thornton. He had the gun."

"What happened?"

"I stabbed him with a letter opener."

The officer looked impressed, but not enough to put his gun away. "Where are the others?"

"In my office. Down the hall. One guy's shot. The others are okay, just tied up."

More police came up the stairs near the elevator, weapons drawn. Rick nodded toward his office. Four officers moved quickly, but cautiously, down the hall.

"Police!" they yelled.

"Over here!" came Kevin's response.

After a moment, Rick heard, "All clear! Get the EMTs up here."

Soon the elevator opened and four medics appeared with stretchers. Two stopped by Ben, and the others rushed down the hall.

Another elevator opened, and Rick recognized Detective Palmer, remembering him from the investigation after Vince's death. More uniformed officers were with him. So was Alex, his face pale.

"That's Rick," Alex said. He rushed over. "Man, am I glad to see you."

Detective Palmer gestured at the officer guarding Rick to take off the handcuffs. "I hear you're the hero," he said.

Rick shrugged off the detective's comment. What kind of a hero stabs his best friend? "Can I see my brother and the guards?" he asked.

Palmer nodded.

Rick limped wearily down the hall. When he reached his office, Kevin and the two guards were untied. The paramedics were working on Bob.

"Will he be all right?" Rick asked.

One EMT nodded. "We're getting an IV into him now."

Detective Palmer had followed Rick. "Everyone else okay?"

Rick sat heavily, dropping his head into his hands. "I think so. Kevin?"

Kevin rubbed his wrists. "Yeah. What happened?"

"I stabbed Ben," Rick said. "I don't know how badly he's hurt."

"He'll live," the detective said without sympathy. "Took guts to stab him. You could have been killed."

Rick looked at his hands, which were shaking now. "He killed Vince. Shot a guard. I couldn't let him hurt anyone else. Not here. Not in my company."

"Once he's patched up, we'll talk to him. We'll need statements from you, too," Detective Palmer said. "Then get you all checked out at the hospital." He separated Rick, Kevin, and the uninjured guard, moving them out of Rick's office. More officers came in with crime scene tape and other paraphernalia.

Rick stopped paying attention, his body drained. His arms and legs shook. He answered questions from one of the officers, refused a ride to the hospital, and went home, waving off the PlayLand employees and media outside.

CHAPTER 29: TUESDAY, APRIL 10

Rick didn't get to work until midmorning Tuesday. He ached when he moved, and his face was bruised and tender when he shaved.

Paige hovered over him as he ate breakfast. "You shouldn't have gone after Ben," she said, pouring his coffee. "You could have been killed. Who knew he was so violent? Poor Vince!"

Her chatter irritated Rick. He left. The office couldn't be any worse than his kitchen.

When Rick walked into PlayLand, the guard on duty rushed around the reception desk. "Everyone's glad you got Thornton, sir," he said, pumping Rick's hand in both of his. "Bob's been here twenty years. He'll work another twenty, thanks to you."

Rick smiled ruefully. "I hired Thornton. I guess I needed to stop him."

As he started down the third floor hallway where he'd fought with Ben, applause broke out. Shit. They thought he was a goddamn hero. When he'd fucked up royally. He was the one who'd hired Ben, kept him around all these years. "Damn it," he said. "No need for all that."

Mary fussed in his office. "The police weren't done in here until midnight," she said. "I had the cleaning crew in for the carpet first thing, but it's not dry yet. Do you want me to set you up in the conference room?"

Rick shook his head. "I'm all right," he said. "Just bring me a cup of coffee, please."

He stood gazing out the window. The mountains were still there. Unchanged. They should look different. Everything else had changed.

Mary returned with his coffee. Maura followed her into the office. "You okay?" Maura asked, shutting the door as Mary left.

He nodded. "Just tired."

"Did you see the papers?" she asked. "They're calling you SuperCEO." She laughed. "You've set quite a high bar. Think Grant can live up to your image?"

Rick snorted. He sipped his coffee. "All I could think about," he said, "was that bastard's not going to shoot anyone in *my* company. Didn't think about anyone else. Not Bob. Not even Kevin. Ben was attacking my space, and I wasn't going to let him do it."

"What's wrong with that?"

"Shouldn't I care more about the people than my goddamn company?"

Maura walked over and touched his arm. "Rick, don't beat yourself up. It doesn't matter what you thought. What matters is you did a really fine thing. You saved a lot of lives. Yours. Kevin's. Both guards'. Probably even Ben's. That's what matters."

Rick glanced at her, then turned back to the mountains. Easy for her to say. "Ben confessed to killing Vince."

Maura's face blanched and her hand went to her throat. "My God! That's awful."

Rick shrugged. "At least we know," he said. "He says it was an accident. Says he struggled with Vince and Vince fell on the hearth."

"Do you believe him?"

Rick shrugged again. "I'd like to." He sat heavily. "He was my best friend," he said, dropping his head into his hands. "How'd we get to this point?"

They sat in silence.

"What's next?" Maura asked when Rick looked up.

"Keep going. Finish the launch. Crank out more product. Keep customers happy. Maybe turn a profit at year end."

"And you?" Maura asked.

"I'll keep playing CEO until the announcement on May 14." Rick paused and laughed cynically. "Did you think I'd change my mind? No way."

"You talked about this being your company."

"Yeah, it's my company. But it's full of crazy people. Why would I want to stay?"

"They aren't all bad. Most of them are really good." She grimaced. "Most of the time."

Rick stared into his coffee. "One of these really good people killed Vince and held a gun on Kevin and me. Shot one of my employees. Another really good employee is paranoid, but created the best new product line we've had in ten years. At any moment we have half a dozen really good people suing the crap out of us. And an equal number of inept managers we should have fired years ago." He sighed. "No, I need to go. I can't play the game anymore. Maybe working with the foundation will help me find the goodness in people again."

"I hope so, Rick," Maura said. She left him alone in his office.

CHAPTER 30: MONDAY, MAY 14

Maura and Kevin had spent the weekend finalizing the press release announcing Grant as Rick's replacement. Even though Kevin no longer managed Communications, Rick had insisted only Rick, Kevin, Grant, and Maura be involved. "Leo's too likely to let something slip to his cronies at Toy Mart," Rick said.

Maura knew Rick's lack of trust meant Leo shouldn't manage the corporate communications group, but there was nothing she could do about it now. Rick would have to handle damage control with Leo after the fact.

She was in her office early Monday morning making last minute changes to the documents. At 8:15 she collected the final copies off the printer.

As she left for the officers' meeting, Maura told her assistant Kay the news and gave her a copy of the press release. "Fax this to the newspaper at nine thirty, unless you hear from Rick or me," she said.

Kay nodded, her eyes wide with shock.

Maura hurried to the conference room. When she arrived, Kevin asked her quietly, "Did you make the changes?"

She handed him a copy of the final press release.

Leo arrived at 8:35 and looked around. "I beat Rick?" he asked. "And Grant? It's a red letter day."

Rick and Grant walked into the room not long after Leo.

"Let's get started, shall we?" Rick said.

He took his usual seat at the head of the table and motioned for Grant to sit next to him.

This caused a flurry of movement, as the other officers shifted down the table to accommodate Grant. Alex, who usually sat next to Rick, picked up his spreadsheets, frowning. Maura hid a grin. She sat in Grant's usual chair, watching her peers.

"I didn't send out an agenda for today's meeting, because I have an unusual topic that I imagine will spawn some discussion," Rick said. "I am stepping down as CEO of PlayLand, effective June 1."

Alex's head jerked up and his pencil lead snapped, the sound audible in the suddenly silent room. Leo's jaw dropped, and his coffee mug thumped on the coaster in front of him, dark liquid sloshing over the side. Even Dewayne's stoic expression faltered.

"I know it's a shock," Rick continued. "But for some time now, since even before my accident, I've been . . ." He appeared to have trouble finding the word he wanted. ". . . dissatisfied. The accident made me realize I need more out of life than being CEO. And Vince's death. Life is too short not to care about what you're doing. Now that the business is back on track, it's time for me to leave."

"Are you leaving PlayLand completely?" Dewayne asked.

"I'll be Chairman of the Board," Rick said. "But I won't be active on a daily basis."

Leo, Alex, and Dewayne, for whom this was new information, glanced around the table. Maura could see them thinking as Rick's words sank in, wondering what this meant for them. If Rick was gone, who would be CEO?

Rick sipped his coffee, then said, "I'm pleased to say Grant will replace me as CEO."

There was silence for a split second. Maura started clapping. She had to make sure Grant got off to a good start. Kevin joined her, and then the others.

"Congratulations, Grant," Maura said.

"Hear, hear," someone else added.

Grant smiled and nodded.

Thank God! Maura sighed. At least they acknowledged Grant positively. For now.

When the applause died down, Rick said, "I'll work with Grant on the transition, but he'll need your support also."

"I can't see you riding off into the sunset," Leo said. "What do you plan to do with yourself all day?"

"Establish a family foundation," Rick said. "That was always my father's intent. It's too late for Dad to see what our money can do for this community, but it's not too late for me."

"More power to you, Rick," Maura said. Others nodded.

"Let's hear from Grant," Leo said, leaning back in his chair, with his arms crossed over his stomach. "What's our new boss have to say?"

Uh-oh, Maura thought. What was Leo thinking?

Grant pushed his chair back, stood and faced his former peers. "When Rick told me he was stepping down, I was as shocked as you are. Hell," Grant said with a grin, "he's younger than I am! I'm honored by his trust, and I'm eager for the challenges ahead. But I'll need help from each of you."

"What changes are you going to make?" Leo asked, his arms still crossed.

"I'll ask Martin Cunningham to replace me in Operations. I don't have plans beyond that."

"When this meeting is over, you're free to tell your staffs about my departure and Grant's promotion," Rick said. "Don't say anything about Martin until Grant says it's okay. He hasn't talked to Martin yet. A press release goes out this morning. You can use it for talking points with your groups. There'll be an email this afternoon to all employees."

Maura passed out copies of the press release.

"How this group presents the news is very important," Rick said. "We need to stay focused on the business. Our progress this year has been good, but we aren't out of the woods yet."

Alex nodded as Rick spoke.

"Make sure our employees know I'm leaving for personal reasons," Rick continued, "I wouldn't be leaving if I didn't believe they're capable of continuing our turnaround. And I believe Grant and the rest of you can lead them through it."

"You should all hold stand-up meetings in your groups this morning," Maura said. "If you get questions you can't answer, please forward them to me." She glanced at Leo, who was scowling. "To me and to Leo as head of Communications," she amended. "Leo and I will draft responses."

Rick and Grant fielded further questions for a few minutes. Then Grant stood. "I need to meet with the Operations staff immediately," he said. "Starting with Martin. Give me fifteen minutes with him before you start your meetings."

The group was quiet as they broke up. There would be a buzz later, Maura knew, but they would wait until they were out of Rick's and Grant's hearing before speculating.

Leo stopped Maura as she followed Grant out of the room.

"I have to go with Grant to talk to the Operations staff," she said. "Can I catch up with you later?"

"Thanks for small favors," Leo said. "I guess getting the Communications guy involved late is better than not at all."

Maura nodded. Leo was right. He should have been involved sooner. "Sorry, Leo. Rick's orders. If you have a problem, take it up with him."

$ $ $

The rest of the day was chaotic.

Maura and Grant met with Martin, who was thrilled to have the chance to lead Operations.

Grant and Martin met with the rest of the Operations staff at headquarters, and Grant faxed the press release to the outlying plants. He held a videoconference with the other locations and promised he and Martin would visit each facility in the weeks ahead.

Maura wandered the hallways, talking to the employees she knew. She ate lunch in the cafeteria, listening to employee conversations. She sat in on Grant's videoconference.

At the end of the day she went to Rick's office for a debriefing. Rick and Mary were packing boxes. Although the transition of power to Grant was not effective for two weeks, Rick wanted Grant to move into the corner office immediately. Rick would move to an office down the hall until he leased space for the foundation in another building nearby. Meanwhile, he wanted Grant to start with all the trappings of a CEO.

"I talked to Leo," Rick told her, before the others arrived. "I think he's okay."

When Grant, Leo, and Kevin joined them, they all recounted what they had heard. "Most of the employee scuttlebutt is very supportive of both Rick and Grant," Maura said. "As usual, there are a few cynics. Someone wants to know whether Rick is hiding something like a fatal disease or a government investigation of

PlayLand. But for the most part, people are happy for Rick. And they're willing to give Grant a chance."

"We need some responses on a few issues," Leo said. "Whether PlayLand will pay employees for time spent volunteering with their favorite charities. Whether we can meet production quotas without Martin in Manufacturing. Whether Martin's promotion means PlayLand will favor internal production over outsourcing."

Leo was showing off, letting Rick and Grant know he was on top of Communications, Maura decided.

"I'll need draft responses from Maura and Martin by ten tomorrow morning, if we are going to make our commitment to respond to these questions promptly," Leo continued. "Communications used to get dinged for slow responses, and that's going to change on my watch."

Kevin grimaced. Kevin should be annoyed, Maura thought, a frown on her face, too. Leo's comments were clearly directed at Kevin. Maybe he wasn't okay with Rick's decision. "My staff's drafting responses already, Leo," she interjected. "Tim Baylor's working with Martin on the Operations questions."

The others reported similar reactions from the employees in their divisions. The biggest concerns appeared to be in the outlying plants and the field sales force. "They're always the most suspicious of changes at headquarters. Because they're so far away and feel like they're left out of the loop," Maura said.

$$\$ \, \$ \, \$$

After the meeting, Maura went back to her office. Her paper inbox and email inbox were full. The voicemail light on her phone blinked. She punched the button to listen to messages.

"Tim Baylor here. The union sympathizer still hasn't turned in his FMLA paperwork. I've called him personally and he refuses. The New Mexico plant's ready to pull the plug. What do you think?" Beep.

"Maura, it's Sara. I had a squirrelly conversation with Gus this morning. He's asking if his college friends have any rights in his drawings. I don't know what he's talking about. What should I do?" Beep.

Maura dropped to her chair and picked up the top document in her inbox. The settlement agreement with Steve Williams—after all the legal haggling, it was ready to sign. She sighed, dropping the agreement back in the inbox.

She wouldn't deal with anything more today, she thought. She was exhausted after Rick's announcement.

To think it all started with Linda's nudge in January about needing a CEO successor. Now it was reality.

Rick's departure would be hard for PlayLand. And for Maura. But Linda was right; Grant was a good choice. Things were in place to groom Kevin for the future. Next time would be easier.

But no more today. It could all wait.

And in three weeks, she had to be ready for Liz's *quinceañera*.

THE END

If you enjoyed Playing the Game, *please leave a review here:*
https://www.amazon.com/gp/product/B00FKH1KHA/

Playing It Straight, *the next book in this series, is now available on Amazon at*
https://www.amazon.com/Playing-Straight-PlayLand-Sara-Rickover/dp/0985324465/

DISCUSSION GUIDE

1. The epigraph in this book is a quote from Winston Churchill: "Play the game for more than you can afford to lose . . . only then will you learn the game." Which characters in *Playing the Game* played for more than they could afford to lose? Which held back? Does this epigraph fit the theme of the book?

2. Which characters in *Playing the Game* changed the most during the course of the story? In what ways did they change?

3. Which characters did you admire most? Least?

4. Which of the characters was most like your favorite boss? Which was like your least favorite boss? How did you manage that boss?

5. Which character in this book was the best leader? Which character would you most want to work for? Is the same character the best leader and your preferred boss?

6. Does this book say anything about balancing work and family time?

7. Have you ever worked for a business that faced serious problems like PlayLand did? How did your employer deal with those problems? What advice do you have for the PlayLand executives?

8. Have you or someone you've known ever been laid off? Have

you had to lay off employees you managed? What impact did the layoff have on both the employees who were let go and the survivors?

9. What were some of the unique challenges of working in a family-owned business described in this book—for the family members and for those who worked for them?

10. In what ways did the relationships between the PlayLand vice-presidents work well? In what ways were they dysfunctional? How do you think these relationships could have been improved?

11. Of the business functions portrayed in the book—Product Development, Operations, Marketing, Finance, Legal, and Human Resources—which contributed well to PlayLand? Which were stumbling blocks to progress?

ABOUT THE AUTHOR

Sara Rickover worked as an attorney, mediator, and Human Resources executive before turning from facts to fiction. She has more than twenty-five years of corporate and legal experience, plus a decade as a mediator. She has navigated the bureaucratic realms described in *Playing the Game*.

One reader said of the characters in *Playing the Game*, "I know these people." But Sara insists the characters are all figments of her imagination. Well, mostly.

PRAISE FOR *PLAYING THE GAME* FROM AMAZON REVIEWERS:

"This is a fascinating, fast-paced novel about the issues facing the modern corporation: corporate succession, office politics, financing, unionization, and so forth. The characters are sharply drawn and the plot is full of interesting twists; I lost a few hours of evening sleep reading this one, as I couldn't put it down. Highly recommended!"

"Playing the Game is a page-turner from page one. The characters are clever, scheming, even diabolical—but also real, and vividly drawn. Rickover does a masterful job of keeping all the corporate balls in the air and keeping her readers guessing about how things will turn out."

"A very enjoyable and enlightening book if you want to know the inside scoop of the corporate world. I couldn't put it down."

". . . this book is fast-paced, entertaining, and wonderfully written!"

Find *Playing the Game* and other books by Sara Rickover on Amazon.

https://www.amazon.com/Sara-Rickover/e/B00FKW6VMO

www.ingramcontent.com/pod-product-compliance
Lightning Source LLC
Chambersburg PA
CBHW070913260626
47162CB00007B/2659